Horace

GEORGE SAND

Horace

TRANSLATED BY
ZACK ROGOW

MERCURY HOUSE
SAN FRANCISCO

First published in French in the *Revue indépendante,* from November 1841 through March 1842; in three volumes by De Potter in spring 1842; and as part of the *Oeuvres complètes* of George Sand by Perrotin in 1843. The illustrated edition published by Hetzel in 1852 (the only edition carefully reviewed by the author), which was reproduced by Editions de l'Aurore in 1982, served as the basis for this translation.

Published in the United States by Mercury House, San Francisco, California, a nonprofit publishing company devoted to the free exchange of ideas and guided by a dedication to literary values.

United States Constitution, First Amendment: Congress shall make no law respecting an establishment of religion, or prohibiting the free exercise thereof; or abridging the freedom of speech, or of the press; or the right of the people peaceably to assemble, and to petition the Government for a redress of grievances.

Mercury House and colophon are registered trademarks of
Mercury House, Incorporated

Printed on recycled, acid-free paper
Manufactured in the United States of America

Library of Congress Cataloging-in-Publication Data
Sand, George, 1804–1876.
 [Horace. English]
 Horace / by George Sand ; translated by Zack Rogow—
 1st ed.
  p. cm.
 ISBN 1-56279-082-X
 I. Rogow, Zack. II. Title.
PQ2403.H813 1995
843'7—dc20

95-11057
CIP

FIRST EDITION
5 4 3 2 1

Translator's Introduction

I have to confess that when I began translating *Horace,* I was not aware of George Sand's many gifts as a novelist. Of course I admired her outlandish behavior, that cigar-smoking woman who bushwhacked her way through the nineteenth century, wearing men's clothes when she went out hunting or when she attended the Paris theater. I enjoyed the stories of her amorous adventures, how she became the lover of famous composers, revolutionaries, writers, and actors, not all of them male. All of that is part of George Sand. But I discovered in reading this book that George Sand the historical figure is only a small corner of the picture. Sand—whose real name was the Baroness Amandine Aurore Lucie Dupin Dudevant—had a style and vocabulary that were the admiration of her literary colleagues, a wide-ranging knowledge of politics and religion, and a wonderfully catty wit, all of which she used ably in her work. *Horace* is one of the best examples of these skills in her oeuvre.

One of Sand's most winning qualities as a novelist, though, is her empathy for her characters, an empathy that leaps over barriers of gender, class, and age. In *Horace,* this shines through in her portrait of the swashbuckling student radical, Jean Laravinière, marked for life by smallpox and unable to form relationships with women. This empathy also surfaces in her surprisingly affectionate depiction of the Marquis de Vernes, an old rake past his prime.

But *Horace* is most remarkable for the vision it displays. Sand was never afraid to take unpopular positions in her novels, positions that seem advanced even today. She stands alone among nineteenth century novelists as the only writer who has given us an image of a "fallen woman" (the character Marthe in *Horace*) who is *not* punished by fate, but who bounces back from being abused and seduced to become successful and loved in her own land. Her declaration in chapter twenty-nine that "Love, devotion, and care are the true paternity" will raise eyebrows a century and a half after it was written, when our courts are arguing over who has the right to be called a parent.

Maybe the reason I underestimated George Sand as a writer is that the works of hers I could find in English in bookstores and libraries tended to be her somewhat corny novels of rural life. These books, such as *The Haunted Pool, François the Waif, The Bagpipers, Little Fadette*, were ground-breaking in their sensitive treatment of French peasants, and had a profound influence on Flaubert and other writers. But Sand's novels of agrarian France sound dated today. And they are not located in the world that Sand knew best.

Horace has none of these shortcomings. It's a novel as sophisticated as Sand herself.

Horace was considered so politically scandalous when it was written at the beginning of the 1840s that her publisher refused to print it. This might help explain why *Horace* has remained untranslated for over 150 years. Try to imagine this book in the England of *Oliver Twist, Vanity Fair,* and *Wuthering Heights,* novels published in the same decade that gave birth to *Horace.* This book is far ahead of those classics in its social thinking. In those English novels, the need for major social upheaval is merely a background rumbling. But in *Horace,* a revolutionary transformation of society is *the* subject on the table for discussion. It is a given for all the characters. I don't mean to say that *Horace* is the better of these books. But the dilemmas the characters face are far more contemporary.

Sand's novel takes place in 1832, during a decade when France was the center for a flowering of unprecedented radical ideas. After the defeat of Napoleon at the Battle of Waterloo in 1815, the victorious royalist powers had imposed on France a return of the Bourbon dynasty, which had been overthrown in the French Revolution. This wildly unpopular monarchy collapsed during the July Days of 1830, when a three-day uprising in the streets of Paris sent King Charles X packing into exile. Two characters in *Horace,* Paul Arsène and Jean Laravinière, are supposed to have fought on the barricades in this rebellion.

Although the July Days marked the long-overdue end of Charles X's reign, the revolt ended in a compromise that allowed Louis Philippe, the Duke of Orleans and Charles X's cousin, to assume the throne as the so-called Citizen King. Louis Philippe ruled over a constitutional monarchy in which, conveniently, the only people who could vote were males owning substantial amounts of property (and they made up less than one percent of this nation of thirty million people). The new monarchy fed its policies right to the rising industrialists. It soon alienated both the radicals, who yearned for a true republic, and the Legitimists, nostalgic for the days of aristocratic supremacy. These two opposite groups found themselves in a peculiar alliance against the status quo, and in *Horace* we see them mingling in the salons of the elite and in the cafés of the Left Bank. Most of the characters in *Horace* come from one of the social extremes in French society, with the notable exception of the protagonist, Horace Dumontet, who hails from an upwardly mobile, middle-class, provincial family.

The discontent of the French Left produced an explosion of ideas on how to rebuild society. These new notions included the utopian movements inspired by Fourier and Saint-Simon (Sand's character Eugénie is a follower of the latter), the first organized efforts of the feminist movement, and the liberation theologies of Abbot Félicité de Lamennais and Pierre Leroux, who combined Christian faith with attacks on the distribution of wealth. This lively opposition to the government culminated on June 5, 1832, in the revolt at the Saint-Merry Cloister in Paris, an armed insurrection against the monarchy that grew out of the funeral of General Lamarque, who had fought for the revolutionary and Napoleonic governments. The Saint-Merry revolt leads directly to one of the dramatic climaxes of *Horace,* just as it does in Victor Hugo's *Les Misérables,* published twenty years later. Sand witnessed firsthand the results of the violent suppression of this rebellion, since from the windows of her Paris apartment she could see the entrance to the city morgue.

The other major historical event of 1832 that shapes *Horace* is the cholera epidemic that swept through France that year. This epidemic claimed over eighteen thousand lives in France. The misery caused by this outbreak gave a push to the Saint-Merry revolt.

One other reason *Horace* created such a scandal at the time of its publication was that several of the characters were based on people whom George Sand knew. If writing well is the best revenge, then George Sand must have been smacking her lips when this book first hit the streets in serialized form. The main character, Horace Dumontet, is largely a portrait of Jules Sandeau, the first man George Sand lived with after her separation from her husband. It was out of Sandeau's name that George created her nom de plume. Like the character Horace, Sandeau was a notoriously indolent dilettante. And as with his fictional counterpart, Sandeau attempted a career as a writer by chronicling a failed romance (his affair with Sand, in fact). Jules began living with George Sand when he was only nineteen, the same age as Horace at the start of the book. Sand and Sandeau spent several months together in 1831 and 1832 in an apartment much like the one that the narrator, Théophile, inhabits in *Horace*. At the end of their affair, George sent Sandeau off to Italy, a fate not unlike that of Horace in the book.

Another character in *Horace* whom Sand based very closely on one of her contemporaries is the Viscountess de Chailly, a portrait of Countess Marie d'Agoult. Initially, Marie d'Agoult might have been the person George Sand had the most in common with. Like Sand, Marie d'Agoult was an aristocrat who had turned her back on her class and her marriage to live with an eastern-European composer: d'Agoult with Franz Liszt, Sand with Frédéric Chopin. Both women embraced the republican movement against the ruling monarchy, and both were active in artistic circles. They were at first the closest of companions. But Sand found out that Marie d'Agoult was telling their mutual acquaintances that George's reckless passion for Chopin was killing him (nothing could be further from the truth), and the friendship moved irrevocably toward a break. The meticulous and devastating satire of Marie d'Agoult in *Horace* was Sand's way of getting even for what she felt was a two-faced betrayal.

George Sand's *Horace* provides us with a window into a not-so-distant past in which women lived under frightening and all-too-familiar constraints. In the Paris of the 1830s, it was terribly unsafe for an unaccompanied female to walk by herself through the streets at night, and apartment doors were barred for protection. Young, single women without independent means were often forced to survive as *grisettes,* working girls who either lived as the mistresses of students, or earned some of their income as part-time prostitutes. (The term *grisette* comes from the French word *gris,* meaning gray, after the gray uniforms that milliners' assistants wore.) The characters Marthe and Eugénie in *Horace* belong to this class. Sand depicts both of them as actively and successfully challenging the limits on what grisettes can achieve, Marthe as an actress, and Eugénie in her ability to win the respect of her peers even as she defies the conventions of marriage. It was tolerated, on the other hand, for upper-class women in society to take lovers, but these women had to fight constantly to ward off the stinging shame that might result if a man bragged to others about his affairs.

A word that I found myself translating over and over again in this book is the French term *esprit,* which has numerous meanings in English: mind, intellect, wit, spirit, soul, understanding, humor, disposition, character, etc. On one level, this novel is a comparison of three *esprits:* those of Horace Dumontet, the Viscountess de Chailly, and Paul Arsène. Horace has the type of mind that dazzles in the conversation of cafés or salons, but lacks a core of conviction. The Viscountess is well-read and surrounds herself with unconventional thinkers, but she herself never goes beyond repeating the witty remarks of others. Paul Arsène, in contrast, is the self-deprecating, uneducated son of a shoemaker, but his concern for others leads him to become a natural student of social theory.

In creating an English version of *Horace,* I've tried to remain true to the diction used in our language during the period when the book was published, without allowing the wording to sound fussy or stiff. The translation is based on the fine, most recent edition of *Horace* edited by Nicole Courrier and published by Editions de l'Aurore in 1982.

I would like to thank Adrienne Guy, who painstakingly read through my manuscript and the French original and made many valuable suggestions. I also would like to thank three other translators who read this text and made helpful comments: William Rodarmor, Sasha Vlad, and Maria Espinosa. And thanks to Marilyn Sachs and Anne Sachs for their useful ideas on smoothing the style of the translation.

Horace

Notice

Horace must accurately portray a widespread modern phenomenon, since this book has made me a dozen dyed-in-the-wool enemies. People I don't even know claim to recognize themselves in the characters, and hate me to death for the cruel way I unmasked them. I repeat here what I said in my first preface: no one posed when I sketched this portrait. I took it from everywhere and nowhere, just as I contrast the type representing blind devotion to an unbridled type. These two types are eternal, and I have heard a very intelligent man say in jest that the world is divided into two groups of more or less thoughtful beings: *the jokers and the suckers.* It is perhaps the former word which struck me and which brought me to write *Horace* around that time. Perhaps I was bent on showing that the exploiters are sometimes duped by their own egotism, that the devoted don't always lack happiness. I proved nothing; one proves nothing with stories, not even true ones; but good people have consciences that bolster them, and it's for them above all that I wrote this book, in which so much malice has been perceived. They do me too much honor: I would much rather belong to the poorer class of *suckers* than the more illustrious one of the *jokers.*

GEORGE SAND
Nohant, November 1, 1852

To Monsieur Charles Duvernet

We have certainly known him, but scattered among ten or twelve specimens, none of whom served as my particular model. God keep me from using a character in a novel to satirize an individual. But I have tried again to poke fun at a failing prevalent in the world of today; and if I didn't improve on my usual attempt, as usual I will say that it is the author's fault and not life's. Today's marquis are no longer ridiculous. Now that society has given birth to a new litter which has pushed aside the old one, the pretensions and impertinences of vanity have certainly changed their habitat and nature. I have tried, with a bit of care, to criticize the handsome young man of our time; and this *handsome man* is not what's called in Paris a *lion*. The latter is the most inoffensive of beings. Horace is a more widespread and dangerous type, because he's worth more. A lion is the successor of neither Molière's marquis nor the rakes of the Regency; he is neither good nor evil; he belongs to the category of children who enjoy bragging. This impotent affectation of great vices which no longer exist is only a very brief episode in the overall picture. Horace had to go through this episode; but his point of departure was different, and he left in search of a different goal. Thank God that one ridiculing is not enough for ambitious youth, which expands and refines itself by means of a thousand errors and mistakes, owing to the powerful engine of self-love. My friend, we often spoke of those among our contemporaries in whom we saw personality developing in frightening excess; we saw them do much evil while desiring to do good. Sometimes we made fun of them, often on several occasions; more often we pitied them. But we always loved them, *nevertheless!*

GEORGE SAND

Those who inspire in us the greatest affection are not always those for whom we have the highest regard. Tenderness does not require admiration and enthusiasm: it is based on a feeling of equality which makes us seek out in a friend a peer, a man subject to our own passions, our own weaknesses. Veneration demands a different sort of affection than that continuously openhearted intimacy we call friendship. I would have a very poor opinion of a man who could not love what he admired; I would have an even worse opinion of a man who could love *only* what he admired. This applies merely to friendship. Love is a different creature entirely: it lives only on enthusiasm, and all that injures its feverish delicacy blights and withers it. But the sweetest of all human emotions, the one that is nourished by calamities and mistakes as well as by greatness and heroic acts, the one that spans every stage of life, that begins to develop in us from our very first sensation of being, and that endures as long as we do, the one that parallels and actually lengthens our life, that is reborn from its ashes and that reties itself as tightly and just as firmly after being broken; that emotion, alas! is not love, as you well know, but friendship.

If I were to say here all that I think and know about friendship I would forget that I have a story to tell you, and I would write a lengthy treatise that might fill goodness knows how many volumes; but I would run a terrible risk of finding few readers in this century where friendship is so out of fashion that it's barely more common than love. Therefore I will limit myself to the matter I just mentioned in order to pose this preliminary goal for my narrative: to know why one of the friends whom I miss the most and whose life was most intertwined with mine, was not the most accomplished and best of the bunch; who, in fact, was a young man full of defects and failings, whom I even despised and hated at certain moments, and yet for whom I felt one of the most powerful and invincible attachments I've ever experienced.

His name was Horace Dumontet; he was the son of a low-level provincial clerk with a salary of fifteen hundred francs, who, having married a country girl with an estate of about ten thousand écus, found himself in command, so to speak, of three thousand francs of income. The collateral for his future, that is to say his advancement, was his work, his health, and his good behavior, in other words his blind allegiance to all the actions and procedures of whatever government and society he was serving.

No one would be astonished to learn that, in such a precarious situation and with such limited means, Monsieur and Madame Dumontet, the mother and father of my friend, decided to give their son what's called an education, that is, they enrolled him in a secondary school in the provinces until he received his baccalaureate, and they then sent him to Paris to take classes at the University, with the end in mind that within just a few years he would become a lawyer or doctor. I say that no one would be astonished by this, because there's hardly a family in a similar position that has not had the ambitious dream of providing their sons with an independent existence. *Independence,* or what this emphatic word represents, is the poor clerk's ideal; he has suffered too many privations and often, alas! too many humiliations not to want to free his progeny from them. He thinks that all possible fates have been scattered around him in abundance, and he has only to bend down to scoop up his family's shining future. Man desires to better himself— it's thanks to this instinct that the edifice of social inequality, so surprisingly fragile and durable, holds up.

Of all the professions which an adolescent can embrace in order to escape poverty, never, to our day, have parents taken it into their heads to choose the most humble and secure. Cupidity or vanity is always the judge; there are so many examples of success all around! From the lowest ranks of society we see all sorts of prodigies rise to the top, although prodigious in nothing at all. "Why shouldn't our Horace," said Monsieur Dumontet to his wife, "succeed as well as *so and so* or *so and so,* and all those others who have less aptitude and courage than he?" Madame Dumontet was a little frightened by the sacrifices her husband was suggesting in order to launch Horace in his career; but their means of persuading themselves was: Had they not given the light of day to the most intelligent child, the most favored by heaven, who had ever lived? Madame Dumontet was a simple and good woman, raised in the fields, full of good sense in the sphere of ideas which her education had allowed her to survey. But, beyond this small realm, there was a world unknown to her that she saw only through her husband's eyes. When he told her that since the Revolution all the French were equal before the law, that there was no more privilege, and that any man of talent could break out of the pack and succeed merely by pushing a little harder than those closer to the goal, she succumbed to this pretty reasoning, afraid of seeming backward, obstinate, and of resembling the peasants from whom she had come.

The sacrifice Dumontet suggested to her was nothing less than half their income. "With fifteen hundred francs," he said, "we can live and raise our daughter under our watchful gaze, modestly; with the remainder of our income, that is, with my salary, we can support Horace in Paris, on a good footing, for several years."

Fifteen hundred francs to be in Paris on a good footing, at nineteen years of age, and when you're Horace Dumontet! . . . Madame Dumontet never recoiled before a sacrifice; the worthy woman would have lived on black bread and walked shoeless to be helpful to her son and agreeable to her husband; but it grieved her to spend in one swoop the savings she had squirreled away since their marriage, which by then had mounted up to roughly ten thousand francs.

For those who do not know the narrow life of the provinces, and the incredible ability of the mothers of families to pare and glean all things, the possibility of saving several hundred écus per year on an income of three thousand francs, without starving one's husband, children, servants, and cats to death, would seem incredible. But those who live that life or who see it close up know that nothing is more typical. A woman without talent, employment, or fortune has no other way of existing and aiding the existence of her loved ones than to practice the strange occupation of stealing from herself and cutting back each day, from what her family consumes, a little bit of the necessities: this makes for a sad life, without charity or gaiety, variety or hospitality. But what does that matter to the rich, who find the public wealth very equitably divided! "If those people want to raise their children like ours," they say, speaking of the lower middle class, "let them scrimp and save! And if they don't want to, let them make their children into tradesmen or ditch diggers!" The rich are quite right to speak this way from the point of view of birthrights; from the point of view of human rights, may God be the judge!

"And why," answer the poor from the depths of their sad dwellings, "why shouldn't our children march in step with the children of the industrialist and the noble lord? Education is the great leveler, and God commands us to work towards this leveling."

You, too, are certainly correct, eternally correct, good parents, in general; and despite the harsh and frequent defeats of your hopes, it is definitely true that we'll march toward equality for a long time along the road of your legitimate ambition and naive vanity. But when this leveling of rights and hopes is complete, when every man finds in society an environment where his existence is not only possible, but useful and fruitful, we must truly hope that each person will evaluate his strengths and judge himself, in calm and freedom, with more reason and modesty than he does at this moment, under the spell of feverish anxiety and in the tumult of struggle. The time will come—I firmly believe this—when every young person will not resolve to stick a pistol in his mouth if he can't become the leading light of his century. Then, when everyone has political rights, and the exercise of those rights is considered to be one of the features of every citizen's life, perhaps the career of politics will no longer be encumbered by the palpitating ambitions of those who rush into it today with so much bitterness, disdainful of any role other than to lead and govern people.

In any event, Madame Dumontet, who was counting on those ten thousand francs for her daughter's dowry, agreed to dip into them for her son's support in Paris, reserving the right to save in the future to marry off Camille, Horace's younger sister.

So here we have Horace, on the beautiful sidewalks of Paris, with his title of graduate and law student, his nineteen years and his allowance of fifteen hundred francs. He had already been studying (or was supposed to have been studying) for a year when I met him in a little café across from the Luxembourg Gardens, where we both went every morning to drink hot chocolate and read the newspapers. His obliging manners, his openness, his lively and gentle expression, won me over at first sight. Young people soon connect. If two of them sit together at the same table for several days running and exchange a few polite words, on the first sunny and expansive morning the conversation will be carried from the café to the far ends of the paths of the Luxembourg Garden. That is, in point of fact, what happened to us one spring morning. The lilacs were in bloom, the sun was shining joyfully on the mahogany counter with its gilded bronzes belonging to Madame Poisson, the beautiful café manager. Horace and I ended up, I have no idea how, at the edge of the large boating pond, arm in arm, chatting like old friends, although we didn't even know each other's names yet; exchanging our general ideas had quickly brought us closer, but we were not yet out of the realm of personal reserve, which is exactly what creates mutual trust among well-mannered people. All I learned about Horace on that day was that he was a law student; all that he knew about me was that I studied medicine. The only questions he asked me concerned how I looked upon the branch of knowledge I had devoted myself to, and vice versa.

"I admire you," he said to me right as we were parting, "or rather, I envy you. You work, you don't waste time, you love science, you have hope, you're marching straight toward your goal! As for me, I'm on a path that's so different that instead of persevering along it I only look for ways to stray from it. Law horrifies me; it's just a tissue of lies that conceals divine fairness and eternal truth. If only it were lies connected by a system of logic! Just the contrary, the lies shamelessly contradict one another, so that anyone can do evil by his own perverse means! Any young man who can take seriously the study of this chicanery, I call base or absurd; I scorn him, I hate him! . . ."

I liked his vehemence, although it was not completely immune from being calculated. Hearing him, one couldn't doubt his sincerity; but

one could also see that he was not fulminating and making these imprecations for the first time. They came to him too naturally not to be
rehearsed—please excuse what seems like a paradox. If my meaning
appears obscure, it may seem difficult to penetrate the secret of Horace's
personality: hard to define, hard enough for me, and I've studied it a
great deal.

It was a blend of affectation and naturalness so delicate that one
could no longer tell one from the other, just as in certain dishes or
essences the taste or the aroma no longer reveals the basic ingredients.
I've seen people who, from the first, disliked Horace in the extreme,
and who considered him as pretentious and bombastic as can be. I've
seen others who immediately became infatuated with him and never let
go of that impression, maintaining that he was the most candid and
easygoing person they had ever met. I assure you that both were mistaken, or rather, that both were correct: Horace was *naturally affected*.

Don't you know some people like that, who come into the world
with borrowed personalities and manners, and who seem to be acting a
part, even as they seriously play out the drama of their lives? These people imitate themselves. With ardent wits drawn by nature to the love of
great things, though their surroundings may be prosaic, their enthusiasm is still romantic; though their abilities may be limited, their ideas
are still excessive. They always drape themselves with the cloak of the
character they have in their imagination. This character is actually the
man, since it is his dream, his creation, his internal engine. The real
man walks side by side with the ideal man; and just as we see two
images of ourselves in a mirror cracked down the middle, we see in
such a person, split down the middle, so to speak, two images which
can't be separated, but which are quite distinct from one another. That
is what's meant by the phrase "second nature," which has become a
synonym for habit.

So, that was Horace. He had nourished in himself such a need to
appear to his best advantage that he was always dressed up, gotten up,
gleaming, both psychologically and physically. Nature seemed to help
him in this perpetual endeavor. He cut a beautiful figure, always assuming elegant and smooth postures. Irreproachably good taste didn't
always govern his wardrobe or his gestures; but a painter could find in

him, at any moment of the day, an effect worth capturing. He was tall, well built, robust without being heavy. His face was noble, thanks to the purity of its lines; and yet it was not distinguished, something very different. Nobility is a work of nature, distinction is a work of art; one we're born with, the other is acquired. Distinction stems from a certain arrangement and habitual expression. Horace's thick, black beard was trimmed with a dandyism that had Latin Quarter written all over it, and his full head of ebony hair bloomed with a profusion that a true dandy would have taken care to restrain. But when he impetuously passed his hand through this inky wave, its disorder was never ridiculous, nor did it diminish his forehead's beauty. Horace knew perfectly well that he could muss his hair ten times an hour with impunity, because, as he expressed it to me one day, his hair was "extremely well landscaped."

He dressed with a sort of studied elegance. His tailor had neither a reputation nor any idea of what real fashion was, but he had the wits to understand Horace, and to risk with him a wider cuff, a vest with a more contrasting color, a more tailored cut, a waistcoat bulging more at the shirtfront than he would make for his other young clients. Horace would have looked perfectly ridiculous on the Boulevard de Gand, but in the Luxembourg Garden or in the orchestra of the Odéon Theater he was the best dressed, the most nonchalant, the tightest around the ribs, the fullest along the thighs, the *flashiest,* as the fashion magazines put it. His hat was cocked to one side, just the right amount, and his cane was neither too thick nor too light. His clothes didn't have the pithiness of the English style, which characterized the truly elegant; on the other hand, his movements were so supple, and he wore his stiff lapels with such natural ease and grace, that from deep inside their carriages or from the heights of their theater boxes, the noble ladies of the Faubourg Saint-Germain, even the young ones, looked him over once.

Horace knew he was handsome and he made you constantly aware of it, although he had enough wits never to talk about his looks. But he was always preoccupied with other people's looks. Minutely and rapidly he would pick apart all their defects, all their unpleasant traits; and naturally he drew you, with his mocking comments, to compare inwardly his appearance with that of his victims. His wit was biting on this subject; and since he had an admirably sculpted nose and magnificent eyes, he had no mercy for badly shaped noses and vulgar eyes. For hunchbacks he had a mournful compassion, and each time he pointed one out to me, I was naive enough to look with an anatomist's eye at Horace's dorsal structure, his vertebrae quivering with a secret pleasure, although his face expressed only an indifferent smile at the frivolous advantage of a beautiful physique. If anyone fell asleep in an embarrassing or disgraceful position, Horace was always the first to laugh at it. This forced me to notice, when he stayed in my room, or when I surprised him in his, that he always slept with an arm folded under the nape of the neck or thrown over the head like a classical statue; and it was this observation, seemingly childish, that led me to understand this natural, innate affectation which I spoke of earlier. Even asleep, even alone and without a mirror, Horace found a way to sleep nobly. One of our friends claimed mischievously that he posed for flies.

Please excuse all the details. I believe they're necessary, and now I'll return to my first conversations with him.

The next day I asked him why, if he found law so distasteful, he didn't devote himself to some other field of study. "My dear sir," said he with an air of self-assurance which belied his age, and seemed borrowed from a man of forty, "there's only one profession today that leads to everything, that of a lawyer."

"What do you call 'everything'?" I asked him.

"For the moment," he answered, "the Chamber of Deputies is everything. But wait awhile, and we'll see something very different!"

"Oh, you're counting on a new revolution? But if it doesn't happen, how will you arrange to become a deputy? Are you wealthy?"

"Not exactly; but I will be."

"Excellent. In that case, all you need is your license; you won't have to practice."

I sincerely thought he had sufficient funds to justify his confidence. He hesitated a few seconds; then, not daring to confirm my error or to brusquely disabuse me of it, he resumed: "One must practice to become known . . . without a doubt, within two years those competent will be chosen as candidates; so one must demonstrate competency."

"Two years? That seems like a very short time to me; in any case, you will need twice that much to be admitted to the bar and to prove your competence; you will still be far short of the age . . ."

"Don't you think the age limit will be lowered as it was for the census, perhaps even in the next session?"

"I don't think so. But in the end, it's a question of time, and I think that sooner or later you will get there, if you're firmly resolved to do it."

"Isn't it true," he said to me with a beatific smile and a glance sparkling with pride, "that resolve is all you need in this world? And that, no matter how low you start, you can climb to society's peaks, if you keep in your heart a vision of the future?"

"No doubt," I answered. "What's important is to know how many obstacles one will have to overcome, and that secret is known only to Providence."

"No, my dear friend!" he shouted, slipping his arm through mine in a familiar manner. "What's important is to know if one's will is stronger than any obstacle—and that," he added, thumping his sonorous thorax, "I have!"

Our chat had ended up opposite the Chamber of Peers. Horace seemed as if he were ready to grow like a giant in a fairy tale. I looked at him and noticed that, despite his precocious beard, the roundness of the contours of his face revealed that he was still an adolescent. His enthusiastic ambitions made the contrast even more glaring. "So, how old are you?" I asked him.

"Guess!" he said, smiling.

"At first sight I would have pegged you for twenty-five," I answered. "But I'm not sure you're even twenty."

"True enough, I'm not quite there. And what do you conclude on the basis of that?"

"That your will is only two or three years old, and for that reason it's still very young and fragile."

"You're mistaken," cried Horace. "My will was born with me, it's as old as I am."

"That's true with respect to aptitude and innate ability; but, after all, I presume that you have not yet exerted your will much toward your political career! You can't have given much thought to becoming a deputy, since you can't even have known for very long what a deputy was!"

"Rest assured that I knew it as early as a child can. No sooner did I understand the meaning of words, than I found in them something magical. This is a question of destiny, you see; mine is to be a member of parliament. Yes, yes, I will speak and be spoken of!"

"I hope it comes to pass!" I answered him. "You have the equipment: it's a gift of God. Now learn the theory."

"What do you mean by that? Law? *Chicanery?*"

"Oh, if only it were that easy! I mean: Learn the science of humanity, history, politics, all the religions; and then, judge, combine, form a definite opinion . . ."

"You mean *ideas?*" he resumed with that smile and that look, imposing in their triumphant conviction. "I already have some ideas, and if you don't mind my saying so, I don't think I'll ever have better ones; because our ideas come from our feelings, and all *my* feelings are grand! Yes, sir, heaven made me grand and good. I know not what trials it has in store for me, but, and I say this with a pride that only fools would laugh at, I feel myself to be generous, strong, magnanimous; my soul shivers and my blood boils at the idea of injustice. Great things intoxicate me to the point of delirium. From that I derive no vanity, nor could I; but, I say to you with confidence, I feel I belong to the race of heroes!"

I could not repress a smile; but Horace, who was watching me, saw that this smile had no malevolence in it.

"You're surprised," he said, "that I indulge myself like this in front of you, whom I barely know, in feelings that ordinarily one doesn't broach even with one's best friend. Do you think it would be more modest for me to keep quiet?"

"Certainly not. And it would be less honest."

"Well then, you should know that I feel I'm better and less ridiculous than all those hypocrites who, believing themselves *in petto* to be demigods, cunningly bow their heads and prudishly affect good taste. Those are the egotists, the ambitious ones in the hateful sense of the word and the deed. Far from displaying that friendly enthusiasm which rallies around itself all vital ideas and generous souls (and how else do great revolutions happen?), they caress in secret their narrow superiority, and, fearing that it will alarm others, they mask it from jealous glances, planning to use it adroitly on the day their fortunes are made. I tell you such men are good only for making money and for serving in a corrupt government; but the men who overthrow the powerful and their iniquity, who rile up a passionate generosity, those who seriously and nobly stir up the world, the Mirabeaus, the Dantons, the Pitts—see if they trifle with the niceties of modesty!"

There was some truth in what he was saying, and he said it with such conviction that it didn't cross my mind to contradict him, even though since then my experience, or perhaps my nature, has made me horrified by such presumptuousness. But what was unique about Horace was that while you were looking at him and listening to him, you were under the spell of his voice and gestures. After parting from him, you would be astonished at not having pointed out his error; but when you saw him again you were once more drawn in by the magnetism of his paradox.

I left him that day very struck by what an unusual character he was, and wondering if he were crazy or a great man. I leaned toward the latter opinion.

"Since you like revolutions so much," I said to him the next day, "you must have fought last year, during the July Days?"

"Alas! I was on vacation," he answered. "But there, in my little province, I took action, and if I didn't encounter any dangers, it was not my fault. I joined the volunteers of the municipal guard, and we kept watch to preserve the victory. We spent nights doing sentry duty, rifles on our shoulders, and if the Old Regime had fought back, if it had sent troops against us as we anticipated, I flatter myself that we would have acquitted ourselves better than those old grocers who were later inducted into the National Guard the government eventually organized. They never even left their shops while the outcome was still in doubt, and we were the ones who patrolled the whole town to protect them against any outside response. Two weeks later, when the danger had already moved on, they would have slit our bodies with their bayonets if we had yelled, 'Liberty forever!'"

That day, after we had chatted a long time, I suggested that he stay with me until the dinner hour and then come and dine with me on the Rue de l'Ancienne-Comédie at Pinson's—the most reasonable and affable of the Latin Quarter restaurateurs.

I gave Horace the best treatment, and Monsieur Pinson's cooking is certainly excellent, healthy, and inexpensive. His little restaurant is the meeting place for the young who aspire to literary glory and for well-established students. Ever since his colleague and rival Dagnaux, cavalry officer in the National Guard, had performed marvels of bravery during the riots, a whole phalanx of students, Dagnaux's regular customers, swore they would never cross the threshold of his domain, and fell back upon the bigger cutlets and thicker steaks of the peaceable and benevolent Pinson.

After dinner we went to the Odéon Theater to see Madame Dorval and Lockroy in *Antony*. From that day on, our acquaintance was set and Horace and I were joined in friendship.

"So," I said to him during an intermission, "you find the study of medicine even more repulsive than law?"

"My dear friend," he answered, "I confess I understand nothing of your vocation. Is it possible that you can plunge your hands, your eyes, your wits into that human mud every day without losing all feeling of poetry and all freshness of the imagination?"

"There's something worse than dissecting dead bodies," I said to him, "and that's operating on the living: that takes more courage and resolution, I assure you. The sight of the most hideous cadaver makes one less sick than the first cry of pain torn from a poor child who understands nothing of the hurt you're causing him. It lies somewhere between the butcher's trade and an apostle's mission."

"They say that the heart dries up in your profession," continued Horace. "Aren't you afraid of becoming so passionate about science that you forget humanity, as did all the great anatomists you hear praised? When I see them I avert my eyes as if I'd glimpsed an executioner."

"I'm hoping," I answered, "to attain just the level of cold-bloodedness required to function, without losing pity and human sympathy. I have a ways to go before I acquire the necessary calm, and I don't believe, actually, that it hardens the heart."

"That's possible. But in the end, the mind becomes unnerved, the imagination slackens, the sense of beauty and ugliness is lost; one sees only a certain material side of life where all ideals end in the idea of usefulness. Have you ever known a physician-poet?"

"I might just as well ask you if you know many politician-poets. It hardly seems to me that a political career, as I see it today, is appropriate for maintaining a freshness of imagination and the fragile coloration of poetry."

"If society were reformed," exclaimed Horace, "that career could be the most beautiful training for the vitality of the brain and the compassion of the heart; but it's definitely true that the path as it's laid out today is withering. When I think that to be able to judge the truth about society, where philosophy should be the guiding light, I have to know the Code and the Digest; that I'm assimilating Pothier, Ducaurroy, and Rogron; that I labor, in a word, to make myself a brute and, in order to put myself in touch with the men of our time, I descend to their level—oh! then I seriously think about pulling out of politics."

"But then what would you do with the enthusiasm that's eating you up, with that greatness of soul overflowing in you? And what would you feed that will of steel which you reproached me for doubting just a few days ago?"

He took his head in his hands, pressed his elbows into the railing that separated the parterre from the orchestra, and remained lost in thought until the curtain rose. Then he listened to act three of *Antony* with great attention and emotion.

"And what about passion!" he declared when the act had ended. "What value do you place on life's passions?"

"Are you talking about love?" I answered. "Life, as we've structured it for ourselves, allows only all or nothing in this realm. It isn't possible to be both a lover like Antony and a citizen like you. You have to choose."

"That's just what I was thinking when I heard Antony speak so disdainfully of society, so incensed by it, so rebellious against everything that impedes his love . . . Have you ever been in love?"

"Perhaps. What does it matter? Ask your own heart what love is."

"Damned if I know!" he exclaimed, shrugging his shoulders. "Have *I* ever had time to love? Do I know what a woman is? I'm pure, my dear boy, pure as a goose," he added, and burst out laughing good-naturedly. "And in case this makes you look down on me, I'll tell you that up to now women have made me more scared than desirous. But I have a lot of hair on my cheeks and a lot of imagination to satisfy. Well! that, above all, has kept me from straying in vulgar ways like my friends. I have not yet met the ideal virgin for whom my heart would take the trouble to beat. Those sad grisettes who gather at the Chaumière and other filthy pens fill me with so much pity that I wouldn't have the fall of one of those plucked angels on my conscience for all the pleasures of hell. And then, that type has such coarse hands, it has such a pug nose, it says 'ain't' when it should say 'isn't,' it accuses you of being the cause of its unhappiness in letters that would make you die laughing. There's no way even to feel serious remorse for that type. If I give myself up to love, I want it to wound me deeply, to electrify me, to break my heart, or to exalt me to the seventh heaven and make me drunk on volup-tuousness. No middle ground: one or the other—one and the other, if you like—but no drama in the back of a shop, no barroom victory! What I want is to suffer, to go crazy, I want to take poison with my mistress or stab myself over her corpse; but I don't want to be ridicu-lous, and above all I don't want to be bored in the midst of my own tragedy and end it with a touch of vaudeville. My friends tease me a great deal about my innocence, they play the Don Juan under my nose to tempt or dazzle me, and I assure you they do it without much ex-pense. I wish them great pleasure; but I want something else for myself. What are you thinking about?" he added, seeing me turn my head to suppress a strong desire to laugh.

"I'm thinking," I said, "that tomorrow I'm having a very likable grisette over for lunch to whom I'd like to introduce you."

"Oh! may God protect me from those sorts," he exclaimed. "I have five or six friends whom I'm condemned never to glimpse except through the flimsy phantoms of their two-week bedmates. I know by heart the vocabulary of that type of female. Fie! You scandalize me, and here I thought you were more sober than all my absurd companions. For a week I've been avoiding them to attach myself to you, who seemed to be a serious person and who, certainly, had elegant ways for a student. And now I hear you have a woman, you, too! My God, where will I hide so I never have to meet another woman like that!"

"You'll have to risk meeting mine, though. I tell you I'm counting on it, and I'll come and get you if you don't have lunch with her at my house."

"If you're tired of her, I warn you I'm not the man to take her off your hands."

"My dear Horace, let me reassure you by telling you that if you were tempted to take her off my hands, you would have to begin by cutting my throat."

"Are you serious?

"As serious as can be."

"In that case, I accept your invitation. It will be a pleasure to see true love up close . . ."

"For a grisette, you realize. Does that shock you?"

"Well, yes, it shocks me. As for me, I've only seen one woman I could have loved, if only she had been twenty years younger. She was a dowager from the provinces, a squire's widow, still blonde, once beautiful, who spoke, walked, greeted, and dismissed in such a way that she made all the women I'd seen before look like turkey-keepers. This woman was from an old family; she had an hourglass figure, hands like a Raphael Madonna, the feet of a sylph, the face of a mummy, and a viper's tongue. But I promised myself never to take a mistress who was beautiful, lovable, and young unless she had hands and feet like hers and, above all, aristocratic manners, and a lot of white lace on blonde hair."

"My dear Horace," I said to him, "it will be a long time before you love, and perhaps you'll never love."

"I hope God was listening to that!" he exclaimed. "If I love once, I'm lost. Farewell to my political career, farewell to my austere and vast future! I don't know how to do anything halfway. Let's see, will I be an orator, a poet, or a lover?"

"Perhaps we should begin by being students," I said.

"Easy for you to say," he replied. "You're a student *and* in love. Me, I'm not in love, and I study even less!"

I developed a lively interest in Horace. I was not absolutely convinced that he had the heroic strength and the austere enthusiasm which he attributed to himself, out of the sincerity of his heart. Rather, I saw in him a wonderful child, generous, candid, more taken with beautiful dreams than able yet to realize them. But his frankness and his constant aspiring to higher things made me like him without my having to see him as a hero. This fantasy of his was not at all unpleasant: it was testimony of his love for ideal beauty. One of two possibilities, I told myself: either he has a calling to be a superior man, and a secret instinct that he naively believes revealed it to him; or he's merely a worthy young man, and, once this fever subsides, a sweet goodness will bloom in him, a weighty conscience, warmed from time to time by a ray of enthusiasm.

All in all, I liked him better from the second perspective. I would have been surer of him if I had seen him shed that openly fatuous manner without losing the love of the beautiful and the good. The superior man has a terrible destiny ahead of him. Obstacles exasperate him, and his pride is sometimes tenacious and violent, so much so that it can make him stray and turn what God gave him for doing good into a disastrous power. One way or another, I liked Horace and he endeared himself to me. Either I had to support him in his strength, or I had to help him in his weakness. I was five or six years older; I was blessed with a calmer nature; my future plans were settled and no longer caused me personal anxiety. In my time of passion, I was saved from mistakes and suffering by an attachment full of sweetness and truth. I felt that all this happiness was the free gift of Providence, that I hadn't deserved it enough to enjoy it alone, and that I should share some of my soul's serenity by placing it like a sedative on another soul that was irritable or snake-bitten. I was thinking like a doctor; but my intentions were good, and, except for repeating the innocent bragging of my poor Horace, I would say that I, too, was good, and felt more affection than I knew how to express.

The one clearly absurd and blameworthy thing that I could find in my new friend was his aspiration to an aristocratic woman, while he, a fierce republican, was a poor judge, to be sure, of fine manners, and exaggeratedly disdainful of rough and naive behavior, when he himself was not as polished as he claimed.

I had decided to introduce him to Eugénie sooner rather than later, thinking that the sight of this simple and noble creature would change his mind or at least steer it toward a wiser course. He saw her, and he was struck by her graciousness, but he didn't find her at all as beautiful as he imagined a woman seriously loved should be.

"She is just *not bad*," he said when she was out of earshot. "She must be quite a wit."

"She has more judgment than wit," I answered him, "and her former girlfriends thought her very foolish."

She served our modest lunch, which she had prepared herself, and this prosaic act stirred up disgust in Horace's supercilious heart. But when she sat down between us, and played the hostess to him with perfect ease and propriety, he was suddenly respectful and changed his tune. Up until then he had overwhelmed poor Eugénie with very witty paradoxes that didn't even make her smile. He had taken this as a sign of her admiration. When he began to sense in her a judge and not a fool, he became serious, and took as many pains to look sober as he had taken to look lighthearted. It was too late. He had already angered Eugénie's severe nature; but she revealed none of her reaction, and lunch was hardly over when she retired to a corner and began to sew, neither more nor less than an ordinary grisette. Horace felt his respect for her shrinking as quickly as it had grown.

My little apartment, located on the Quai des Augustins, consisted of three rooms, and cost me no less than three hundred francs rent. It was a home of my own: luxury for a student. I had a dining room, a bedroom, and, between the two, a study, which I decorated with the name of parlor. That's where we had coffee. Horace, noticing the cigars, lit one up without hesitation. "Excuse me," I said, taking his arm, "but it bothers Eugénie. I only smoke out on the balcony." He took the trouble of begging Eugénie's pardon for his heedlessness; but at heart he was surprised to see me treat with consideration a woman who was busy hemming my cravats.

My balcony crowned the top floor of the building. Eugénie had shaded it with convulvulus and sweet pea, which she had sown in two planters with orange trees. The orange trees were in bloom, and a few pots of violets and reseda completed the delights of my divan. I gave Horace the place of honor on the bit of old tapestry which served as my oriental rug, and the leather cushion on which I used to lean my elbow to smoke as voluptuously as a pasha. A windowpane separated the divan from the chair where Eugénie worked in the study. In this way I saw her, I was with her, without annoying her with my tobacco smoke. When she saw Horace on the rug instead of me, she gently and without affectation lowered the muslin curtain in the casement window between us, pretending to be screening herself from the sunlight, but clearly out of a sense of modesty, which Horace understood perfectly. I was sitting on one of the orange-tree planters, behind him.

There was just enough room for two people and four or five flowerpots on that narrow belvedere; but in a glance we could take in the most beautiful stretch of the river Seine, the entire length of the Louvre, yellow in the sun and sharply contrasting with the blue of the sky, all the bridges and quais as far as the Hôtel-Dieu. Opposite us, Sainte-Chapelle raised its somber gray steeples and sharp pediment above the houses of the Ile de la Cité; a little farther off the beautiful tower of Saint-Jacques-la-Boucherie lifted its four giant lions to the heavens; and to the right the façade of Notre Dame completed the picture with its elegant and solid mass. It was a banquet for the eyes: on one side, the old Paris, with its venerable monuments and its picturesque disorder; on the other, Renaissance Paris, mingling with Paris of the Empire, the work of the Medicis, Louis XIV, and Napoleon. Each column, each doorway, was a page in the history of royalty.

We had just read *The Hunchback of Notre Dame,* fresh off the presses; naively, we were completely taken with it—as was everyone, at least everyone young—taken with the charm by which this Romantic work on the ancient beauties of our capital had pumped new blood into poetry. It was like a magic coloring through which forgotten memories came back to life; and, thanks to the poet, we looked at the pinnacles of our old edifices, we examined their distinctive shapes and their picturesque effects with different eyes from those of our predecessors, the students of the Empire and the Restoration.

Horace was passionate about Victor Hugo. He loved furiously all of his strangeness and daring. I didn't argue with him, although I didn't always agree with him. My taste and my instincts drew me to a less uneven form, to a type of painting with gentler contours and softer shadows. I compared him to Salvator Rosa, who saw with the eyes of the imagination more than the eyes of science. But why would I have waged a war of words and countenances against Horace? At nineteen years of age one doesn't recoil from a manner of expression that makes a sensation livelier, and one doesn't condemn it at age twenty-five. No, joyful youth is not at all pedantic; for it there is no such thing as a translation that's too energetic in rendering what youth experiences with such energy. And it's certainly something when a poet gives his thoughts so wide and striking a shape that almost an entire generation opens its eyes with him and begins to enjoy some of the same emotions that inspired him!

That's the way it was with Hugo: even the most recalcitrant among us, those who, after shutting *The Hunchback of Notre Dame,* needed to refresh their vision by reading a page of *Paul et Virginie* or quickly reviewing, as an elegant critic put it, the most "crystalline of Petrarch's sonnets," nonetheless placed over their delicate eyes those multicolored glasses which revealed so many new things; and after they enjoyed their emotion-filled shows, these ingrates claimed that those were indeed strange glasses. Strange, if you like, but without the master's whims, and with your naked eye, would you have even noticed any of it?

Based on my criticisms, Horace made minute concessions; I made bigger ones based on his enthusiasm; and after our discussion our glances, following the flight of the swallows and crows which buzzed our heads, rested, like them, on the towers of Notre Dame, eternal object of our contemplation. It had a part of our love, that old cathedral, as with forsaken beauties who come back into fashion and whom the crowd presses itself around as soon as they have found a new and fervent admirer whose praise rejuvenates them.

I'm not claiming to turn this narrative of a part of my youth into a critical examination of my era: my powers are not up to it: but I couldn't go over certain days in my memory without recalling the influence certain readings had on Horace, on me, on all of us. They're part of our life, of ourselves, so to speak. I don't know how to separate in my memory the poetic impressions of my adolescence from my reading of *René* and *Atala*.

In the midst of our Romantic discourse, the doorbell rang. Eugénie alerted me by tapping on the windowpane, and I went to answer the door. It was a painting student from the school of Eugène Delacroix, whose name was Paul Arsène, nicknamed Masaccio Junior in the studio, where I went every day to teach a class in anatomy for painters.

"Greetings, Signor Masaccio," I said, introducing him to Horace, who cast a glacial look at his dirty tunic and uncombed hair. "Here's a young master who will go far, they assure me, and who, in the meantime, has come to take me to class."

"No, not yet," Paul Arsène answered. "You have over an hour; I came to speak to you about something that concerns me personally. Do you have a moment?"

"Certainly," I responded. "And if my friend is in the way, his cigar awaits him on the balcony."

"No," the young man continued, "Nothing I have to tell you is confidential, and since two heads are better than one, I wouldn't be angry if Monsieur listens as well."

"Have a seat," I said to him, and went to look for a fourth chair in the next room.

"Don't mind me," said the art student, climbing onto the chest of drawers; then, having tucked his cap between his elbow and knee, he pulled out a checkered handkerchief and wiped his face, which dripped with sweat, and spoke in these terms, his legs dangling down and the rest of his body in the pose of the *Pensieroso:*

"Monsieur, I want to give up painting and go into medicine, since they tell me it's a better way of life; so I've come to ask your opinion."

"You're asking me a question," I said to him, "that's more difficult to answer than you may think. I believe all the professions are very crowded, and therefore every way of life, as you call it, is precarious. Great knowledge and great ability are no guarantee of a future; in the end, I don't see where medicine would offer you more opportunities than the arts. The best choice is the one that our aptitude points out to us; and since you have, they assure me, the most remarkable talent for painting, I don't understand why it already repels you."

"Repels me? Me? Oh, no!" answered Masaccio. "It doesn't repel me at all, and if one could make a living as a painter, I would prefer it to anything. But it seems to take such a long, long time! My patron says you have to draw from life for at least two years before handling brushes. And then, before exhibiting, it seems you have to work at painting for at least two or three more years. And when you've exhibited, if you're not rejected, you're often no further along than before. This morning I went to the museum, I thought that everyone would stop in front of my patron's painting, since, after all, he's a master, and famous! Well, half the people passing by didn't even raise their heads, and they all went to look at a gentleman who had had himself painted in an artillery man's uniform. He had wooden arms and a cardboard face. Put those people aside for the moment: they were poor and ignorant. But then along come some young people, painting students from different studios, and each one had something to say: some criticized, some admired, but not one spoke as I would have liked them to speak. Not one understood. Then I said to myself: What's the use of making art for a public that doesn't see or understand a bit of it? It *used* to be good enough for me. Now I'm going to take up another profession, provided it brings in some money."

"What a complete idiot!" Horace whispered in my ear. "His soul is as filthy as his shirt!"

I didn't share Horace's contempt. I hardly knew Masaccio, but I knew him to be intelligent and hard working. Monsieur Delacroix sang his praises, and his comrades were his admirers and friends. A thought that I didn't understand must have been hidden beneath these displays of ingenuousness and cupidity. And since he had declared, at the beginning, that he had nothing confidential to tell me, I foresaw that this confidence would not be coaxed out of him easily. To be convinced of Masaccio's obstinacy, and at the same time to have a presentiment of some decent motive in him, one had only to look at his face and observe his deportment.

He was the people embodied in an individual; not the robust and peaceful people who till the soil, but those who are crafty, puny, bold, intelligent, and alert. That is, he was not handsome. Nevertheless he was the sort of person about whom his comrades at the studio said: "You could make something amazing with that head." That's because his head had, in fact, a magnificent expression beneath the vulgarity of its features. I've never seen an expression more energetic or penetrating. His eyes were small, almost veiled, under short and narrow lids; and yet those eyes shot flames, and his glance darted so quickly that it always seemed as if it were about to tear his sockets. His nose was too short, and because of the short distance from the corner of his eye to his nostril, his face made a first impression that was common, even lowly; but that impression lasted only a second. If there were still something of the slave and vassal about his shell, the genie of independence was brooding inside him and revealed itself in flashes. A thick mouth, shadowed by a budding black mustache, irregularly rooted; a wide face, a square and straightforward chin, slightly cleft in the middle; high and projecting zygomas—everywhere firm and straight planes, broken at right angles, proclaimed an unusual will and an indomitable uprightness. At the junction of the nostrils there was a delicateness which a follower of Lavater would find exquisite, and a sculptor would have admired his forehead no less than a phrenologist. As for me, I was in the thick of my research, and I never stopped looking at him; and when I did anatomical presentations at the studio, I always instinctively addressed myself to this young man, who was for me the epitome of intelligence, courage, and goodness.

It also hurt me, I admit, to hear him speak in such a trivial manner.

"What, Arsène?" I said to him. "You would give up painting for another career where you can make a little more profit?"

"Yes, Monsieur, I'd do it, just as I said," he answered without the slightest embarrassment. "If I could be sure right now that I would net a thousand francs a year, I would become a cobbler."

"One of the fine arts," said Horace with a contemptuous smile.

"It's not an art at all," said Masaccio coldly. "It's my father's trade, and I could do it as well as the next man. But it wouldn't earn me the money I need."

"So you need a great deal of money, then, my poor boy?" I said to him.

"I tell you, I have to earn a thousand francs; if I can't, I'll cut my expenses in half."

"Then how can you even think of studying medicine? You would need about thirty thousand francs, as much for the years of study as for those where you're building a clientele. And then . . ."

"And then you have not taken the required classes," said Horace, impatient with my patience.

"That's true," said Arsène. "But I will take them, or at least I'll do the equivalent. I'll shut myself in my room with a pitcher of water and a morsel of bread, and it seems to me that I could learn in a week what the students learn in a month. Students, in general, don't like to work; and when you're young, you play, you lose time. When you're twenty and more reasonable, and when, moreover, you're forced to hurry, you hurry. But from what you tell me about the rest of the training, I see clearly that I can't be a doctor. What about becoming a lawyer?"

Horace doubled over with laughter.

"You're going to hurt yourself," Masaccio said to him calmly, struck by Horace's pretentiousness.

"My dear child," I said, "put some distance between yourself and all these projects. At your age they're not realistic. Your future is in arts and industry. If you have neither money nor credit, there is no more certainty in one path than another. Whatever choice you make, you need time, patience, and resignation."

Arsène sighed. I decided to wait and question him later.

"You were born a painter, that much is certain," I continued. "That's still the direction in which you will advance the fastest."

"No, Monsieur," he replied. "I might as well begin working tomorrow in a novelty shop and earn some money."

"You could always be a lackey," added Horace, increasingly indignant.

"I'd dislike that very much," said Arsène, "but if there were no alternative . . ."

"Arsène! Arsène!" I cried. "It would be a great sorrow for you and a loss for art. Is it possible that you fail to understand that a great gift is a great responsibility imposed by Providence?"

"That's a pretty word," said Arsène, "one which makes eyes light up. But there are other responsibilities than to oneself. Too bad! Well, I'll go tell them at the studio that you're coming at three o'clock, right?"

And he jumped off the chest of drawers, shook my hand without saying another word, barely acknowledged Horace, and plunged like a cat into the depths of the staircase, stopping at each floor to put his heels back into his dilapidated shoes.

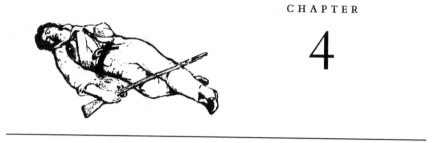

Paul Arsène came to see me again; and when we were alone, I got out of him, not without difficulty, the secret that I had sensed was coming. He began by telling me his life story:

"As I mentioned to you, Monsieur, my father is a cobbler in the provinces. There were five children; I'm the third. The oldest was fully grown when my father, already old and able to retire with a small nest egg, made a second marriage, this time to a woman who was neither beautiful nor good, neither young nor rich, but who had gotten hold of his mind, and who is now wasting his honor and his money. My father, cheated, unhappy, more captivated by her as she gave him more grounds for jealousy, took to the bottle to numb himself, as our class does when we have sorrows.

"Poor father! We were very patient with him, since we genuinely pitied him. We remembered when he was so sober and so good! Finally, it reached a point where we could stand it no longer. His personality had changed so much that for a word, for a look, he pounced on us and beat us. We were no longer children, we couldn't put up with it. What's more, we had been raised with gentleness and we were not used to our family being a hell. And then—wouldn't you know it? —he became jealous of my older brother! The truth is, my stepmother had made advances to him, since he was a handsome boy and a good child; but he threatened to tell my father the whole story, and so she beat him to it, as in the tragedy of *Phaedra,* which I can no longer see without crying. She accused my brother of her own wicked ways.

Then my brother sold himself as a substitute for the draft, and he left. The second child, who foresaw that something similar might happen to him, came here to seek his fortune, promising to send for me as soon as he had found a means of survival.

"Me, I stayed at home with my two sisters, and I lived peacefully enough, since I'd decided to let that evil woman scream all she liked without answering her back. I enjoyed keeping busy; I knew my school lessons fairly well; and when I was not helping my father in the shop, I amused myself by reading or by doodling on paper, since I've always had a taste for drawing. But since I thought it would never do me any good, I wasted as little time on it as possible.

"One day, a painter who was traveling through the region to do studies for landscapes ordered a pair of boots at our shop, and I was given the task of measuring his foot. His albums were spread out on the table of his little room at the inn. I asked his permission to look at them; and since my curiosity aroused his own, he told me to draw a sketch of a man from my imagination, on a scrap of paper that he gave me along with a pencil. I thought he was making fun of me; but the pleasure of drawing with such a black pencil on such a smooth piece of paper triumphed over my self-respect. I drew whatever came into my head; he watched, and didn't laugh. He even wanted to glue my sketch into his album, and to write on it my name, profession, and my town. 'You're wrong to remain a worker,' he told me. 'You were born to paint. If I were in your shoes, I would throw it all over and go study in a big city.' He even suggested that he would take me there, since he was a good and generous man. He gave me his address in Paris, so that if I were moved to do so, I could go and find him. I thanked him, but I didn't dare follow him or believe in the hope he gave me. I returned to my leather and my boot-trees, and another year passed without a storm between me and my father.

"My stepmother hated me; since I always gave in to her, our quarrels didn't go far. But one fine day she remarked that my sister, Louison, who was already fifteen years old, was getting to be pretty, and that the people in the neighborhood had noticed. Then she began to hate Louison, to criticize her for being a little flirt—and worse. Poor Louison was still as innocent as a ten-year-old, and to add to that, she was as proud as our poor mother had been. Louison, desperate, instead of being all submissiveness as I counseled her, lost her temper, answered back, and threatened to run away. My father wanted to back her up; but his wife soon had the upper hand. Alas, Monsieur, Louison was scolded, insulted, hit. And little Suzanne, too. She tried to take her sister's side, and screamed loud enough to rouse the whole neighborhood. Then one day I took my sister Louison in one hand and my little sister Suzanne in the other, and all three of us left, on foot, without a sou or a change of clothes, and we cried to the heavens along the main road. Then we went to find my Aunt Henriette, who lived over ten leagues from our town, and the first thing I said to her was:

"'Aunt, give us something to eat and drink—we're dying of hunger and thirst; we don't even have the strength to speak.' And when my aunt had given us dinner, I said to her:

"'I've brought you your nieces. If you don't want to take care of them, they will have to beg for bread from door to door, or they will have to go back home and perish from the beatings.'

"'My father had five children. None remains at home. The boys will get along by working; but if you don't take pity on the daughters, they will get what I'm telling you.'

"My aunt answered: 'I'm quite old, quite poor; but I'd go out begging before I abandoned my nieces. In any case they're well behaved, brave, and all three of us will work.' That said and agreed upon, I accepted twenty francs which the poor woman insisted on giving me, and I turned on my heels and left for here.

"Right away I went looking for my second brother, Jean, who found me employment in the shop where he worked as a cobbler, and then I went to see my young painter to ask his advice. He received me kindly and wanted to advance me some money, which I refused; I had enough to eat from my work. But that devil painting which he'd planted in my brain wouldn't leave, and I never started my day without sighing and thinking how much I'd prefer handling a pencil and a brush to an awl. I'd made some progress since, despite myself, during my leisure time on Sundays I always doodled faces or copied pictures from an old book my mother had given me. The young painter encouraged me, and I didn't have the strength to refuse the free lessons he offered me. But I had to live on something during that time, and the question was what.

"The painter knew a man of letters who gave me some manuscripts to copy. I had a fine hand, as they say, but I didn't know how to spell. They tried me out, and in the five or six lines they dictated, they found no mistakes. I'd read enough books to have learned the language a bit just by rote; but I didn't know the rules, and I didn't dare tell them, for fear of losing the work. Yet I didn't make mistakes in my copying because I paid close attention. This attention caused me to lose a good deal of time, and I saw I'd do better to learn grammar by writing essays on my own. Actually, I made rapid progress, but since this time came out of my sleep, I fell ill. My brother moved me to his garret, and worked for two. The little bit of money I'd earned copying the author's manuscripts went to pay the pharmacist. I didn't want to let my young painter know of my situation. I'd seen with my own eyes that he himself often came up short, not yet having either a reputation or wealth. I knew that his good heart would lead him to rescue me; and since he'd already done that once, against my inclinations, I would have preferred to die on that pallet rather than induce him to spend any more on me. He thought me an ingrate, and finding an opportunity to make a trip to Italy, the object of all his desires, he left without seeing me, taking with him an impression of me that caused me much pain.

"When my health returned, I saw that my brother had grown thin and feeble, our small savings were spent, and the shop was closed to us, since, to nurse me, Jean had missed many days of work. This was in July of last year, when it was hot as hell. We chatted sadly of our little problems, me still in bed and so weak that I could barely understand what Jean was saying. Then we heard a cannon blast, and it didn't even occur to us to ask why. But the door flew open, and two of our comrades from the shop, all disheveled, all afire, came to get us 'for victory or death'—that's how they put it. I asked what it was all about.

"'To overthrow the monarchy and set up a republic,' they said. I jumped out of bed, and in two seconds I donned a sorry pair of pants and a tattered shirt, which I'd been using as a robe. Jean followed. 'Better to die from a bullet than from hunger,' he said to me, and we left.

"We arrived at the door of a gunsmith's, where young people like us were distributing rifles to whoever wanted them. We each grabbed one, and took up positions behind a barricade. At the first shots from the troops, my poor Jean fell stone dead next to me. I lost my mind, I went into a fury. Ah! I would never have thought myself capable of spilling so much blood. For three days I bathed in it up to my waist, you could say, because I was covered with it—and not just the blood of others, but mine as well, which flowed from several wounds; but I felt nothing. Finally, on August 2nd, I ended up in the hospital, without knowing how I'd gotten there. When I left there, I was more miserable than before, and my heart was broken: my brother Jean was no longer with me, and the monarchy had been restored.

"I was too weak to work, and those July Days had left who knows what fever in my head. It seemed to me that anger and despair could make an artist out of me. I dreamed frightening paintings; I doodled faces on the wall which I imagined worthy of Michelangelo. I read the *Iambes* by Barbier, and in my mind I molded them of living pictures. I dreamed, I was idle, I was dying of hunger, and I didn't even notice.

"This couldn't continue very long, but it did go on for a few days with such intensity that I had no idea what was going on around me. It was as if my head contained all of me, as if I no longer had legs or arms or stomach or memory or consciousness or relatives or friends. I walked in front of myself down streets, not knowing where I wanted to go. My steps always brought me, without my knowing how, to the graves of the July rebels. I didn't know if my poor brother was buried there, but I felt that whether it was he or the other martyrs, it made no difference, and that to press my knees to the earth was paying homage to my brother's ashes. I was in an inflamed state of mind which made me talk to myself out loud endlessly. I have no memory of those long speeches; it seems to me that most often I spoke in verse. It must have been ridiculously bad, and passersby must have thought I was mad. But I saw no one, and I only heard myself from time to time. Then I would try to force myself to shut up, but I couldn't. My face was bathed in sweat and tears, and the strangest part was, this state of despair was not without a certain sweetness. I would wander all night long, or sit on some milestone in the moonlight, prey to endless, unconnected dreams, like the ones in sleep. And yet I didn't sleep, since I was walking, and on the walls or on the pavement I saw my shadow walking and gesticulating next to me. I don't understand how it happened that I was not picked up even once by the Guard.

"Finally I met a student I had seen sometimes in the studio of my young painter. He was not proud—since I looked like a beggar—and he approached me first. I exercised no caution, and had no idea if I was well or poorly dressed. I had other things on my mind, and I walked next to him along the quais, talking painting with him, since that was my obsession. He appeared to be interested in what I was saying. Perhaps he did not mind being seen with one of the "unwashed" of the glory days and making the gawkers think he'd fought then. At that time, all the young bourgeois took great pride in showing off gendarme's sabers they had bought from urchins after the 'festivities,' or scratches they had gotten when they ran too quickly to the window to see what was going on. This fellow seemed to have a bit of the braggart in him: he claimed to have seen me and talked to me on this or that barricade, where I didn't remember meeting him at all. Finally he asked me to have lunch with him, and I accepted without pride; it had been I don't know how many days since I'd eaten, and my brain had begun to behave in very peculiar ways. After lunch he was going to visit the studio of Monsieur Dusommerard in what used to be the Cluny mansion; he suggested I come with him, and I followed automatically.

"The sight of all those rare and marvelous art objects amassed in that collection made me so excited that I forgot all my sorrows in an instant. In one corner, several painting students copied enamels for the engravings collection which Monsieur Dusommerard is assembling at his own expense. I glanced at their work; it seemed to me I could do as well, and that I even could be more observant than some of them. Just then, Monsieur Dusommerard came back, and was greeted by the student who was introducing me—he knew him somewhat. They stood for a few minutes a little ways away from me, and I could tell from their glances that I was the subject of their conversation. The lunch had restored some of my composure, and I began to realize that my tawdry appearance must be shocking, and that the antique dealer might have taken me for a thief if the other man had not answered for me.

Monsieur Dusommerard is very kind; he doesn't like troublemakers, but he gladly puts up with poor devils who display zeal and unselfishness. He came over to me, asked me some questions, and, seeing my desire to work for him—and also, I'm sure, taking into consideration my need—he right then and there gave me some money for buying pencils, so he said, but in fact it was to enable me to purchase the basic necessities. He showed me the objects I was to copy. From the next day on, I dressed cleanly and settled into the spot where I was to work. I did my best, and I worked so quickly that Monsieur Dusommerard was satisfied and gave me more to do. I've had a lot to be pleased about, and it's thanks to him that I'm alive today; since he not only had me copy many art objects, but he also gave me letters of introduction that provided me with an entrée into many jewelry stores to paint flowers and birds for enameled jewelry, and heads for imitation cameos.

"As a result, I've been able to practice my vocation and enter the studios of Monsieur Delacroix, whom I've admired and been drawn to since the first time I saw him. I'm not the begging type, and I never would have dreamed he would have given me so much. The first time I went to tell him that I wanted to take lessons from him, I thought I should bring along a few sketches. He looked at them and said to me: 'They're really not bad.' They had warned me that he didn't make small talk, and that if he said even that much I should consider myself lucky. So I did, and I was just leaving when he called me back to ask if I had the means to pay. I answered yes, blushing to the whites of my eyes. But whether he guessed that the expenses would cut deep, or whether someone had spoken to him about me, he added: 'Good, pay the student who collects the fees.'

"That meant, as I soon found out, that I contributed money to the general fund that went to pay the models and the room rental, but that the master would receive nothing for himself, and that my lessons would be free. So, you see why that master is close to my heart!

"Six months went by quickly, and I would have been happy if things could have gone on like that forever. But it was not to be; my situation had to change, and instead of patiently advancing in the most wonderful of careers, I have to start running as fast as possible in whatever one I can find."

Here Masaccio became visibly distraught; he no longer told the story spontaneously, as it welled up in his thoughts. He hunted for pretexts, yet he found none that was a plausible explanation for the indecision into which he had fallen. He showed me a letter from his sister, Louison, which contained new information about his Aunt Henriette. This good elderly relative had become completely infirm, and helped her nieces only by lending them respect, since they had to work all day to support her. Her doctors said she wouldn't recover, and the family couldn't hope to keep her among them for more than three or four months.

"When we lose her," Paul Arsène said, "what will become of my sisters? Will they stay on their own in a little town where they have no other relatives than Aunt Henriette, exposed to all the dangers that surround two pretty young girls who have been abandoned? Besides, my father wouldn't allow it; it would be his duty not to allow it; then their fate would be worse, since they would not only be exposed to ill treatment by my stepmother, but they would also be faced with the bad example of that woman, who's worse than just nasty. The only choice I have is either to rejoin my sisters in the provinces and find work there as a laborer, so I won't have to leave them again, or to send for them here, and to support them until they, through their own labor, can support themselves."

"All that is very proper and very well thought out," I said to him; "but if your sisters are as strong and hard working as you say they are, they won't be a burden to you for long. I don't see that you will be forced to find a way of life that provides a steady salary as large as you were saying the other day. It's only a question of finding the money to bring Louison and Suzanne here, and to help them out a little at first. Well then, you have friends who could advance you that sum without much difficulty. I myself . . ."

"Thank you, Monsieur," said Arsène. "But I don't want to . . . We know when we borrow, we never know when we can pay back. I already owe too much to others' benevolence, and times are hard for everyone, I know. Why add privations that I can bear to the burdens of others? I love painting; if I'm forced to abandon it, so much the worse for me. If you make a sacrifice so that I can continue to paint, it might prevent you tomorrow from doing the same for someone who is worse off than I. After all, as long as one lives honestly, what difference does it make if one is an artist or a laborer? One doesn't have to be fastidious. There are so many great artists who complain, they say. There have to be some poor shoemakers who say nothing."

Everything I said to him fell on deaf ears: he remained unshakable. He had to earn a thousand francs a year and begin his employment, even if it were as a lackey, as soon as possible. It was only a question of finding a new position.

"But what if I undertook," I said to him, "to give you more work at home than you now have, either copying additional manuscripts, or some drawings, would you still insist on giving up painting?"

"If only that could be!" he said, shaken up for a moment; "but," he added, "it would be a burden on you and it would never be steady work."

"Let me at least try," I said. He shook my hand again and left, taking with him his resolve and his secret.

Horace visited me more and more often. He showed a friendship for me that I responded to, even though Eugénie didn't share my feelings at all. Several times he happened to run into Masaccio Junior at my apartment; and despite the good I told Horace about this young man, far from agreeing with the high opinion I held of him, Horace felt an insurmountable antipathy for him. Nevertheless, he treated him with more consideration after he saw him attempt a portrait of Eugénie; the sketch turned out so well, with such a noble resemblance and done with such a free hand, that Horace, infatuated with all intellectual superiority, couldn't help but pay him a sort of deference. But he was all the more indignant about that inexplicable lack of noble ambition which contrasted with his own exuberance. He got carried away by his own vehement declarations on the subject, and Paul Arsène, listening to him with a smile at the corner of his lips, was content to offer only this response, which he turned to me and uttered: "Monsieur, your friend speaks so well!"

Other than that, Paul seemed neither positively nor negatively disposed toward him. He was one of those people who marches so undeviatingly in the direction of his goal that no distraction along the road can make him stop. He said nothing frivolous; he expressed an opinion on almost nothing, always pleading ignorance, whether it were real or it served as an infallible pretext for cutting short any discussion. Always shut inside himself, he exercised his will only to calm that of others, but without becoming didactic, or to accommodate them, but without ostentation; and, while waiting to make the decision he was turning over in his mind, he studied the models, learned anatomy, and did designs for porcelain with as much care and zeal as if he had never thought of changing careers. That calm in the present, mixed with that restlessness for the future, filled me with admiration. It's one of the rarest combinations of qualities; youth in particular tends to fall asleep in the present without a worry for tomorrow, or else to devour the present in feverish anticipation of the future.

Horace seemed to be the deliberate and systematic opposite of this personality. It took me only a few days to be convinced that he didn't work, although he claimed that a few of his sleepless hours could compensate for a week's worth of indolence. It was not true at all. He had not been to three law classes in his life; perhaps he hadn't cracked a book more often than that; and one day when I was examining the shelves in his room, I found only novels and books of poetry. He confessed that he had sold all his law books.

This confession led to others. I feared that his need for money might be the result of wanton behavior. He justified himself by telling me that his parents were not wealthy; and without acquainting me with his exact budget, he assured me that his good mother was under a strange illusion in telling herself that she was sending him enough to live on in Paris.

I didn't dare push my inquiry further; but I cast an involuntary glance at my young friend's elegant and well-furnished wardrobe: he lacked nothing. He had more waistcoats, suits, and frock coats than I, who enjoyed an inheritance of three thousand francs' income. I guessed that his tailor had become the scourge of his existence. I was not mistaken. Soon I saw Horace's forehead cloud over, his speech become more brusque, and his tone sharper. It took more than a week to get him to confess. Finally I coaxed him into confiding in me about the insult that had occurred. His filthy tailor had had the gall to present his bill, the wretch! He deserved to be caned! Horace's indignation was a sign that he still had virtue; he hadn't reached that stage of perversity where one brags about one's debts or laughs with bluster at the idea of seeing a bill for three or four thousand francs land in one's parents' laps. What's more, he deeply cherished his mother, although he found her limited;

and he was a good son, even if he had a secret contempt for his father's dependence on the government.

Seeing him turn melancholy, I took it upon myself to say a few soothing words to the tailor; and Horace, after thanking me with extreme effusiveness, regained his serenity.

But his idleness didn't end, and his style of living, for someone with only an ordinary student income, surprised me greatly whenever I observed it. How, in fact, could he reconcile his ardor for glory, his dreams of parliamentary service and political power, with his profound inertia and the voluptuous nonchalance of such a temperament? It seemed that life was a hundred times longer than he needed, he had so little to do. He lost hours, days, and weeks with a truly royal heedlessness. He was a thing of beauty, that proud young man with his athletic build, his head of black hair, flaming eyes, reclining from morning till night on the divan on my balcony, smoking an enormous pipe (whose bowl I had to remake every day, since while shaking it out against the balcony railing he never failed to let it fall to the street), and leafing through a Balzac novel or a volume of Lamartine, never deigning to read an entire chapter or section. I left him there when I went to work, and when I came back from the clinic or the hospital, I found him dozing in the same spot, almost in the same position. Eugénie, condemned to endure this strange tête-à-tête, and not having, what's more, grounds to complain personally of him, since he barely condescended to speak a word to her (viewing her more as furniture than a person), was indignant about his princely laziness. As for me, I broke into a smile whenever Horace, his eyelids still weighed down by a sleepy daydream, resumed his discourses on glory, politics, and power.

My skepticism, however, had no tinge of blame or contempt. Every day after dinner, Horace and I met in the Luxembourg Gardens, at our café, or at the Odéon, with a fairly large group consisting of his friends and mine; and there, Horace held forth with rare ability. On all subjects he was the greatest authority, even though he was the youngest; in all matters he was the bravest, the most passionate, his ideas were the most *advanced,* as we said then, and as they still say, I believe, today. Even those among his listeners who didn't like him were compelled to hear him out with interest, and those who contradicted him generally exhibited more distrust and spite than justice and good faith. This is because Horace was at an advantage there: the discussion was on his turf; and everyone admitted that even if Horace was not an infallible logician, still he was a prolific, ingenious, and fervent orator. Those who didn't know him thought to pull the rug out from under him by saying that he was a man without depth or ideas, who had done an immense amount of work, and whose inspiration was only the result of meticulous study. As for me, who knew so well that the contrary was the case, I admired his powers of intuition, which allowed him to assimilate something merely by grazing it in passing, and to develop it at the drop of a hat using random improvisation. He was certainly privileged to have such a nature, the kind one could predict would always be timely, since he needed so little time to broaden and perfect himself.

His constant presence at my apartment tortured Eugénie. Like all active and hardworking people, she couldn't stand to witness the spectacle of prolonged inactivity without it causing her an unease which bordered on suffering. Being active not by nature, but out of reason and necessity, I was not as revolted as she, and in any case, it pleased me to think that this inaction was merely a temporary shortfall in my young friend's energies and that soon he would be, as he put it, yanking at his leash.

And yet, since two months drifted by without bringing any alteration in this way of life, I thought it my duty to help rouse the tiger in him. I attempted to broach this delicate subject while we were having coffee at Poisson's. The day had been stormy, and long bolts of lightning periodically blued the greenery of the chestnut trees in the Luxembourg Garden. The lady behind the counter was as beautiful as always—perhaps more beautiful, since the habitual melancholy of her countenance harmonized with this languid and half-somber evening.

Horace's glance fell on her several times, and turning back to me he said: "I'm amazed at you! You can be seriously smitten with that type of woman, but you haven't developed a great passion for her."

"I admire her beauty," I said to him, "but I'm lucky enough to have eyes only for the woman I love. Rather, it's *I* who should be amazed that *you,* whose heart is free, are not paying more attention to her classical profile and her nymphlike figure."

"Polyhymnia in the Museum is just as beautiful," Horace answered, "and she has several advantages over this one. First, she never talks, and that one would break her spell over me as soon as she opened her mouth. Then, the one in the Museum isn't a barmaid; and third, her name is not Madame Poisson. Madame Poisson! What a name! You will say I'm a snob, but look at yourself! If Eugénie had been named Margot or Javotte . . . "

"I would have preferred Margot or Javotte to Léocadie or Phoedora. But let me tell you, Horace: you're hiding something from me—are you falling in love?"

Horace held out his arm to me. "Doctor," he exclaimed, laughing, "take my pulse; it must be a very calm love, since I don't notice it. But what makes you think that?"

"Because you're no longer thinking about politics."

"Where did you get that idea? I'm thinking about it more than ever. Is there only one path to a goal?"

"Oh? And which one are you walking on? I know that *dolce far niente* would be happiness enough for me, but for one who loves glory . . ."

"Glory comes and finds those who worship it with a sensitive and proud love. As for me, the more I think about it, the more I find the study of law incompatible with my nature, and the legal profession impossible for anyone with self-respect. I'm renouncing it."

"Is that so?" I exclaimed, stunned by how easy it was for him to announce such a decision. "Then what will you do?"

"Oh, who knows?" he answered, indifferently. "Maybe literature. It's a wider path; or rather, it's an open field one can enter from all sides. It suits my impatience and my laziness. It only takes a day to reach the highest ranks; and when the hour of the great revolution chimes, the parties will be able to recognize in letters, much more so than at the bar, the men who will suit them."

As he was saying this, I saw in the mirror a face that seemed to me to be Paul Arsène's; but before I could turn my head to make sure, it had gone.

"And what branch of letters will you pick?" I asked Horace.

"Verse, prose, the novel, drama, criticism, polemics, satire, poetry—all forms are open to me, and none intimidates me."

"So much for form. What about content?"

"The content is overflowing," he answered, "and form is a narrow vase in which I have to learn to contain my thoughts. Calm down, you will soon see that the idleness that frightens you is hatching something. Still waters run deep."

My eyes, flitting around, again found Paul Arsène, but in an unfamiliar outfit. His shirt was very white and fine, he had on a white apron, and, to finish off the metamorphosis, he was carrying a tray filled with cups.

"There goes," said Horace, whose eyes had followed the same path as mine, "a waiter who looks uncannily like Masaccio Junior."

Although he had trimmed his long hair and little mustache, it was impossible to doubt for a moment that it was indeed Masaccio in person. The sight of him was frightfully heartrending, and, making an effort, I called out to him, "waiter!"

"*Voilà,* Monsieur!" he responded forthwith; and, coming over to us without the slightest embarrassment, he presented us with our coffee.

"Is it possible, Arsène," I cried, "that you chose this place?"

"Until I find a better one," he answered, "and it's not so bad here."

"But you can't have a moment to draw!" I said to him, knowing full well that it was the only objection that might sway him.

"Oh! it's a sad thing, but only for me," he answered. "Don't blame me, Monsieur. My elderly aunt is about to die, and I want to bring my sisters here; once you've been bitten by this rascal Paris, you see, you can't go back to the provinces. At least here I can listen to young students talk about art and painting; and when Monsieur Delacroix has a show, I can steal away for an hour to see his pictures. Will art die because Paul Arsène is not mixed up in it anymore? It's only the cups that are in danger," he added gaily, rescuing the platter that was about to fall from his inexperienced hand.

"Oh ho, Paul Arsène," exclaimed Horace, bursting out laughing, "either you're a little Jew, or you're in love with the beautiful Madame Poisson."

He made this joke, as was his wont, with so little tact that Madame Poisson, whose counter was right nearby, heard it and blushed to the whites of her eyes. Arsène became pale as death and dropped the platter, Monsieur Poisson hastened to the site of the racket, glanced at the damage, and then went behind the counter to record it in a book he kept for such purposes. (The café waiter is held accountable for all he breaks.) We heard the owner, seeing his wife's reaction, say to her harshly:

"Why do you always jump and scream at the slightest noise? You've got the nerves of a princess."

Madame Poisson turned her head away and closed her eyes, as if the mere sight of the man horrified her. This little bourgeois drama took only three minutes. Horace paid no attention to it: but for me it was like a flash of lightning.

The deep and sincere interest I felt for poor Masaccio Junior made me return to Poisson's café often; I would sit there longer than usual, and consume more, in order not to attract the proprietor's unfriendly attention, since he seemed like a jealous brute. But although I always expected to witness some tragedy in their household, over a month went by and that savage order seemed undisturbed. Arsène performed his servile duties with rare alacrity, irreproachable neatness, unexpected and good-humored politeness, which won the goodwill of all the regular customers and even of his rude employer.

"Do you know him?" the latter asked me, seeing that I often chatted at some length with him. Arsène had charged me to reveal nothing of the fact that he had been an artist, for fear of losing his employer's trust, and in keeping with his instructions I answered that I used to see him in a restaurant, where he was much missed.

"An excellent fellow," Monsieur Poisson answered, "perfectly honest, not a blabbermouth, shirker, or drunkard, always content, always at the ready. Business has been good since he entered my service. Well, Monsieur, would you believe that Madame Poisson, who is weak and indulgent to the point of absurdity with all these lads, can't bear this poor Arsène!"

When he said this, Monsieur Poisson was standing two steps from my table, his elbow leaning majestically on the outside of that mahogany counter where his wife held court, looking bored as a true queen. Her husband's round and red face emerged from a frilled muslin shirt, and his obesity spilled over his nankeen trousers, stretched ridiculously tight against his enormous thighs. Horace had nicknamed him The Minotaur. While he was deploring his wife's injustice to poor Arsène, I thought I detected an almost imperceptible smile stray over her lips. But not a word escaped those lips, and when I tried to continue this conversation with her, she responded with an imperturbable calm:

"What would you have us do, Monsieur? Those people (she indicated the boys in the café in general) are the bane of our existence. Their manners are so brutal and unfeeling! They value the establishment and never the people in it. My cat is worth more: at least he values both me and the establishment."

And as she spoke in this vein in a voice both sweet and drawling, her snowy hand stroked the tiger-striped back of the magnificent angora that was frolicking adroitly among the dishes on the counter.

Madame Poisson was not lacking in intellect, and I often noticed that she read good novels. As a regular, I had purchased the right to pass the time of day with her, and my respectful manners inspired her husband's trust. I often complimented her on her choice of books; I had never seen in her hands even one of those trashy works, half obscene, which are the delight of shopkeepers. One day, when she was finishing *Manon Lescaut,* I saw a tear roll down her cheek, and I approached her, saying that it was the most beautiful romantic novel ever written in France. She cried:

"Oh, yes, Monsieur! At least it's the most beautiful I've ever read. Ah, that false-hearted Manon! That sublime Desgrieux!" and her glance fell on Arsène, who was dropping money into his little wooden bowl. Was it by chance, or by impulse? It was difficult to say. Arsène never raised his eyes to look at her; he continued to circulate from the tables to the counter with a calm which would have baffled even the most astute observer.

Little by little Horace deigned to pay attention to the beauty and fine manners of Laure: that was the nickname Monsieur Poisson gave his wife.

"Now, if *she* had been born on a throne," Horace often remarked while looking her over, "the entire world would have prostrated itself before such majesty."

"What good would a throne do?" I responded. "Beauty is the true royalty."

"What distinguishes her from most barmaids," he resumed, "is that cool dignity, so different from the others' teasing flirtation. In general, they sell you their glances for a glass of sugar water; it could take away your thirst forever. But that woman, in the midst of all the crass compliments surrounding her, is a true pearl in the dung; she genuinely inspires a sort of respect. If I could be sure she wasn't foolish, I'd almost like to fall in love with her."

The sight of several young men who, every day, fell over themselves to grab the attention of the beautiful cafékeeper, and who had actually committed foolhardy acts for her, succeeded in awakening Horace's conceit; but such pride prefers not to follow the same path as naive admirers. He didn't want to be confused with this retinue; what he needed to do, said he, was to pull the staging area out from under the noses of those laying the siege. He meditated on his methods, and one night he tossed an impassioned letter onto the counter; then he remained out of sight until the next day, believing that this aura of preoccupation, discouragement, or disdain, to be explained later depending on the outcome, would have an effect, in contrast to the behavior of his obsessive rivals.

I had allowed myself to get mixed up in this folly, privately persuaded that it would serve as a lesson to Horace, with his budding fatuousness and the pains he took on his epistolary eloquence. The following day I was busier than usual, and so we planned to meet that evening at Poisson's café. The lady was not behind the counter: Arsène performed by himself both the roles of master and servant, and he was bustling about so much that he responded to all our questions with an "I don't know" tossed off with an air of indifference while on the run. Nor did Monsieur Poisson show his face. Although we hadn't found anything out, we had just decided to make our exit when Laravinière, President of the Bousingots, came in noisily, surrounded by his merry phalanx.

Somewhere I once read a rather lengthy definition of the word *student,* which, though certainly not composed without talent, seemed altogether incorrect to me. It belittles the student too much, and, I would even say, degrades him; he plays a lowly and coarse role in it which isn't truly his. In fact, the student has more bad habits and ridiculous traits than vices; and when he has them, those vices have such shallow roots that he need only take his examinations and cross again the threshold of his paternal home to become calm, positive, reliable—too positive, most of the time, since the student's vices are those of society's as well, a society where adolescence is consigned to an education that is at once superficial and pedantic, encouraging presumptuousness and vanity; where youth is abandoned, without rule or restraint, to all the disorders engendered by skepticism; where manhood follows immediately after in the sphere of ego rivalry and struggle. If students were as perverse as they are portrayed to be, France's future would be extraordinarily compromised.

You must excuse forthwith the writer I am now blaming, recognizing how difficult it is, in fact well nigh impossible, to summarize in one type a class as numerous as that of students. What? Is it literate youth taken as a whole you wish to convey in a simple effigy? But what infinite nuances there are in that population of children, or half-men, which Paris continually sees renewing itself, like dissimilar victuals mixed in the vast stomach of the Latin Quarter! There are as many classes of students as there are rival and various classes within the bourgeoisie. Hate the crusty bourgeoisie, which, master of all the power of the State, uses that power to traffic in misery; but don't condemn the young bourgeoisie, which feels generous instincts developing and growing within itself. In several instances in our recent history, youth has shown itself to be brave and openly republican. In 1830, it intervened again between the people and the fallen ministers of the Restoration, still a threat behind the walls where their sentence was read—that was youth's ultimate day of glory.

Since then, youth has been so closely monitored, so mistreated and discouraged, that it has not shown itself publicly. Nevertheless, if the love of justice, the passion for equality, and the enthusiasm for higher principles and higher devotion of the French Revolution still have a home other than among the people, it is in the soul of that young bourgeoisie that it must be sought. It is a fire that seizes them and consumes them rapidly, I agree. A few years of that noble exaltation, that they seem to receive as if by transfusion from the burning pavements of Paris, and then the boredom of the provinces, or the despotism of the family, or the influence of society's seductions soon erases even the slightest trace of this generous spirit.

Then we return to ourselves, that is, to ourselves alone; we regard as youthful foolishness those courageous theories that we once loved and professed; we blush at the thought of having been a Fourierist, a Saint-Simonian, or a revolutionary of any stripe; we hardly dare recount what audacious motions we put forward or supported in political groups; and finally, we're astonished that we ever hoped for equality with all its consequences, that we loved the people fearlessly, that we voted for the law of brotherhood with no amendments. And after a few years—that is, when we're well or poorly established—whether we be right smack in the middle, royalist, or republican, of the shade of opinion of the *Débats,* the *Gazette,* or the *National,* we inscribe over our doorway, or on our diploma, or on our license, that we never, in all our life, intended to commit any offense against sacrosanct Property.

But this is the case to be made, I repeat, against the bourgeois society that oppresses us. Let's not make a case against youth, since youth has been what youth, taken in the aggregate and in contact with itself, is and always will be: enthusiastic, romantic, and generous. Students are what is best about the bourgeoisie: never doubt it.

I won't undertake to contradict point by point the author's assertions, which I indict without any bitterness, I assure you. It's possible that he is better informed about current student customs than I could be; but I'm forced to conclude either that the author is mistaken or that students have changed, since what I've observed is quite different.

In my day we were not divided into two species—one, called the *carousers,* very numerous, who spent their days at the Chaumière, at cabarets, at the Panthéon dance hall, screaming, smoking, vociferating in the foul and hideous air; the other, called the *grinds,* very restrained, who shut themselves in, lived in poverty, and gave themselves over to a material labor resulting in cretinism. No! It is true there were many idlers and lazybones, even bad sorts and idiots; but there was also a very large number of active and intelligent young people, whose morals were chaste, whose loves were romantic, and whom life stamped with a sort of elegance and poetry in the midst of their moderate resources and even their poverty. It's true that these young people were quite egotistical, that they wasted a good deal of time, that they preferred any kind of fun to their studies, that they spent more money than a virtuous devotion to their families would have permitted, and finally, that they involved themselves in politics and socialism with more fervor than reason, and in philosophy with more feeling than knowledge and profundity. But if they had, as I've already admitted, bad habits and ridiculous traits, they were far from being vicious, far from frittering their days away in degradation, their nights in orgies. In a word, I saw many more students who resembled Horace than ones like those in *The Student* sketched by the writer whom I venture to contradict here.

The one whose portrait I would now like to draw for you, Jean Laravinière, was a tall boy, twenty-five years of age, nimble as a chamois and strong as a bull. His distracted parents were guilty of not having had him vaccinated, so his face was furrowed all over by smallpox—and this was, happily, an inexhaustible source of jokes on his part. Though ugly, his face was pleasant, his appearance original, as were his wits. He was as generous as he was brave, and that was no small measure. His instinctual *combativeness,* as it's called in phrenology, drew him impetuously into every brawl, and he always brought along a cohort of intrepid friends, fanaticized by his coolheaded heroism and his bellicose joyfulness. He had fought very hard during the July Days; later, alas! he fought too well elsewhere.

He was a blusterer, a *carouser,* if you will; but what a loyal personality, what magnanimous devotion! He had all the eccentricities of his role, complete recklessness about his impetuosity, all the swagger of his position. You might have laughed at him; but you would have been forced to love him. He was so good, so naive in his convictions, so devoted to his friends! He was supposed to be a medical student, but really was and only wanted to be a student rioter—a *Bousingot,* as it was called back then. And since this is a historical term which will be lost if we don't take care, I will attempt to define it.

There was another class of students whom the rest of us (students who were slightly aristocratic, I confess) called—without disdain, however—*café students.* This class invariably consisted of the majority of the freshmen, children newly arrived from the provinces, whose heads had been turned by Paris, who believed they could make men of themselves in the blink of an eye by smoking themselves sick and by pounding the sidewalks from morning till night, their caps (since freshmen rarely own a hat) cocked over their ears. Beginning with the sophomore year, students in general become more serious and natural. By their junior year they have completely given up this way of life. That's when they sit in the orchestra circle at the Italiens, and when they begin dressing like the rest of the world.

But a certain number of the young people remain attached to their habits of strolls, billiard rooms, and endless smokes in taverns, or walks in noisy groups in the Luxembourg Gardens. In a word, they make of the recreational activities that others partake of in moderation, the foundation and the habitual practice of their lives. It's completely natural that their manners, their ideas, and even their features, instead of taking shape, remain in a sort of vagabond and disheveled infancy, in which one must take care not to encourage them, though it may certainly have its sweetness and even poetry. They always find themselves naturally carried away by riots. The youngest go just to observe, others go to take part; in those days almost everyone threw himself into it for a moment and then quickly withdrew, after having delivered and received a few good blows. This activity didn't change things on the surface, and the only alteration produced by these efforts was a doubling of the fear of the shopkeepers and brutal cruelty on the part of the police. But not a single person who so casually disturbed public order back then need blush at the present hour for having had a few days of youthful warmth. When youth cannot demonstrate the greatness and courage in its heart except by attacking society, that society must be evil indeed!

They were called Bousingots because of the sailor hats of that name, made of shiny leather, which they adopted as their rallying sign. Later they wore a scarlet headpiece in the form of a military stocking cap, with a black velvet band all around it. Pointed out again and again to the police, and attacked in the street by stool pigeons, they next adopted a gray hat; but they were no less frequently rounded up and mistreated. Their conduct has been much denounced; but I don't think the government has been able to justify that of its own officers, veritable assassins who beat to death a good number of Bousingots while shopkeepers looked on, showing not the slightest indignation or pity.

The name Bousingots stuck. When *Le Figaro*, which kept up a teasing and caustic opposition under the loyal management of Monsieur Delatouche, changed hands, and little by little changed its stripes, the name Bousingot became an insult; after that there was no mockery too bitter or unjust with which to smear them. But the true Bousingots remained unmoved, and our friend Laravinière joyously kept his title of President of the Bousingots till he died, without fearing that he deserved either ridicule or contempt.

He was so sought after and adored by his companions that we never saw him walking by himself. In the midst of this ambulant group that was always singing or yelling around him, he rose above them like a robust and proud pine in the heart of a thicket, or like Fénélon's Calypso among the small-fry nymphs, or, finally, like the young Saul among the shepherds of Israel. (He preferred the latter description.) He could be spotted from afar by his pointy, wide-brimmed gray hat, by his goatee, by his long, smooth hair, by his enormous red cravat that clashed with the enormous white lapels of his Marat-style vest. Generally he wore a blue jacket with long tails and metal buttons, pants with large gray and black checks, and he carried a heavy walking stick of service-tree wood which he called his "Friar John," in honor of the wooden cross with which Friar John Hackem wreaked, according to Rabelais, such a *horrifick* carnage on Picrochole's armed men. Add to all that a cigar as big as a log, jutting out of a half-burnt auburn mustache; a raspy voice that broke in the first days of August 1830 while singing the "Marseillaise" off-key; and the benevolent aplomb of a man who had embraced Lafayette over a hundred times, but who no longer spoke of him after 1831 except as *My poor friend*—and there you have him in his full glory, Jean Laravinière, President of the Bousingots.

"Were you asking after Madame Poisson?" he said to Horace, who in general did not take kindly to his acting in a familiar manner. "Well! you'll see Madame Poisson no more. On vacation, Madame Poisson. Serves him right. Monsieur Poisson will never strike her again."

"If she had picked me to be her protector," exclaimed little Paulier, hardly bigger than a fly, "she wouldn't have been hit twice. But since it was the *President* she honored with her choice . . ."

"Excuse me! That's not true," answered the President of the Bousingots, raising his husky voice loud enough so that everyone could hear him. "Arsène, a shot of rum! My throat is burning. I have need of refreshment!"

Arsène came over to pour him some rum and remained standing next to him, watching him attentively with an indefinable expression.

"Well, my poor Arsène," resumed Laravinière, not setting eyes on him while he sampled the contents of his shot glass; "you won't see your shop owner's wife again! Perhaps that will make you happy? She didn't care for you, your shop owner's wife?"

"I have no idea," answered Arsène in his clear and firm voice; "but where the devil could she be?"

"I tell you she's gone. *Gone,* do you hear me? That means she's wherever she pleases: everywhere but here."

"You're not afraid of distressing or seriously offending her husband, speaking so loudly about such things?" I said, throwing a glance at the rear door, where Monsieur Poisson ordinarily appeared twenty times an hour.

"Citizen Poisson is not within," responded Louvet, one of the Bousingots. "We just ran into him at the entrance to the police station, where he undoubtedly went to inquire after her. Oh, yes! He's searching, he'll search for a long time to come. Search all you want, Poisson. Go fetch!"

"Poor brute!" another interjected. "That ought to teach him not to try to catch flies with vinegar. Arsène! Bring me some coffee!"

"Good for her!" said a third. "But I would never have thought her capable of such impulsive behavior! She looked as though her sorrows had worn her out, the poor woman! Arsène, a beer!"

Arsène briskly served everyone, and he always came back to plant himself behind Laravinière, as if he were waiting for something.

"Hey! Why are you looking at me like that?" Laravinière said to him, seeing him in the mirror.

"I'm waiting to refill your glass," Arsène calmly replied.

"Such a good boy!" said the President, handing him his glass. "Your heart understands mine. Ah! if you had been playing Hebe at the Rue Montorgueil barricade this time last year! I was so abominably thirsty! But that kid was thinking only of plugging gendarmes. Brave as a lion, that kid! Your shirt was not as white as it is today, eh? Red with blood and black with powder. But where the devil have you been hiding since then?"

"Tell us instead where Madame Poisson spent the night, since you know," Paulier said.

"You know?" exclaimed Horace, his face burning.

"So, that interests you, does it?" answered Laravinière. "Seems to me you're devilishly curious! Well, I'm not telling, and I hope my saying that doesn't anger you; I gave my word, you understand."

"Oh, I understand," said Horace bitterly. "You want us to think that you were the one who put Madame Poisson up for the night."

"At my residence? I wish it had been; that assumes there is a 'my residence.' But no bad jokes, please. Madame Poisson is a very honest woman, and I'm sure she would go neither to your residence nor mine."

"So tell them how you helped her get away," said Louvet, seeing how eager we were to guess the meaning of his reticence.

"Fine, here! Listen!" answered the President. "I can say one thing for sure: this will bring no shame to the lady. Ah, you are listening, eh?" he added, seeing Arsène still behind him. "You would like to sneak in and tattle about this to your shopkeeper."

"I don't even know what you're talking about," answered Arsène, sitting on an empty table and spreading out a newspaper. "I'm here to serve you: if I'm in the way, I'll go."

"No, no, stay, child of July!" said Laravinière. "What I have to say will compromise no one."

It was dinnertime for the inhabitants of the neighborhood. In the café were only Laravinière, his friends, and us. This was how he began his narrative:

"Last night . . . I might as well say this morning (since midnight had struck almost an hour before), I was returning to my quarters alone, taking the long way around. I won't tell you where I was coming from, nor where this encounter took place; I've told you my reservations in this matter. Walking in front of me I saw a real hourglass figure, and she had such an air of propriety, so little of the provocative in her way of walking, as we know, that I did a triple take . . . Finally, convinced that this had to be quite a rare butterfly, I followed her; but something mysterious and indefinable (a certain style, my dears) prevented me from acting like a churl, even though gallantry is not your President's customary mode of behavior.

"'You charming woman,' I said to her, 'may I offer you my arm?'

"She doesn't answer or turn her head. That amazes me. Oh, no! Maybe she's deaf. Must be. I press my advance. She walks twice as fast. 'Don't be scared!' 'Oh!' A little scream, then she leans against the parapet."

"Parapet? I thought this was along the quai," said Louvet.

"I said parapet, but I could have said milestone, window, any kind of barrier. What does that matter! I see her shake like a woman who's about to faint. I stop, dumbfounded. Is she making fun of me? 'But Mademoiselle, don't be afraid.' 'Oh, my God! Is that *you*, Monsieur Laravinière?' 'Oh, my God, is that *you*, Madame Poisson?' (What a dramatic surprise!) 'I'm very pleased I ran into you,' she says in a resolute tone. 'You're an honest man, you'll escort me. I place my fate in your hands, I put my trust in you. Keep this secret.' 'Madame, I'm ready to brave water or fire *for* you and *with* you.' She takes my arm. 'I could ask you not to follow me, and I'm sure you wouldn't insist upon it; but I'd prefer to confide in you. My honor will be in good hands; you won't betray it.'

"I hold out my hand, she puts hers in mine. My head is spinning a little, but no matter. I offer my arm like a marquis, and, without allowing myself a single question, I accompany her . . ."

"Where?" demanded Horace impatiently.

"Where she pleased," answered Laravinière. "On the way: 'I am leaving Monsieur Poisson for good,' she says, 'but I'm not leaving him to misbehave. I have no lover, Monsieur; I swear to you before God, who watches over me, since he sent you to me at this moment, that I have none and want none. I'm fleeing ill treatment, and that's all. I have a refuge, at a friend's home, an honest and good woman; I'll live by my own hands. Don't come to see me; I must keep myself well sequestered after such an escape. But remember me with friendship, and know that I will never forget . . .' Another handshake; a solemn adieu, perhaps forever, and then, goodnight, no one. I know where she is, I don't know at whose home or with whom. I won't seek to find out, and I will put no one else on her trail. It doesn't matter, I haven't slept all night, and here I am lovesick as a dog! What good is it to me?"

"And you believe," Horace said with emotion, "that she doesn't have a lover, that she's at a woman's house, that . . ."

"Oh, I don't believe anything, I don't know anything, and it doesn't concern me! She has taken hold of me. So I'm forced to keep my promise, since I've been conquered. Those devil women! Arsène, some rum! The orator is fatigued."

I looked at Arsène: his face did not betray the slightest emotion. I ceased to believe he loved Madame Poisson; but, seeing Horace's restlessness, I started to think that his feelings were taking on a more serious character. We parted ways at the Rue Gît-le-Coeur.

I came home overwhelmed with exhaustion. I had spent the previous night by the side of a sick friend, and I hadn't been home all day.

Although I saw a light shining in my windows, I was tempted to believe that no one was home, so slow was Eugénie to answer the door. It was only after the third ring that she made up her mind to open it, after looking me over thoroughly and questioning me through the grating.

"Are you that scared?" I said to her, going in.

"Very scared," she told me. "I have my reasons. But since you're home, I'm not worried anymore."

This beginning greatly troubled me. "What happened, then?" I exclaimed.

"Only something very good," she answered, smiling, "and I hope you won't retract my decision: while you were gone I gave away your room."

"My room! Great God! And I didn't sleep all last night! Why did you do that? And what's the meaning of all this mystery?"

"Shhh! Be quiet!" said Eugénie, covering my lips with her hand. "Your room is being occupied by someone who has more need of sleep and tranquillity than you."

"This is a strange invasion! What you're doing is well and good, Eugénie, but after all . . ."

"Enough, my friend. Won't you leave right now and ask your friend Horace or someone else (you don't lack friends) to lend you half of his room for the night?"

"But will you at least tell me for whom I'm making this sacrifice?"

"For a woman who is a friend of mine, who came in desperate straits to seek refuge."

"Oh my God!" I exclaimed. "Someone is giving birth in my room! The lout whom we owe that child to should go to the devil!"

"No, no, nothing of the sort," said Eugénie, blushing. "But speak more softly. This isn't a question of love, strictly speaking; it's a completely pure and Platonic story. Out with you now!"

"So, are you taking such deferential precautions because this is a kidnapped princess?"

"No, she's a woman like me, and she certainly deserves your respect."

"And you won't even tell me her name?"

"What good would that do tonight? We shall see tomorrow what we can confide in you."

"And you're sure it's a woman?" I said with great difficulty.

"You suspect me?" answered Eugénie, bursting out laughing.

She pushed me toward the door, and I obeyed mechanically. She gave me my candle and, affectionately and playfully, led me as far as the landing, then went back inside, and I heard her turn the bolt twice, at the same time locking the door with a bar I had had installed for additional security when I left Eugénie home alone at night in my garret.

When I reached the foot of the stairs, I became dizzy. I'm not at all jealous by nature, and besides, my sweet and sincere companion had never given me the slightest reason to mistrust her. I more than loved her, I had boundless respect for her character, I trusted her word absolutely. Nevertheless, I was seized with a sort of delirium, and I couldn't make up my mind to walk down the last flight. Twenty times I went back upstairs as far as my door; the same number of times I went back down the stairs. The deepest silence reigned in my garret and in the house as a whole. The more I struggled with my folly, the more it took hold of me. A cold sweat trickled down my forehead. Several times I considered breaking down the door: despite the lock and the iron bar, I think I would have been strong enough then; but the fear of frightening and offending Eugénie with such violence, and the insult of such a suspicion, prevented me from giving in to the temptation. If Horace had seen me like that, he would have pitied me or scoffed at me bitterly. After all I had said to him about combating the instincts of jealousy and despotism that he allowed to enter into his theories of love, I would have looked perfectly ridiculous.

Nevertheless, I couldn't bring myself to leave the building. I thought seriously about spending the night strolling along the quai; but our building had a backdoor that opened onto the Rue Gît-le-Coeur, and while I was walking around it, someone could leave from the other side. Once I went out the main entrance, if the concierge had been warned or had gone to bed, I would certainly not be able to get back in after midnight. Concierges are terribly inhumane to students, and mine was among the most intractable. *The devil with that mysterious guest and her compromised reputation!* I thought; and not willing to lose sight of my treasure, or able to fend off my fatigue, I lay down on the straw mat in the embrasure of my doorway and finally went to sleep.

Luckily we lived on the top floor, and the only apartment that opened onto our landing was vacant. I didn't run the risk of being surprised in that ridiculous position by scandal-mongering neighbors.

As one might expect, I didn't sleep long or deeply. The morning chill woke me early. I was shattered, I had a smoke to revive myself, and when, toward six o'clock, I heard the door to the building open, I rang my own bell. Once again I had to wait and undergo an interrogation at the grating. Finally I was permitted to enter.

"Oh, my God!" said Eugénie, rubbing eyelids that were weighed down by a better sleep than I'd had. "You look different! Poor Théophile! Did you sleep very badly at your friend Horace's?"

"It couldn't have been worse," I answered. "A very hard bed. And your guest, has he finally left?"

"*He?*" she said with an astonishment so candid that I was filled with shame.

When a person is guilty, he rarely thinks of repenting in time. I felt spite overcome me, and, having nothing sensible to say, I set my cane down somewhat brusquely on the table and I threw my hat peevishly on a chair: it rolled onto the floor, and I gave it a good kick; I needed to break something.

Eugénie, who had never seen me like that, was stupefied: silently she picked up my hat, stared at me fixedly, and finally guessed how much I was suffering, seeing the serious change that had come over my features. She stifled a sob, held back a tear, and softly entered my bedroom, whose door she carefully closed again. Inside was the mysterious personage. I no longer dared, I no longer wanted to suspect her, but despite myself, I still suspected. Unjust thoughts, once we let them gain the upper hand, can take hold of us so completely that they dominate our imagination, even though reason and our conscience may protest. It was torture for me; I paced restlessly in my study, stopping each time in front of that fatal door, my feelings close to rage. Minutes seemed like centuries.

Finally the door reopened, and a woman, hastily dressed, her hair still mussed from sleep, and her body wrapped in a huge shawl, stepped toward me, pale and trembling. I recoiled in surprise: it was Madame Poisson.

She bowed before me, almost touching her knee to the ground; and in that sad pose, with her pale complexion, her disheveled hair, and her beautiful naked arms emerging from her scarlet shawl, she could have disarmed a tiger. But I was so happy to see Eugénie vindicated that I would have welcomed even my awful concierge with as much courtesy as the beautiful Laure. I raised her up again, had her sit down; I asked her to excuse me for coming back so frightfully early, not yet daring to ask forgiveness or even to venture a glance in the direction of my poor mistress.

"I feel very unhappy and guilty," Laure said to me, still quite moved. "I almost brought sorrow into your household. It's my fault, I should have warned you, I should have refused Eugénie's generous hospitality. Oh, Monsieur, put the blame on me: Eugénie is an angel. She loves you as you deserve, as I would like to have been loved, even for only one day of my life. She will explain everything, Monsieur; she will tell you my troubles and my errors, my errors, which are not what you believe, but a thousand times worse, and which I'll atone for my whole life."

Her tears cut short her words. I took her two hands tenderly. I don't know what I said to reassure and console her, but she seemed to respond, and pulling me over to Eugénie, she expedited, with a completely feminine grace, the outpouring of my remorse and my dear companion's forgiveness. I received it on my knees. Her response was to draw Laure into my arms and to say to me, "Be a brother to her, and promise me to protect her and to help her as if she were my sister and yours. Look, *I'm* not jealous! And yet how much more beautiful she is, how much better educated, and how much better suited than I to turn your head!"

Lunch, modest as usual, but imbued with politeness and even a tender playfulness, was followed by Eugénie's making arrangements to move Laure into the other apartment on our landing, which the concierge had not yet managed to put at her disposal, even though, unbeknownst to me, he had been commissioned to do so several days before. While our new neighbor, under the name of Mademoiselle Moriat (that was Eugénie's last name, and she was passing her off as her sister), settled into her secret haven with a sort of melancholy sluggishness, my companion returned to tell me what I needed to know to assist her.

"Are you friendly with Masaccio?" she said, to begin with. "Are you concerned about his fate? And would you love Laure more if you knew that Paul Arsène cherished her?"

"What, Eugénie!" I cried, "you know Masaccio's secrets? Those secrets have been impenetrable to me and he's already confided them to you?"

Eugénie blushed and smiled. She had known the whole story for quite some time. While Masaccio was painting her portrait, she had been able to instill in him an extraordinary trust. He, so reserved, even mysterious, had been won over by Eugénie's sincere goodness and her discreet kindness. And besides, the son of the people, suspicious and proud around me, opened his heart in a brotherly way to a daughter of the people: it was only fair.

Eugénie had promised to keep his secret; she did so religiously. She put me through a very discerning and scrupulous interrogation, and when she felt assured that my curiosity was based only on a sincere and devoted interest in her protégé, she let me in on many things. First, Madame Poisson was in fact not Madame Poisson, but rather a young working girl born in the same town and province and on the same street as Masaccio Junior. The latter had felt for her, almost since childhood, a romantic and completely star-crossed passion. But the beautiful Marthe, still a youth herself, let herself be seduced and spirited away by Monsieur Poisson, then a traveling salesman, who took her with him when he set up his café just outside the fence of the Luxembourg Gardens, no doubt counting on her beauty to be the signpost that would attract customers to his establishment. This secret plan didn't prevent Monsieur Poisson from being jealous, however, and at the slightest provocation he would fly into a rage against Marthe, which made her most unhappy. It was even rumored in the neighborhood that he often beat her.

In the second place, Eugénie told me that Paul Arsène, having one evening, contrary to his sober habits, given in to the temptation to drink a mug of beer, had entered, about three months ago, Poisson's café; and that there, after glimpsing the beautiful lady decked in white with lush black hair like a medieval princess, and recognizing her as poor Marthe, his first, his only love, he had nearly become ill. Marthe signaled to him not to speak to her, because her fierce overseer was there; but she found a way, while giving him change of his five-franc coin, to slip him a note, which read as follows:

"My poor Arsène, if you don't despise this girl from your hometown too much, come and chat with her tomorrow. That is Monsieur Poisson's day to take his turn as watchman. I need to talk about my town and my lost happiness."

"No doubt," continued Eugénie, "Arsène arrived punctually for their rendezvous. He left more in love than ever, finding Marthe even handsomer for her pallor, and ennobled by her sorrow. And what's more, since she had read many novels behind the counter, and some-times more serious books, she had acquired a beautiful way of speaking and all sorts of ideas that she hadn't had in the past. Besides, she had confided in him her unhappiness, her regrets, her desire to escape from the shameful and miserable situation her seducer had put her in, and Arsène imagined that the duties of Christian charity and friendship alone bound him from then on to his compatriot. He prowled around her constantly, but managed not to provoke the jealous man's suspi-cions, and he succeeded in chatting with Marthe each time Monsieur Poisson was absent.

"Marthe had made a firm decision to flee her tyrant; but not with the intent, she said, of trading another shame for the one of which she wanted to rid herself. She entrusted Arsène with the task of finding her a situation where she could live honestly by her own two hands, either as a housekeeper in the home of a wealthy person, or as a salesgirl in a novelty shop, etc.; but all the situations that Paul envisioned for her seemed to him unworthy of the woman he loved. He wanted to find a position for her that was honorable, but at the same time comfortable and free: and that was not easy. So he conceived and executed the plan of leaving the world of art and of resuming some sort of trade, even if it were domestic work. He told himself that because his aunt was about to die, he would send for his sisters to join him in Paris, and he would set them up along with Marthe as seamstresses working out of their home; he would support all three of them until they could get on their feet, even abandoning painting forever if his funds and their work didn't prove sufficient for them to live in comfort. That's how Paul sacrificed the passion of art to that of devotion, and his future to his love.

"Finding no more lucrative employment at the time than that of a café waiter, he pretended to *be* a café waiter, and in fact he chose Monsieur Poisson's café, where he was able to devise a plan to carry Marthe off, and he plans to remain there for a while to deflect suspicion. Now that his Aunt Henriette has in fact died, Arsène's sisters are on their way, and I've taken upon myself the task of setting them up in an honest home: this one is clean, and the neighbors are good. The apartment next to ours has two little rooms; the rent is one hundred francs. Those young ladies will be just fine there. We'll lend them the linens and furniture they need until they have the funds to purchase their own, and that shouldn't take long; since Paul, who has worked two months now, has already been able to buy a fairly nice set of furniture, which has been up there in your attic, unbeknownst to you.

"Finally, two nights ago, when you were nursing your sick patient, Laure—or, to put it more accurately, Marthe, since that's her real name —mustered all her courage, and at the stroke of midnight, while Monsieur Poisson took his turn as watchman, she left with Arsène. He was to escort her here, and quickly return before his employer came back in; but they had gone barely thirty paces when they thought they saw a light in Monsieur Poisson's chambers in the entresol, and they considered returning right away. Then Marthe, in despair, made up her mind to force Arsène to go back. She began to run as fast as she could down the Rue de Tournon, counting on the swiftness of her journey and heaven's protection to escape alone from the dangers of the night. She was followed by a man on the quais; but by good fortune he turned out to be your friend Laravinière, who promised to keep her secret. He escorted her to our door. Arsène dashed out to see us this morning. The poor boy was supposed to be running an errand clear on the other side of Paris. He was so drenched in sweat, so short of breath, so moved, that we thought he would faint dead away at the top of the stairs. Finally, in the five minutes he had to converse, he informed us that their fear at the moment of flight had been a false alarm, that Monsieur Poisson had not returned until morning, and that in his confusion and fury he didn't suspect Arsène in the least of complicity."

"And now," I said to Eugénie, "what do they have to fear from Monsieur Poisson? No legal action, since he's not married to Marthe."

"No, but some violence in his first flush of anger. Since he's a coarse man, at the mercy of all his passions, incapable of real affection, he will soon find consolation in a new mistress. Marthe, who knows him well, says that if we can keep her whereabouts secret for a month at the most, there will be nothing to fear."

"If I understand the role you've picked out for me in all this," I continued, "it is: *first of all,* to let you put all of our means at the disposal of our unfortunate neighbors; *second of all,* to keep behind the door a good strong cane reserved for Monsieur Poisson's shoulders, should he attack. Well, then, here, *first of all,* is a quarter of my income, which I received yesterday, and with which you will do, as usual, as you see fit; *second of all,* here is a pretty good rattan cane which I will place on sentry duty."

That done, I threw myself on my bed, where I literally fell asleep before I could even remove my clothes.

I was awakened two hours later by Horace. "What the devil is going on at your house?" he demanded. "Before anyone will open the door, you have to negotiate at the grating, there's whispering behind the door, someone is being hidden in the kitchen, or the wood bin, or the armoire, who knows where? And, when I pass by, she laughs up her sleeve. Who is the object of this hoax? Is it you or me?"

I, too, started to laugh. I got dressed, and I was going to take my place in the meeting that Marthe and Eugénie were convening in the kitchen. I was of the opinion that we had to let Horace in on the secret, as well as a small number of friends whom I was in the habit of receiving at home. By trusting Marthe's secret to their honor and prudence, there was a much greater chance of keeping it than if we tried to hide it from them. It was impossible that they would not find out, even if Marthe never entered our room from hers, and even if I routed all my friends via the concierge. The instructions would never be followed; and all it would take would be a door slightly ajar, just for an instant, for one of our young men to catch a glimpse of the beautiful Laure and recognize her. So I began the chapter of solemn disclosures with Horace, while still concealing from him, as I did with the others, the interest which Arsène had in Laure, his role in her escape, and even their long-standing acquaintance. Laure, who had once again become Marthe, was, to Horace and to all our friends, a childhood friend of Eugénie's; Eugénie, for her part, took care not to say that she had only known Marthe for two days. Supposedly, she was the only one who would offer her refuge and take her under her protective wing. As a chaperone she was fairly respectable; all my friends held Eugénie in high regard, and with good reason, and I never bragged, rest assured, of my ridiculous attack of jealousy.

Even so, Eugénie didn't forgive me as easily as I had hoped. I might even say that she never forgave me. As much as she made, I'm convinced, every effort to forget it, she always thought about it with bitterness. How many times she made me feel it, when she denied energetically that a man's love was as exalted as a woman's?

"The best, the most devoted, the most loyal of men is always ready," she said, "to suspect the woman who has given herself to him. He will insult her, if not by his actions, at least by his thoughts. In our society, man has assumed over us a right that is strictly material; so all of our fidelity, and often all of our love, is summarized for him by one fact. For us, who only command moral power, we place more weight on moral proofs than on appearances. Even when we're jealous, we're capable of denying the evidence of our eyes; and when you utter a vow, we abide by your word as though it were infallible. But is our word any less sacred? Why have you made your honor and ours so different? You would tremble with anger if a man told you that you were lying. And yet you live on distrust, and you surround us with precautions that prove you suspect us. For a man, who should be reassured forever by years of chastity and sincerity, just one unusual circumstance, one mysterious word, a gesture, a door open or shut, can destroy all his trust in an instant."

She addressed all these lovely sermons to Horace, who was in the habit of assuming the pose of a future Othello; but, in fact, it was on my heart that these steely blows rained.

"Where the devil does she get these things she says?" Horace observed. "My dear friend, you let her go too often to hear them preach at Taitbout Hall."

Paul Arsène's relationship with Marthe was as strange as could be. Whether he never dared express his love to her, or whether she never wanted to acknowledge it, they remained, as on the day they met, like brother and sister. Marthe was unaware of that young man's devotion; she didn't know what sorts of hopes he'd had to renounce in order to interest himself in her fate. He didn't hide from her the fact that he had studied painting; but he hadn't told her what admirable abilities nature had endowed him with in this domain; and besides, he attributed his renunciation to the need to send for and support his sisters. Marthe owned nothing, and hadn't wanted to take anything with her from Monsieur Poisson's. She expected to work, and the advance of money that she accepted she attributed only to Eugénie. She wouldn't have fled on Arsène's arm if she had believed she would owe him for more than a few simple favors, such as his introducing her to Eugénie and his setting up a haven for her with his sisters, which she fully expected to pay back by contributing her share of the expenses. Framing his devotion in this way, Paul burned his bridges and lost the right ever to say to her: "Look what I've done for you," since, on the surface, he had only done for her what is permitted in the most casual of friendships.

The poor boy was so overwhelmed with work, and kept on such a short leash by his employer, that he was not able to meet his sisters' coach. Marthe never went out, fearing that she would run into someone who would put Monsieur Poisson on her trail. So Eugénie and I took responsibility for helping out at the arrival of Louison and Suzanne, our new neighbors. Louison, the older, was a rustic beauty, a bit of a shrew, with a loud voice, a touchy personality, and the habit of being in command. She had acquired this habit at the home of her old, infirm aunt, who looked upon her as an oracle, and who left her in charge of five or six apprentice seamstresses, among whom the younger sister, Suzon, was only a secondary power, a sort of minister of public works, but subordinate to her older sister without recourse to appeal. Louison also put on queenly airs, and she had the insatiable desire for power that eats up sovereigns.

Suzanne, without being beautiful, was pleasant and had a more refined nature than Louise. It was easy to see that she was capable of understanding all that Louise would never understand. But Louise was over her and all around her like a lead bell, preventing her from breaking out or being exposed to other influences.

They welcomed our attention, one with surprise and shyness, the other with a somewhat brutal stiffness. They had no idea what life in Paris was like, and couldn't imagine that Arsène faced an overriding difficulty that prevented him from coming to meet them. They thanked Eugénie distractedly, Louise repeating at every turn, "Still, it's very unpleasant that Paul ain't here!" And Suzanne adding, in a tone of consternation, "Ain't it funny that Paul didn't come!"

One must admit that, having just made a fairly long coach journey for the first time in their lives, finding themselves in the clutches of customs agents who were examining their trunks, and not knowing what to make of the noisy throng of travelers arriving and departing, of horses being harnessed and unharnessed, of clerks, mailmen, and porters, it was fairly natural that they should lose their heads and display a bit of fatigue, ill humor, and fright. They became milder when they saw that I had come to help them, that I was watching out for their bundles, and that I was handling their bill with the office. Hardly had they gotten settled into a hackney cab with their belongings, their innumerable baskets and cartons (since they had brought with them, as country people are accustomed to do, a swarm of objects whose freight cost exceeded their value), when Louison rummaged through her two-handled basket, her arm plunged in to the elbow, and shouted, "Wait, Monsieur! I have to pay you! What did you give them for our coach fare? Wait a minute!"

She couldn't comprehend that she didn't have to reimburse me right away for the money I had paid out of pocket for them; and this dash of grandeur, which I was far from appreciating myself, began to win me their esteem.

We got into a cabriolet, Eugénie and I, so we could arrive at our shared domicile at the same time.

"Oh, my God! What a huge house!" they cried, measuring it with their eyes. "It's so tall you can't see the summit."

It seemed even taller to them when they had to climb the ninety-two stairs that separated our apartment from the ground. At the third floor, they acted surprised; at the fourth, they broke out laughing; at the fifth, they were furious; at the sixth, they declared that they could never live inside such a lighthouse. Louise, discouraged, sat down on the top step and said, "This is one awful town."

Suzanne, who had more desire to mock than to fly into a fury, added, "Convenient, eh? To go up and down those steps fifteen times a day! You could break your neck!"

Eugénie immediately showed them into their apartment. They found it small and sordid. One room looked out on an extension of my balcony. Louise moved toward it, and, recoiling immediately, fell back into a chair.

"Oh my God!" she exclaimed. "That gives me vertigo; I feel like I'm at the top of our steeple."

We wanted to give them supper. Eugénie had prepared a light meal in my apartment, hoping, at that time, to introduce them to Marthe.

"You're very kind, Monsieur and Madame," said Louison, throwing a warning glance at Suzanne, "but we ain't hungry."

She looked despondent; Suzanne hastened to unpack the trunks and to arrange their belongings, as if that were the most pressing task in the world.

"Now, why are there three beds?" Louise observed suddenly. "So Paul is going to live with us? Very good!"

"No, Paul can't live with you yet," I answered her. "But you will have a woman from your hometown, an old friend, whom he wants to introduce to you himself . . ."

"Really? And who's that? Ain't many people from our town here that I ever heard of. How come he never told us in his letters?"

"He had many things to tell you about it and he will explain them to you in person. Meanwhile, he entrusted me with the task of introducing her to you. She's already living here; in fact, right at this moment she's preparing your supper. Would you like me to bring her in?"

"We'll go see for ourselves," Louison responded, her curiosity piqued. "So, where is she, this girl from our town?"

She followed me quickly.

"Look, it's Marton," she cried harshly, recognizing the beautiful Marthe. "How's by you, Marton? Are you a widow, then, if you're going to live with us? You did an ugly thing, nothing less, by running away with that man who made you rebel against your father. But they say you finally married him, and mercy on all our sins."

Marthe blushed, turned pale, and looked abashed. She hadn't expected such a welcome. The poor woman had forgotten what her former playmates were like, just as Arsène had forgotten his sisters. Homesickness has that effect on everyone: it transforms the objects of our memories into poetic ideals, whose good qualities grow in our eyes, while their defects always soften with time and absence and are almost erased by our imagination.

And then, when Marthe had left the region five years before, Louise and Suzanne were just children who never thought about anything. Now they were two dragons of virtue, particularly the elder, who had all the pride of a beauty famous at a radius of two leagues, and all the intolerance of uncontested wisdom. When they left the soil where they shone in their full brightness, these two wildflowers had to lose (Arsène had not foreseen this) much of their charm and worth. In their village they set a good example, binding the girls in their circle to habits of industriousness and good behavior. In Paris, their merits remained buried, their precepts useless, their example invisible; and the qualities required by their new station in life—goodness, judgment, charity— they did not possess, could not possess.

These thoughts came much too late. Marthe's first act was to throw herself into the arms of Arsène's sister, her second was to wait for the latter's first show of affection, the third was to close herself up in a justified feeling of shyness and pride; but a profound sadness betrayed itself on her pale visage, and large tears formed in her eyes.

I took her hand, and, squeezing it affectionately, sat her down at the table; then I forced Louise to sit next to her.

"You have no right to interrogate or reproach her," I said to the latter in a firm tone of voice that astonished and swiftly mastered her: "She has the respect of your brother, and ours. She's been unhappy, and unhappiness demands the respect of honest souls. When you've gotten to know her again, you will like her, and you will never speak of her past."

Louison lowered her eyes, stymied and unconvinced. Suzanne, who had followed behind, giving in to her heart's impulse, leaned toward Marthe to kiss her; but a terrible look that Louise threw back at her paralyzed her. She limited herself to shaking Marthe's hand; and Eugénie, fearing that Marthe would be uneasy between the two women from her hometown, seated herself next to her, making a point of showing more friendship and regard for her than for the others. The meal was sad and awkward. Either out of spite, or because the dishes were not to her liking, Louison didn't touch her food. Finally, Arsène arrived. After the initial embraces, he guessed, with that amazing presence of mind he possessed, what was going on with all of us, and he took his two sisters off into another room, where he remained shut in with them for over an hour.

After delivering and receiving this lecture, they were all red in the face. But the influence of fraternal authority, so little a part of the customs of the provinces, had checkmated Louise's resistance. Suzanne (who did not lack in refinement), seeing in Arsène a useful counterweight to her sister's authority, was not upset, I believe, to change masters a bit. She was sincerely friendly toward Marthe, while Louise overwhelmed her with affected politeness that was very clumsy and almost offensive.

Arsène tried to send them off to bed almost immediately.

"We'll wait for Madame Poisson," Louise said, not realizing she was turning the knife in Marthe's heart by addressing her in that manner.

"Marthe has not traveled," responded Masaccio coldly. "She doesn't have to go to sleep before she wants. The rest of you, who are tired, you must rest."

They obeyed, and when they had gone:

"I beg you to forgive my sisters," he said to Marthe, "for certain provincial biases which they will soon shed. I'll see to it."

"No, don't call them biases," answered Marthe. "They're right to scorn me: I've committed a shameful error. I yielded to a man whom I would soon hate, and who was not made to be loved. Your sisters are scandalized only because my choice was vile. If I'd let myself be carried off by a man like you, Arsène, I'd be treated leniently, and perhaps even esteemed in all hearts. You see yourself that everyone who encounters Eugénie respects her. She's considered your friend's wife, even though she's never tried to pass for that; and me, even though I took the name 'spouse,' everyone sensed that I was not that at all. Seeing what a brute I'd taken for a master, no one believed that love could have tossed me into that abyss."

With those words, she cried bitterly, and her sadness, too long confined, broke through her chest.

Arsène stifled the sobs that almost escaped him.

"No one ever said or thought ill of you," he exclaimed. "As for me, I know very well how to make my sisters share the respect I feel for you."

"Respect! Is it possible that you respect me, you! You don't think, then, that I sold myself?"

"No! No!" shouted Paul forcefully. "I believe that you loved that hateful man; and where is the crime in that? You didn't know him; you believed in his love; you were deceived like so many others. Ah, Monsieur!" he added, turning to me, "you don't believe that Marthe could ever sell herself, do you?"

My response revealed my embarrassment. In the few days we had known about Marthe's situation with regard to Monsieur Poisson, Horace and I had already asked each other several times how such a beautiful and intelligent creature could have fallen for that Minotaur. Sometimes we told ourselves that the man in question, so heavy and coarse, could have had, a few years ago, youth and a certain handsomeness; that his Vitellius profile, now odious, might have added character before the rapid and disorderly advance of obesity. But sometimes we also lingered over the notion that jewels and promises, the lure of finery and the hope of a carefree life, had intoxicated that child before her intellect and feelings had developed. In the end we thought that her story could well resemble that of all seduced girls who are pushed toward evil by the needs of their vanity and the influence of their laziness.

Despite my hastening to reassure her, Marthe saw what was going on inside me. She felt the need to justify herself.

"Listen to me," she said, "I'm very guilty, but not as guilty as I seem. My father was a worker, a poor and gloomy man who sought to forget his hardships and his worries in wine, as so many others do. You don't know what the people are really like, Monsieur! No, you don't know! Among the people you find the greatest virtue and the greatest vice. There you can find men like him," and she placed her hand on Arsène's arm, "and there you find men whose lives seem to be given over to the soul of evil. A dark fury eats them up, a deep despair of their situation feeds a continual rage in them. My father was like that. He complained constantly, with oaths and imprecations, about the unfairness of chance and the injustice of fate. He wasn't born lazy; but he became that way out of discouragement, and poverty was the boss in our household. My childhood slipped away between two alternating pains: on the one hand a sad compassion for my unfortunate parents, on the other a profound terror of my father's outbursts and frenzies. The straw pallet where we slept was just about our only belonging; yet every day greedy creditors argued who would reclaim it. My mother died young, of ill treatment by her husband. I was still a child. I felt her loss keenly, although she took out on me, the scapegoat, the injuries and blows showered on her. But it never occurred to me to insult her memory and to rejoice in the sort of freedom that her death won for me. I put all these injustices at the feet of poverty, hers as well as my father's. Poverty was our only enemy, but it was a common, terrible, hateful enemy which, from the day I was born, I was used to detesting and fearing.

"My mother, despite it all, was hardworking and forced me to be that way, too. When I was alone and left to my own inclinations, I gave in to the one that dominates childhood: I fell into the habit of being lazy. I barely saw my father: he left in the morning before I woke up, and only came home at night after I'd gone to bed. He was a good and quick worker, but as soon as he got his hands on some money, he drank it up; and when he came home drunk in the middle of the night, shaking the paving stones under his heavy and uneven tread, shouting obscenities in a tone that resembled a roar more than a song, I woke up drenched in a cold sweat, my hair standing on end with fear. I hid in a corner of my bed, and whole hours went by with me not daring to breathe, him pacing, agitated and talking to himself in his delirium, sometimes arming himself with a chair or a stick, and pounding on the walls and even on my bed, because he thought he was being followed and attacked by imaginary enemies. I was very careful not to speak to him, since once, when my mother was still alive, he wanted to kill me, to save me, he said, from the misery of poverty. After that time, I hid when he came near; and often, to avoid being struck by the blows which he landed at random in the darkness, I slid under my bed, and I stayed there till daylight, half naked, numb with fear and cold.

"During that time, I often ran through the meadows that surrounded our little town with the children who were my age; we often played there together, Arsène. And you know quite well that this child, who always dragged along the remnants of a shoe, held in place by a thread around her leg by way of a buskin, and who had so much difficulty getting her undisciplined hair back under her rag of a bonnet, you know quite well that this child, fearful and melancholy even in her play, was as pure and as modest as your sisters. My only crime, if it is a crime, when one's existence is so sad, was to desire, not wealth, but the calm and gentle manners that affluence can procure. When I went into a businessman's home, and I saw how polite and tranquil his family was, how clean his children, how simple and elegant his wife, my whole ideal was to be able to sit and read or knit on a clean chair in a quiet and peaceful home; and when I reached the height of dreaming of an apron of black taffeta, I thought I had stretched my ambition to its furthest limits. I had learned, as did all the daughters of artisans, how to do needlework; but I was always slow and awkward at it. Suffering had wilted my active abilities; I lived only on daydreams, happy when I was not mistreated, terrified and almost stupefied when I was.

"But how can I tell you the main and the most awful cause of my error? Must I, Arsène? Or wouldn't it be better to incur a bit more blame than to place such a hateful curse on my father's head?"

"You have to tell it all," answered Arsène, "or rather I'll tell it for you; because you can't let yourself be accused of a crime when you're innocent. I know the whole story, and I've just told it to my sisters, who hadn't heard it before. Her father," he said, turning to us, "(forgive him, my friends; poverty is the cause of drunkenness, and drunkenness is the cause of all our vices), that miserable man, debased, degraded, certainly deprived of his reason, developed a sordid passion for his daughter, and this passion burst forth precisely on that day when Marthe, who had, unbeknownst to her, been noticed at a dance by a traveling salesman, stimulated her father's insane jealousy. This traveler had gushed when he was with her; he hadn't neglected to speak to her of love and of running away together—they all do with young girls they meet in the provinces. Marthe barely listened to him.

"He had to leave the following night, and the next night, just at the moment when he was leaving, he saw a disheveled woman running after him, who leapt into his carriage. It was Marthe fleeing, a latter-day Beatrice, escaping the sinister violence of a latter-day Cenci. She could have, you say, chosen otherwise, found refuge elsewhere, invoked the protection of the law; but in the last scenario, she would have had to bring dishonor on her father, face the shame of one of those scandalous trials where the innocent party is often as sullied in public opinion as the guilty. Marthe believed that she had found a friend, a protector, even a spouse, since the traveler, seeing her childish simplicity, had talked to her of marriage. She believed she could love him out of gratitude, and, even after he'd betrayed her, she believed she still owed him some thanks."

"And then," resumed Marthe, "my first steps in life were marked by such terrible scenes and such frightening dangers that I no longer had the right to expect better. I had merely exchanged tyrants. But the second one, with his jealousies and his frenzies, had a sort of education that made him seem to me less harsh than the first. Everything is relative. That man, whom you find so crude, and whom I also found to be so once I could compare him with others, seemed to me good, sincere, at the beginning. The exceptional meekness that I had acquired in such a trying and hard life encouraged and quickly pushed to extremes the despotic instincts of my new master. I put up with his behavior with a resignation that a woman who had been brought up under better circumstances wouldn't have. To some extent I'd become blasé about dangers and injuries. I always dreamed of being independent, but I no longer thought that was possible for me. I was a broken soul; I no longer felt I had the energy required to make any effort, and without Arsène's friendship, advice, and help, I would never have found it. Anything that resembled an amorous advance, even simple and polite praise, only frightened and saddened me. I needed more than a lover, I needed a friend: and I found him, and now I'm astonished that I suffered for so long without hope."

"And now you will be happy," I said to her, "since you will find yourself surrounded only with tenderness, devotion, and deference."

"Oh! from you and Eugénie," she cried, throwing her arms around my companion, "I can count on it; and as for this one's friendship," she added, taking Arsène's head in her hands, "it will get me through anything."

Arsène alternately blushed and turned pale.

"My sisters will respect you," he exclaimed with emotion, "or else . . ."

"No threats," she replied. "Oh! never make threats for my sake. I'll disarm them, don't worry; and if I fail, I'll endure their little snubs. It's such an insignificant thing to me! It seems like child's play. Don't be anxious, dear Arsène. You wanted to save me, in fact you have saved me, and I'll bless you all the days of my life."

Ecstatic with love and joy, Arsène returned to Poisson's café, and Marthe, stepping softly, claimed her little bed next to the two sisters, whose vigorous snoring covered up the light tread of her footsteps.

Arsène's sisters did, in fact, soften. After several days of fatigue, shock, and uncertainty, they seemed to have made up their minds to mix, without any reservations, with the company imposed on them. True, Marthe's behavior toward them was so obliging, it was almost submissive. The good manners she had acquired, combined with her natural sweetness and an always lively and never giddy disposition, made her company the most agreeable of any woman I've ever known. It took Eugénie and me only two or three days to develop a genuine affection for her. Her politeness impressed even the haughty Louison; and when the latter felt the need to pick a quarrel with her, Marthe's gentle voice, her carefully chosen words, her kindness calmed or at least dulled the argumentative mood of the country girl.

For our part, we did our best to reconcile Louise and Suzanne with the Paris that had made such a poor first impression on them. They had imagined in their village that Paris was an Eldorado where, relatively speaking, the poor lived like the wealthy in the provinces. To a certain extent their dream actually came true, because when they rode in a hackney cab (two or three times I gave them this luxurious pleasure) they looked at each other dumbfounded, saying, "We ain't doin' so bad here, we're steppin' out in a carriage!" And then, at the sight of even the smallest shop they were dazzled with admiration. The Luxembourg seemed like an enchanted garden to them. But if the sight of new things thrilled them almost to distraction for several days, that didn't prevent them from reflecting sadly on their new state when they found themselves in that little room six flights up in which their life was now confined.

What a change, in fact, from their existence in the provinces! No more air, no more freedom, no more chatting on their neighbors' doorsteps; no more friendly interactions with all the inhabitants of their lane; no more strolls after work with all the local girls on a little rampart planted with chestnut trees; no more country dances on Sundays. As soon as they were settled into their jobs, they saw that in Paris the days are too short to do all that one has to accomplish, and that even if one earns twice what one does in the provinces, one must also spend twice as much, and work three times as hard. Each one of these discoveries was a surprise that angered them. Nor had they comprehended that female virtue would be exposed to so many dangers, that they could not go out alone at night, or go dancing in a public place and still be respected. "Oh my God!" cried Suzanne in dismay. "Is the world really so wicked here?"

And yet they submitted to it, not without grumbling to themselves. Arsène's frequent exhortations kept them respectful, and they no longer showed their discontent as savagely as they had on their first day. The close proximity of the two sisters, dissatisfied and fairly ill bred, would have been quite disagreeable if work, sovereign remedy for all ills when it's proportionate to our strength, hadn't come along to pacify everyone. Thanks to the careful preparations Eugénie had made in advance, commissions did arrive; and she gave serious thought, seeing the respect and trust her customers showed her, to setting up a dressmaking workshop. Marthe was not terribly diligent, but she had a good deal of taste and inventiveness. Louison sewed quickly and with cyclopian resolve. Suzanne was not unskillful. Eugénie would handle the business end, try on the dresses herself, and supervise the work, and she loyally divided the proceeds with her partners. Each of them, having an interest in the success of the phalanstery, would work, not for piecework and without consciousness, as do day laborers, but with all the zeal and attention of which she was capable.

This grand idea was agreeable enough to Arsène's sisters; it remained to be seen if Louison's personality would be tractable enough to make the partnership work. Used to being in charge, she was distressed to see that the good-for-nothing Marthe (as she called her when whispering in her sister's ear) had more talent than she for concocting a sleeve ornament, or for arranging the delicate parts of a bodice. When, true to her antediluvian traditions, she cut a piece of cloth as she was accustomed to, and Eugénie came along to upset all her plans, the virago had great difficulty not hitting her over the head with her chair. But a gentle word from Marthe and a knowing smile from Suzon made all that anger retreat, and she had to content herself with moaning indistinctly, like the sea after a storm.

While we were making this important attempt to begin a new life in our garrets, Horace, who had retreated to his own, devoted himself to literary endeavors. As soon as I had some free time I went to see him, since I'd been deprived of his company for several days. I found his apartment strangely altered. He had arranged his little furnished room in an affected way. He had put his foot-coverlet on the table, to give it an office-like appearance; he had placed one of his mattresses in the doorway, to muffle the sounds of his neighbors; and he had wrapped his cotton-print curtain around him to use as a dressing gown, or rather as a theatrical cloak. He was seated before his table, his elbows jutting outward, head in hands, his hair in disarray; and when I opened the door, twenty manuscript sheets, raised by the breeze, fluttered around him and fell in every direction, like a flock of startled birds.

I ran after them, and while collecting them I snuck a glance at them. Each one had a different title at the top of the page.

"It's a novel," I exclaimed, "called *The Curse,* Chapter One! No, it's called *The New René,* Chapter One . . . No again! here's *A Deception,* Book the First. Ah! Now another, *The Last Believer,* First Part . . . Wait! Look, a few verses! A poem! First Canto, *The End of the World.* Aha, a ballad! *The Moorish King's Beautiful Daughter,* First Stanza; and on this page, *The Creation,* A Dramatic Fantasy, Scene One. And then here's a light comedy, God forgive me! *The Beggar Philosophers,* Act One. And by my soul! Something else! A political pamphlet, page one. Why, if all of these march abreast, my dear Horace, you will stage quite an invasion of the literary world."

Horace was furious. He complained about my curiosity, and tearing all his beginnings out of my hands, none of which had gone beyond half a page, he crumpled them into a ball and threw it into the fireplace.

"What! So many dreams, so many projects, so many ideas completely abandoned over a joke?" I said.

"My dear friend, if you've come here to amuse yourself," he answered, "fine! Let's gossip, let's laugh as much as you want. But if you're going to scoff at me before my ship has even been launched, I'll never be able to get a head of steam going again."

"I'm leaving, I'm leaving," I said, picking up my hat. "I don't want to disturb you at the moment of inspiration."

"No, no, stay," he said, physically detaining me. "Inspiration isn't coming today. I'm in a stupor, and you came in the nick of time to distract me from myself. I'm worn out, my head is spinning. I haven't slept in three nights, and I have not been out for five days."

"Well, that takes courage, and I congratulate you. You must have something in the works. Do you want to read it to me?"

"I haven't written a thing, haven't edited one line. This scribbling on paper is much more difficult than I imagined. It really is tedious. My subjects haunt me. When I close my eyes, I see an army, a world of creations teeming in my brain. When I reopen my eyes, it all disappears. I gulp down quarts of coffee, I smoke dozens of pipes, I get drunk on my own enthusiasm; it feels as if I'll burst like a volcano. And as soon as I approach this cursèd table, the lava hardens and my inspiration cools again. In the time it takes to get a sheet of paper ready and to trim my pen, boredom triumphs; the smell of the ink makes me nauseous. And then that horrible necessity of translating my thoughts into words and putting them into ink-scratches—my thoughts, as fiery, as alive, as changeable as rays of sunlight tinting the clouds in the air! Oh, it's a calling, all right! Where can you hide from a calling, great God? That calling will follow me everywhere!"

"So you have pretensions," I said to him, "of finding a way of expressing your thoughts that does not take a material form? I know of none."

"No," he said, "but I'd like to express myself, right from the word go, without fatiguing myself, without effort, the way water murmurs and the nightingale sings."

"The murmur of water is produced by work, and the nightingale's song is an art. Have you never heard young birds chirp in a wavering voice, stumbling through their first tunes? Every precise expression of ideas, feelings, and even instincts requires training. Do you hope, with your first attempts, to write as prolifically and easily as you would after you've had a good deal of experience?"

Horace claimed that he lacked neither ease nor prolificacy, but the actual time to delineate the characters overwhelming all his faculties. He lied: I offered to take dictation from him while he improvised out loud, but he refused, and for good reason. I knew well that he could draft a witty and charming letter as fast as the ink could flow from his pen; but it truly seemed to me that giving a form, however short and incomplete, to any idea required patience and work. Horace's mind was certainly not sterile; he was right to complain of the excessive activity of his thoughts and the multiplicity of his visions; but he was thoroughly lacking in the power of elaboration which must govern the use of a form. He didn't know how to work; later, I learned that he didn't know how to suffer either.

But that was not even the primary obstacle. I think that to write, one must have a definite and reasoned opinion about one's subject, not to mention a certain number of other ideas, equally definite, to back up one's arguments. Horace had no firm opinions about anything. He made his convictions up as he went along, developing them in a rather brilliant way; he also changed them often, and Masaccio, hearing him, was in the habit of repeating this proverbial axiom under his breath: "One day is never the same as the next."

Provided that one limits oneself to small talk, one can act in this manner and entertain and amuse one's listeners, at one's own risk. But when one uses words to a more serious purpose, one must perhaps know a bit better what one claims to say and prove. Horace was never at a loss for that in a discussion; but his opinions, which he only believed in at the moment he uttered them, could not warm the depths of his heart, move his imagination, and bring about in him the internal, mysterious, powerful labor that results in inspiration, like the work of the Cyclopes, which was evidenced by the glow of Aetna.

Despite the absence of general convictions, individual feelings can move us and make us eloquent; that, in general, is youth's power.

Horace did not yet have that power, and having neither felt passionate emotions nor seen their effects on society—in a word, having learned what he knew only from books—he could not be impelled, by a higher revelation or by a generous need, to choose this or that plot, this or that image. Since he was rich in fictions amassed in his intellect by the culture, and all set to become fecund when his life was complete, he considered himself ripe to produce. But he could not develop an attachment for those fleeting creations that did not stir his soul and that, to tell the truth, did not come from it, since they were the product merely of certain memory combinations. They also lacked originality, no matter what form he tried to pour them into—and he knew it, because he had taste, and his vanity had no trace of foolishness. So he scratched out, tore up, started over, and ended up abandoning one piece to try another that succeeded no better.

Not understanding the cause of his impotence, he mistakenly attributed it to a dislike of form. Form was the only richness he *could* acquire at that time with patience and will; but it would never have made up for a certain depth which he was fundamentally lacking, and without which literary works, no matter how shot through with metaphors, how freighted with ingenious and charming turns of phrase, have no merit.

I often repeated these things to him, but I could not convince him. After the attempt that, for more than a month, he persisted in making, he continued to delude himself. He believed that his boiling blood, the impetuosity of his youth, his feverish impatience to express himself, were the only obstacles he had to overcome. In the meantime, he acknowledged that everything he had attempted took on, after ten lines or three verses, such a resemblance to the authors on whom he had been nurtured that he blushed at doing only imitations. He showed me several verses and sentences that could have been signed Lamartine, Victor Hugo, Paul-Louis Courier, Charles Nodier, Balzac, even Béranger, the most difficult of all to imitate, because of his clean and compact style; but these brief attempts, which one could call fragments of fragments, would only have been, in the work of his idols, appendices functioning as ornaments to unique thoughts, and this uniqueness was something Horace didn't possess. If he wanted to express an idea, it was shocking (even to him) how obvious the plagiarism was, since the idea was not his at all: it belonged to them; it belonged to the whole world. To put his stamp on it he would have had to hold it in his mind and his heart deeply enough and long enough for it to undergo some personal modification; since no intellect is identical to any other, and the same causes never have the same effect on one as on another; several masters may simultaneously render the same fact or feeling, or handle the same subject, without there being the slightest danger of their colliding with one another. But for him who has not experienced that cause, for him who has not witnessed that fact nor felt that emotion himself, individuality, originality, are impossible. So, many more days passed with Horace getting no further than he was when the first hour struck. I should say that this effort completely squandered what little willpower he had amassed to pull himself out of inertia. When he was weary with fatigue, saturated with disgust, almost ill, he came out of seclusion and burst out of doors, seeking distractions and even wanting to try passion, he said, to see if it would revive his benumbed muse.

This resolution made me tremble for him. To disembark without a destination on that stormy sea, with no experience for protection, is to risk more than one might think. He had ventured the same way into a literary career; but since he hadn't had to find an accomplice, the only disaster he had endured was a bit of lost ink and time. But what would become of him, blind as he was, under the direction of that *blind god?*

His ship was not wrecked as promptly as I had feared. When it comes to passion, not everyone who wants to can lose himself in it. Horace was certainly not born passionate. His personality took on such a large dimension in his mind that no temptation was worthy of him. He would have had to meet sublime beings for his enthusiasm to be awakened; and while waiting, he preferred himself, with some reason, to all the vulgar beings with whom he might become connected. There were no grounds for fearing that he would risk his precious health on prostitutes of the lower depths. He was incapable of lowering his pride so far as to implore those who succumb only to magnanimous offers or shows of infatuation to rouse their spent hearts and revive their sated curiosity. In fact, he professed to feel for them a contempt verging on the cruelest intolerance. He didn't understand the religious and truly great significance of *Marion Delorme*, a work he loved without having assimilated the profound moral which it conceals. He struck the pose of Didier, but only as he appears in a certain scene, the one in which Marion's lover, stunned by his discovery, crushes that unfortunate woman with sarcasm and curses. As for the forgiveness at the end, Horace said that Didier would never have bestowed it if he hadn't been on the verge of having his head severed a minute later.

What I feared was that when Horace turned his attention to more precious lives, he might stain or break them by a whim or with his pride, and that he might fill his own life with regret or remorse. Fortunately, such a victim was not easy to find. One can no more find love with cool composure and a set purpose than one can find poetic inspiration with those ingredients. To love, one must begin by understanding what a woman is, what protection and respect she is owed. To the man who is imbued with the holiness of reciprocal commitments, the equality of the sexes before God, and the injustices of the social order and of vulgar opinion in this matter, love can reveal itself in all its grandeur and beauty; but to him who is permeated with the common misconceptions on the inferiority of women, on the difference between her duties and ours with respect to fidelity, to him who seeks emotion rather than an ideal, love will not reveal itself. And for this reason, love, this feeling that God created for everyone, is known only to a few.

Horace had never turned over this important human question in his thoughts. He laughed freely about what he didn't understand, and, judging Saint-Simonianism (then the subject of much propaganda) only by its defects, he refused to examine such charlatanism. Those were his words; even if they were deserved in many respects, his knowledge didn't derive from any serious connection. He only saw in it the blue outfits and the plucked foreheads of the *fathers* of the new doctrine, and that was enough for him to declare the entire Saint-Simonian idea absurd and false. So he was not searching for light, but, not wanting to steep himself in any brand of pedanticism—neither, he said, that of the conservatives nor that of the innovators—he let himself be swept up in the brutal instinct of masculine priorities which society consecrates and sanctifies.

With these vague notions and a total absence of religious or social dogma, he wanted to experience love, the most religious of the manifestations of our moral life, the most important of our individual acts with regard to society! He had neither the sublime impetus that can revive love in a bold intellect nor the fanatical persistence that can preserve at least the appearance of order and a sort of virtue in following the traditions of the past.

His first passion was for Malibran.

Sometimes he went and sat in the orchestra at the Italiens; he borrowed money and went there whenever the divine soprano appeared on stage. There was certainly enough there to kindle his enthusiasm, and I would have liked that incessant adoration to occupy his imagination longer. It would have prepared him for receiving more lasting and complete impressions. But Horace couldn't wait. He wanted to make his dream come true, and he committed acts of *folly* for Madame Malibran; for example, he threw himself under the wheels of her carriage (after lying in wait for it at the exit), though he made sure that no harm came to him; then he tossed one or two bouquets onto the stage; finally he wrote her a rapturous letter, such as he had written a few weeks before to Madame Poisson. He received no more of a response this time than the first, and he didn't even know the letter's fate, whether it had been looked on with contempt, or if it had been received favorably.

I feared that this initial failure might cause him sharp pain. He got off with feeling only a bit spiteful. He made fun of himself for having believed for an instant that "the pride of genius would lower itself long enough to perceive it had won an ardent and 'pure' homage." I found him one day writing a second letter, which began as follows: "Thank you, woman, thank you! You have disabused me of glory"; and which ended: "Adieu, Madame. Be great, be intoxicated with your triumphs! And may you find, among the illustrious friends who surround you, a heart who understands you, an intellect that mirrors your own!"

I got him to throw the letter on the fire by telling him that Madame Malibran probably received similar ones at least three times a week, and she no longer wasted her time reading them. This observation gave him something to think about.

"If I believed," he exclaimed, "that she was base enough to show my first letter to her friends and laugh about it, I would go and hiss at her tonight in *Tancrède,* since, after all, she does sing off-key sometimes!"

"Your hiss would only be drowned out by the applause," I said to him, "and if it reached the soprano's ears, she would say to herself with a smile: 'That's one of my love letters booing me; it's the other side of the day-before-yesterday's bouquet.' So your hissing would just be one more homage among all the others."

Horace pounded the table with his fist.

"I must be an idiot three times over to have written that letter!" he shouted. "Fortunately, I signed it under an assumed name, and if some-day I do honor to the name I bear, *she* won't be able to say: 'He's a feather in my cap.'"

After these initial crises, Horace put aside his letters and his loves for a while and came over to relax on the divan on my balcony, examining the four women in our garret like a sultan, and breaking my pipes, as was his wont.

Forced to absent myself for part of the day for my studies and business, I had to leave him stretched out on my rug, since to draw him out of his superb indolence, I would have had to indicate to him that it displeased me, and, in short, that was not the case. I knew quite well he wouldn't try to court Eugénie, that Arsène's sisters would smash his face with their irons if he tried to affect the role of a rakish young lord with them; and since I genuinely liked him, it pleased me to find him there when I came home, and to share with him our modest family meal.

As for Marthe, she appeared to take no more note of him in her secret thoughts than she did when she had been the object of his glances behind the counter at Poisson's café. From that time on, his actions had reflected hers—he hadn't forgiven her for slighting his declaration, which, in reality, she had never received. In the meantime he was still struck, despite himself, by her exquisite bearing, her sober, sensitive, and delicate way of conversing. Her beauty seemed to deepen right before his eyes. Still melancholy, she no longer had the slave's dejected expression. Monsieur Poisson had already replaced her, and had ceased to frighten her. At our house she became like a Sunday in the country; and her health, which had suffered for a long time, prospered under the gentle and sound regimen I had prescribed for her, and which she followed without whims or revolts in a way that was rare for a nervous woman. Her presence in my house certainly attracted more friends than we'd had in the past—though Eugénie undertook to show the door to those whose friendship was too blatantly feigned. As for our old friends, we forgave them for being a bit more attentive than usual. These little gatherings were in themselves useful and noble, since students who acted bold and roguish on the streets suddenly displayed, under our roof, polite manners, chaste good cheer, and proper language, in order to please honest young ladies and amiable women. Only a cold heart and savage temperament would not have savored, in this attempt at benevolent and pure sociability, such uplifting pleasure. Everyone enjoyed it. Horace became less selfish and bitter. Our young people acquired the concept of, and a taste for, manners more gentle than those they saw exemplified elsewhere. Marthe forgot the horror of her past. Suzanne laughed goodheartedly, and her judgment became sounder than her former provincial ideas had allowed. Louison made less progress than the others, but she mastered her harsh frankness, and although she remained fiercely strict, she was not upset to be treated as a lady by young men whose elegance and distinction she perhaps overestimated a good deal.

Horace was gradually coming to find Marthe's company extremely charming. Having no way to find out if she had ever received his letter, he had the intelligence to act like a man who does not want to be rejected twice. He displayed a sort of devoted sympathy for her which could turn into love if its progress were not brusquely interrupted, and which, should he meet with sustained resistance, allowed good taste to make amends for the past.

This situation is the most favorable for passion to develop. With it, one leaps great distances without even noticing. Although my young friend was not predisposed, either by his nature or his education, to the refinements of love, he was initiated into them by a respect that he couldn't help but feel. One day, he instinctively spoke the language of passion, and was eloquent. It was the first time Marthe had heard such language. It didn't scare her the way she had thought it would; she even found it charming in a new way, and instead of rebuffing him, she admitted she was surprised, moved; she asked for time to understand what was going on inside her, and left him with hopes.

Although I was Horace's confidant, I was also indirectly Arsène's, through Eugénie. I was interested in both of them; I was the friend of both of them. If I valued Arsène more, I can say that I felt more friendship for Horace and was more drawn to him. I would have been fairly hard put to choose between these two suitors of the Penelope for whom I was the guardian, if I had been asked to give my counsel. My affection prevented me from harming either of the two, but Eugénie guided my conscience.

"Arsène loves Marthe with an eternal love," she said to me, "and Horace has merely taken a fancy to her. In one she will find, no matter what she does, a friend, a protector, a brother; the other will dally with her tranquillity, perhaps her honor, and will throw her over for a new whim. Don't let your friendship for Horace be childish. It's Marthe alone with whom you should concern yourself. Unfortunately, she likes to listen to that harebrain; it torments me. I think the more I criticize him, the better she thinks of him. It's up to you to enlighten her: she will believe you more than me. Tell her Horace doesn't love her and will never love her."

That was very hard to prove, and very reckless to assert. What did we know about it, after all? Horace was young enough to be ignorant of love; but love could create a major turning point for him, and suddenly ripen his personality. I admitted that the noble Marthe should not run the risk of such an experience, and I promised to try the strategy Eugénie suggested to me, namely, to take Horace out into society to distract him from his love, or to test its durability.

Into society! you will say to me, you, a student, a medical student, no less? Oh, God, yes. I had connections with several noble houses, connections that were not exactly constant, but nevertheless regular and durable, so that whenever I felt the impulse I could always be in touch with what was most sparkling and appealing in the Faubourg Saint-Germain. I had one black suit, which Eugénie carefully maintained for me for these grand occasions; some yellow gloves, which she made last three times longer by rubbing them with bread crumbs; and an irreproachable linen shirt, by means of which I came out of seclusion once a month. I went to see old family friends, and I was always welcomed with open arms, although they knew quite well that I didn't make a point of being a Legitimist. The clue to this mystery, and forgive me, dear reader, for not having thought to tell you this earlier, is that I was born a gentleman and of very good stock.

Legitimate and only son of the Count de Mont—, ruined before my birth by the revolutions, I was raised by my respectable father, the fairest, most upright, and wisest man I have ever known. He himself taught me everything that one learns in grade school; and at the age of seventeen, I was able to go to Paris with him and pursue a diploma for a bachelor's degree. Then we returned together to our modest home in the provinces, and there he said to me: "You see that I am beset with a serious illness; it is possible it will bear me away sooner than we think, or at the least that it will weaken my memory, will, and judgment. I want to use the little lucidity remaining to me to discuss seriously your future, and to help you crystallize your ideas.

"Whatever those of our class may say who cannot be consoled for the loss of the reign of piety and chivalry, the century is progressing and France is heading toward democratic ideas, which I find more and more just and providential, the more I approach the end when I will return naked to Him who sent me naked to earth. I raised you with a religious conviction in the equal rights of all men, and I consider this conviction to be the historic and necessary complement to the principle of Christian charity. It would be good if you practiced this equality while you work, according to your own lights and abilities, to win and maintain your niche in society. It is not my wish at all that this niche be glittery. For your sake, I want it to be independent and honorable. The slim inheritance that I will leave you will only suffice to give you a professional education, after which you will support yourself and your family, if you have one, and if this education has borne fruit. I know that the titled members of our circle will find a great deal of fault with me at first, for giving my son a profession instead of placing him under the government's protection. But perhaps the day is not far off when they will deeply regret having limited those of their own blood to profit only from the favors of the court. As an émigré I learned what a sad thing a gentleman's education is, and I wanted to teach you other arts besides horsemanship and hunting. I found in you a warmhearted tractability which I thank you for in the name of the love I bear you, and one day you will thank me even more for having put it to the test."

I spent two years by his side, busy completing the foundation for my studies, and developing the ideas he had given to me in embryo. He had me investigate several branches of knowledge, in order to see where I had the greatest aptitude. I don't know if it was the sorrow of seeing him continually suffer without being able to alleviate his pain that influenced me, but a decided calling certainly pushed me toward the study of medicine.

Once my father was persuaded of this, he wanted to send me to Paris; but he was in such a deplorable state of health that I obtained his consent to let me stay a few months longer in order to care for him. We were heading, alas, toward an eternal separation! His illness grew continually worse; the months and the seasons followed one after another without bringing him any relief, but also without diminishing his courage. With each crisis in his illness he wanted to send me away again, saying I had more important things to do than care for a moribund man, but he gave in to my tenderness and allowed me finally to close his eyes. A moment before expiring, he made me renew the solemn promise I had made to him many times to begin my studies right away. I kept my word religiously, and, despite the sadness that weighed on me, I pushed forward the preparations for my departure. He himself had put my affairs in order by leasing his property for nine years so that I could have a secure income during my years of work in Paris. And that is how I got along for four years, living on my three thousand francs of income, and seeing the time when I would take my examinations approach without having neglected to obey the last wishes of the best of fathers, and without having broken my former ties to those of our acquaintances for whom he felt respect and affection.

Among these was the Countess de Chailly, who, in her youth, despite the difference in their wealth, had felt for my father, so they say, very tender sentiments. A loyal friendship survived this love, and my father, when he was dying, had said to me, "Never forsake her; she is the best woman I have ever met in my life."

Indeed, she was as good as she was intelligent. Although very rich, she was not at all vain, and although very well born, she had no aristocratic prejudices. She owned several chateaux, one of which bordered my father's small estate, and it was in that one that she preferred to spend the summers. Moreover, she had a little townhouse on the Rue de Varennes, and since she enjoyed artful conversation, she brought together there fairly pleasant company. Ceremony and conceit were banished; one saw there worldly people, all belonging to the former aristocracy or of the Legitimist persuasion, and at the same time a few men of letters and artists of all shades of opinion. One could profess there the newest ideas; but the happy medium and the upstart middle class found no favor with Madame de Chailly; like all Carlists, she could more easily put up with republican opinions and proud but discreet poverty.

That year she had been detained in Paris on important business, and although it was late in the season, she was not yet inclined to leave. Her circle had greatly narrowed, and the artistic and literary element, who hardly went to the country except in autumn (if they went at all), was more in evidence than the noble element in her salon. She graciously accorded me the favor of introducing one of my friends, and one evening I brought Horace there.

He had quite ingenuously asked me for instructions on how to present himself in society, and how to behave suitably once there. This was not the first time he had had the chance to see people from this class; but he was not unaware that they were more indulgent in the country than in Paris, and he was anxious not to appear like a bumpkin in Madame de Chailly's salon. He made an entertainment out of what he called "this game"; he promised himself to observe, investigate, and collect facts for his next novel; and in the meantime he was very nervous about the idea of slipping on a heavily waxed parquet floor, of stepping on the foot of a lapdog, of crashing into a piece of furniture: in a word, of making himself a ridiculous character in a classical comedy.

When he had put on his best suit, his smartest waistcoat, his straw-yellow gloves, and when he had brushed his hat, Eugénie, who was pinning all her hopes for Marthe's welfare on this "debut among the countesses," enjoyed adjusting his tie with more distinction than he could; she made him tuck in two inches of cuff, instructed him not to wear his hat cocked over one ear, and managed, in a word, to make him look almost *comme il faut*. He submitted himself to these corrections with excellent grace, marveling at the delicacy of tact that allowed this woman of the people to fathom a thousand little points of taste which he would never have thought of on his own, and was astonished by the indifference, perhaps affected, with which Marthe witnessed the preparations. At heart, Marthe was very worried about his fantasy of going out into society, and although she had not at all acknowledged to herself that she loved Horace, her heart was gripped by a secret terror. There was a moment when Horace, rehearsing his entrance and bursting with laughter, approached her in a comic manner, giving her the role of the Countess de Chailly. At that moment, Marthe, struck by the respectful greeting he addressed to her, started to tremble; and turning to me she said:

"Is that really the way you greet great ladies?"

"Not bad," I answered, "but it's still a bit too free: Madame de Chailly is an elderly woman. Start from the top, Horace. And then, look, when you make your exit, Madame de Chailly will certainly invite you to come back; she will address a few cordial words to you, and it's possible she will hold out her hand, since she is in the habit of being extremely maternal to my friends. Then you must take her hand with the tips of your fingers, and bring it up to your lips."

"Like this?" said Horace, trying to kiss Marthe's hand.

Marthe quickly withdrew her hand. Her face showed acute pain.

"Like this, then?" said Horace, taking Louison's coarse, red hand, and kissing his own thumb.

"Would you stop your nonsense?" cried Louison, scandalized. "They're right to say that the highest society is the most indecent. You see that? That old countess getting young men to kiss her hand! Look, you! Don't try that again; I ain't no countess, and I'll land you such a box on your ear . . ."

"Gently, my dove," answered Horace, pirouetting. "We're not eager for that. What do you say, Théophile, shall we go? I feel completely at ease, and you'll see how I can act the part of a marquis. I'm going to enjoy this!"

He made his entry better than I had expected. He crossed the paths of a dozen people on his way to greet the mistress of the house, without any blunders, and with an air that was neither too free and easy nor too humble. His face made an impression on everyone, and the Viscountess de Chailly, daughter-in-law of my old Countess, miraculously displayed toward him none of the haughty distrust that she generally showed for new arrivals.

They had just had coffee; they were moving to the garden, and were breaking into two groups: one was walking with the mother-in-law, active and lively, the other was around her daughter-in-law, romantic and nonchalant.

It was a little garden in the old style, with shaped trees, puny statues, and a thin stream of water that was turned on at the Viscountess's command. She claimed that she loved "that sound of fresh water burbling under the foliage at nightfall, because then, no longer seeing that wretched fountain and that greenish water, I can picture myself in the country by water flowing freely through the meadows."

Speaking in this manner, she stretched out on a settee that was rolled out for her from the salon onto the slightly yellowed grass, smooth as a gaming table. An exotic bush leaned over her head, pretending to be a palm tree. Her court, composed of the youngest and most stylish in society at that time, sat around her; and they exchanged, with a somewhat forced beatitude, a swarm of pretty remarks signifying nothing at all. This group was not the one I would have chosen, if the need to watch over Horace in his debut performance had not forced me to listen to the *affected* manner of the Viscountess, much inferior, from my point of view, to the *affectionate* manner of her mother-in-law. I feared that Horace would soon grow weary of it; but to my great surprise, he took great pleasure in it, although the role he was playing was fairly delicate and hard to fill.

In fact, it was more than a small test of his aplomb and good sense. It was obvious that, from the first glance, the Viscountess had taken an interest in sounding him out, to find out if "his warbling was as pretty as his wings." Instead of keeping him at a distance until he had proved his wit in the thick of battle, she made it easy for him, with a sly complacency, to have a chance to show from the start if he were a man of sense or a fool. She immediately steered the conversation to subjects on which he would unquestionably express his opinion, and attacked him on literature, throwing out to the first to arrive this insidious question: "Have you read Monsieur de Lamartine's latest piece of verse?"

"Is it to *me,* Madame, that this remark is addressed?" asked a young monarchist and religious poet who had sat down almost at her feet with a contemplative look.

"As you wish," replied the Viscountess, using the breeze from her fan to flutter her long wisps of chestnut hair, rolled into buoyant spirals.

The young poet declared that he found the latest *Meditations* very weak. Since he had lost all hope of imitating Monsieur de Lamartine, he bitterly disparaged him.

The Viscountess made him feel that she knew something of his motive, and Horace, encouraged by a distracted look she let fall on him, braved a few syllables. Of the three or four other people who were lying in wait for him, at least three were, at heart, the Viscountess's adorers, and because of this felt fairly negatively disposed to the new arrival, whose becoming mane and emphatic speech announced some pretension to superiority. Generally they took sides against him, even with some malice, hoping that he would lose his temper and say something foolish.

The expectation was only half fulfilled. He flared up, talked much too loudly, and was more obstinate and acrimonious than good taste and polite society would dictate; but he didn't at all say the foolish things they were expecting.

He said other things which they were not expecting, but which gave an exalted impression of his mind to the Viscountess and even to his adversaries; because in certain superficial and bored company, one is forgiven more easily for a paradox than a platitude, and, if one demonstrates one's originality, one is certain to find approval from more than just a blasé woman.

Shall I say all I think about this matter? For the sake of the truth I must. Even if I should be accused of betraying my own, or at least of distancing my aims from the class I was born to, I am obliged to declare here that, with few exceptions, Legitimist society was still, in 1831, an incredible intellectual mediocrity. The old French art of conversation, so bragged about, has been lost in today's salons. It has fallen several notches; and if one wishes to find something that still resembles it, one must look in the wings of certain theaters or in certain painting studios. There you will hear a discourse that, though more trivial, is as quick, as playful, and much more colorful than that of the former high society. Only that could give a foreigner some idea of the verve and the sarcasm our nation has had a monopoly on for so long. If one speaks merely of the wit that is abundantly consumed in student or artist garrets, I could safely say that one hears enough of it in one hour, among young people enlivened by cigar smoke, to entertain all the salons of the Faubourg Saint-Germain for a month. One must have heard it to believe it. I, who, without bias or preconceptions, often went back and forth from one circle to the other, was confounded by the difference, and I was often struck by seeing a certain witticism make the rounds of a salon like a precious jewel passed from hand to hand, which had already been beaten to death at our house until no one wanted to scrape it up any more. I'm not speaking of the bourgeoisie as a whole: that class has certainly proven that it has the wit to govern, more, in fact, than the nobility. As for wit itself, only the second generation of the bourgeoisie has it. The newly rich of that era shoved their soul into the shadow of industry, in the heavy atmosphere of factories, a soul preoccupied with the love of gain, and completely paralyzed by egotistical ambition. But their children (raised in public schools with the children of shopkeepers, who, for want of money, desire to succeed as well, but on the pathways of the intellect) are in general incomparably more cultivated, livelier, and more refined than the washed-out heirs of the aristocracy. These unfortunate young people, dazed by tutors whose intellectual freedom has been shackled, because of religious and political prescriptions, are rarely bright, and never educated. The absence of a court, the loss of positions and employment, the resentment caused by the triumph of a new aristocracy, succeed in eclipsing them; and their role, which nevertheless seems to be improving insofar as they understand and accept it, was, at the time of my story, the saddest in France.

I've said nothing about the people, and the French common people, particularly in the major cities, are considered to have infinite wit. I question the epithet. Wit only exists when one is purified by a taste that the people cannot have, this taste itself being the result of certain vices of civilization which are not those of the people. So the people have no wit, from my point of view. They have more than that: they have poetry, they have genius. With them, form is nothing. They don't waste their minds hunting for it; they take it as it comes to them. But their thoughts are full of grandeur and power, because they rest on the principle of eternal justice, disregarded by societies and preserved in their hearts. When this principle sees the light of day, no matter how it is expressed, it startles and strikes like the lightning of divine truth.

Horace talked a good deal. Carried away as he always was by the heat of discussion, he defended his Romantic authors, whom the others challenged both as a group and one by one. He defended all of them, and was given lively support by the Viscountess de Chailly, who prided herself on eclecticism in the arts and letters. True, his adversaries were quite weak, and I couldn't imagine why Horace would waste his time and words standing up to them.

The old Countess, who passed by several times with her friends on a nearby path, motioned me over to her.

"Your friend is very loud," she said. "Why is he storming against fate? Is my daughter-in-law making fun of him? Look after him. You know she is cruel, and she takes advantage of her wit with those who have none."

"Don't worry, Mother," I answered (since my childhood I had addressed her this way), "he has quite enough wit to defend himself, enough even to make himself popular."

"Oh, indeed! Have you brought me a dangerous man? He is certainly pleasant to look at, and he seems very romantic. Fortunately, Léonie is not the romantic type. But call him over here for a moment, so I can also enjoy his wit."

I tore Horace away (much to his displeasure) from the congregation he had already captivated, and I stayed behind the arbor awhile to hear what they said about him.

"He's a funny one, that little man," said the Viscountess, playing with her fan again.

"He's a fop!" replied the Legitimist poet.

"A fop! You're being harsh," said the old Marquis de Vernes. "I think *presumptuous* would be a more fitting word. But he is a young man with much merit who could become a witty man if he sees the world."

"If it's wit you want, he has it," said the Viscountess.

"Rather! He has it to spare," said the Marquis, "but he is wanting in tact and decorum."

"He amused me," she continued. "Why did Mother get ahold of him? You have no opinion, Monsieur de Melleraie?" she said to a young dandy over whom she seemed to hold sway.

"By God, Madame!" answered the latter with a cool tartness, "you express your own opinion so well that I can only bow my head and say amen."

The Viscountess Léonie de Chailly had never been beautiful, but she absolutely wanted to be, and by resorting to artifices she could pass for a pretty woman. At least she had all the mannerisms of one, all the poise, all the charm, and all the privileges. She had beautiful green eyes with a changeable expression, which, though they could not exactly charm, could trouble and intimidate. She was frighteningly thin, and her teeth were problematical; but she had superb hair, always arranged with remarkable care and taste. Her hands were long and dry, but white as alabaster, freighted with rings from every country in the world. She had a certain grace which deceived many people. In short, she had what could be called artificial beauty.

The Viscountess de Chailly had never had wit; but she absolutely wanted to have it, and she made others believe she did. She repeated the latest commonplace with perfect refinement, and the most absurd paradox with stupefying self-possession. And then she had an infallible method for eliciting admiration and homages: she was a shameless sycophant with all those she wished to be attached to, and was caustic without pity to all those whom she wished to sacrifice to them. Cold and mocking, she pretended to be enthusiastic and sympathetic artfully enough to captivate those wits who were subject to a bit of vanity. She liked to think of herself as knowledgeable, erudite, and eccentric. She had read a little of everything, even politics and philosophy; and it was curious indeed to hear her recite to the ignorant, as if it came from her, what she had learned that morning in a book or heard the night before from some serious man. In short, she had what could be called artificial intellect.

The Viscountess de Chailly was the offspring of a family of financiers who had bought their titles under the Regency; but she wanted to pass for well bred, and wore her crowns and coats of arms even on the handle of her fans. She was unbearably haughty with young women, and never forgave her friends for marrying for money. The Viscountess, however, received young people in the arts and letters fairly graciously. With them she assumed the role of the well-off patrician, pretending in their company that she cared only for merit. In short, her nobility was artificial, like all the rest of her: her teeth, her bosom, her heart.

Women like that are more numerous in society than one would suppose, and if you have seen one, you have seen them all. For Horace, the pleasure of this novelty was combined with an ingenuousness so complete that he took the Viscountess seriously from the first word that she spoke, and she turned his head.

"My dear boy, she's adorable!" he said to me coming home that evening on the long, deserted streets of the Faubourg Saint-Germain. "She has wit, grace, and a *je ne sais quoi* that has no name I know, but that penetrates me like a perfume. What a precious jewel a woman is who is so well wrought, so studiously fashioned for pleasing! You call that coquettishness? Fine! I'm for coquettishness! It's very beautiful and likable, in any case. It's a science, I'm telling you, and a science that serves all the others. I really don't know why people speak ill of coquettes: a woman who is busy doing something other than pleasing is no longer a woman in my eyes. This is certainly the first real woman I've ever met."

"Yet there are men who don't like the Viscountess, and if you ask me . . ."

"That's because she wants those men to dislike her; she finds them unworthy of even the slightest attention. She's discerning."

"Thank you very much for the lesson," I said. He didn't even hear me; his head was full of the Viscountess. He didn't scruple to talk about her in front of Marthe the next day, and said such harsh things against common and austere women that she was offended and took her work into another room.

"It's working like a miracle," Eugénie whispered to me. "The experiment succeeded even better than I'd hoped. He caught fire like straw; I hope Marthe is cured."

Arsène came over, and found Marthe more affectionate and cheerful than usual, although she was suffering horribly. He announced that since it was no longer necessary for him to be at Poisson's café, he was changing his employment.

"Aha!" Horace said to him, "you're taking up painting again?"

"Perhaps later," answered Masaccio, "but not now. My sisters have not yet secured enough work for the year. Could you possibly find me a position somewhere as a clerk, doing some sort of bookkeeping, in the office of a theater, for a bus company, anything of that sort? You people know people!"

"My dear friend," said Horace, "you don't write well enough or fast enough. And besides, do you know how to keep books?"

"I'll learn," said Arsène.

"He believes that," said Horace. "If I were to give you any advice, it would be to persevere in the area you just tried; you acquitted yourself quite well. The only drawback is a little fatigue. Serve in a good household instead of in a café; you'll earn a lot, and you'll hardly ever have to work. If Théophile wants, he could find you a position in the house of a great lord, or at least in the home of some fine lady of the Faubourg Saint-Germain. Wouldn't the Countess hire him as a servant, if you recommended him? What do you say, Théophile!"

"That's quite enough about servants," answered Arsène, who well understood that Horace intended to lower him in Marthe's eyes. "I'll go back to it if I can't find better. But since it's a way of life that is looked down upon . . ."

"Who dares look down at you?" exclaimed Louison, hot under the collar, tracing the direction of Paul's involuntary gaze. "Are you the one, Marton, who's lookin' down at my brother?"

"Back to your sewing!" said Masaccio to Louison severely, to make her lower the hostile glance she directed at Marthe.

"Well," she resumed, "I find it funny that someone would look down at you: I don't know who gave them the right, and I don't see how Mademoiselle Marton . . ."

Marthe looked sadly at Arsène, and gave him her hand to appease him. He was ready to explode at his sister.

"She's crazy," said Arsène, shrugging, and he sat down next to Marthe, turning his back on Louison, whose eyes filled with tears.

"And it's shameful, too!" she yelled as soon as he had left. "You see, Monsieur Théophile, I can't put up with that and keep calm. Mademoiselle Marthe and Monsieur Horace, who get along very well, I'm sure, only try to bring *disrepute* on my brother."

"You *are* crazy," answered Eugénie, "and your brother, who called you that, had his reasons. Marthe has never said a word about Paul that didn't honor and praise him."

"I ain't crazy," exclaimed Louison, sobbing, "and I don't want you all to judge me. I didn't want to say it in front of him, for fear of startin' a quarrel; but since he's gone, and the guilty are present," she pointed in turn at Marthe, who listened to her in pity and pain, and Horace, his back stretched out on the dresser, his legs on the back of a chair, not deigning to interrupt her: "I'll tell you what I heard, not two days ago, when Monsieur and Madame were havin' their little tête-à-tête, as they so often do, thank God she's in one room and we're in the other! It's easy that way to get along while we work! Comin' and goin', gaddin' about; and as that man says, lovers have time to spare."

"Charming, charming!" said Horace, raising himself up on one elbow and gazing at her with a calm full of contempt. "Well, proceed, daughter of Herodias! Later I'll see my head on a platter for your dinner. What did I say? Go ahead, speak, since you eavesdrop behind doors."

"Yes, I eavesdrop behind doors when I hear my brother's name! And you said so offhandedly that it was too bad that he became a servant, and that he was lost. And Mademoiselle Marton, instead of treatin' you as you deserved for sayin' that, said, a little shocked, 'What? What do you mean, lost?' 'Yes,' you said, 'He changed his work in vain, now he will always have something of the lackey about him, a brand of shame that he can't erase. In fact, you might even say he's marked for life as a galley slave.'"

"If you had listened awhile longer," said Marthe with angelic sweetness, "you would have heard my response: I said that if that were true, Arsène would ennoble the most vile position."

"And you call that pretty, sayin' that? Ain't that admittin' that my brother is in a vile position? I'd like to know what your ancestors were made of—weren't all of us brought up to work for a livin'?"

I cut this quarrel short; it could have lasted all night; there is no one harder to convince than a person who doesn't understand the value of words, and who changes the meaning of them in his imagination. I sent the two sisters off to bed, finding fault with them, as I often did, and threatening, for the first time, to complain to Paul about the bitter vexation they caused their companion.

"Fine, fine, do that!" answered Louison, sobbing bitterly. "That would be kind of you! It wouldn't be difficult, since he's so smitten with that Marton that, when we've worked enough to feed her, he will show us the door the first time she says anything against us. Go ahead, go ahead, ladies and gentlemen. And you, Marton! It ain't pretty to set brothers and sisters fightin' one another; you will repent for it on Judgment Day! I call down God's own judgment!"

She left with a tragic air about her, dragging Suzanne along, cursing us and slamming the doors with a crash.

"Those companions of yours are some abominable she-devils," said Horace, calmly relighting his cigar. "Paul Arsène did you, my poor friends, a strange service. He let hell loose in your apartment."

"It hardly worries us personally," answered Eugénie. "The storm will blow over. But it really is cruel to you, Marthe; and if you listened to me, there would be a remedy for all the persecutions to which you are victim."

"I know what you're trying to say, my good Eugénie," said Marthe, sighing, "but rest assured that it's impossible. Besides, I'd be even more hateful to Arsène's sisters if . . ."

"If what?" demanded Horace, noticing that she hadn't finished her sentence.

"If she married him," said Eugénie. "That's what she imagines. But she's wrong."

"If you married him?" exclaimed Horace, suddenly forgetting the Viscountess and returning to the feelings Marthe had formerly evoked in him. "You, marry Arsène? Who could have thought up such an idea?"

"It's a very reasonable idea," Eugénie resumed, who wanted more and more to nip in the bud their nascent attraction. "They come from the same town, from the same circumstances, and are close in age. They've loved each other since they were children, they still love each other. Only a tiny scruple prevents Marthe from saying yes. But I know, and I will clearly state it, since the moment has come to speak. It's Arsène's only desire, his only thought."

The effect of this declaration surpassed Eugénie's expectations. Marthe, who became in Horace's eyes the fiancée of Paul Arsène, fell so low in his estimation that he blushed for having ever loved her. Humiliated, wounded, believing she had toyed with him, he took his hat, and, as he placed it on his head before leaving:

"If you're talking about your affairs," he said, "three's a crowd, and I'm going to see Odry, who's performing tonight in *The Bear and the Pasha*."

Marthe was stunned. Eugénie kept on talking to her about Arsène; Marthe didn't answer, tried to stand up to leave, and fell into a faint in the middle of the room.

"My poor friend," I said to Eugénie while helping her pick up her companion, "nothing can turn back destiny! You thought you could spare her. It's already too late: Horace is loved!"

CHAPTER

13

This fainting spell ended in long sobs. When Marthe had calmed down, she wanted to pick up the previous topic of conversation, and showed more initiative than she had previously manifested in two months of our living together. She spoke of leaving us, and of going to live alone in a garret, where our friendly relationship would no longer be troubled by Louison's intolerant and intolerable moods.

"You will continue to employ me in your work," she said. "I'll come every day to bring back work you consign to me. That way, your tranquillity will no longer be disturbed by my presence. I feel that I overestimated my strength in believing I could stand these harsh quarrels and cowardly accusations. I see they would kill me."

We also felt strongly that she could not long withstand such domination; but we didn't want to abandon her to the anxieties and dangers of being alone. We resolved to explain our position to Arsène so that he would set up house for his sisters somewhere else. We would continue to work together, and Marthe, whom we loved like a sister, would remain our neighbor and keep sharing our bread.

But this arrangement didn't satisfy her. She had second thoughts that we could certainly guess: she no longer could bear Horace's presence, and wanted to flee from him at any cost. It was certainly the quickest way to cut short this dangerous attachment; but how to make Arsène understand her reason, which would ring the death knell for all his hopes? At least at this point, Eugénie still flattered herself that she could fix everything by buying time. Marthe would be cured; Horace's disdain would help her along the more smitten he became with the Viscountess de Chailly; and little by little Arsène would make his pleas heard. Those were the dreams she still nourished. The most pressing matter was to banish Louison and Suzanne, whose company was beginning to weigh heavily on us, a single moment of anger and folly on their part destroying the effect of days of patience and discretion.

It was Louison who put an end to our perplexity through a sudden and unforeseen change.

The next day, at first dawn, she went and whispered by her sister's bed, so low that Marthe, who was hardly sleeping, and who thought they were weaving some foul scheme against her, could hear nothing of what they were confiding. But she suddenly saw Louison approach her bed, go down on her knees, and say to her with joined hands, "Marthe, we've offended you; forgive us. The fault is all mine. I'm a hothead, Marton; but at heart, I pity you, and I want to correct my mistake. Come, Suzon, come my sister, help me to rid Marthe of the pain I caused her."

Suzanne approached, but with a repugnance that Marthe attributed to a pronounced antipathy for her. Marthe was good and she was generous; Louison's humility touched her so deeply that she threw her arms around her neck and forgave her with all her heart. Marthe no longer had the courage to distress Louison by following through on her plans of the previous night, not knowing what pretext to give for her removal, which she felt so keen a need for because of Horace.

We were all very moved by Louison's repentance, and we spent the day pouring out our hearts, which seemed to assuage some of Marthe's sadness.

That evening, Eugénie, to avoid receiving Horace, who had announced that he would be coming to visit, suggested we go out for a stroll. Marthe quickly accepted, and we were already on the stairs when Louison said she didn't feel well and suggested we leave her at home.

"I'll go to bed early," she said, "and by tomorrow I'll feel better; it's my usual migraine."

So she remained behind, but, instead of going to bed, she slipped out onto the balcony. This was not unplanned. Horace, whom the concierge had assured we were all out, raised his eyes and saw a woman on the balcony. Since he was a bit myopic, he imagined it must be Marthe. The idea occurred to him to use cruel banter to get even for what he called some "trickery" on her part, since he believed that, by agreement with Arsène, she had accepted Horace's attentions and halfway welcomed his declaration simply to toy with him or conduct two liaisons at the same time.

Quickly he climbed the stairs, and, out of breath, rang the bell, his heart filled with a bitter and piercing pleasure. But when instead of Marthe, "Herodias's daughter" came to open the door for him, he recoiled three paces, and didn't balk at swearing.

That was not enough to startle Louison, though; and, broaching the subject right away, she made as sweet and polite excuses to him as she was capable of, for the manner in which she had acted toward him the night before.

Horace, utterly astonished by this conversion, promised to forget it completely; and finding that a bit of boldness would give him, in his own eyes, a Don Juan manner by which he could perfect his role with Marthe, he placed a big kiss of familial protectiveness on the village girl's plump vermilion cheek. Despite her usual prudishness, she was not too upset, and spoke to him as follows:

"If I was in a bad mood yesterday evening, Monsieur Horace, it was because I'd made a mistake. I'd imagined, seein' my brother so taken with Mademoiselle Marthe, that she had agreed to welcome his attentions at the same time as yours, and that the two of you were in cahoots to deceive my poor Arsène."

"I thank you for the assumption," answered Horace. "Permit me to show my gratitude by kissing that other cheek that reproaches its neighbor."

"This is the last one, though," said Louison, allowing herself to be kissed a second time, not without blushing a great deal. "That's enough reconciliation now. So then I said to myself, it was very nasty of Marthe to let herself be courted by two suitors; upon my honor I didn't know that my brother hadn't even said a single flirtin' word to her."

"Ah!" said Horace in a different tone of voice, "that's curious!"

And then he began to listen with interest.

"Well, by my stars, maybe you already know," Louison continued, "it seems (in fact it's certain) that Marton doesn't want to hear talk of marriage. And then, you see, Monsieur (I can tell you this just between the two of us), Marton is proud, too proud for a girl who ain't got two sous to her name. But that one fancies herself a princess; *she* reads books, and *she* would like to have a perfect love with a young man who's well dressed and educated. She finds my poor brother too common, and besides, her mind is set on someone else, and you know very well who that is."

"The devil take me if I know who it is," said Horace, amazed at Louison's big, cunning eyes.

"Go on!" she said, crudely nudging him with her elbow. "You're not that dense; you know she's crazy about you."

"You don't know what you're saying, Louison."

"Look, look! Then why has she been gettin' herself up so grand recently? And who is it then she's thinkin' of when she spends half the night sighin' and moanin' instead of sleepin'? And why did she swoon last night when you left all in a huff?"

"She fell into a faint? What! What are you saying, Louison?"

"Stiff on the floor; and tears, and sobs! And look at her now, wantin' to leave here so she can avoid seein' you, since she thinks you don't hold her in such high regard anymore."

"Who told you all this, Louison?"

"Oh, my word, Monsieur, I got eyes and ears! Use yours, and you'll see for yourself."

"But haven't your brother and Marthe loved each other since they were children? They were supposed to be married!"

"Don't bet on it; that's Eugénie's idea. She wants to get them hitched now, and God knows Marthe doesn't fancy the idea at all. But Eugénie doesn't understand at all; *you* just have to say a word to her, and she'll speak clearly and openly to my brother."

"And why hasn't she done that earlier? Then she's deceiving *him!*"

"It ain't like that, Monsieur. She's goodhearted and she's afraid of hurtin' him. Besides—like I told you—my brother never asked anythin' of her. It's Eugénie who's done all that, like the crazy woman she is. Fine favor she's doin' Paul to make him marry a woman who's thinkin' about another! It can't be."

When we returned home (and our walk was short, because, being just about to take my examinations, I devoted at most an hour a day to my pleasures), we found Horace quite changed from the way he had seemed the previous day. He came forward to meet us, and pressed Marthe's hand with a strange ardor. Desire, if not love, had entered his soul. Up until then, his uncertainty about succeeding had vexed his pride and dragged down his pursuit. Now, convinced of his triumph, he was enjoying it in advance with a sort of beatitude. His face had an emotional and thoughtful expression that made him singularly handsome. He was pale; his moist and slow look penetrated poor Marthe like a poison arrow. She hadn't expected to see him that evening: she thought herself out of danger for the day. She felt herself getting dizzy as she surrendered her trembling hand to him, which he kept in his own until Eugénie brought the lamp.

He sat down facing her, never taking his eyes off her, and while I wrote in a neighboring room, the door ajar, and the women worked around the table, he made conversation with as much taste and elegance as if he had been in the Viscountess de Chailly's salon. I didn't have the leisure to listen to him; I only heard his voice rise into a most sonorous and exquisite diapason. Eugénie told me that evening that she had never seen him as amiable, as flirtatious in his wit and language, as close to naturalness and simplicity as he was for almost two hours.

Marthe didn't dare speak or breathe; Eugénie contributed nothing to the conversation, not wanting to let her adversary shine. Louison, all mildness, was the only one to play the role of the interlocutor. She kept asking questions; and, however foolish and senseless they were, Horace responded to them with the charm of ingenuous condescension, and found for her the most playful explanations, sometimes shiningly poetic, like those one gives to children one loves when one wants to aim at their level while still telling the truth.

Although Eugénie brought into play all her mental resources to interrupt him, confound him, even make him go away, she didn't succeed; Marthe was under his spell, and nothing could save her. Bent over her work, her chest breathless, her eyes clouded, she sometimes ventured a timid glance; and always meeting Horace's eyes, she averted her own with a confusion full of fear and delight.

It was, as I've said, the first time Marthe was sought after by an intellect. Her own, dormant and isolated, in a secret and continual exaltation, had renounced the sort of soulful love that no one had ever expressed to her. Poor Arsène had never dared, had never been able to speak of more than friendship. His looks had nothing seductive about them, his speech had no poetry, or at least no art. The other loves Marthe had inspired were impertinent flirtations which she had suppressed, or brutal passions which had terrified her. But ever since the day Horace had spoken to her of love, she had kept it in her head and heart like the memory of intoxicating music. She thought about it by day, she dreamed of it by night. Chaste and contemplative, she aspired to no greater happiness than to hear the same things spoken again the same way. The thought of being forever deprived of them was already a regret so deep that it seemed her happiness had lasted years. That evening, she would have given her life to spend an instant with him, and to relive the quarter of an hour she had experienced the day of her first intoxication. Horace well understood her silence.

"Marthe is lost," Eugénie said to me when everyone had gone to bed. "She can't understand Arsène any more; his love is too plain for ears full of that other one's pretty words. You should take Horace to the Viscountess's house tomorrow."

"You can see that it takes him less than a day to forget her," I answered, "because today he's certainly smitten with Marthe. But why always despair of him? The day he truly loves, he will be transformed."

"Speak softer," Eugénie continued. "I think they can hear us on the other side of this wall."

"It's Louison's bed that's right there, and she snores so loudly . . ."

"I have a feeling," she responded, "about that girl—she's not as simple-minded as she appears, and she guesses what she doesn't understand."

Despite Eugénie's diligent surveillance, glances, words, and even notes were exchanged between Marthe and Horace. I suggested to my friend that we return to the Countess's house, but he refused. I advised Eugénie to stop trying to thwart this passion, which seemed true, and which obstacles only made more ardent. From then on, Louison was sweetness and goodness itself. She displayed a charming friendship for

Marthe; and Marthe was increasingly willing to give herself over to it, the more Louison favored her love for Horace, and helped her turn it into a thousand fruitless little mysteries for Eugénie's penetrating eyes.

One day Eugénie, who was suffering a great deal, scolded Louison for sending Marthe on an errand in her stead.

"And why shouldn't she go out like anyone else?" said Louison, pretending to be extremely surprised.

"Marthe is so pretty that she will be stared at and followed in the street."

"Well!" said Louison with a bitterness that pierced despite herself, "you think she's the only pretty girl in the whole world? They look me over, too. But they don't follow me; they see very well that I wouldn't cotton to it . . . And they wouldn't follow Marthe, either," she added, correcting herself, "because they see very well that she doesn't encourage anyone."

Louison had taken care to tell Marthe the night before, in a voice that only Horace could overhear:

"Tomorrow at noon you'll go to the Rue du Bac, to Petit Saint-Thomas, to fetch that little jaconet remnant we were asked to match."

There was something so deliberate about this manner of arranging an opportunity for Horace to meet Marthe outside that the latter was horrified. Thinking about it, she believed she had detected only a certain thoughtlessness on the part of her companion; and although with the beating of her heart she felt that Horace would indeed be waiting for her in the designated spot, she wanted to be persuaded that he hadn't paid any attention to Louise's words. The following day, as she drew near the store, she saw, in fact, that Horace was strolling on the sidewalk waiting for her. She passed right near him; he didn't stop her or greet her at all; but he gazed at her with such passion that this lapse in proper decorum was an eloquent testimony to the love that filled him. She smiled at him in a way that was simultaneously fearful, happy, and tender; and this look, this exchanged smile, lasted as long as a few halting steps could prolong it. It was a century of happiness for them both.

Although they hadn't exchanged a word, Marthe, doing her shopping in a hurry, was very sure of finding him again on the same sidewalk, by the same shop window. In fact she did find him there; and he waited for her with the intention of seeing her back home, to be able to talk with her without witnesses. But just at the moment when he came up to her and was about to slip Marthe's arm into his own, an open carriage stopped at the porte cochère facing the shop. A male servant decked with braid stepped down from the back of the carriage and went into the establishment to deliver some message, while the lady who had given it to him leaned over to look at Horace, blinking as if trying to place him. Horace tipped his hat: it was the Viscountess de Chailly. She acknowledged him in a cursory manner, with an expression of doubt and uncertainty; then she put on her pince-nez, as if to reassure herself that she actually knew him. Horace found it quite unnecessary to await the results of this slightly impertinent exploration, and he made ready to approach Marthe. But that cursèd pince-nez wouldn't leave him alone. The farther away he moved, the more the Viscountess leaned out her door, and the coach was turned in such a manner that she could follow him with her eyes as far as the bend in the road. Horace, only too aware of this, was in torment. Marthe was dressed simply, but with a sort of distinction that gave her the appearance of being a very proper woman. But alas! she was carrying a package wrapped in a scarf, and that was the unmistakable stamp of the grisette. This futile circumstance and the Viscountess's indiscreet curiosity held enough sway over Horace's vanity to prevent him from giving in to the commands of his heart. He hesitated, started to follow Marthe ten times, retraced his steps to throw the Viscountess off the scent; and when the carriage had left, he began running. Marthe, who believed he was on her heels, had thought it prudent to cut to the right, and went down the Rue de l'Université, to avoid the numerous pedestrians of the Rue du Bac. She counted on his rejoining her. But when she turned around, she saw no one behind her; and Horace, going up the Rue du Bac as fast as his legs could carry him and as far as the Seine, didn't encounter her ahead of him.

That's how he lost the chance to make his pleas of love heard. But Louison knew how to get it back for him.

Eugénie, who had barely recovered her own health, was obliged to spend several days at Saint-Germain caring for one of her sisters, who had fallen terribly ill. Our garret was left in Marthe's hands. Horace spent whole days there, and Louise and Suzanne took care not to disturb them. Left to her destiny, Marthe lent her ear to this love that was expressed so charmingly and powerfully. When I questioned Horace, he swore to me that he was seriously smitten with her, and that he was capable of any devotion to prove it to her. I insinuated to Marthe that she should use her influence to make him work, since I saw his debts swelling from day to day, and, if I hadn't provided for his daily existence, I don't know where he would have eaten dinner. This assistance I gave him out of the goodness of my heart put me in the delicate and ridiculous position of not daring to reproach him for his laziness. When I ventured a word on the subject, he replied in a despondent tone: "It's true, I've become dependent on you, and you should despise me." If I tried to take exception to this theme, hurtful to both of us, by invoking his own self-interest, his future, he shut my lips by saying:

"In the name of the present, I beg you not to speak to me of the future. I'm in love, I'm happy, I'm drunk, I feel alive. How and why would you have me think of other things than this fortunate moment where I exist superabundantly?"

Wasn't he right? "Up till now," I said to myself, "there's been something too personal about his ambition, which portrayed the future in the light of egotism. Now that he's in love, his soul will open to ideas that are more ample, truer, more generous. Devotion will reveal itself to him, and with devotion, the need and the courage to work."

14

When Eugénie came back and saw that all her efforts had been in vain, she thought it was time to let Arsène know the truth, or at any rate to sound him out about it. She asked for my advice on how to break the news, and after we had examined the question from all angles, she decided on the following approach.

No longer trusting the walls of our garret, which she said had ears, she wanted to surprise Horace in the middle of his thoughts by taking a grave step that only her good reputation and the dignity of her character gave her the right to risk.

"Look" she said to him, "you were able to make yourself loved; but you don't know the extent of the duties you've taken on with regard to Marthe. You've made her lose Arsène's protection, a courageous and persevering protection, which she would never have wanted for and which would always have been fruitful. She doesn't know how much she owes him, how much more she would have owed him if she hadn't been put in the position of having to renounce his help. But *I'll* tell you, because you should know everything. Arsène would never have given up painting, which he loved with a passion, if his secret plan hadn't been to shelter Marthe from need, by his own labor. He would never have considered sending for his sisters from the provinces, if his one goal hadn't been to give her a circle and protection that would always disguise his own role as her protector. Finally, at present he's found a very minor position in the offices of an industrial firm. Nothing in the world is further from his desires, his work habits, his quick and generous mind; I know that, and I fear he'll succumb because of it. But I also know that he wants to earn money, and that he earns enough there to subsidize all of Marthe's needs, while seeming only to take care of his sisters. I know our little bit of needlework doesn't bring in enough to support three women (if you deduct my share) in the comfort, cleanliness, and freedom which Marthe and Arsène's sisters enjoy. Everything I know, everything I'm telling you Marthe is not aware of yet. She has never kept house herself; she is as inexperienced as a child in that respect. Arsène is fooling her, and we are helping him do it, so that she should know neither want nor excessive labor. As a consequence, we also have to fool his sisters, on whose discretion we can't count. Up till now I've done the accounting; I've made them all believe that our receipts outweigh our expenses, while the contrary is actually the case. But this state of affairs can't last any longer. Arsène has always secretly hoped that Marthe would develop a serious affection for him once, recovered from her terrors and cured of her wounds, her soul opened to gentler impressions. I've shared his illusion, I confess, and I have done my all to save Marthe from any other attachment. I didn't succeed. Now, tell me what you would do in my place about Arsène's secret, and what advice you would give them both."

This beginning quite disconcerted Horace. "I'm not wealthy," he said. "How can I act as a woman's protector, when I have not been able to help and guide myself?"

He paced around his room agitatedly, and little by little his thoughts turned gray. "I hadn't counted on all this!" he exclaimed, with a sorrow that was not without a tinge of humor. "Nothing like this had ever occurred to me. Why is it absolutely necessary that between two beings who love one another there must be a protector and a protected? You, Eugénie, who are always clamoring for equality for your sex . . ."

"Oh, Monsieur," she answered, "I clamor for it and I practice it, even though it's very hard to win in present-day society. I know how to limit my needs to the little that my industry can procure for me. You know how I live with Théophile, and you know that consequently I never waste a day, not an hour. But do you know in what way I consider him my legitimate and natural protector? If I were to fall ill and be deprived of work for a long time, instead of going to the poorhouse, I'd find in his heart a refuge from loneliness and poverty. If a man were cowardly enough to insult me, I'd have support and someone to avenge me. And then, if I became a mother . . ." she added, lowering her eyes in a display of modest dignity, and raising them again to his with firmness to make him feel the possible consequences of his love affair with Marthe, "my children would never have to worry about lacking bread and education. There you have it, Monsieur, that's why it's important to women like us to find in their lovers lasting affection and a devotion equal to their own."

"Eugénie, Eugénie," said Horace, falling into a chair, "you're confusing me terribly. I'm not Marthe's lover to the extent that I've reflected on the serious consequences of this intoxication lighting my brain. Look, my dear Eugénie, I confess to you, I accuse myself: I can't fool you, nor would I want to. I desire Marthe with all the might of my being, and I love her with all the power of my heart; but can I promise to be for her what Théophile is to you? Can I commit myself to rescuing her from all dangers, from all future evils? Théophile is rich compared to me; he has a small fortune that's secure; he can work for the future. And I, who have nothing but debts, I would have to work for the future, the present, and the past all at the same time!"

"But Arsène has nothing," Eugénie pointed out, "and what's more, he's supporting his two sisters."

"So," exclaimed Horace, struck by the allusion and falling into a sort of fury, "I have to become a café waiter, do I? No, there isn't a woman in the world for whom I would choose to debase myself in a line of work that was unworthy of me. If Marthe thinks that . . ."

"Oh, Monsieur, don't blaspheme," said Eugénie. "Marthe doesn't think anything, since I've kept her in the dark about all of this; and the day she realizes that this sort of question has been raised in regard to her, I'm sure she will flee from us all out of fear of becoming a burden to any of us. I see quite clearly that you don't love her, since you don't understand her in the least, and you don't value her at all. Oh, poor Marthe! I knew she was fooling herself!"

Eugénie got up to go. Horace detained her.

"And now," he said, "you're going to keep working against me?"

"Just as I've done up till now; I've got nothing to hide."

"You're going to present me as a hateful being, an egotistical monster, because I'm so poor that I can't keep a woman and because I respect myself enough not to want to be a lackey? Oh, there's no question that if a man is measured by the weight of the gold he can earn, Paul Arsène is a hero and I'm a poor wretch!"

"Everything you say," Eugénie answered, "is insulting to Marthe and to me, and I will not deign to reply. Let me go, Monsieur. The truth hurts, but Marthe must learn it, and she must renounce both her friend Arsène, because of you, and you, because of herself. Luckily, she still has us! Théophile will be able to replace Arsène, and with more disinterested motives; I, too, will work for her and with her; and the idea will never cross our minds to call it *keeping* a woman!"

"Eugénie," said Horace, fervently seizing her hands, "don't judge me without understanding me. One day you will repent having disparaged me in Marthe's eyes and in my own. I don't have the sordid thoughts you attribute to me. Perhaps I'm speaking without propriety or discernment; but because of your touchiness you've been scared off by words alone, and because of mine I've gotten carried away by the hurtful comparison you're always making between Masaccio and me. It's not in my nature to emulate examples—models of supposed virtue horrify me. But without pretense, without oaths, it seems to me I can show devotion when it's called for, to the point of self-sacrifice. What can you know about me, when I know so little myself? I haven't been put to the test yet; but I've mulled this over and questioned myself in vain, and I find in myself neither the makings of cowardice nor the seeds of ingratitude. So why do you condemn me before the fact? You have cruel prejudices against me, Eugénie; and I can't breathe, take a step, or say a word without your interpreting it to my shame. Marthe can no longer stifle a sigh or shed a tear that's not ascribed to me. Finally, we can no longer exist, she and I, without the name Arsène hanging over our heads like a judgment. It already cramps and saddens all the enthusiasm in my heart; my future is losing its poetry, and my soul, its trust. You're cruel, Eugénie, to tell me all these things."

"And that's the extent of your courage?" said Eugénie. "You're afraid you would be humiliated if you told me that Arsène's example doesn't scare you, and that you feel yourself capable, like him, of great acts of self-denial for the object of your love?"

"What do you want me to do? What commitment must I make? Do I have to marry? But there's no common sense in that! I'm a minor, my parents would never give their consent . . ."

"You know that I believe in the Saint-Simonian religion in some respects," answered Eugénie, "and that I look on marriage as a voluntary and free commitment—a justice of the peace, witnesses, and a sacristan do not make it more sacred than love and integrity do. Marthe, I know, agrees with these ideas and I believe neither she nor I will ever speak to you of the legalities of marriage. But there is a truly spiritual marriage, which is contracted before heaven; and if that makes you recoil . . ."

"No, Eugénie, no, my noble friend," Horace shouted, "I reject nothing in that. My only complaint is the distrust you show toward me; and, if you make your friend share in it, we will turn—great God!—the most spontaneous and truest of passions into something arranged, stiff, and false, which will chill both of us."

While Eugénie was attentively probing Horace's heart, at the same time, at the same moment, more serious injury was being done to Arsène's. He had gone to see his sisters, or rather Marthe, with the former as pretext; and since Louison had just gone out, Suzanne, who was upset with the older sister's despotism, seized the opportunity to strike a decisive blow of her own. She took Arsène aside.

"Brother," she said to him, "I'm askin' for your protection, and I'll start by askin' that what I'm about to confide, you keep just to yourself."

When Arsène promised, she told him all about how Louison had conducted herself with Marthe.

"You believe," she said, "that she has made up with Marton in good faith, and that she ain't causin' her any more pain? Well, you should know that she's plannin' much worse for her, and that she hates her more than ever. Seein' that you love her, and that she couldn't pry you apart with words, she has decided to lower her in your eyes. She wanted to dishonor her, and I truly believe she's already succeeded."

"Lower her! Dishonor her!" cried Paul Arsène. "Is this my sister speaking? Is it my sister I'm hearing about?

"Listen, Paul," Suzanne continued, "this is what happened. Louison heard, through the partition of our room, what Monsieur Théophile and Eugénie were sayin' in theirs. That's how she learned that Eugénie wanted you to marry Marthe and that Marthe was beginning to love Monsieur Horace. Then she said to me, 'We're saved, and our brother will soon know that he's being toyed with. We just have to get him the proof; and when he discovers what a lost woman he's given us for a companion, he will kick her out and from then on he will only believe us.' 'But what proof will you give him of that?' I said to her; 'Marthe ain't a lost woman.' 'If she ain't, she will be soon, take my word for it,' said Louison. 'Just do what I do and obey me every step of the way, and you will see how that crazy girl plays right into my hand.' Then she pretended to ask Marthe's forgiveness, and she began to always agree with her in order to please her. And then she said who-knows-what to Monsieur Horace to encourage him to court Marton; and then she told Marton all day long how Monsieur Horace was a handsome young man, a fine fellow, that in her shoes she wouldn't make him pine so long. And then, finally, she arranged secret meetings for them, she gave them chances to meet outside, and, when Eugénie was sick, she left them alone in a room all day, on purpose, sent me into the other one, and two or three times Marthe came in as if to seek refuge, you could see she was afraid and moved, but Louison shut the door in her face, and pretended not to hear her knock. God only knows what happened as a result of all that! It's certainly awful for a girl like Louison, who delivers horrible sermons to me if my shawl ain't pinned just below the chin, and who wouldn't let a man touch even the tip of one of her fingers, to throw a poor girl into the devil's own trap and to show favor toward a young man whose intentions are hardly Christian. It made me very ashamed of her and harmed Marthe a great deal. I tried to make Marthe understand that no good was meant to her by these actions, and that Monsieur Horace was only a seducer. Marthe took it the wrong way: she thought I hated her. Louison threatened to beat the daylights out of me if I said another word to Marthe, and Eugénie, seein' how sad I was, criticized me for my ill humor. Finally, the moment has come when the blow they have been readyin' for you is about to fall. Don't be surprised when it does, my brother, and be lenient with poor Marthe, who ain't the most guilty party here."

Arsène managed to contain the awful feeling that this revelation produced in him. For a while he even doubted it. He wondered if Louison was a monster of treachery, or if Suzanne was guilty of the most sordid slander; in both cases he felt wounded and horror-stricken at having such a being in his family. He waited for Louison to come home so he could question her in a calm and confident manner about the relationship between Marthe and Horace. "I've been told they're in love," he said to her. "I see no wrong in it, and I have no right at all to take offense. But I would have thought that you, as my sisters, would have warned me earlier, since you thought I had such an interest in her."

Louison could clearly see that despite his resigned manner, Paul's lips were pale and his voice choked. She believed that a pent-up jealousy was the sole cause of his suffering, and she rejoiced in her triumph. "Really, Paul!" she said to him, "you shouldn't speak unless you're sure of the facts, and you took it so badly when we tried to warn you! But now I can speak to you frankly, if you need me to, and if you promise Marthe won't know."

Speaking in this manner, she pulled out of her pocket a letter that Horace had entrusted to her to deliver to Marthe. Arsène wouldn't have opened it if his life had depended on it. Besides, in his plain and rigid way of seeing things, a letter by itself was conclusive evidence. He put it in his pocket and said to Louison: "That's enough, thank you; I'd already made up my mind when I came here. I give you my word of honor that Marthe will never know the service you've just done me."

He went into my study, which I had just returned to myself, and a few moments later Eugénie came in. "Here," he said, delivering Horace's letter, "this is a letter for Marthe that I found on the ground in my sisters' room. It's Horace's handwriting; I recognize it."

"Paul, it's time we had a talk," said Eugénie.

"No, Mademoiselle, it's no use," said Paul. "There's nothing I want to know. I'm not loved, and the rest doesn't concern me. I've never intruded, I never will. I've only been indiscreet with you, in speaking to you often about myself and in imposing the company of my sisters on you, and that has not always been particularly pleasant. Louison is hard to live with; and since the chance has come up to move her elsewhere, I came to tell you that, starting tomorrow, you're free of her, and of Suzanne as well, but I thank you for the kindness you've shown them, and ask that you will maintain your friendship for me, which I will return and reclaim as soon as I can, as long as Monsieur Théophile sees no harm in it."

"Your sisters are not a burden to me," Eugénie answered. "Suzanne has always been very sweet, and Louison has been so for a while now. I gather that since your ideas about the future have changed, you want to break up the unit we formed under more auspicious circumstances; but why are you in such a hurry?"

"My sisters must leave right away," Arsène resumed. "They may not be as good as they seem, and I am perfectly capable of setting them up in a place of their own. Listen, Eugénie," he said, taking her aside, "I hope you keep Marthe with you as long as she has no objection, and that you see that all her desires are met, as long as no one else takes over the responsibility for that. Here is a part of the money I received this morning; allocate it as usual, and, as usual, keep my secret."

"No, Paul, that's not possible any more," said Eugénie. "It would be degrading poor Marthe to do her such favors given what you now know. It's time she learns to whom she owes the well-being she's enjoyed up till now, so she may thank you and renounce it forever."

"Eugénie," said Paul animatedly, "if you do that, I will no longer be able to set foot inside your door, and I could never see Marthe again. My presence would make her blush, she would be humiliated, perhaps she would even hate me. Leave me her trust and her friendship, since I may never lay claim to anything else. As for refusing on her part the last favors I wish to do for her, you don't have the right, nor do you have the right to betray the secret you swore to me you would keep."

When I discussed the matter with Eugénie, I supported Arsène's decision, and it was agreed that Marthe would know nothing. Soon she came home with Horace, whom she had been waiting for, I believe, on the staircase. Arsène bade her good day, and, calmly discoursing on general topics, he carefully observed both her and Horace, without either of them noticing; lovers have, in this regard, a truly miraculous ability to be distracted. After a quarter of an hour, Arsène withdrew once he had squeezed Marthe's hand and calmly acknowledged Horace. I understood Eugénie's look, and accompanied Arsène downstairs. I was afraid that stoic resolution hid some desperate plan, even more so since he was doing everything possible to keep me away from him. Finally, no longer able to struggle against both himself and me, Arsène leaned against the parapet and swooned. I forced him to go into a pharmacist's and take some drops of ether. I spoke to him for a long time; he seemed to listen, but I really don't think he heard me. I took him back to his apartment, and didn't leave him until I saw him get into bed. At the end of his street, beset with the tragic memory of so many nighttime suicides caused by the despair of love, I retraced my steps and went back to his house. I found him sitting up in bed, suffocating on torturous sobs that he could not get out. My testimony of friendship made a few tears fall from his eyes, assuaging him a bit. When he had slightly regained his composure, and seeing my concern:

"Rest assured, Monsieur," he said to me, "I give you my word of honor that I will be *a man*. Perhaps when I'm alone I'll be able to cry; that would be best. So leave me, and depend on me. I'll come see you tomorrow, I swear it."

When I arrived home, I found Marthe to be charmingly gay. Horace, at first bothered by his rival's presence, went overboard to be friendly, and the woman who loved him didn't need much coaxing to find his wit delightful. She had no idea that Paul was dying inside, and my false face did not give her the slightest clue. Oh, the egotism of love! I thought.

The very next day Arsène came to fetch his sisters, and almost without giving them time to say goodbye he silently led them to the new home he had hastily set up for them.

"Now," he said to them, "you're free to tell me if you want to stay here or if you would prefer to go back home to the country."

"Go back home?" exclaimed Louison, stupefied. "So you want to send us back, Paul? You want to abandon us?"

"Neither," he answered. "You're my sisters, and I know my duty. But I thought you hated the capital and that you wanted to leave."

Louison answered that she had grown accustomed to life in Paris, that she wouldn't be able to find work again in the country, since her departure had caused her to lose her clientele, and that she wanted to stay.

Since by listening through the partition Louison had discovered all the secrets of our household, she had become reconciled to remaining in Paris, thanks to the advantages she believed she could derive from her brother's incomparable devotion. Up until then she hadn't really known Arsène; she had counted on a sort of comfort, but not on his completely forfeiting his likes and dislikes, his freedom, his entire existence. Nor had she understood the activity, the courage, the capacity for breadwinning, if one could call it that, that developed in him when he was moved by a generous passion. Once she understood the extent to which she could take advantage of him, she looked on him as certain prey, and she took measures to monopolize him. The only passions that govern badly brought up women, when an innate greatness of soul does not counterbalance variable impressions, are vanity and avarice. The latter leads them to confusion, the former to the most narrow and merciless egotism. Louison, deprived early of a mother's care, sacrificed to her stepmother, and abandoned to bad examples or bad inspirations, had to be subject to one or the other of these disastrous passions. She reacted by leaning toward the one that her stepmother did not have, and virtuous in hating the vice before her eyes, gave herself up instinctively to the one passion that poverty and deprivation suggested to her. She became covetous; and no longer thinking of anything but how to satisfy her pressing need, she derived from it a skill and a knavery of which her limited intelligence didn't seem capable. That is how she lured Marthe into the trap, and from then on she flattered herself that she reigned exclusively over her brother's conscience.

"What he did for us because of that heathen," she whispered to Suzanne, "he will do that much more when he knows, thanks to us, how unworthy she was."

Suzanne was far from having a soul as black as her sister's; but accustomed to trembling in Louison's presence, she only felt remorse in retrospect or aborted her reactions. Arsène did not suspect the calculating baseness of Louise's plans. He attributed her frightful treachery toward Marthe to one of those female hatreds founded on prejudice, religious intolerance, and a dominating spirit suppressed to the point of vengeance. He certainly found a monstrous inconsistency between her officious conduct toward Horace and her furiously prudish homilies; he attributed these contradictions to her ignorance, to her poor understanding of devotion. It upset him deeply; but full of compassion and courage as he was, he resolved to entomb in a secret part of his soul the crime of this haughty and cruel sister. He promised himself that he would convert her little by little to truer and more noble sentiments, and not reproach her until the day when she would be capable of understanding her mistake and making amends for it. When Eugénie found out, despite Arsène's discretion, what had gone on between him and his sister, he said:

"What would you have me do! If I'd told you how much harm she had done to me, you would all have hated and scorned her; you would have said: She's a monster! And since the greatest misfortune is to lose the respect of honest people, I pitied my sister so much then that I felt hardly any anger."

He displayed a sweetness so full of sadness that Eugénie's affection for him doubled.

"If you want to stay in Paris and if that would be in your best interests," he said to his sisters, "I'm not opposed to it. I'll find you work, and I'll support you in the meantime. We are not well-to-do enough to have separate lodgings; I'll live with you. That's the agreement until further notice."

"What do you mean until further notice?" Louison demanded.

"That means, until such time as you can do without me," he answered, "since my life isn't insured, like a house against fire. So, little by little look into how you may become independent, either by making honest marriages or by acquiring with your intelligence or diligence a good clientele."

"You can be sure," said Louison, somewhat disconcerted and affecting pride, "that we won't remain your charges without doin' anything; just the opposite—we want to get off your hands as soon as possible."

"It's not a question of that," Arsène resumed, fearing that he had wounded her. "As long as I'm alive, everything that's mine is yours; but as I said, I'm not immortal, and you have to think . . ."

"What notions have gotten into his head today!" exclaimed Louison, turning to Suzanne with a look of fear. "Wouldn't you say he *wanted* to die? Oh, my brother, is your sorrow eatin' you up alive? Are you goin' to do harm to yourself for that . . ."

"I forbid you ever to utter Marthe's name in my presence!" said Arsène, with an expression that made his sisters blanch. "I forbid you ever to speak to me of her, even indirectly, whether it's to speak well or ill of her, do you understand? The first time that happens, you'll see me leave here and never return. You've been warned."

"Enough," said Louison, crushed, "we'll follow your instructions. But I ain't bringin' up the subject of her, Paul, when I urge you not to be so sad."

"That's no one's business," he said, just as vigorously, "and I don't want anyone asking me about it, either. I spoke of death just now, and

I must tell you that I'm not the type to kill myself. I'm not a coward; but it seems that war is coming, and if a revolution is proclaimed, I'm not saying I won't take part as I did last year. So, get used to the idea that one day you may have to make do for yourselves, as honest artisans must and can do. I'm going to my office now. Mend your old clothes while you wait, since in a few days you'll have work. But I forbid you to ask Eugénie for any work or to accept any from her."

"You see," said Louison to her sister once he had left, "it all turned out as I wanted. He also detests Eugénie now. He thinks she's the one who lost Marthe for him."

Suzanne lowered her head in embarrassment, then said, "His heart is heavy; all he thinks of is dyin'."

"Bah! It's because this is the first day," the other replied. "Soon you'll see, he won't think about it anymore. Arsène is proud; he won't want to cause himself pain for a girl who trifles with him; and you'll see, he'll be the first to speak to us about it, and he'll be happy when we speak ill of her."

"I don't care, I won't ever do it," said Suzanne.

"Oh, you, *the heartless one,* a fool who would have put up with anythin' from Marton without sayin' a word! You're too indulgent, Suzon. If you had principles, you would know that it ain't right to go too soft on women without morals. You'll see, I tell you the ain't far off when my brother will reproach you for your indifference on this score."

"I don't care, and I'll say it again," said Suzanne, "that I'll never risk sayin' a word against Marthe to him, even if it seems like he's encouragin' me to do it. I'm certain he'd never put up with it. Try it yourself, since you think you're so clever!"

The day was spent quarreling, as usual. Nevertheless, when Arsène came home, he found his room nicely straightened up, all his linen mended, his personal effects cleaned, folded, and the dinner vegetables cooked and properly served. Louison made him loudly praise all these fine services, and overwhelmed him with irksome attentions, which he suffered without impatience. She forced herself to cheer him up, but she could not coax a smile out of him; he had hardly gulped down a few mouthfuls when he left, without having answered any of the questions she had asked him. The next day he behaved the same, and the day after, and every day following. With his wits and zeal he was soon able to find them work, and he always put at their disposal, for their shared upkeep, two-thirds of the money he earned; but he put aside a portion of the other third, and they never knew where it went. In vain Louison searched even in his bed straw, even under the squares in the flooring of his room, to see if he had his own private nest egg, she found nothing; in vain she ventured ingenious questions, she received no response; in vain she tried to get him to spend this invisible money on furniture, on linens, on objects she said would be useful to their household, he turned a deaf ear, not letting them want for anything necessary to their well-being, but constantly refusing the smallest personal luxuries. This was a great worry to Louison, who thought nothing of disposing of the greater part of her brother's means, and she racked her brains to find a way to gain the rest. It seemed to her that Arsène was committing an injustice, almost a theft, in holding back a few écus for some mysterious purpose. She didn't sleep because of it; if she had dared, she would have shown the spite it made her feel, but with his impassive sweetness and his icy silence, Arsène dominated her in a way she hadn't imagined could be so austere. Yet she had to submit to it, renounce ever knowing the depths of that heart that was shut forever, or surprising a thought on that face that had turned itself to stone.

I give these particulars of her inner thoughts, even though at this point I hadn't yet penetrated them; but everything that pertains to the people whose story I tell here was unveiled to me little by little with such precision that I can follow them through events of their lives in which I played no part with the same fidelity I use to portray those where I personally was present.

The departure of the two sisters was a true relief to us; but the mystery and haste with which Arsène effected this separation remained inexplicable to us for a long time. At first we surmised that he never wanted to see Marthe again and that he had courageously used this move as his chance and pretext. Yet he came to see us just as he always had; and when Marthe asked him where his sisters were living, he evaded her questions, and ended up telling her that they had been placed with a master dressmaker in Versailles. I knew that was not true, since I had encountered them a few times in the neighborhood of the place of business where Arsène worked; their pretense of avoiding me gave me a presentiment of, and made me respect, Arsène's wishes. It was impossible for Eugénie to get a word out of this enigma; she couldn't even coax Arsène to provide her with a new explanation of his secret feelings and resolve with regard to Marthe. Afraid of his calm demeanor, and fearing that he kept a reserve of foolish hope, she frequently tried to disabuse him of such feelings; but he cut short all exchanges along these lines, hastily saying to her, "Oh, I know! I know! No point in discussing it."

What's more, not a word, not a glance, that might make Marthe suspect that she was the object of an ardent and deep passion. He played his part so well that she convinced herself she had never been anything but a friend in his eyes; and we ourselves began to believe that he had conquered his love and was cured.

Eugénie, who foresaw the confusion and sorrow Marthe would feel once she learned of the pecuniary services he had done, unbeknownst to her, forced him to take back all that he had most recently given. From that moment on she wished to be solely responsible for her friend, and that responsibility was slight indeed. Marthe was excessively sober, she dressed with simple modesty, and she assiduously helped Eugénie in her work. The one trace of Arsène's beneficence that we did not whisk away, for fear of afflicting that excellent young man, was a small set of furniture he had purchased for her, which consisted of a narrow, iron-frame bed, two chairs, a table, a walnut chest of drawers, and a little vanity he had chosen himself—alas! with so much love! We led Marthe to believe that those furnishings belonged to us and that we were lending them to her. She received our attentions with such candor and charm that we would have been glad to have her receive them all our lives; but it was not to be. An evil genie was hovering over Marthe's destiny: Horace.

After Eugénie's formal declaration, Horace expected a struggle with Arsène. He was quite humiliated to have such a rival; and yet, since he knew him to be very refined, very fearless, very respected by all of us, above all by Marthe, he was willing to accept the challenge. A few days earlier, he had been ready to throw in the towel rather than match his elegant and cultivated wit against the slightly coarse and rustic malice of

Masaccio; but just at that moment his love reached a feverish paroxysm, and he wouldn't have blushed at vying for the object of his desire with Monsieur Poisson himself.

Much to everyone's surprise, Paul Arsène appeared calm to the point of indifference, and Horace thought that Eugénie had very much exaggerated his love. But once he knew that Paul was no longer unaware of his own love, and once I had recounted to him how I had surprised this courageous young man in a state of anguished sadness, Horace began to worry about Paul's perseverance in continuing to appear in his presence, and about the sort of triumphant calm he seemed to assume when he faced him. Horace's jealousy caught fire; the strangest suspicions were roused in his mind, and he let them show their faces. At first Marthe understood none of this: her conscience was too pure to allow her to take offense at doubts that made no sense to her. Horace's somber spite disturbed without enlightening her. Eugénie had the delicacy not to interfere in what was going on between them, but she hoped that Marthe, realizing the insult done to her, would rise up proud and offended.

In his fits of jealousy, Horace begged me, out of spite, to escort him to Madame de Chailly's. He went back there two or three times, and pretended that he found the Viscountess more and more adorable. This wounded Marthe's heart all the more; but love in its infancy is like a serpent newly cut into sections, which finds in itself the power to pull itself back together and reconnect itself. The sorrows, the sleepless nights, the sharp and bitter quarrels are followed by heady and intoxicating reconciliations; vows never to see one another again are followed by vows never to part. It was a stormy happiness blended with tears; but it was an intense happiness, made more sharp by its opposite.

One day when Horace started to ridicule and denigrate Arsène in his absence, and Marthe heatedly defended him, he grabbed his hat, as he did when he had his outbursts, and left without saying a word. Marthe knew quite well that he would be back the next day, and that he would beg forgiveness for his misdeeds; but she was one of those tender and passionate souls who don't know how to wait proudly for the end of a distressing crisis. She stood up, threw her shawl over her shoulders, and dashed toward the door.

"What are you doing?" Eugénie asked her.

"See for yourself," Marthe answered, beside herself, "I'm running after him."

"But my friend, you're not thinking. Don't encourage that sort of injustice, or you'll regret it later."

"I know that perfectly well," said Marthe, "but it's stronger than I, and I have to put it to rest."

"He will come back on his own, at least let him get credit for that."

"He will come back tomorrow!"

"Well, yes, tomorrow, definitely."

"Tomorrow, Eugénie? You don't know what it means to wait till tomorrow! Spend the whole night in a fever, with a swollen heart, with an insomnia that counts the hours, the minutes, with that horrible thought impossible to drive away: he doesn't love me! and this even more horrible one: he's not good, not generous, I shouldn't love him! Oh, no, you wouldn't know about that."

"My God," exclaimed Eugénie, "you understand that you're wrong to love him, but when a glimmer of reason reaches you, you're impatient to shut it out."

"Let me shut it out quickly, then," said Marthe, "because that brightness is the most intolerable pain in the world." And, unleashing herself from Eugénie's grasp, she dashed to the stairs and disappeared like a lightning bolt.

Eugénie didn't dare follow her, for fear of attracting attention to Marthe and causing a scandal in the building. She hoped that these senseless lovers would run into each other at the foot of the stairs, and that after a few moments they would return together. But Horace, furious, was walking extremely fast. Marthe could see him ten paces ahead of her. She didn't dare call out to him along the quai; she didn't have the strength to run. With each step she felt herself about to faint; she saw him striking the parapet with his cane in a gesture of uncontrollable rage. She started to follow him again, no longer thinking of her personal pain, but of her lover's. He bowled over two or three passersby, caused half a dozen others to cry out and swear when he ran into them, proceeded down the Rue de la Harpe, and arrived at the Narbonne Apartments, where he lived, without even noticing that Marthe was following in his footsteps and had almost caught up with him at least ten times. At the moment when he collected his key and his candlestick from the concierge, he saw her scowling face looking over his shoulder:

"Just where do you think you're going, Miss?" said the concierge in a wrathful voice to the person who prepared to go up the stairs without saying a word to her.

Horace turned around and saw Marthe, with no gloves or hat, pale as death. He seized her in his arms, half lifted her, and, pulling her shawl over her head like a veil to screen her from hostile glances, he drew her onto the stairs and swiftly escorted her to his room. There, he threw himself at her feet. It explained everything. The very subject of their quarrel was forgotten in that first instant. "Oh, I'm so happy!" he exclaimed, delirious with love. "Here you are, you're with me, we're alone! For the first time in my life, I'm alone with you, Marthe! Do you understand my happiness?"

"Let me go," said Marthe, frightened. "Perhaps Eugénie followed me here, perhaps Arsène. My God! am I dreaming? Somewhere, following you, I saw Arsène's face, I don't know where. No, I'm not sure about that . . . Maybe! . . . It doesn't matter, you love me, you still love me! Let's go, take me home."

"Oh, not yet! Not yet!" said Horace. "Just a second longer! If Eugénie comes, I won't answer; if Arsène comes, I'll kill him. Stay right there, stay another second!"

Meanwhile, Eugénie, alone, worried, terrified, counted the minutes, paced back and forth from the landing to the window, and saw no sign of Marthe returning. Finally she heard someone coming up the stairs. Her at last . . . No, it was a man's footstep.

She rejoiced at the thought that it was I, and that she could send me to look for Marthe. She ran to meet me, but instead it was Arsène.

"So where is Marthe?" he said in a lusterless voice.

"She went out for a minute," said Eugénie, disconcerted. "She'll be back any minute."

"Went out alone at night?" said Arsène. "You let her go out like that?"

"She's coming home with Théophile," said Eugénie, distraught.

"No, no! She's not coming home with Théophile," said Arsène, letting himself fall into a chair. "Don't take the trouble to deceive me, Eugénie. She won't even come back with Horace. She'll come back alone; she'll come back despondent."

"So you saw her?"

"Yes, I saw her running along the quai in the direction of the Rue de la Harpe."

"And Horace wasn't with her?"

"I only saw her."

"And you didn't follow her?"

"No, but I will wait for her," he said.

And he got up precipitously.

"But why didn't you run after her?" said Eugénie. "Why did you come here?"

"Ah! I don't know any more," said Arsène, bewildered. "I had some idea, though! . . . Yes, yes, that's it; I wanted to ask you, Eugénie, if this was the first time she had gone out alone at night, or alone with him? . . . Tell me, is it the first time?"

"Yes, it's the first time," said Eugénie. "Marthe is still pure, I will testify to it. God, why didn't you run after her?"

"Oh! maybe there's still time to kill the wretch!" cried Arsène furiously. And springing up like a wildcat he dashed outside.

Eugénie understood the disastrous results that such an exploit could bring about. Terrified, she began to run after Arsène. Fortunately, I was coming up the stairs, and I stopped the two of them.

"Where do you think you're going?" I said to them. "Why do you both look so distraught?"

"Stop him, follow him," Eugénie said to me with some urgency, seeing Arsène already getting away. "Marthe's gone with Horace, and Paul is going to do something disastrous. Get going!"

I started running after Masaccio, and I caught up with him. I grabbed hold of his arm, but I couldn't detain him, even though I was much taller and more muscular than he. Fury had increased his strength tenfold, and he pulled me along as if I were a child.

I learned from his broken exclamations what had happened, and I saw how imprudent Eugénie had been. A lie was the only means left to prevent a tragedy.

"How can you believe," I said to him, "that this is the first time they have gone together? It's at least the tenth."

This assertion fell on him like water on a fire. He stopped short, and looked at me gloomily.

"Are you quite sure of what you're saying?" he asked me in a heartrending voice.

"I'm certain. She's been his mistress for more than a month now."

"So Eugénie fooled me?"

"No; they're fooling Eugénie."

"His mistress! So he doesn't want to marry her, the villain!"

"What do you know about it?" I said to him, thinking only of calming him and getting him to turn back. "Horace is a man of honor, and what Marthe wants, he also wants."

"You're sure he's a man of honor? Swear that to me, on your own."

Using evasive assurances and indirect answers I succeeded in bringing him back to his senses. He thanked me for the service I had done him, and he left me, swearing to me that he would go home right away.

As soon as I saw him head in that direction, I ran to the Narbonne Apartments and obtained information about Horace. "He's upstairs, shut in with a young woman or lady," answered the concierge "—well, with whom you please. But I'm going to make her come downstairs; I won't hear of there being any scandal here."

I pleaded with her to speak more softly, and I enlisted her cooperation with Figaro's "irresistible arguments." She explained to me that the lady was pretty, that she had long black hair and a scarlet shawl. I doubled my persuasive efforts, and I obtained a promise from her that she would not bruit the news about and that she would let the fugitive leave, no matter what time of night it was, without saying a word to her and without letting anyone know what she had seen.

When my mind was at ease about this, I went home to reassure Eugénie. I couldn't keep myself from laughing a little at her consternation. Once Arsène had come to his senses and was out of trouble, the somewhat brusque but inevitable conclusion of Horace and Marthe's love seemed less surprising and less dismal than my generous friend wanted to see it. She scolded me severely for what she called my levity.

"You see," she said to me, "since she's been in love with him, she looks to me as if she'd been condemned to death, and now I'd no sooner laugh about it than I would if I saw her walking up the gallows."

We waited up part of the night. Marthe didn't come back. Sleep ended up winning out over our concern.

At the first light of dawn the door of the Narbonne Apartments opened and closed even more gently, letting through a woman who covered her head with a red shawl. She was alone, and took a few quick steps to put some distance between herself and the building. But soon she stopped, weak and broken, at the edge of a milestone, and leaned against it so as not to fall. That woman was Marthe.

A man took her into his arms: that man was Arsène. "What, alone! Alone!" he said to her. "He didn't even walk you back!"

"I forbade him," said Marthe, her voice dying away. "I was afraid someone would run into us together, and then I didn't want him to see me again by daylight! I didn't want to see him ever again! But what are you doing here at this hour, Paul?"

"I couldn't sleep," he answered, "and I came to wait for you so I could take you back; something told me you would be coming out of his house alone and despondent."

Marthe was so confused and distracted that she didn't want to go back home.

"Take me to your sisters," she said to Arsène. "At least they won't know where I spent the night."

"You have no more loyal and devoted friend than Eugénie," replied Arsène. "Don't make your position worse by staying away any longer. Come, I'll walk with you to her apartment, and I'll make sure she doesn't rebuke you."

He led her back to the door of her room. She wanted to shut herself in and cry as long as she needed to before seeing us again; but just when she was about to leave Arsène, to whom she had poured out her heart as if to a brother, she suddenly remembered that his love for her was less calm than that. She had forgotten this, since she was so used to counting on his blind devotion to her.

"Well, Arsène," she said to him with deep feeling in her voice, "do you regret now not marrying me?"

"I'll regret it my whole life," he replied.

"Don't speak to me that way, Arsène," said she. "You're tearing me to shreds. Oh! if only I could love you the way you want and deserve! But God hates me and curses me."

When she was alone, she threw herself on her bed fully clothed and cried bitterly. Eugénie, who could hear her sobs through the partition, knocked in vain at her door; she didn't answer. Worried, and fearing that Marthe might have fallen prey to the nervous convulsions to which she was prone, Eugénie took several keys and, trying each in the lock, found one that worked. She rushed over to Marthe, who lay with her face sunk into the bolster, her hands clenched in her beautiful black tresses, and her face streaming with tears.

"Marthe," Eugénie said, pressing her to her bosom, "why are you in such despair? Are you regretting the past, or afraid of the future? You made your own choice and acted freely; no one has the right to humiliate you. Why are you hiding instead of coming to me, when I've waited so anxiously for you and I'm so happy to see you?"

"Dear Eugénie, I'm more than regretful, I'm ashamed and sorry," answered Marthe, kissing her. "I didn't act of my own free will and with the calm of my own volition. I gave in to raptures that I didn't share, since I was frozen by the memory of recent injuries and by the fear of new insults. Eugénie! Eugénie! He doesn't love me; I feel my unhappiness so deeply! He has passion without love, enthusiasm without respect, effusiveness without trust. He's jealous because he doesn't believe in me at all, because he judges me unworthy of inspiring a serious love, and incapable of sharing one."

"That's because he's unworthy and incapable himself!" cried Eugénie.

"No, don't say that; it all comes from me, from my miserable fate. He, who has never loved before, whose heart is as virginal as his lips, he deserved to meet a woman as pure as he."

"And that's why," said Eugénie, shrugging, "he fell for the Viscountess de Chailly, who has three lovers at the same time!"

"At least *that* woman," responded Marthe, "has intelligence, a brilliant education, and all the seductiveness of high birth, fine manners, and luxury. Look at me: I'm a narrow-minded, ignorant nobody of a woman. I can barely read; I only know how to understand. But I can express nothing, I have no ideas of my own, at no time could I dominate the heart and mind of a man like Horace! Oh! how clearly he spelled that out for me, how clearly he told me that last night in the heat of our quarrel, and now I see that I was crazy to complain about him. I have only myself to blame, only my own past to curse."

"What! Have you already gotten to that stage?" said Eugénie, dismayed. "Has he already gone that far toward acting your master and superior? I would have thought that, at least during the first headiness, he would have forgotten himself a little, so he would see and admire only you; but instead of throwing himself at your feet and thanking you for the solemn proof of love and trust that we give when we open our arms and soul unreservedly, he's already elevated himself to the role of the merciful ruler, to honor you with his indulgence and forgiveness! Really, Marthe, you have reason to be ashamed, because you have indeed been humiliated . . ."

"Don't say that, Eugénie. If you had only seen the turmoil he was in, his suffering, his tears, and how he said such cruel things to me humbly and tenderly! No, he didn't realize he was hurting me, he didn't think about it. He was suffering so much himself! He had only one thought: ridding himself of the suspicions that were torturing him; and when he accused me, it was to get me to reassure him with my answers. But I didn't have the strength to do it. I was so afraid when I saw that noble pride, that pure youth, that great intelligence, which demanded so much of me, and which had the *right* to demand so much; and I could think of so few things to answer to all that! I was overwhelmed, and right away he took my sadness for remorse over some fault or for the return of some nasty feeling. 'What's the matter?' he said to me; 'you're not happy in my arms! You're gloomy, distracted; are you thinking of someone else?' Then he imagined I had secret contacts with Paul Arsène, and he begged me to drive Paul away from here and never see him again. I would have consented, yes, I would have been that weak, if he'd persisted in asking me tenderly. But as soon as I showed the slightest hesitation, he revealed a spite and bitterness that gave me the strength to resist him, since I, too, became spiteful and bitter. And we said very hard things to each other, which weigh on me like a mountain."

"You were right to say he doesn't love you," Eugénie said, "but you're mistaken when you say it has to do with you and your past. The evil only comes from his pride; it's rooted in an egotism that you encourage with your weakness. The man whose heart is made for love doesn't question whether the object of his love is worthy of him. From the moment he loves, he no longer examines the past; he enjoys the present and believes in the future. If his mind tells him there's something in that past to be forgiven, he forgives it in a secret place in his heart, without ringing church bells as if his generosity were a miracle. This forgetting of faults is so simple, so natural, for someone who loves! Did Arsène ever blame you, did he? Has he not always defended you against yourself, as he would against the whole world?"

"I even suspect Arsène," said Marthe, sighing. "I think that in love we're humble and generous when we're rejected, but happiness makes us demanding and cruel. That's what's happening to me with Horace. In the hours of the night we spent together, we continually alternated between sweetness and pride. When he revolted me, he threw himself at my feet to calm me; but as soon as he'd led me to humble myself before him, he crushed me again. Oh! I think love makes us wicked!"

"Yes, the love of wicked people," answered Eugénie, sadly shaking her head.

Eugénie was being unfair; she didn't see the truth any more clearly than Marthe. Both were mistaken, each in her own way. Horace was neither as worthy of respect nor as wicked as they imagined. With his triumph he quickly became insolent; he had that in common with so many others that if one were to rigorously condemn this failing, one would have to scorn and curse the majority of our sex. But his heart was neither cold nor depraved. He certainly loved Marthe very much; it was just that, lacking a moral education with regard to love, as all men do, and since he was not among that small group whose natural sense of devotion makes them an exception, he loved with only an eye to his own happiness, and, if I can state it this way, out of love for himself.

He came by that day, and, instead of being embarrassed in front of us, he had an air of triumph, which I myself found to be in fairly bad taste. He was waiting for me to make jokes, and he was prepared to answer them by taking a strong stand. Instead, I permitted myself the luxury of rebuking him.

"It seems to me," I said to him as I led him into my study, "that you could have had more discreet meetings with Marthe that wouldn't have compromised her. This night spent away without preparation or pretext could give rise to a good deal of gossip in the building."

Horace took this observation very badly.

"I greatly admire," he said, "your taking such umbrage on her account, since you live openly with Eugénie!"

"That's the reason that Eugénie is respected by everyone around me," I replied. "She's my sister, my companion, my mistress, my wife, if you will. From whatever angle you look at our union, it's absolute and permanent. I've taken considerable pains to make sure that she is accepted by all those who love me, and to surround Eugénie with enough devoted friends that intolerant cries won't reach her ears. But I did not lift the veil hiding our secret love until reflection and experience had made me sure of the strength of our mutual affection. After the first night of intoxication I did not introduce Eugénie to my friends by saying, 'Here's my mistress, respect her because of me.' I hid my happiness until I could say to them with confidence and loyalty, 'Here's my mate, she's respectable for her own sake.'"

"Well, I feel stronger than you," said Horace haughtily. "I'll say to the whole world, 'Here's my lover, I want her to be respected. I will demand that any recalcitrants bow down, if it pleases me, before the woman I've chosen.'"

"You wouldn't succeed that way, had you the invincible arm of the ancient avenging knights. In the times we live in, men are not afraid of one another; and your lover, as you call her, will be respected only as much as you yourself respect her."

"How strange you are, Théophile! In what way, then, have I offended the one I love? She came to me and threw herself into my arms, and I kept her there one or two hours longer than was proper according to your code of decency. I was certainly not aware that a woman's virtue and reputation could be regulated like the powers of bailiffs, according to the rising and setting of the sun."

"Your comical remarks are inappropriate," I said to him, "for a day as solemn as this should be in the chronicle of your love. If Marthe were to take her part as lightly as you do, I'd have little respect for her. But she looks on this quite differently, as far as I can tell, because she hasn't stopped crying since this morning. I'm not asking you to explain the cause of her tears; but I'd hope that you'll ask her what it is with a less gleeful expression and a less free-and-easy manner."

"Listen, Théophile," said Horace, becoming serious again, "I'll speak to you honestly, since you force me to do so. The friendship I feel for you prevented me from offering an explanation that your severity toward me now renders necessary. Know, then, that I am not a child anymore, and if I've allowed myself to be treated like one, it's not a right you've acquired irrevocably and that I can't take back from you when it seems fitting to me. I am declaring to you today that I am tired, extremely tired, of the kind of war you and Eugénie are waging, in the name of Monsieur Paul Arsène, against my love for Marthe. I'm not acting as lightly as you think in putting aside all pretenses and discretion in this matter. It's best that you all know, you and your friends, that Marthe is my mistress and not another's. It is important, to my dignity and my honor, that I'm not treated here as superfluous; but for you, for them, for Marthe, for everyone, and for myself as her actual lover, her only lover, that is, as my mistress's master. And since for some time now, thanks to the odd role that you've had me play, thanks to the obstinate claims of Monsieur Paul Arsène, thanks to the thinly disguised support accorded him by Eugénie (thanks to your neutrality, Théophile), thanks to the equivocal friendship that governs the relationship between Marthe and me, thanks finally to my own suspicions, which make me suffer most cruelly, I haven't known where I stand in all this, nor how I stand here—I've finally resolved to know whom I can count on, and to define my position clearly. It's for that reason that I come here this morning with my head held high, to tell all of you, without equivocation or ambiguity: 'Marthe spent the night in my arms, and if anyone thinks that's wrong, I am prepared to know what his rights are, and to yield him my own, if mine are not better grounded.'"

"Horace," I said to him, looking him straight in the eye, "if those are your thoughts this morning, very well, I accept; but if that's what you were thinking last night while holding Marthe close to you and compromising her, that's a very cold calculation for a man as ardent as you appear to be, and I see in it more politics than passion."

"Passion doesn't preclude a certain diplomacy," he replied, smiling. "You know very well, Théophile, that I began my life with politics. If I become a man of feelings, I still hope some portion of the man of ideas will remain. But rest assured, and don't be shocked by this. I swear to you that last night I was hardly diplomatic, that I was not thinking of anything, that I gave in to the intoxication of the moment. But this morning, in summing things up for myself, I recognized that instead of a foolish repentance I should have the contentment and energy of someone happy in love."

"Then have it," I said to him, "but be sure that your face and your countenance don't express something other than what you're feeling; because at this moment you have, despite yourself, the look of a fop."

I was quite irritated by something vain and arrogant in him that day, which, for all the affection I had for him, I wanted to wipe off his face. I feared that Marthe would be wounded by it; but the poor woman no longer had the power to react in such a way. She was intimidated, downhearted, and as if seized by a convulsive shiver at his approach. He reassured her as sweetly and tenderly as he knew how; but between them there was an extreme sense of unease. Horace wanted to be alone with her; and Marthe, restrained by a feeling of shame, didn't dare leave us again to grant him a private interview. For a few seconds he hoped she would have the courage for it, and he created various pretexts that she pretended not to understand. Eugénie feared that it would seem forced if she left the two of them alone. And in the midst of all this Paul Arsène arrived on the scene.

Despite his efforts at self-control, and although he had been quite prepared to encounter Horace, he couldn't completely disguise the horror that Horace's presence evoked in him. Horace saw the sudden alteration in his face, already pale and sunken by the anguish of the preceding night; and seized by a burst of irrepressible arrogance, he proudly raised his head and offered his hand to him in the manner of a sovereign to a vassal who is paying him homage. Arsène, with his generous candor, didn't understand this gesture, and, attributing it to a completely opposite emotion, he energetically grabbed and squeezed his rival's hand, with a look of sadness and openness that seemed to say: "You're promising me that you'll make her happy, and for that I thank you."

This mute explanation sufficed for him. After inquiring after Marthe's health, and also squeezing her hand effusively, he exchanged a few words of small talk with us and withdrew after five minutes.

Horace was not really jealous of Arsène to the extent that he was concerned about Marthe's feelings for him, but he feared that in the past there had been a more intimate bond between them than she cared to admit. He thought that for a man to be so devoted to a woman who was giving him up, he must retain either some hope or a well-founded gratitude; and both of these suppositions offended Horace equally. Ever since Eugénie had revealed to him the full extent of Arsène's devotion, he had taken even greater umbrage at it. As he had naively admitted, he was hurt by a comparison that was not favorable to him, according to Eugénie's way of thinking, and that would become deadly to him, according to Marthe's way of thinking, if it were always staring her in the face. And then, our circle saw only dimly what was happening between them. Those who didn't like Horace preferred to doubt his triumph, or at least they pretended in his presence to believe in Arsène's. Those who liked Horace blamed Marthe for not declaring herself openly in his favor and dismissing his rival, and they spelled this out for Horace. Finally, other young people who, being mere acquaintances, did not visit our home and judged us with a levity that was a bit brutal, permitted themselves the sort of cruel remarks that are dropped so lightly and spread so quickly. Giving in to that unthinking jealousy which one feels for every man happy and in love, they disparaged Marthe in order to disparage Horace's happiness in their eyes. Many of these, who had courted the beauty of Poisson's café, avenged themselves for not having had their advances favored by saying it was not such a difficult or glorious conquest, since she favored a braggart like Horace. Some of them even said that she had taken as a lover her first café waiter. Finally, I don't know which of these wits was so low, and what tongue so coarse, as to circulate the opinion that she was simultaneously Arsène's mistress, Horace's, and my own.

These calumnies did not reach my ears at that time; but someone was imprudent enough to repeat them to Horace. And he was weak enough that they had an effect on him, and soon he could think of nothing else but dazzling and crushing these detractors by providing unimpeachable proof of his triumph over all his rivals, real or imagined. He tormented Marthe so cruelly that he made the calm and pure life she led with us into a crime and a torture. He wanted her to appear alone with him attending the theater and walking in the street. This temerity grieved Eugénie, and seemed to her only useless bluster against gossip. Everything she did to prevent her friend from taking part in it pushed Horace's impatience and bitterness to the limit.

"How long," he said to Marthe, "will you remain under the thumb of that annoying and hypocritical chaperone, who finds exactly the same behavior scandalous in others that she considers legitimate for her? How can you put up with the pedantic admonishments of that prude, whose point of view is not disinterested, I'm sure of that, and who considers as a preferable lover the man who can give his mistress the most comfort and ease? If you loved me, you would immediately reduce her to silence, and you wouldn't stand to hear her endlessly criticize me in front of you. Can I be content when I see this indiscreet third party meddling in all the secrets of our love? Can I be calm when I know that your one friend is my sworn enemy, and that in my absence she embitters you and puts you on guard against me?"

He demanded that she repudiate Paul Arsène completely, and included in this expulsion that he imposed on her was a very specific condition. He greatly feared the ridicule that follows those who are jealous, and the idea that Masaccio could crow about having caused him anxiety was unbearable to him. He wanted Marthe to act as if with personal resolve and not to appear to be under any outside influence. He encountered a great deal of opposition from her to this unjust and cowardly demand; but he gradually induced her to give in by mercilessly pestering her in a thousand ways. She no longer had the right to press her friend's hand, she could no longer smile at him. Anything between them became a crime: a glance, a word, and she was bitterly reproached for it. If Arsène, obeying a habit he had acquired as a child, used the "tu" form while chatting with her, it was flagrant proof of a former liaison between them. If, when we all went out for a walk together, she let him take her arm, Horace used this as a ridiculous pretext to leave us in a pout, saying under his breath to Marthe that he didn't care to be Paul's rival and that it was quite enough to follow in the footsteps of Monsieur Poisson without also sharing with his lackey. When Marthe rebelled against this iniquitous persecution, he sulked for weeks at a time; and that unlucky woman, unable to bear his absence, sought him out and begged his forgiveness for the wrongs of which *she* was the victim. But if she then offered to have a frank talk with Masaccio before dismissing him:

"That's right," exclaimed Horace, "make him take me for a madman, or a tyrant, or a fool, so Monsieur Paul Arsène can go around making fun of me and slandering me everywhere! If you act that way, I'll have to pick an argument with him and strike him, one fine morning, right in the middle of a café."

Exhausted by this hateful struggle, one day Marthe took Arsène's hand, and bringing it to her lips:

"My best friend," she said to him, "you will do me this one last service, the most painful of all for you, and especially for me. You will say to me your eternal goodbye. Don't ask me the reason; I cannot and do not wish to say it."

"No point, I've guessed it for a long time," answered Arsène. "Since you said nothing to me, I thought that it was my duty to remain as long as you seemed to need my protection. But since, rather than being useful, my presence does you harm, I'm withdrawing. But don't say that it's forever, and promise me that if you ever need me, you will call on me. Just say the word, or make a gesture, and I'll be at your disposal. Look, Marthe, if you like, I'll spend every day under your window: all you have to do is hang a handkerchief from it, a ribbon, any sign, and that same day you will see me come running. Promise me that."

Marthe promised in tears; Arsène came no more. But that was not enough to satisfy Horace's pride. One day when, as was his wont, he had led Marthe away to his apartment, we waited in vain for her to come back for dinner, and that evening we received from her the following note:

"Don't wait for me, my dear and worthy friends. I will no longer enter your home. I discovered that I didn't owe my well-being there only to your generosity, but that Paul had contributed to it for a long time, and that he was still contributing to it, since all the furniture, which you supposedly loaned to me, belongs to him. You understand that, knowing that, I can no longer avail myself of it. Besides, the world is so evil that it slanders even the most virtuous of affections. I can't repeat to you the vile remarks of which I have been the subject. I prefer, in putting a stop to them and in tearing myself sadly away from you, to speak only of my eternal gratitude for your goodness to me, and of the unalterable attachment that will always be felt for you by

Your friend, MARTHE."

"More of Horace's cowardice," cried Eugénie, indignantly. "He revealed a secret to her that I'd confided to him on his honor."

"These things slip out despite oneself in bursts of anger," I answered her. "It happened because they were quarreling."

"Marthe is lost," Eugénie continued, "lost forever! since now she belongs utterly and irreversibly to an evil man."

"Not to an evil man, Eugénie, but to something even more dire for her: to a weak man ruled by his vanity."

I, too, was incensed, and I cooled off on Horace completely. I had foreseen all the ills that would befall Marthe, and in vain I had tried to deflect them. Every measure we had taken had proved fruitless. Horace, anticipating that we wouldn't abandon his prey to him without a fight, had immediately changed residences. He had rented, in another neighborhood, a room where he lived with Marthe, so hidden away that it took us more than a month to find them. By the time we got there, it was too late to make them change their minds or their habits. Our remonstrances only made them annoyed with us. Horace held sway over his mistress so thoroughly that from then on she withdrew all her trust from us. Forgetting that for a long time she had recounted to us all her complaints against him, from then on she wanted to make us believe in her happiness, and reproached us for groundlessly assuming the fact of her suffering, although her face already bore its deep impression. Predicting that she would lack, that she already lacked, money and work, we still couldn't get her to accept the slightest help. She even rejected our offers with a haughtiness we had never seen in her before.

"I would be afraid," she said to us, "that a favor of Arsène would still be hidden behind yours; and, though I know how generous your conduct has been toward me, I confess that I find it difficult to forgive you for the all-too-justified suspicions of me which that state of affairs provoked in Horace."

Eugénie pushed the constancy of her devotion to her unfortunate companion to the point of heroism; but it was all in vain. Horace detested her and had turned Marthe against her. All her attentions were received with a coolness bordering on ingratitude. In the end we were hurt and fatigued by it; and, seeing that they were avoiding us, we decided not to become irksome. In the course of the winter that followed, we saw one another barely three times; and in the spring, one day when I ran into Horace, I clearly saw that he was pretending not to recognize me, in order to escape a moment's conversation. It seemed we had irrevocably fallen out with them, and I suffered a good deal because of it, Eugénie even more: she couldn't utter Marthe's name without her eyes filling with tears.

Horace had absorbed, from the novels in which he had studied women, ideas so vague and changeable on the species in general that he played with Marthe like a child or like a cat plays with an unknown object that attracts and scares it at the same time. After the shadowy and delirious female characters with which Romanticism filled youthful imaginations, the feminine element in the eighteenth century, "the Pompadour," as we were beginning to say, was in the first bloom of resurrection, and infused into our dreams sharper and more dangerous beauties. Around this time Jules Janin gave what I believe is an ingenious definition of *the pretty,* in style, in the arts, in fashion; he gave it at every turn, and always with grace and charm. The school of Hugo embellished *the ugly,* and used it as a vendetta against *the beautiful* in Classicism, with its pedantic proscriptions. The school of Janin, however, ennobled *the mannered* and gave back to it all its seductiveness, too long denied and insulted by the somewhat brutal contempt of our republican memories. Without our even realizing it, literature performs its miracles. It revives the poetry of former days; and, putting to rest in the past all that had been for intellectuals of the past the object of just criticisms, it brings to us, like a forgotten perfume, the unrecognized riches of a taste that is no longer open to discussion, since it no longer reigns arbitrarily. Art, although it poses as egotistical ("art for art's sake"), creates progressive philosophy without realizing it. It makes its peace with the mistakes and shortcomings of the past, to preserve, as in a museum, the monuments of its conquest.

Horace, who had one of the most impressionable imaginations of an already impressionable era, living more on fiction than reality, looked at his new mistress through the different character types that his reading had left in his head. But although these types were charming in poems and novels, they were not real and living in present-day reality. They were phantoms that belonged to the past, laughing or terrifying. Alfred de Musset used Shakespeare's phrase as an epigraph for his lovely sketches: *false as water,* and when de Musset, used to seeing in women of all epochs the dangerous Daughters of Eve, traced purer and more ideal forms, he drifted between a fresh and candid coloration and somber and variable shades, which demonstrated his own indecision. This youthful poet had a tremendous influence on Horace's brain. When the latter had just read *Portia* or *La Camargo,* he wanted poor Marthe to be one or the other. The next day, after he had consumed a feuilleton by Janin, she had to become for him an elegant and coquettish patrician. Then, following Alexandre Dumas's romantic chronicles, she was to play the tigress, and he the tiger; and after Balzac's *The Magic Skin,* her role was that of a mysterious beauty whose every glance and word concealed profound abysses.

In the midst of everyone else's fantasies, Horace forgot to examine the depths of his own heart and to look there, as in a limpid mirror, for the true image of his friend. At first, she was cruelly volleyed back and forth from the women of Shakespeare to those of Byron.

This artificial appreciation finally fell away when intimacy showed him that his companion was a real woman of our time and country, just as beautiful, perhaps, in her simplicity as the eternally true heroines of the great masters, but modified by the surroundings she lived in, with no notion of turning a modest student household of our day into a drama of the Middle Ages. Little by little Horace gave in to the charm of that sweet affection and that limitless devotion of which he was the object. He no longer steeled himself against imaginary dangers; he tasted the happiness of living as a couple, and Marthe became as necessary and as beneficial to him as she had seemed fatal before. But this happiness didn't open his heart or give him confidence: it didn't bring him back to us; it didn't inspire any generosity on his part toward Paul Arsène. Horace never did justice to Marthe the way she had deserved in the past and deserved in the present; and instead of acknowledging that he had misunderstood her, he attributed the triumph that he thought he had scored over Masaccio's memory to his own domineering jealousy. Marthe would have liked to have inspired in him a more noble trust: it pained her to always see the fires of anger and hatred ready to reignite at the slightest positive word she ventured about her disavowed friends. She blushed at the minute and constant precautions she was forced to take to maintain the calm of her enslavement, to dispel any shadow of suspicion. But since she never had whims of independence beyond the borders of her love, and since on the whole she saw that Horace was satisfied by her sacrifices and proud of her devotion, she, too, was happy, and she wouldn't have switched masters for anything in the world.

This state of affairs constituted an incomplete happiness, blameworthy in a sense, since neither of the two lovers benefited morally and intellectually, as they should have in a purer love. I believe we should define a noble passion as one that exalts and strengthens us in the beauty of our feelings and the grandeur of our ideas; a harmful passion, as one that returns us to egotism, fear, and all the pettiness of blind instinct. Every passion is either legitimate or criminal, depending on whether it produces one or the other effect, although society, which bestows humanity's seal of approval, often sanctifies the harmful and proscribes the good.

Because most of the time we are born and die in ignorance of these truths, we must endure the evils brought about by their violation, without knowing where the harm comes from and without finding its remedy. Then we persist in nurturing the causes of our suffering, believing that we will soften them by means that inflame them to no end.

That is how Marthe and Horace lived: he believed that he had achieved security by redoubling his distrust and precautions so as to horde all the power; she believed that she had calmed his worried soul by making sacrifice after sacrifice, allowing his sad tyranny to increase day by day; since in every type of despotism, the oppressor suffers at least as much as the oppressed.

And so the slightest blow disturbed this fragile felicity, and, once his jealousy was appeased, Horace had to be satiated. That was how things remained until his life became unpleasant again. An enemy kept watch at his door: poverty. For three months he had succeeded in avoiding it, entrusting to Marthe a small sum that his parents had sent in addition to his stipend. Horace had asked for this sum to pay "unforeseen" debts, of which he only dared admit to a very small part, they were so far beyond his family's budget; and instead of devoting the money to paying off that portion of his debt, he allocated it for the daily needs of his new household, just conceding to his creditors certain flimsy and partial installments, with which they were willing to content themselves.

His tailor was the least compromised by this imminent bankruptcy. I had given him my guarantee, and I began to regret it somewhat, since the expenses continued to mount, though each time it was brought to Horace's attention he got out of it by means of new promises and orders, larger and larger in proportion to the increase in his debt. As soon as Horace tried to limit his dandyism, this purveyor, very well informed about his rights, came every day to insist on them. When I saw that the latter was continually raising the stakes and that Horace was extraordinarily unthinking in this regard, I thought I was within my rights to limit my guarantee to expenses he had already incurred, and to communicate to the tailor that it did not extend to future expenses. I had already committed over a year's worth of my small income, and I foresaw financial difficulties, of which, in fact, I have felt the effects for ten years, and which I did not have the right to impose on ones closer and more precious to me than this newfound friend, so little solicitous of his honor and my own. When he learned of my reservations, he became indignant about what he called my "distrust" and wrote me a letter full of pride and bitterness to announce to me that he no longer wanted me to do him any service, that he had submitted to my protection unawares, having completely forgotten my offers and the measures I had taken, and he begged me not to interfere further in his affairs, claiming that the tailor would be paid in a week's time. Yes, he was paid—but by me, since Horace forgot the promises he had made to him as quickly as the ones he'd accepted from me; and likewise I forced myself to forget his insane letter, which I didn't respond to at all.

But the other creditors, whom I could not hold off, fell upon him.

True, they were quite small debts that would make a spendthrift of the Chaussée-d'Antin laugh; but everything is relative, and these encumbrances were enormous for Horace. Marthe knew nothing of all this. He wouldn't permit her to earn a living and hid his situation from her, so that she would feel no remorse. He had such an aversion to anything that might remind him of the grisette, that it was all he could do to let her sew her own apparel. He himself would have preferred to walk about with his wardrobe in tatters than to see the object of his love mending it. Modest Marthe had to busy herself with reading and making herself look pretty, on pain of losing all poetry in Horace's eyes, as if beauty lost its value and luster by leading a simple and unaffected life. For three months she had to play the role of Marguerite to this makeshift Faust; had to water the flowers in the window boxes; had to plait her long, ebony hair several times a day before a Gothic mirror he had purchased for her, at a price much too high for his billfold; had to learn to read and recite verses; and, finally, had to conduct an offhand tête-à-tête with him from morning till night. And when she gave into his whims, Horace didn't realize that this was not the real Marguerite, an ingenue walking from church to the fountain, but a contrived Marguerite, a keepsake heroine.

Yet the time came when Faust had to admit to Marguerite that he had nothing to give her for dinner, and that Mephistopheles wouldn't intervene on their behalf. Horace, having courageously kept his secret for a long time, having drained his friends' slender wallets one by one for several weeks, having feigned a lack of appetite for several days in order to leave his companion some food, was suddenly seized by a violent fit of despair; and, after a day of ferocious silence, he confessed his disaster with a dramatic solemnity not called for by the circumstances. How many students go to bed hungry but happy twice a week, and how many patient and robust mistresses have shared their fate without ill humor or terror? Marthe was born poor; she had grown up and developed into a beauty despite the frequent distress of barely pacified hunger. The tragedy Horace was acting out so seriously did scare her; but she was astonished that the ending put him at such a loss. "I still have two rye bread rolls here," she told him. "That's enough for dinner, and tomorrow morning I'll pawn my shawl. It will bring us twenty francs, and we can live on that for more than a week, if you allow me to run our household economically."

"You speak of such things so cold-bloodedly!" exclaimed Horace, flouncing into his chair. "My situation is vile, and I don't understand why you want to share it. Leave me, Marthe, leave me. A woman like you shouldn't stay twenty-four hours with a man who doesn't know how to keep her from such degradation. There must be a curse on me!"

"You can't be serious," Marthe replied. "Leave you because you're poor? Did I ever think you were rich! I knew all along that a time would come when you would have to let me work again; and if I agreed to live at your expense, it's because I counted on necessity to give me the chance to pay off my debt to you soon. So, tomorrow I'll go look for work, and in a few days I'll be earning at least enough to make sure we have our daily bread."

"How wretched!" Horace exclaimed again, irritated at seeing his pride conquered. "And when you've provided for the needs of our hunger, how will we be farther along? Will we pawn our belongings one by one?"

"Why not, if we have to?"

"And our creditors?"

"We'll sell this jewelry you gave me despite my pleas; that can always buy us some time."

"You fool! That would be only a drop in the bucket. You know nothing about real life, my poor Marthe; you live in the clouds, and you think people manage by a stroke of fortune, like in a novel."

"If I live in novels and in the clouds, it's because you make me, Horace. But let me come down from there, and you'll see that I haven't lost my taste for work or forgotten how to tighten my belt. Was I born in opulence? Did I have everything? Do I have the right to be so demanding?"

"That's just it," said Horace, "that's what I find so humiliating and revolting. You were born poor; I forgot that, because I saw you as worthy to sit on a throne. I jealously guarded the fragrance of your natural nobility. I took pleasure in adorning you, in preserving your beauty like something precious that had been entrusted to me. Now I have to watch you run through the dung, bargaining with shopkeepers over a few sous, cooking dinner, sweeping the dust, spoiling and fouling your pretty fingers, growing older, more pale, wearing old shoes and patching your dresses, being in the end what you wanted to be at the beginning of our union? Bah! All of that horrifies me, just thinking about it. Have a poetic life and lofty ideas in the midst of such a life? I could never dream, never think, never write. If I have to live that way, I'd rather shoot myself!"

"For the three months we've lived like princes, you have not written a word," said Marthe sweetly. "Perhaps necessity will give you an unexpected push. Try—maybe you can win both honor and wealth in a flash."

"She preaches to me and jokes with me into the bargain!" Horace exclaimed, kicking the log in the fire with his boot. "Oh, no! The last log that was still burning in our fireplace."

"God forbid!" Marthe replied. "I wanted to console you by telling you that I'm not proud, and that the day you live in affluence I won't blush at enjoying it. But in the meantime, let me work, Horace, please, I beg of you, let me live the way I know how."

"Never!" he cried energetically. "I'll never consent to your becoming a grisette again, a student's woman; that can never be. I'd prefer you to leave me."

"That's the third time you've said that awful word. Don't you love me anymore now that poverty has scared you away from me?"

"Oh, my God! Am I afraid for myself? Haven't I already gone through several hopeless crises? Do I even know if I suffered from them? I don't even remember what I did to get out of them!"

"So you're worried about me? Well, set your mind at ease, since the inactivity to which you condemn me weighs on me and is killing me; work, at the same time that it deters our poverty, will make my life sweeter and my heart gayer."

"But the work you speak of and the poverty you defy, they're one. Yes, Marthe, to me they're the same. No, no, I can't bear that! I'll find a way, I'll come up with something. I'll borrow little Paulier's last écu, and I'll try the roulette table. Maybe I'll win a million!"

"Don't do it, Horace, in heaven's name, don't resort to such awful measures!"

"You really want to go to the pawnshop, don't you? To the pawnshop! With the most vile women, with lost women! It would be the first time in your life, wouldn't it? Answer me, Marthe! Tell me you've never been there before!"

"When I go there, I won't be humiliated by it. It's a measure for which society bears the shame. You see more mothers of families there than lost women, believe me, and many miserable creatures have thrown down their last rags there rather than sell themselves."

"Aha, you've been there, Marthe! I can see that you've been there! You speak with a familiarity that proves that this wouldn't be your first time . . . But why did you go there? You lacked for nothing when you were with Monsieur Poisson, and then Arsène wouldn't have let you go there!"

And, instead of pondering his mistress's calm devotion, Horace racked his brains to find in her past some fault that would have reduced her to the measures she had just thought of in order to save him.

"I swear to you," Marthe said to him, "on the head of him who in juxtaposing the name of Monsieur Poisson with that of Arsène has just brought on himself a cloud of shame and sadness, that when I go there tomorrow it will be for the first time in my life."

"But who gave you the idea of going there?"

"I read this morning, in *Memoirs of a Contemporary,* a scene where she recounted her poverty. She had brought her last jewel to the pawnshop, and, noticing a poor woman crying in the doorway because they had refused to let her sell some memento, she shared with her the ten francs she had just received. That's quite beautiful, isn't it?"

"What?" said Horace. "I was not listening. You're telling me stories, as if I were in the mood for stories!"

It has often been said, not without reason, that it's always during a streak of bad luck that sorrows and impediments join forces and attack us relentlessly. Horace was dreaming of a way to rid himself of the newest of his creditors, with whom he'd had, two hours earlier, a stormy discussion, when Monsieur Chaignard, proprietor of the furnished apartment he was living in, came to collect from him two months' back rent on two rooms at twenty francs a fortnight. Horace, already negatively predisposed, received him haughtily, and, pressed by him, threatened, pushed to the limit, threatened in turn to toss him out the window. Chaignard, who was not brave, withdrew, declaring an armed invasion would follow the next day.

"Now you see, we have to go to the pawnshop tomorrow, to prevent a scandal," said Marthe, striving to calm him with her caresses. "If you let him put you out on the street, the other creditors will press even harder, and there won't be any way to buy time."

"Well, you won't go," said Horace. "I'll go myself. I'll take my watch."

"What watch? You don't have one."

"What watch? My mother's. Ah, what a curse! It's already been at the pawnshop a long time, and no doubt it will stay there. My poor mother! If she only knew that her beautiful watch, her antique watch, her fat watch, is there in the midst of tatters, and that I don't have the means to redeem it!"

"What if I exchanged it for the chain you gave me?" said Marthe, timidly.

"You're not at all attached to the proofs of my love," said Horace, tearing down the chain, which was hanging on the chimney and rolling it in his hands angrily. "I don't know what keeps me from throwing it out the window! At least some beggar would benefit from it, instead of it falling into a usurer's pit tomorrow, without it helping us. A fine expedient, on my soul! Come on, I still have some good suits; I've got an overcoat I can certainly do without."

"Your overcoat! When it's this cold out! When winter is beginning!"

"Well, what does it matter? You want to pawn your shawl."

"I never catch cold, and you already have. Besides, can a man pawn his clothes? It's one thing to do without a watch, a luxury! But the necessities! What if someone recognized you?"

"Oh, if Arsène recognized me, he'd say: Here's the man who took responsibility for Marthe; she must be very unhappy, poor Marthe! Maybe he's already saying it."

"How could he say what isn't true?"

"How do I know? At least admit that it would be a fine victory for him, if he knew to what circumstances we've been reduced."

"But we won't boast about it, what good would it do?"

"Bah! Tomorrow you will go out, every day you'll run around looking for work: it won't be long before you bump into him, he's always prowling around here . . . You know as well as I, Marthe, don't look so surprised. Well, you'll see him; he'll ask you questions, and you'll tell him everything one sad day. And you'll have days like that, my poor child! You won't always take things as philosophically as you do today."

"Alas, I do foresee days like that," Marthe answered, "but poverty won't be the direct cause. Your jealousy will grow."

Her eyes filled with tears. Horace wiped them with his lips, and gave in to the raptures of a love more feverish than delicate, especially that night.

Marthe had been awake a long time when Horace woke up. It was late. Horace had slept well; his mind was calm and refreshed. Cheerful thoughts came to him when he heard the sparrows calling to one another on the rooftops, where the sun of a beautiful winter morning was melting the previous night's snow. "Hey, hey!" he said, "are you cold and hungry up there? It's even worse than in this place. If you don't have any more bread, my poor Marthe, your regular customers won't have any crumbs, and they'll complain about you."

"That won't happen," said Marthe. "I saved them some of my last night's supper, a bit of rye bread. Those gentlemen aren't hard to please, they ate quite a good lunch."

"They're better off than we are, aren't they?"

"What difference does it make?" said Marthe. "We'll have a better dinner tonight."

"You talk about dinner; that's always a consolation for someone who really wants lunch. So, you've been to the pawnshop, eh?"

"Not yet, you practically forbade me yesterday. I'm waiting to get your permission."

"I thought you had already come back," said Horace, yawning.

Marthe was delighted by his change of mood, which she attributed to wiser notions, but which was nothing other than the result of a more imperious appetite. She threw her old red shawl over her shoulders and folded the new one in a pretty sheaf of paper; then, fearing that Horace might change his mind, she hastened to leave. But several minutes later she came back looking pale and dismayed: Monsieur Chaignard had forced her back upstairs, telling her in a manner that was hardly courteous that he wouldn't suffer the smallest personal effect to be removed from his premises as long as the rent wasn't paid.

Horace, indignant about this insult, rushed downstairs, where Monsieur Chaignard was still grumbling, and a violent discussion began between them. Chaignard was even more firm now, since he had witnesses. Foreseeing a storm, he had flanked himself with his concierge and a sort of attorney who looked like someone imitating a bailiff. These two acolytes played their roles: one, the defender of his master's sacred person; the other, the keeper of the peace, yet ready to draw up a written complaint. Horace realized that the law was not on his side, and that in the end he would have to capitulate; but he gave himself the satisfaction of overwhelming poor Chaignard with biting epithets and of criticizing him for his stinginess in the most bitter and wounding terms he could imagine. All he expended in bilious wit and effort in this instance would have gone completely to waste if the noise hadn't attracted other malicious listeners, whose presence avenged his vanity. Chaignard was red in the face, foaming, furious; the bailiff, finding nothing he could sink his teeth into amidst assaults of a sort as delicate as sarcasm, waited attentively for a more decisive word that would constitute a misdemeanor, punishable by law. The concierge, who didn't like his master, laughed into his gray and dirty beard at Horace's jokes; and a few students had left the doors of their rooms ajar to enjoy this quaint dialogue. Finally one of those doors, opening all the way, revealed a large face with red bristles, wrapped in an old foot-rug from which emerged two thin and shaggy arms. The owner of this bizarre face and these enormous arms was none other than the illustrious Jean Laravinière, President of the Bousingots, who had moved the night before into a room costing fifteen francs a month, a delicious mezzanine, he called it, whose front door and window he had to open when he extended his two arms to don his frock coat.

"This is quite an uproar, my dear landlord," he said to the fiery Chaignard. "You might have an apoplectic fit; but that's the least of the inconvenience here: the worst is that you woke up one of your tenants at eight in the morning and he didn't get home till six."

"Why are you interfering?" exclaimed Chaignard, beside himself.

"Manners, manners, Monsieur Chaignard, not to mention morals," Laravinière replied. "You will not long have the honor of my presence or the benefit of my rent in your building if you treat the children of the fatherland that way right before my very eyes!"

"The fatherland wants us to pay our debts," cried Chaignard. "I'm a lieutenant in the National Guard . . ."

"I know that quite well," replied Laravinière coolly. "That's why I'm entreating you to calm yourself."

"And I know my rights as a citizen," Chaignard continued.

"In that case, we'll come to an understanding with you," Laravinière resumed. "I'm well acquainted with Monsieur Horace Dumontet, and if you need a guarantee for him, I offer mine."

I don't know to what extent Laravinière's guarantee reassured the landlord, but he was eager for a pretext to cut the scene short, annoyed at having become the laughingstock. The storm subsided, and awaiting further developments, everyone returned to their apartments.

A quarter of an hour later, Jean Laravinière, having changed from what he called his "Roman outfit" to more modern and decent clothing, knocked on Horace's door. Since Horace had begun living with Marthe he had taken care to distance himself from all his acquaintances, with the exception of two or three friends who couldn't incite his jealousy, and who had the respectful admiration for him that an intelligent and presumptuous young man always inspires in half a dozen of his more credulous and unassuming comrades. One might even say, incidentally, that the principal cause of the pride that preys upon the majority of the young talents of our era is the naive and bountiful infatuation of those surrounding them. But this reflection is beside the point here. Laravinière was not at all among Horace's admirers; *his* only infatuations concerned political abilities. If he had sought Horace out under the pretext of having a laugh at Monsieur Chaignard's expense, he probably had other motives than that of reestablishing a connection which had never been very intimate, and which for two or three months seemed to have been completely dropped by both sides.

Horace had always felt a profound disdain for those republicans cut from the same cloth (that's how he referred to them) who professed a certain contempt for the arts, letters, and even the sciences, and who, somewhat tainted with Babouvism, were not far from wanting to demolish the palaces and replace them with cottages. Such blunt methods were irreconcilable with the need for elegance and the dreams of his own grandeur that Horace nourished. So he considered Laravinière one of those instruments of destruction whom the more prudent revolutionaries gladly let march in the front ranks, but to whom they would not wish to entrust their personal futures.

Be that as it may, Horace welcomed him with open arms, without quite knowing why. Horace was well disposed toward him; he was in the midst of laughing: he had just recounted to his female companion the mockery with which he'd overwhelmed poor Chaignard, and he was very pleased to present a witness to his triumph. And then, which of you young people with a precarious fate has not experienced this? When we're in distress, a familiar face, whoever it may be, always gives us a flicker of courage or security that predisposes us in its favor.

Seeing Marthe, Jean took a step back, muttered some excuse, and seemed to want to withdraw; but Horace detained him, introduced him to his companion, who held out her hand to him in memory of a nocturnal encounter when he had protected and respected her, and who asked him with a smile to recount the story of the scene with Monsieur Chaignard.

When that tale had raised their spirits, Laravinière drew Horace into the hallway and said to him, "After what happened just now, I see that you're in one of those financial crises that we all know from experience. I'm not offering to pay off Monsieur Chaignard for you, I couldn't do it, and besides, a few evasive measures will suffice to muzzle him until further notice. But if you are short of those few always essential écus, often impossible to find just when you need them the most, I could share with you the five or six remaining to me."

Horace hesitated. He had often spoken fairly ill of Laravinière to Marthe and to me; he bore a sort of grudge against him for the help he had bragged of giving to the fugitive from the café Poisson; in a word, he felt repugnance at accepting the services of a man he barely knew. But in thinking of poor Marthe, who had not had breakfast, he thought better of it, and accepted with frank gratitude.

"One day you'll do the same for me," Laravinière said to him. "You don't owe me any thanks: when we trade places, we'll trade roles. Each in his turn."

"My thoughts exactly," answered Horace, who, as soon as he had the money in his pocket, felt cooler and more uneasy with Laravinière.

So the pawnshop, that veritable Calvary of distress, was avoided on that day. Marthe nevertheless insisted on looking for work; and after Horace had made her swear that she wouldn't ask Eugénie, he let her take steps to obtain some. At first the measures she took didn't produce any brilliant successes. Yet after a few weeks she was able to provide, as she had announced her intention, for their daily bread; a few new advances from Laravinière provided for the rest; and Horace, too, gave serious thought to working to pay his debts.

Despite her efforts and his resolutions, the two lovers fell into ever increasing financial difficulties. Marthe resigned herself to them with a sort of melancholy satisfaction. In the midst of her fatigue, she was proud that from now on she would be the cornerstone of her lover's existence; since it must certainly be admitted that, without her, dinner would often have eluded them. She had, at certain moments, enough authority over him to get him to increase his creditors' patience by making small sacrifices. And then, a student's creditors are less temperamental than those of a dandy. They know quite well that when it comes to a son of the middle class, what is put off is not lost, and that, once in the bosom of his family again, the young citizen of the provinces can be depended upon to honor his debts. It happens slowly, but in the end, with that class, there is no real bankruptcy, and disarray is only temporary. So Horace could still obtain enough credit from his suppliers to feign a certain elegance.

Strange, though (and yet it never fails), his taste for spending increased as a result of the anxieties and the impediments it created. Giddy personalities are unique in that obstacles and privations only excite their thirst for pleasure and double their boldness in procuring that pleasure for themselves. After confessing to his scrupulous companion the true state of his finances, after letting her read the letters of gentle reproach and well-founded complaint his mother wrote to him, it was no longer possible to preserve the illusion, and to tear her away from her work, her conscientious and austere economy plan. That would have incurred Marthe's censure, and Horace clung to the idea of being admired just as much as being loved. So he had to get used to seeing her resume her humble habits, and he had to play the role of the stoic. But this role weighed on him horribly—from then on, the sanctum that had been his delight no longer gave him pleasure. Boredom got the better of his jealousy. He had one of those voluptuous, artistic temperaments in which love succumbs under the weight of prosaic reality. The sight of this austere and impoverished household became too gloomy for his cheerful imagination. Instead of drawing from Marthe's example the courage to work, he felt work becoming more of a burden to him, more impossible than ever. He was cold in that poorly heated room, and the cold, which didn't numb Marthe's diligent fingers, paralyzed this young man's brain. And then, that sober nourishment, which Marthe prepared with enough care and tidiness to sharpen the appetite, was neither substantial enough nor abundant enough to fuel the energy of a twenty-year-old male, used to denying himself nothing.

He reproached his patient homemaker with a coarseness that made him blush one minute and cry the next, but even so his reproaches began again the very next day. He accused her of being shabby and parsimonious; and when she responded, with her eyes full of tears, that she only had twenty sous a day to spend on their table, he sometimes questioned her bitterly about what she had done with the hundred francs he had handed to her the week before—forgetting that he had taken that money back little by little without counting it, and that he had spent it elsewhere on baubles, shows, ice cream, lunches, and loans to his friends. Horace was, after all, the soul of generosity: he didn't like paying debts, but he loved to give; and at the same time that he would forget to return ten francs to some poor devil with holes in his boots, he would play the magnifico with a merry companion who asked him for forty to regale his mistress. He took perfumed baths, and tipped the boy who gave him a massage a hundred sous; he tossed a gold coin to a little chimney sweep to see him jump for joy and call him "my prince"; he bought Marthe a silk dress that was quite useless to her, since she lacked even a cotton print one; he rented saddle horses to go rambling through the Bois de Boulogne. In short, when Madame Dumontet managed to send him a tiny pool of money by wringing out the family's budget a thousand times, Horace wasted it in three days, and they had to go back to potatoes, to forced seclusion, and to the melancholy yawns of home life.

Yet a just and sincere witness was present at the long torment that poor Marthe was undergoing. It was Jean the Bousingot, whose presence in the house was not as accidental as he had led them to believe. Jean was devoted body and soul to a man who, being unable to approach that sad sanctuary where the object of his love was growing pale, wanted at least to watch over her stealthily, and to continue his mysterious solicitude for her. That man was Paul Arsène. The deep dejection he had experienced at first had given way to thoughts of political commitment. He had always told himself that he had enough strength left in him to get his head broken in the name of the republic. As a result, he had gone to look for the one man he knew in the organized movement, and Jean had greeted him with open arms.

During that period the most important and best-organized political group was the Friends of the People. Several of its leaders had already played a role in the Carbonari; they and others who were younger had played an even more splendid role since 1830. Among these men, who rose to prominence and grew in stature during this decade, and whose names are already historic, the organization Friends of the People counted among its ranks Trélat, Guinard, Raspail, et cetera; but the one who had the most influence on young college students like Laravinière, and on the younger supporters of a republic among the people, like Paul Arsène, was Godefroy Cavaignac. He was practically the only one of the remarkable men of our time who was not tainted by that puerile conceit which makes affectation second nature. His majestic height, his noble face, something chivalrous that permeated his manners and his language, his joyful and frank way of speaking, his activism, his courage and devotion—all that would have been enough to set Jean's bellicose head on fire, to warm the heart of the generous Arsène, even if Godefroy hadn't expressed the most comprehensive and logical social ideas, I would even say the most philosophical, that found form in that period in mass organizations. Only this man, the president of the Friends of the People, professed in the clubs what could be called a doctrine; a doctrine which, in many respects, didn't yet satisfy the secret instinct and the vast aspirations of Arsène's soul toward the future, but which, at least, represented immense and incontestable progress from the liberalism of the Restoration. In the estimation of Arsène, and in the people's ever severe and suspicious estimation, the other republicans were a bit too preoccupied with overturning the powers that be, and not at all with laying the groundwork for the republic; when they tried to do that, it was more rules and discipline that they envisioned than moral law and a new society. Cavaignac, in the course of the beautiful opposition that he had so grandly and forcefully waged in the previous year, even faced with the pale and lying opposition in the legislature, had busied himself with ripening his ideas, with establishing principles. He thought about the people's emancipation, about public education, about universal and free suffrage, about progressive changes in property, and he didn't confine, as certain republicans do today, these two distinct and vast principles to the hypocritical question of *the organization of work* and *electoral reform;* very elastic words, and if one isn't careful their meaning can contract as easily as expand. In 1832 one wasn't afraid, as one is today, of being considered a *communist,* nowadays everyone's bugbear. A jury acquitted Cavaignac after he had said, among other admirably bold things, "We do not dispute property rights. We simply place above them society's right to regulate them according to the greatest common good." In that same speech, the most comprehensive and exalted of all those made during the political trials of that era, Cavaignac further stated, "We dispute your [established society's] monopoly on political rights. And don't think it's just to demand them in the name of ability. From our point of view, whoever is useful is able. All service carries rights along with it."

Arsène attended this trial; he listened with restrained emotion; and, while most of the listeners, conquered by the magnetism an orator's delivery and bearing can exercise on the masses, burst into passionate applause, he remained deeply silent. But the speech pierced him most deeply of all, so much so that he didn't hear the other pleas made that day. He was completely absorbed by the ideas that Godefroy awakened in him, and he went away full of them, and repeated them to me, word for word:

"Religion, as we, *we* understand it, is humanity's sacred right. It is no longer a question of threatening crime with a bugbear after death, of providing consolation to the miserable on the other side of the tomb. It is in this world that we must ground morality and well-being, that is to say, equality. All those who bear the title 'human' are entitled to the same religious respect for their rights, to a pious sympathy for their needs. Our religion, *ours,* is one that will transform horrible prisons into hospices of repentance, and that, in the name of all that is inviolably human, will abolish the death penalty . . . We will no longer adopt a faith that places all in heaven, that reduces equality before God to that posthumous equality which paganism proclaimed just as well as Christianity.

"Théophile," exclaimed Arsène, putting his hand in mine, "those are great words and a new idea, at least for me. It gives me so much to think about that all my past, that is, everything I've believed up till now, is turned upside down right before my eyes."

"It's not an idea entirely unique to the orator you just heard," I answered. "It's an idea that belongs to our century and that has already been expressed in many forms. One might even say that it's the idea which has dominated our revolutions for the last hundred years, and all of humanity as long as it has existed, through an instinctive revelation of its rights, more powerful than the religious theories of asceticism and renunciation. But it's always a new and great thing to see human rights, looked at from a religious point of view, proclaimed by a revolutionary. For quite a long time your republicans had forgotten to give their theories the divine sanction they should have. As for me, a Legitimist . . . ," I added, smiling.

"Don't talk like that," Paul Arsène replied with spirit; "you're not a Legitimist in the way that word is usually used. You feel that legitimacy stems from the rights of the people."

"That's true, Arsène, I feel it deeply; and although my father was attached, by deed and by the scruples of his conscience, to the men of the past, the closer he got to his grave, the more he grew to understand and respect the institutions of the future. Do you think he was the only one in that generation of thinkers? Don't you believe that Chateaubriand said to himself a hundred times that God was above kings, in the same way that Cavaignac proclaimed before you today the rights of society above those of the rich?"

"Yes, indeed," said Arsène. "So it's true that we have a right to happiness in this life, that it's not a crime to seek it, and that God himself has made it our duty? That notion hadn't dawned on me yet. I was split between a revolutionary feeling that almost made me an atheist, and a turning back to the devotion of my youth that made me compassionate to the point of weakness. Ah! if you only knew how cold and cruel I was for three days in the throes of my delirium! I killed men and I said to them: Die, you who made others die! Killers, I'm killing *you!* It seemed to me the workings of a savage justice; but I felt myself compelled to do it by a supernatural impulse. And then, when I calmed down, when I knelt on the tombs of July, I thought of God, of that God of submissiveness and humility of whom I'd been taught, and I no longer knew where to seek refuge for my thoughts. I wondered if my brother was damned for having raised his hand against tyranny, and if I would also be for having avenged my brother and my brothers, men of the people. So I preferred to believe in nothing, since I couldn't understand how in the name of Jesus on the cross we had to let ourselves be crucified by the representatives of his ministries. That's where we stand, we, the other offspring of ignorance: atheist or superstitious, and often both. But what are our teachers thinking of, our republican leaders, in not speaking to us of the very core of our being, the mover of all our actions! Do they take us for brutes that all they ever promise us is the satisfaction of our material needs? Don't they believe we have a more noble need, that of a religion, just as they need one? Or don't they have one themselves? Could they be coarser, more incredulous than we? Well!" he finished, "Godefroy Cavaignac will be my preacher, my prophet; I'll go and ask him what we should think about all this."

"I'm sure he will tell you excellent things, my dear Arsène," I answered him, "but don't make the mistake again of believing that his opinions are the only font of new ideas. Elevate your mind to a broader notion of the time we live in. Don't give yourself exclusively to this or that man as if he were truth incarnate; men are changeable. Sometimes, thinking they're moving forward, they retreat; thinking they're making things better, they wander astray. There are even those who lose their generosity with their youth, and who become strangely corrupted! Apply yourself to the very ideas whose antidote you seek. Educate yourself by drinking from several streams. Look, read, compare, and reflect. Your conscience will be the logical connection among several ideas that may seem to contradict one another. You will see that upright men don't differ so much on the heart of things as on their words; that amongst them a bit of jealous vanity is sometimes the only obstacle to a unity of belief; but between them and men in positions of power, there is an immense abyss that separates want from enjoyment, devotion from egotism, right from force."

"Yes, I need to educate myself," said Arsène. "Alas! If I only had time! But when I spend the entire day doing figures, I no longer have the strength to read; my eyes close in spite of myself, or I even become feverish; and, instead of following with my wits what I'm reading with my eyes, I follow my own ramblings, turning pages I've filled myself. For a long time I've wanted to learn what Fourierism is. Cavaignac mentioned it today, as well as the *Révue Encyclopédique* and the Saint-Simonians. He said of the Saint-Simonians that in the midst of their errors, they upheld useful ideas with devotion, and developed the principle of association. Eugénie, I'll go hear them preach."

That was Eugénie's territory; she was quite a fervent believer in restoring the rights of women. She began to indoctrinate her friend Masaccio, something she had never done before; since she was one of those delicate and prudent minds who don't risk their influence unless it's on a safe bet. She knew how to wait, just as she knew how to choose. She hadn't spoken to me ten times about her Saint-Simonian beliefs; but she had never done so without making a strong impression on me. Perhaps I knew better than she, by scrutiny and reading, the strong and weak points of this philosophy; but I always admired the purity of intent and the subtle tact with which she, her noble and modest instincts in rebellion, tacitly dismissed the discussions whereby second-rank disciples elaborated on their doctrine, inferring instead, often a priori, the secret teachings of the masters, which resonated with her natural pride, with her integrity and her love of justice. I often said to myself that the strong and intelligent woman called upon by the apostles to formulate the rights and duties of woman should have been Eugénie. But aside from the fact that her reserve and modesty would have prevented her from mounting a stage where too often the social comedy was playing instead of the human drama, among the Saint-Simonians, in the inevitable deviation that their principles had now taken, some would have judged her too rigid, some too independent. The moment never came. Saint-Simonianism was going through a first phase and there would be a gap before the second one. Eugénie felt this, and foresaw a hiatus of ten, perhaps twenty, years before the forward march of Saint-Simonianism could resume.

Paul Arsène, struck by the glimpse he got in their initial conversation on the subject, went to hear the Saint-Simonian preachings. He struck up a friendship with some of the young apostles; and without even having had time to educate himself on the subject, he leapt into the discussion, and his ideas took shape, sides, and hope. It was a rapid and profound revolution in the intellectual life of this child of the people, who up until then was not without prejudices, and from then on shed them or at least acquired the strength to combat them within himself. The love he still nourished, for want of being able to smother it (since he had done all he could), steeped itself in this source of investigation that he had not yet tapped, and took on a calmer and more noble character, a religious character, so to speak.

In fact, up until then Marthe had only been for him the object of an invincible and tenacious passion. He had cursed it a hundred times over, this passion that drew new power from everything that should have destroyed it; but since it reigned over a great soul, even though it was mysterious, incomprehensible to the very one who felt it, it produced nothing but magnanimous results in him, a generosity without precedent or limits. That proud and rigid soul then gave itself up to such awful battles! How Arsène blushed at being the slave of an attachment that the somewhat narrow severity of his common upbringing had taught him to condemn! For him, whose morals were so pure, to be smitten to such a degree by Monsieur Poisson's ex-mistress, currently another's mistress! Never would he have wanted to profit from the sort of weakness and rapture that Marthe's conduct had allowed him to glimpse, to wrest secretly from gratitude, from an exalted friendship, favors that he would have liked to owe only to an exclusive and durable love. But despite the little hope he had left, he always caught himself wishing that Horace's chance at this love would end, and cherishing the dream of a legal marriage to Marthe. That's where his old prejudices were waiting to make him suffer—the accusation of his peers, his sister Louise's indignation, his sister Suzanne's dread, the fear of being ridiculed, a sort of bashfulness, sometimes all-powerful for lofty personalities since that shyness is taught to them by opinion, as is respect for oneself and others. That's when Arsène tried to tear his love out of his chest, like a poison arrow. But his evangelical nature objected: he was forced to love. The hatred and contempt he called on to help him couldn't enter that heart so filled with indulgence, because it was also filled with justice.

During that winter which he spent far from Marthe, and which he, to the best of his ability, devoted to studying religion, nature, and society, under their new aspects opening up before him on all sides, in turn and simultaneously Fourierist, republican, Saint-Simonian and Christian (since he also read *l'Avenir* and ardently venerated Monsieur Lamennais), Arsène, if he couldn't succeed in constructing an overall philosophy, purified his soul, elevated his mind, and prodigiously developed that great heart of his. Each day I was more struck by him, and, from week to week, I admired his rapid progress. I finally discovered his hiding place; and, braving the harsh reception of his older sister, I sometimes went there in the evening to surprise him in the midst of his meditations. While the two sisters worked, exchanging the most foolish ideas, he, seated at the foot of the table, head in hands, a book open between his elbows, his eyes half closed, studied or dreamed by the glow of a sad lamp whose brightness barely reached him. If you had seen his yellowish complexion, his tired eyes, his mournful expression, you would have taken him for a man consumed by fatigue and poverty; but as soon as he spoke, the fire returned to his eyes, serenity to his forehead, and his speech displayed a tempered energy. I would take him out for a stroll along the quais, and there, smoking our stately cigars, we would chat. When we had gone over general ideas, we came around to our personal feelings; and he often said to me, speaking about Marthe: "The future is mine; Horace's reign can't last long. The poor boy doesn't understand the happiness he possesses, he doesn't enjoy it, he won't profit from it; and you will see, Marthe will learn what true love is by experiencing all that's missing in the way of grandeur and truth from the love she now inspires. You see, my friend, I won a great victory the day I understood that what are called a woman's faults were attributable to society and not to evil inclinations. Evil inclinations are rare, thank God; they're the exception, and Marthe only has good ones. If she chose Horace over me, it was because I was not worthy of her, and because Horace seemed more worthy to her. Wavering and wild, at the same time that I devotedly offered myself to her, I didn't know how to tell her what she wanted to hear. The memory of her unhappiness only inspired pity in me; she felt that, and she wanted respect. Horace was able to express enthusiasm to her; she was fooled by it, but the fault isn't at all hers. Now I would certainly be able to tell her what she needed to close her old wounds, reassure her of her integrity, and give her the confidence in me that she didn't have before. My austerity scared her, she feared my reprimands; she only had that cool esteem for me which a wise and reasonably humane man inspires. She needed to be buttressed, saved, initiated into a new life that was all exaltation and charity. I repeat: Horace, with his beautiful eyes and his great phrases, seemed to her a revelation of love. She followed him. *Mea culpa!*"

I thought Arsène was being unfair to himself, out of generosity. One definitely had to take into account, when it came to Marthe's blindness, a certain weakness and vanity that, in women, is the result of poor education and a false way of looking at things. Particularly in Marthe's case, it was the effect of a total absence of instruction and judgment in this realm of thought, so necessary and so neglected in women of all classes.

Marthe had learned everything she knew from novels. That was better than nothing, one might even say it was a lot, since her stimulating reading at least developed poetic feeling and ennobled defects. But it was not enough. A moving account of passions, the drama of modern life, as we conceive it, doesn't encompass causes, and only creates effects that are more contagious than useful to the minds of those severed from all other culture. I have always thought that good novels were extremely useful, but as a diversion and not as the sole and constant nourishment for one's mind.

I imparted this observation to Masaccio, and he concluded from it that Marthe was even more innocent than she was limited in certain respects. He promised himself to instruct her one day on the true destiny proper to women; and as he was expounding his views on this subject, I admired that he had been able, just as Eugénie had, to reject in

Saint-Simonianism all that was not applicable to our era, to extract from it that apostolic and truly divine sense of the rehabilitation and emancipation of the human race in the *person of woman*.

I also admired the beautiful nature of this young man who, to his artist's perceptive faculties, added such surprising meditative faculties. His mind was capable of simultaneously synthesizing and analyzing; and when I saw him walking next to me, with his shredded clothing, his huge shoes, his common quality and his worker manners, I wondered, as the true phrenological anatomist that I was, why I saw all around us luxurious livery and elegant graces ornamenting so many beings disfavored of heaven, bearing on their foreheads the obvious marks of intellectual, physical, and moral degradation.

Laravinière was a good man but no where near as good a philosopher. His mind was lofty, rather than broad; that is to say that he had more capacity for enthusiasm than for investigation. There was only room in that ardent brain for one idea, and that was the idea of revolution. Worthy and devoted with a passion, he entrusted the care of the future to the numerous idols with whom he had furnished his republican pantheon: Cavaignac, Carrel, Arago, Marrast, Trélat, Raspail, the brilliant lawyer Dupont, and *tutti quanti:* they made up the directorate of his conscience without his having thought much about whether these men, no doubt of superior ability, but as vague and incomplete as the ideas of that time, could agree on how to govern a new society. The fiery young man desired the overthrow of bourgeois power, and his goal was to fight in order to hasten its fall. Everything in the opposition had earned the right to his respect, his love. His favorite expression was "Give me work to do."

He developed a lively friendship with Arsène, not that he understood all the beauty of his intellect, but because, with regard to the intrepid bravura and absolute devotion by which he could judge him, he found him to be his equal in courage and selflessness. Laravinière was quite astonished to see that he cultivated, with a sort of painstaking care, a passion that was not requited; but he fondly gave in to what he called Arsène's fantasy by going to live under the same roof as the beautiful Marthe, and by eliciting a sort of trust and intimacy from Horace. It was a fairly delicate role for a man as frank as he. Still, he conducted himself as loyally as possible, by not showing Horace any friendship, since he didn't feel any for him. Following Arsène's instructions, he was obliging, sociable, and jovial with him; nothing more. Horace's self-confident vanity did the rest. He imagined that Laravinière was drawn to him by the wit that he had used to entrance so many others. That was possible; but it wasn't the case. Laravinière treated him like a husband one doesn't want to deceive, but whom one humors and conciliates in order to cultivate the friendship or the agreeable company of his wife. In all walks of life this is practiced in perfect good faith; and not only did Laravinière make no pretense about himself, but he had expressed his reservations to Arsène, declaring to him that, not wanting to act like a traitor, he would never speak to Marthe either against her lover nor in favor of another. This was perfectly agreeable to Arsène; it was enough for him to have news of Marthe every day, and to be warned in time of the break with Horace that he foresaw and for which he waited, to pre-serve the strong and calm hope that nourished him.

So Laravinière saw Marthe every day, sometimes alone, sometimes in the company of Horace, who didn't do him the honor of being jealous. And every evening he saw Arsène, and discussed Marthe with him for a quarter of an hour, on the condition that afterward they would talk about the republic for half an hour.

Although Jean wasn't playing the role of watchman, it was impossible for him not to observe immediately the bitterness and coolness of Horace toward poor Marthe, and it shocked him. He had thought no more about the nature and fate of woman than he had about the other fundamental questions of society; but this man's instincts were so good that reflection could find nothing to correct in them. He had a prodi-gious respect for women, as strong and worthy men usually do. Tyranny, jealousy, and violence are always marks of weakness.

Jean had never been loved. His ugliness made him extremely reticent around the women he would have found worthy of his respect; and although the coarseness of his speech and manners would never have led one to suspect his shyness, it was so pronounced that he wouldn't raise his eyes to Marthe except on the sly. This mistrust of himself was perfectly disguised by a carefree air, and he never spoke of love except with a satirical tone that one had to laugh at despite oneself. Generally women concluded that he was a brute; and once this judgment was pronounced against him, it would have required great eloquence and courage for poor Jean to overturn it. He felt it keenly, and the need for love that he had stemmed in his heart of hearts was too fragile for him to want to expose it to the mocking doubts that his initial explanations might have provoked. Not being able to give up even for a moment the role he had cast himself in, he had condemned himself to keeping company only with women who were too easy to inspire in him a serious attachment, but whom he nonetheless treated with a sweetness and regard to which they were not accustomed.

This is the story of quite a few men. A singular pride prevents them from revealing themselves as they are, and all their lives they bear the pain of an innocent dissimulation in which they are forced to persist. But since one's true nature always comes to the surface, despite the bantering contempt that our Bousingot professed for romantic feelings, he couldn't stand to see a woman humiliated and distressed, whoever she might be, without experiencing a profound indignation. If he saw a prostitute struck in the street by one of those sordid men who are linked with them, he took her part heroically, and protected her even if it meant risking his life. With even more reason he had difficulty containing himself when he saw a delicate woman receiving those wounds which are more cruel to the heart of a noble being than blows are to the shoulders of a debased one. Since the beginning of his stay in Chaignard's house, he had seen on Marthe's cheeks the traces of her tears; he often came upon Horace during the fits of anger that the latter had difficulty repressing in front of him. Little by little Horace, growing accustomed to considering him a witness of no account, also grew accustomed to containing himself no longer, and Laravinière could not remain for long an impassive spectator to his outbursts.

One day he found him in a veritable fury. Horace had spent the night at the Opera Ball; his nerves were on edge, and he considered it an insult on Marthe's part, an encroachment on his freedom, an attempt at despotism, that she had made certain criticisms about his prolonged absence. Marthe was not jealous, or at least if she was, she never let it show; but she had been anxious all night, since Horace had promised to come home at two o'clock. She feared a brawl, an accident, perhaps an infidelity. Although she had suffered, she only complained of not having been forewarned, and her altered countenance was eloquent testimony to her anguish and the cruel insomnia it had caused her.

"Isn't it hateful, I ask you," said Horace, addressing Laravinière, "to be treated like a child by his nursemaid, like a schoolboy by his master? I don't have the right to go out and come back at the hour I choose? I have to ask permission; and if I forget myself a bit, I find that the time limit is before me like a sentence, like the exact and official amount of time I am permitted to amuse myself. Now, isn't that pleasant! I am to sign a pass with a forfeit of so much per minute of lateness."

"You can see she's suffering!" Laravinière said to him under his breath.

"Why, of course! And you think *I'm* on a bed of roses?" Horace continued in a loud voice. "Should puerile and unjust suffering be met with caresses, while poignant and legitimate suffering like mine festers day after day?"

"Then I really am making you very unhappy, Horace!" said Marthe, raising to him, with a look of severe pain, those big, dark blue eyes of hers. "Truthfully, I didn't think I was working on making you unhappy here."

"Yes, you make me unhappy," he exclaimed, "horribly unhappy! If you want me to tell you in front of Jean—your eternal sadness makes my home hateful to me. It has gotten to the point where when I go out, I breathe, I blossom, I come back to life; and when I come back home, my chest contracts, and I feel like I'm dying. Your love, Marthe, is a vacuum pump, it's suffocating. That's why for some time you've seen less of me."

"I think you've got your dates mixed up," answered Marthe, whose wounded pride was giving her courage. "It's not my constant sadness that forces you to be absent; it's your constant absence that forced me to be sad."

"Do you hear that, Laravinière!" said Horace, who needed someone to believe his alibi, though Jean's doubtful expression made him fear a severe judgment. "So it's because I go out, because I live the life that suits a man, because I use my independence as it pleases me, that I'm condemned to find, when I come home, a distressed face, a bitter smile, doubts, reprimands, coldness, accusations, verdicts! It's the most un-bearable torture in the world!"

"I see," said Laravinière getting up, "that you both have a lot to com-plain of. Listen: take my word for it, you should leave each other."

"That's exactly what he wants!" shouted Marthe, clasping her face between her hands.

"And that's precisely what you're asking for through Laravinière's mouth," Horace resumed heatedly.

"One second," said Laravinière. "Don't make me play a character I must repudiate. I haven't been privy to anyone's secrets here, and what I just said, I said of my own accord, since it's my opinion. You don't suit one another, you've never suited one another; you waver between infatuation and hatred, and you would do better to allow forgiveness and friendship to guide you."

"Granted that this pretty speech was Laravinière's own inspiration and improvisation," said Horace, "at least tell me, Marthe, if it expresses your own thoughts."

"He might easily have surmised that, or guessed it perhaps," she answered with dignity, "hearing you accuse me of being the cause of your unhappiness."

That's not how Horace understood the matter. He was willing to forsake Marthe, but he didn't want her to leave him. The strength she showed at that moment, which the presence of a third party had inspired in her, pushed Horace into one of his most violent outbursts of spite yet. He got up, smashed his chair, gave free rein to his anger and sorrow. Even his old jealousies were reawakened, the detestable name of Monsieur Poisson returned to his lips with a vengeance, and that of Arsène was about to escape them when Laravinière, taking Marthe's arm, said to her forcefully:

"You've chosen as your protector a child without reason or dignity; in your shoes, Marthe, I wouldn't stay another moment in his house."

"Then take her to yours, Monsieur!" said Horace with bitter con-tempt. "I give my consent with all my heart; since I understand now what's going on between you and her."

"In my house, Monsieur," Jean resumed calmly, "she would be hon-ored and respected, while in your house she's humiliated and insulted.

Oh, my God!" he added with sudden emotion, "if only I'd been loved by a woman like Marthe, even for a day, I wouldn't forget it my whole life . . ."

And suddenly he lost his voice, as if his entire heart were ready to escape in one word. There was so much truth in his intonation that Horace's feigned or sudden jealousy evaporated in an instant; Laravinière's emotion got the better of him through a sympathetic reaction; and giving in to the sort of response that violent scenes often produce in us, Horace dissolved into tears; and holding out his hand to him effusively, he said:

"Jean, you're right. You have a wonderful heart, and I'm a coward, a wretch. Beg forgiveness for me of that woman of whom I'm not worthy."

This frank and noble resolve ended the quarrel, and even won over Jean's sincere heart.

"Well," he said, placing Marthe's hand in that of Horace, "you're better than I'd thought, Horace; it's a fine thing to know how to acknowledge one's faults as quickly and generously as you've just done. Certainly Marthe can ask no more than to forget them."

And he fled to his room, either to avoid being a witness to Marthe's joy, or to hide the welling up of a sensitivity he was used to repressing.

Despite this beautiful ending, similar scenes soon recurred, and became more and more frequent. Horace loved dissipation; he gave into it with an unbridled giddiness. He could no longer spend even one evening at home; he lived only in the orchestra of the Italiens Theater and the Opera House. There he was condemned not to shine at all; but he enjoyed just setting eyes on women who displayed, in the boxes, their beauty or their luxury before a crowd of impoverished young men, avid for pleasure, glitter, and riches. He knew by name all the women of fashion whose titles, money, and pride seemed to erect an impermeable barrier to his covetousness. He knew their private boxes, their clothes and their retinues, and their loves; he stood at the foot of the staircase to see them parade slowly before him, their shoulders barely hidden by furs that sometimes slipped right off, grazing him, and who boldly braved his brave looks. Jean-Jacques Rousseau didn't exaggerate at all in painting the singular impudence of women in high society; but it was with a philosophical brutality that Horace could hardly think of sharing. His daring ambition was not wounded by the cold and provocative looks by which this sort of woman seemed to say, "Admire me, but don't touch." In the end the emotion of the scene, the power of the music, the contagion of the applause, everything, down to the phantasmagorical decor and the glitter of the lights, intoxicated this young man, who after all, committed no other fault than to aspire to the pleasures society continually offered to and then pulled back from the poor, like water for Tantalus's thirst.

Besides, when he returned to his dark and shabby garret and found Marthe cold and pale, drowsy with fatigue next to a fire that had burnt down, he experienced a malaise painfully tugged at both ends by remorse and resentment. Then, at the least provocation, the storm would begin again; and Marthe, with no hope of curing such a gloomy passion, energetically desired and called on death.

With this sort of domestic secret, once the first veil has fallen, both sides feel the need to invoke the judgment of a third party; they seek him out, sometimes as a confidant, sometimes as an arbiter. At the beginning, Laravinière played the role of mediator. He was angry at being dragged into choosing sides in the quarrel, and he confessed to Arsène that, despite his resolve to remain neutral, he couldn't help feeling a sort of friendship for Horace. In fact, the latter evinced a good deal of trust in him and often showed a heartfelt generosity toward him that entangled him more and more. Horace had, despite all his faults, his seductive qualities; he was as quick to soften as he was to flare up. A wise word always found a way into his thoughts; a fond word found an even quicker way into his heart. In the midst of an unprecedented outburst of pride and vanity, he could revert suddenly to a modest and ingenuous repentance. In fact, he acted out the most contradictory dispositions one right after the other, and the dispute that I reported sketchily above sums up all those that followed, disputes that Laravinière was called upon to settle.

Meanwhile, once these arguments had been repeated a certain number of times, Laravinière, obeying, as Arsène had counseled him, his spontaneous impressions, felt himself becoming less indulgent of Horace. There is, in the frequent recurrence of the same fault, something that aggravates it and that wears down the patience of a just soul. Little by little Laravinière became so tired of the facility with which Horace blamed himself and begged to be forgiven that his admiration for that facility changed into a sort of contempt. In the end he came to see him as just a sentimental braggart, and he felt his conscience extricating itself from an affection he hadn't been able to prevent. This final break was quite severe, but inevitable in a personality as firm and impartial as Jean.

"My poor friend," he said to Horace one day when the latter was calling on him to intervene, "I can no longer keep you in the dark about my total indifference to your loves. I'm tired of seeing madness on the one hand and, on the other, incurable weakness. Or should I say weakness and madness on both sides. Marthe must be a monomaniac to love you with such constancy, and on your part there's a wretched weakness in all these violent displays that you regale us with. At first I thought you an egotist, and then I thought you were good. Now I see that you're neither good nor bad; you're cold, and you love to work yourself up into a storm of forced passion. You have an actor's nature. When we're there to be moved by your foot stamping, your pronouncements, and your sobs, you amuse yourself at our expense, I'm sure of it. Oh, don't get angry! Don't roll your eyes like Bocage playing Buridan, and don't clench your fists. I've seen it all so many times that to everything you can do or say I'd respond, 'Seen it already!' I'm a used-up spectator, and from now on as cold as a man who always has free passes to the theater. I know you're good at drama; but I know all your roles by heart. If you want me to listen to you, be serious, throw away your dagger, and talk sense to me. Tell me quite prosaically that you no longer love your mistress because she bores you, and authorize me to inform her with all the respect and deference that she deserves. That's the only way you can regain my esteem and I would consider you a man of honor."

"Well!" said Horace, holding in his rage, "I'll agree to speak coolly to you, very coolly, since I know how to contain myself, and I'll begin by saying to you seriously and calmly that you will have to answer for all the insults you've just uttered . . ."

"Let's get down to facts," Jean countered. "This is the tenth time this month you've provoked me, and I'd be doing you a service if I took you at your word; but I have better uses for my blood than to risk it on an oaf like you. Remember how I make your foil fly every time we play at fencing, and allow me to refuse your new challenge."

"I could force you to accept it," said Horace, deathly pale.

"Will you insult me publicly? Will you slap me across the face? But tripping me up, and with a backhand from my Friar John . . . God help me, Horace! Methods like that are only good for stool pigeons and gendarmes. Look, even though I don't like you anymore, I still feel enough for you to make me put up with your folly rather than respond to it. So be quiet. I warn you that I won't defend myself, and that it would be cowardly on your part to attack me."

"Who here is attacking and provoking? Who is cowardly, thrice cowardly, me or you? You overwhelm me with insults, you treat me with the utmost contempt, and you say you won't grant me any satisfaction! Ah, right now I understand the way the Malays duel, tearing out their own entrails in the presence of their enemy."

"That's a pretty phrase, Horace, but it's another pronouncement, because I'm not your enemy, and I swear that I don't wish to insult you. I'm giving you a friendly lesson and you might do well to take it to heart, since you've asked for it so many times. I've been saving it for you for a long time, and accepting excuses from you, and I don't believe I ever took unfair advantage of you because of that."

"You're taking horribly unfair advantage right this moment; you make me blush at how open and loyal I once was to you."

"I'm not taking advantage, since it's to prevent you from humiliating yourself again that I'm forbidding you to go back to that."

"My God, my God! What have I *done*," exclaimed Horace, crying with rage and wringing his hands, "to be treated this way?"

"I'll tell you what you've done," answered Laravinière. "You've made a poor creature who adores you, suffer and waste away, and you don't even appreciate her."

"Me! Not appreciate Marthe! Do you dare tell me that I don't appreciate the woman to whom I've given my youth, my life, my heart's virginity?"

"I don't think it was much of a sacrifice on your part, and in any case, I'm hardly inclined to pity you."

"Because you understand nothing about love! You're the one who is cold and has no understanding of passion."

"That's possible," said Jean with a bitter smile, "but I don't pretend the contrary. Well, then explain to me, in that case, on what grounds you're so much to be pitied."

"Jean," cried Horace, "you don't know what it's like to love for the first time, and to be loved for the second or third."

"Ah, now we have it," said Laravinière shrugging his shoulders. "Only the Virgin Mary is worthy of Monsieur Horace Dumontet! *Seen it already,* my friend. You've said it enough in my presence to poor Marthe. But to say things like that, you see, or even to think them, proves that you are worthy at most of Mademoiselle Louison. You are so vain and foolish! There are certain lost women who are worth more than certain adolescents."

"Jean, you're a boor, a brute, an insolent character."

"Yes, but I'm telling the truth. There are pure hearts under dirty dresses, and rotten hearts under magnificent waistcoats."

At that Horace tore up his crimson velvet waistcoat and threw the tatters in Laravinière's face. Jean dodged them and said, pushing them away with the heel of his foot: "That's right. As if you weren't already up to your neck in debt to your tailor."

"As I am to you, sir," said Horace. "I hadn't forgotten; but thank you kindly for reminding me."

"If you remember, so much the better," said Laravinière heedlessly. "In the prisons there are some poor patriots who buy cigars that way. So, light yours up again, and let's talk a little without losing our tempers. You've unquestionably done wrong to Marthe, you can't deny that; and I, knowing what a spoiled child you are, and that you have wit, fine words, and a superb countenance, forgive you up to a point. I know very well that it's the privilege of handsome boys, as it is of beautiful women, to have their whims; and I can't demand that you have the wisdom of a man like me, who resembles a wild boar more than a Christian, and whose face was worked over one day when the rain was pounding on our door. But what I don't forgive you for is that you enjoy making someone else suffer and that you refuse to break off a liaison you're disgusted with. You lack frankness, in a word, and you don't want to remedy the evil you've done."

"But I love her, that woman I'm making suffer! I can't separate from her! And I couldn't get used to living without her!"

"Even if that's true—and I have my doubts, since you manage to spend the least possible amount of time with her—it's your duty to overcome a love that's harmful to her."

"Even if I wanted to, she would never consent."

"Are you sure of that?"

"She would kill herself if I abandoned her."

"If you abandon her coldly and brutally, that's possible; but if you do it out of loyalty or devotion, in the name of honor, even in the name of your love . . ."

"Never! Marthe would never resign herself to losing me, I know it all too well."

"That's what I call fatuousness. Authorize me to speak to her with the same frankness I've just used with you, and we shall see."

"Jean! Another blow: you have designs on her!"

"Me? That would require three things: first, that all mirrors be banished from the universe; second, that Marthe lose her sight; and third, that she and I have no memory of my face."

"But why are you so determined to separate us?"

"I won't mince words: I'm looking out for someone else."

"Are you assigned to seduce her or kidnap her? For what Russian prince or Don Juan of the Café de Paris?"

"For a shoemaker's son, for Paul Arsène."

"What! You see him?"

"Every day."

"And you've kept me in the dark about it? . . . Now, that's strange!"

"On the contrary, it's quite simple. I knew you didn't care for him, and I didn't want to hear him spoken ill of, since I do care for him."

"So you're the Mercury of this Jupiter, who has already transformed himself into a shower of gold coins to supplant me?"

"A triple insult to *him,* to *her,* and to *me.* Thanks so much! Is that one of your lines? You said it very well! If I were your claque, I'd swoon with admiration."

"But look here, Laravinière, this is enough to drive me crazy! You're acting against me here, you betray me, you speak on behalf of another. And I trusted you!"

"And you were right to, Monsieur. I never uttered Arsène's name in Marthe's presence. And as for stirring things up between you, I always did just the opposite. Today I'm renouncing my efforts at reconciling you: my heart and conscience forbid it. Either I leave this household today and never see you or Marthe again, or I undertake, with your authority, to break a bond that weighs on you and is killing her."

Horace, won over by Laravinière's harsh frankness and unforgiving resolve, his back against the wall, and no longer knowing how to regain the respect of this man whose judgment he feared, promised to think about his proposal and requested a few days to make his final decision. But the days glided by, and he was unable to decide a thing.

He was not lying when he said that he couldn't do without Marthe. Solitude terrified him, and he craved the devotion of another, two things that made Marthe even more precious to him than he dared tell Laravinière, since the latter was no longer inclined to illusions with regard to Horace, and, if Laravinière had guessed the real motive behind this perseverance, he would have accused him of egotism and exploitation. Marthe was easier to fool or mollify. It was enough for her if Horace uttered one word of fear or regret about the idea of separation; then she heroically accepted all the suffering bound up in this unhappy union.

"He needs me more than people realize," she said. "His health isn't as good as it seems. He's frequently indisposed on account of a nervous irritability that sometimes has made me fear, if not for his life, at least for his reason. It frightens me how upset he gets at the slightest unhappiness. And then he's distracted, listless; he doesn't know how to take care of himself: if I weren't there, in the midst of his reveries and ravings, he'd forget to sleep and eat. Not to mention the fact that he would never take the trouble or the precaution to put aside twenty sous a day for dinner. In the end, he loves me, despite all his tantrums. He's told me a hundred times, in those uninhibited, repentant moments when one is really oneself, that he'd prefer to suffer a thousand times more for his love than to be cured of it and cease to love."

That's how Marthe explained it to Laravinière, since the latter, seeing that Horace could decide nothing, had broken the ice with her, after having informed Horace thoroughly of what he was going to do. Horace, who, because of Laravinière's biting criticisms, had developed a veritable aversion to him, foresaw that it would take nothing short of a serious quarrel to get rid of him; and he had ironically challenged him to steal Marthe's heart, and from then on gave him a free hand with her.

Although he was outraged by the disdainful aplomb with which Jean moved against him, Horace didn't fear him. He knew Jean to be awkward, timid, more scrupulous and compassionate than he wanted to appear; and Horace felt strongly that with one word he could destroy, in the mind of his indulgent friend Marthe, the entire effect of the longest speech Laravinière could make. And so it was, and he threw himself into the effort of regaining his hold over Marthe, as if he were trying to win a bet. How many unhappy loves have been prolonged in this way and, with difficulty, reignited in hearts that were worn out or had cooled off for fear of conceding victory to those who predicted the end was near! Repentance and forgiveness, in these cases, are not always completely disinterested, and there is more loyalty than one would think in braving the scandal of a break that has become necessary.

So Laravinière struggled in vain. Since he had resolved to save Marthe, she had become more than ever the enemy of her own salvation. He soon saw that instead of bringing her into the plan he had devised, he had strengthened her resolve to undertake a contrary plan. He admitted to Arsène that instead of serving him, he'd made the situation worse; and so he returned to his neutral stance, consoling himself with the idea that Marthe was apparently not as unhappy as he had believed her to be.

At this point Laravinière would have left Monsieur Chaignard's building, if reasons unknown to our lovers hadn't rendered this dwelling safer and more propitious for certain projects that were secretly occupying him. Why shouldn't I say it today, now that the worthy Jean is no longer at the mercy of mankind, and those who shared his fate are, either from death or from absence, shielded from all persecution? Jean was conspiring. With whom, I never knew; I still don't know. Perhaps he was conspiring with himself; I don't think he was exploited, seduced, or dragged into it by anyone. With that ardent personality I well knew and the impatience to act eating him up inside, I always thought that he was a man more given to chiding the heads of his own party for their cautiousness and to going beyond their intent than to letting himself be outdone by them in an armed undertaking. My situation didn't permit me to be his confidant. Nor did I know or attempt to find out to what extent Arsène was in his confidence. What's certain is that Horace, brusquely entering Laravinière's room one day when he had forgotten to lock himself in, found him surrounded by standard-issue rifles that he had just taken out of a large trunk and that Laravinière was inspecting like a man well versed in the care of arms. In the same trunk were cartridges, powder, lead, a bullet mold, all that was needed to put the possessor of these dangerous relics before a court of law, and from there to the Place de Grève or Mont-Saint-Michel. Horace was in quite a state of gloom and destitution. He still had moments like that with Laravinière, although he had promised himself not to have them anymore.

"Oh, my!" he exclaimed, seeing Laravinière shut the chest precipitously. "So, you're playing that game? Well, don't hide them away. I sympathize with that way of seeing things; and, if you like, at the right time and place, entrust one of those clarinets to me, I also know how to play it."

"Are those your true thoughts, Horace?" answered Jean, fixing his little shiny green eyes on him like a cat. "You've scoffed bitterly at my revolutionary outbursts so often that I don't know if I can count on your discretion. Meanwhile, however little sympathy my struggle and my self may inspire in you, if you will remember that my head could be on the chopping block here, you won't amuse yourself, I hope, by joking out loud about my taste for firearms."

"I hope you're not anxious about that; and I repeat that, far from criticizing you, I approve of you and envy you. I, too, would like to have hope, to have convictions strong enough to get myself slashed up behind a barricade by a saber."

"Well, if you're so inclined, come see me. Look, Horace, isn't this a pen that a young poet like you could write a fine page with and make his name immortal?" As he said this he lifted quite a pretty carbine that he'd put aside for his personal use. Horace took it, weighed it in his hands, cocked and uncocked it, then sat down with it on his knees and fell into a deep reverie.

"What good is it to live in times like these?" he exclaimed when Laravinière, having locked up his dangerous treasures, gently took his favorite weapon from him. "Isn't it a life of failure and agony? Isn't it a dirty trap this society sets for us, when it says to us: Work, become educated, be intelligent, be ambitious, and you will succeed at everything! And, there's no seat so high up that you can't sit in it! What does it do, this lying and cowardly society, to keep its promises? What means does it give us to develop those abilities it demands of us and to use the talents we acquire for it? None! It shoves us aside, it refuses to recognize us, it abandons us, when it doesn't outright suffocate us. If we get restless about succeeding, it locks us up or shoots us; if we keep quiet, it looks on us with contempt or forgets us. Oh, you're right, Jean, exactly right to prepare for a glorious suicide!"

"Oh, if you imagine I'm thinking about my own glory, and that of my friends, you're very wrong," said Laravinière. "I'm perfectly content with society from my own standpoint. I enjoy absolute independence in it, I savor a delicious *dolce far niente*. I go through it as a veritable bohemian, and I have but one line of work, which is to conspire to overthrow it; since the people are suffering, and honor calls on those who are devoted to them. It's in God's hands!"

"The people! Now there's a big word for you," Horace responded. "But, and please don't take offense at this: I believe that you're as little concerned about them as they are about you. You love war and you're looking for it. That's it, my dear President: each obeys his own instincts. Look here, why should you love the people?"

"Because I'm one of them."

"You came from them; you're no longer one of them. The people sense so clearly that you have different interests from them that they leave you to conspire all by yourself, or practically."

"You don't know anything about it, Horace, and I don't have to justify myself; but rest assured that I'm sincere when I say I love the people. It's true I haven't lived much among them, and that I'm a sort of bourgeois, and that I have Epicurean tastes that will bother me one day if we have a Spartan regime that bans beer and my smokes. But what difference does all that make? All the people get are unacknowledged rights, friendless suffering, justice betrayed. It's an idea, if you like, but it's the great and true idea of our time. It's beautiful enough to fight for."

"It's an idea that will turn against you once you've proclaimed it."

"Why should it, if I don't disavow it myself? And why would I do that? How could I change? Does an idea die like a passion, like a need? Universal self-determination will always be a right: establishing it won't take just a day. There's enough work for my whole lifetime, if I don't meet death right at the beginning of it."

This was not the first time they had debated this subject. Jean always got the worst of it, even though he had truth and conviction on his side; his intellect was not quick and subtle enough to beat back all of his adversary's objections and mockery. Horace also wanted a republic, but he wanted it for the benefit of the talented and ambitious. He said that the people would get their due by placing their interests in the hands of intelligence and knowledge, that the duty of a leader was to work for the intellectual progress and well-being of the people; but he would not admit that the people themselves had to have some right to rule the actions of the men above them, or that they could make good use of such a right. A good deal of bitterness often entered into these discussions, and Horace's major argument against the bourgeois democrats was that they were always talking and never taking action.

When he had proof that Laravinière was playing an active role, or was about to, he began to respect him more, and felt sorry that he had hurt him. While still disputing the idea of a revolution for the benefit of the people, he believed in that revolution, and wanted to take part in it, to find glory, feeling, and impetus for his ambition, betrayed by the constitutional government. He asked Jean to trust him and became reconciled with him; and, either because it appeared that the masses were sympathetic, or because Laravinière had groundless illusions, Horace accepted that the movement would prove effective, and he enlisted under oath before Jean and threw himself into it at the first call, ready for any eventuality. He bought himself a rifle and made cartridges with childish ardor and joy.

From that point on Horace became calmer, more sedentary, and his temperament was smoother. The role of conspirator completely absorbed him. This role revived his dejected hopes; with it he secretly avenged himself on an indifferent society; and it gave him some bearing in his own eyes and a posture for the eyes of Jean and his comrades. He loved to worry Marthe, to see her turn pale when he made her anticipate the dangers to which he was dying to expose himself. He also lamented those dangers a bit ahead of time, and spread flowers on his grave, going so far as to write his own epitaph in verse. When he ran into Madame the Viscountess de Chailly at the Opera and she barely acknowledged him, he consoled himself by thinking that she might come and beg a favor of him when he became a powerful man, a great orator, or an influential pamphleteer in the republic.

Whether because the approaching events were not foreseen by others besides himself, or whether because hidden circumstances had delayed their realization, Laravinière was busy doing nothing but furbishing rifles while waiting for the revolution when cholera broke out in Paris and tragically distracted the masses from all political concerns.

I was in the field hospital, wrapped in my coat, on one of those cold nights in spring that seemed to increase the plague's intensity, and I was waiting, stealing from the enemy a quarter of an hour of restless sleep, for them to come and call me to attend to some new outbreak, when I felt a hand on my shoulder. I awoke abruptly, and getting up by habit, I was ready to follow the person who required me before I had completely opened my eyes, weighted down as they were with fatigue. It was only when she passed close to the red lantern suspended in the entry of the field-hospital that I thought I recognized her, despite the changes she had undergone.

"Marthe!" I exclaimed, "is that really you? God Almighty, whom have you come to get me for?"

"Whom do you think?" she said, clasping her hands together. "Oh, please hurry! Come on!"

I had already started off at her side.

"Does he have a very bad case?" I asked on the way.

"I have no idea," she told me, "but he's suffering a great deal, and his wits have been so affected that I fear for the worse. For several days now he's had forebodings, and today he told me several times that he was lost. Meanwhile, he ate a good dinner, he went to a show, and when he came home he had his supper."

"Any problems?"

"None; but he's in pain, and he told me in such strong terms to run to the field hospital that dread seized me at once, and I could barely hold myself up."

"You certainly are shivering, Marthe. Lean on my arm."

"Oh, it's just a touch of cold!"

"You're hardly dressed for such a cold night; bundle yourself in my coat."

"No, no, that would slow you down, let's walk!"

"Poor Marthe! You've gotten skinny," I said to her, walking briskly, while by the glow of the pale streetlamps I examined her thin cheeks, hollowed out even more by the shadow of her black hair, wafted at the will of the dry north wind.

"Just the same, my good health stays the same," she said to me, preoccupied. Then, suddenly, certain ideas connected for her that hadn't before: "Tell me instead," she exclaimed poignantly, "how Eugénie is doing."

"Eugénie is fine," I told her. "Her only complaint is having lost your friendship."

"Oh, don't say that!" she answered in a heartrending voice. "My God! Spare me that reproach! God knows I don't deserve it! Tell me instead that she still loves me."

"She still loves you tenderly, my dear Marthe."

"And do you still love Horace?" Marthe resumed, forgetting her personal interest and pulling me by the arm to make me run.

I ran, and soon we were by his side. He let out a piercing scream when he saw me, and threw himself into my arms:

"Ah, now I can die," he exclaimed warmly. "I have my friend back." And he fell into his armchair, pale and broken, as if he were ready to expire.

This prostration scared me a great deal. I took his pulse, which was barely perceptible. I examined him, put him to bed, questioned him attentively, and set about preparing to spend the night by his side.

He truly was sick. His brain had fallen prey to a melancholy exasperation, all his nerves were on edge; he was in a sort of delirium, he spoke of death, civil war, cholera, the scaffold; and mixing in his dreams the many ideas that possessed him, he took me first for an undertaker's assistant who had just thrown him into the fatal hearse, then for the executioner who was leading him to his doom. These moments of overexcitement were followed by fainting spells, and when he returned to his senses, he recognized me, squeezed my hands energetically, and clinging to me, begged me not to abandon him and not to let him die. I hadn't the least intention of doing so, and I went to torturous pains to diagnose his illness; but no matter how I looked at it, all I could see was a nervous excitation caused by an affectation of the mind. He hadn't the slightest symptom of cholera: no fever, no poisoning, no identifiable illness. Marthe hovered over him with a zeal that he didn't seem to notice, and, looking at her, I was so struck by her anxious, pining look that I begged her to go to bed. I couldn't get her to agree. Meanwhile, at daybreak, once Horace had calmed down and fallen asleep, she in turn fell into a doze in an armchair at the foot of the bed. I was at her bedside, and I couldn't help comparing Horace's face, full of strength and health, with that of this woman, so beautiful not long ago, and now no more than a ghost.

I was falling asleep myself, when, without waking anyone, Laravinière entered on tiptoe and sat down next to me. He himself had spent the night by the side of one of his friends who had been stricken with cholera, and, returning home, he had learned that Marthe had gone to the field hospital on Horace's behalf.

"What's the matter with him?" he asked me, leaning over to examine him. When I confessed to him that I didn't see anything serious, and yet he had kept me busy and worried all night long, Jean shrugged.

"Do you want me to tell you what it is?" he said to me, lowering his voice even more. "It's panic, nothing more. He's played these scenes two or three times for us; and if I'd been here tonight, Marthe wouldn't have gotten so frightened and troubled you. Poor woman! She's sicker than he is."

"So it seems. But you seem very hard on our poor Horace."

"No, I'm fair. I don't claim that Horace is what people call a coward;

in fact, I'm sure he's quite brave, and that he would resolutely stride into the heat of battle or a duel. No, his is the sort of cowardice common to all men who love themselves too much: he's afraid of sickness, pain, a death that's slow, obscure, and sad, of being found lifeless in his bed. He's what you would call 'effeminate.' I saw him once in the street resisting some suspicious characters who were trying to attack him, and his resolve made them back off; but I've also seen him faint dead away because of a little cut he got at the tip of a finger while sharpening his pen. He has a woman's nature, despite his Olympian Jupiter beard. He's capable of rising to heroism, he can't stand a little nick."

"My dear Jean," I answered, "every day I see men in the prime of their life and willpower, who are considered solid and wise, and for whom the thought of cholera (and even of a much lesser disease) renders them pusillanimous in the extreme. Don't think Horace is any exception. It's the exception who confronts illness with stoicism."

"Indeed, I'm not," he replied, "making a case against your friend; but I'd like poor Marthe to get used to his ways and not become alarmed every time it crosses his mind to think he's dead."

"Then that's the cause," I asked, "of her sad and crushed look?"

"Only one of many. But I don't want to play the role of the informant here. Up till now I've abstained from telling you what was going on. Since you've come back to their apartment, you'll judge for yourself soon enough."

In fact, when I returned the next day to reassure myself that Horace was in perfect health, I obtained from him, without too much urging, a confession of his troubles. "Well, yes," he said to me, responding to an observation I'd made, "I'm discontent with my fate, discontent with my life, and, why shouldn't I say it? Completely weary of living. One more drop of gall in my cup and I might just cut my throat."

"But only yesterday, when you thought you had caught cholera, you charged me eagerly not to let you die. I hope that you're exaggerating today's gloom."

"It's because yesterday my brain was ailing, I was crazy, I clung to life with an animal instinct; today I've regained my reason, I've regained my boredom, my disgust and horror for life."

I tried to talk to him about Marthe, for whom he was the one mainstay, and who might not survive if he succeeded in the crime of putting an end to his days. He made a gesture of impatience that approached fury; he looked into the next room, and after assuring himself that Marthe hadn't come back from her morning shopping: "Marthe!" he exclaimed. "Well, you've just named my scourge, my torture, my hell! I thought after all the predictions you had made to me about this that it would preserve my honor if I concealed from you the extent to which they have come true. Well, I don't have such foolish pride, and I don't know why, now that I've regained my best, my one friend, I should make a mystery of what's going on with me. So here's the truth, Théophile: I love Marthe, and yet I hate her; I idolize her, and yet I feel utter contempt for her; I can't separate myself from her, and yet I only exist when I don't see her. Explain that, you, who can explain everything, you who can theorize about love and who claims to be able to treat it like other illnesses."

"My dear Horace," I responded, "I believe it would be easy for me to at least describe the state of your soul. You love Marthe, I'm quite sure; but you want to love her more and you can't."

"That's exactly it!" he cried. "I aspire to a sublime love, I only experience a wretched one. I yearn to embrace the ideal, and I only grasp reality."

"In other words," I continued, trying to soften with a caressing tone what might sound like harsh words, "you would like to love her more than yourself, and you can't even love her as much."

He thought that I was treating his sorrow a trifle cavalierly; but everything he told me to try and modify an opinion that didn't seem to him to do justice to his suffering only served to confirm it. Marthe came back home, and Horace, who had to go out, left me with her. What I saw of their home life hardly inspired me to hope that I might be of use to them. Yet I didn't want to leave them without having fully confirmed for myself that I could do nothing to soften their misfortune.

I found Marthe as little disposed to let me penetrate the depths of her heart as Horace was prompt to open his to me. I should have expected as much: she was the offended party, she had just complaints against him, and her noble generosity condemned her to silence. To overcome her scruples, I told her that Horace had blamed himself, and had confessed all of his wrongdoing: which was true. Horace hadn't spared himself; he had unveiled his faults, while defending them against the egotistical cause to which I ascribed them. But this encouragement did nothing to alter the resolution Marthe seemed to have made; I noticed in her a somber courage and mournful despair that seemed inconsistent with the excitable enthusiasm and the sensitive openness I knew in her. She made excuses for Horace, told me that the fault was society's, whose implacable opinion forever tarnishes the fallen woman and keeps her from recovering by inspiring a true love. She refused to explain her future plans to me, speaking to me vaguely of religion and resignation.

She also refused the offer I made to bring Eugénie to her, saying that this reconciliation would soon be broken off by the same causes that had led to the original dissolution; and while protesting her deep affection for my friend, she implored me never to mention her again. The only idea that seemed rooted in her brain, because she came back to it several times, was that of a duty she had to fulfill, a mysterious duty, whose nature she didn't specify at all.

Carefully observing her bearing and her gestures, I thought I noticed that she was pregnant; she was so little disposed to confide in me that I did not dare to interrogate her on this matter, and put it aside for a more opportune moment.

When I had left her, my heart profoundly saddened by her suffering, by chance I passed a café where Horace was in the habit of going to read newspapers; he happened to be there, and he called to me and motioned for me to sit down next to him. He wanted to know what Marthe had said to me. I began by asking him if Marthe was indeed pregnant. It's impossible to convey the change that this word caused in his expression. "Pregnant!" he exclaimed. "Good God, *what* are you talking about? You think she's pregnant? Did she tell you she was? What a devil of a curse! That's all I need!"

"Why should news like that be so frightening?" I said to him. "If Eugénie announced the same to me, I'd count myself very lucky." He struck the table with his fist so hard that he made all the crockery in the place quake.

"You speak about it so nonchalantly," he said. "In the first place, you're philosophical, and add to that your three thousand francs of income and an estate. But me, what would I do with a child? At my age, with my poverty, my debts, and my parents who would be outraged! What would I feed it with? How would I raise it? Not to mention that I hate the little brats, and that a woman in confinement is for me the epitome of the horrible! . . . Oh, my God! That reminds me that she's done nothing but read *Emile* for the last two weeks! That's it, she wants to nurse her baby! She'll bring him up Jean-Jacques–style, in a room that's six feet square! Here I am a father—I'm lost!"

His despair was so comical that I couldn't help but laugh. I thought this was one of those inconsequential tirades that Horace loved to launch into, even on the most serious subjects, merely to create a little drama for his wit, just as one lets a fiery horse gambol a bit before making him take a measured pace. I had a positive impression of his heart, and I would have thought I was insulting him by solemnly instructing him on the duties his youthful paternity imposed on him. Besides, I might have been mistaken. If Marthe was in the predicament I supposed, could Horace not have known about it? We separated, with me still laughing about his sarcastic aversion to brats, and him continuing to declaim against them with inexhaustible verve.

At home, I found a list of new patients who had signed in. I had been a certified doctor since the previous autumn, and I was beginning my career with the sinister and grievous test of cholera. Suddenly I had a clientele more numerous than I would have liked, and my time was so monopolized for several days that I didn't see Horace again until a fortnight later. It was owing to a strange event that cut short all his bitter facetiousness about offspring.

He came into my apartment one morning, pale and worn out.

"Is she here?" was the first comment he addressed to me.

"Eugénie?" I said to him. "Yes, of course, she's in her room."

"Marthe!" he exclaimed agitatedly. "I'm speaking of Marthe; she's not at my apartment, she's disappeared. Théophile, I was right when I told you I should slit my throat; Marthe has left me, Marthe has fled with despair in her soul, perhaps with suicidal thoughts."

He let himself drop into a chair, and this time his terror and his consternation had nothing affected about them. We ran to Arsène's. I thought that this loyal friend of Marthe's might know about whatever arrangements she had made. We only found his sisters, whose astonished expressions immediately proved to us that they knew nothing about the matter and that they hadn't even had a presentiment of the motive for Horace's visit. As we were leaving we ran into Paul, who was coming home. Horace ran to meet him, and throwing himself into his arms with one of those spontaneous outbursts that made up for all of his past injustices:

"My friend, my brother, my dear Arsène!" he cried out of the fullness of his heart. "Tell me where she is, you know, you must know. Ah! Don't punish me for my crimes with your pitiless silence. Reassure me:

tell me she's alive, that she's entrusted herself to your safekeeping. Don't think I'm jealous, Arsène. No, at this late hour, I swear to God that I have only respect and affection for you. I consent to everything, I submit to everything! Be her support, her savior, her lover. I give her to you, I entrust her to you. Bless you if you can, if you must give her happiness; but tell me that she's not dead, tell me I'm not her executioner, her murderer!"

Although Marthe hadn't been named, since there was no other *she* in the world who could interest Arsène, he understood immediately, and I thought he was going to collapse as if struck by lightning. He was unable to respond for several seconds. His teeth chattered, and he glanced at Horace with a bewildered look, keeping in his cold, clenched hand the hand that the latter had held out to him. He made no comment. A mixture of dread and hope threw him into a sort of fierce delirium. He began running with us. We were going to the morgue. Horace had already thought about going there, but he hadn't had the courage.

We went in without him; he stayed on the porch, and leaned on the rail for support, but he avoided turning his eyes toward that atrocious sight, which he wouldn't have been able to stand if it included among the victims of poverty and passion the object of our search. We entered the hall, where several cadavers, laid out on the fatal slabs, offered to our glances the most hideous social plague, violent death in all its horror, the proof and result of destitution, crime, or despair. Arsène seemed to muster his courage again at the moment when Horace's grew weak; he approached a woman, the body of her baby entwined with her own; with a firm hand he lifted the black hair that the wind had plastered onto the face of the dead woman, and as if his sight had been muddied by a thick cloud, he leaned over that livid face, contemplated it for a second, and letting it fall back with an indifference that was certainly not habitual with him:

"No," he said in a strong voice; and he dragged me to repeat this *No* to Horace right away, which soothed him for the time being.

After a few steps, Arsène stopped: "Show me again," he said, "the note she left you."

Horace had told us about this note. He gave it back to Paul, who reread it carefully. It went as follows:

"Don't worry, dear Horace, I was mistaken. You won't have the burdens and vexations of fatherhood; but after all you've said to me for the last two weeks, I understood that our union could not continue without bringing about your unhappiness and my shame. We both should have prepared each other a long time ago for this separation, which will grieve you, I'm sure, but to which you will become resigned, when you think that we owed each other this act of courage and reason. Farewell forever. Don't look for me, it would be useless. Don't worry about me, I'll be strong and calm from now on. I'm leaving Paris; perhaps I'll go back to the region from which I come. I need nothing, I don't blame you for anything. Don't remember me with bitterness. I leave, calling down on you heaven's blessing."

This letter did not announce any sinister intentions; yet it was far from reassuring. I, in particular, had recently found in Marthe the symptoms of an irretrievable despair and the fierce energy that leads to extreme decisions.

"You must," I said to Horace, "concentrate again on the two of you, and tell us precisely what happened between you for the last couple of weeks; based on that, we'll judge what weight we should give our fears. Perhaps yours are exaggerated. It's impossible that you could have conducted yourself so cruelly as to push her to an act of madness. Marthe has a religious mind, she has perhaps a stronger character than you give her credit for. Speak, Horace, we pity you too much to think of blaming you, whatever you might say."

"Confess to you?" Horace answered, looking at Arsène. "That's a rough punishment; but I deserve it, and I accept it. I knew he loved her, that one, and that his love was more worthy of her than mine. My pride suffered from the idea that another besides myself could give her the happiness that I denied her; and I think that, in my fits of delirium, I would have killed her rather than see her saved by you!"

"May God forgive you!" said Arsène. "But own up to every last bit of it. Why did you make her so unhappy? Is it because of me? You know she didn't love me."

"Yes, I knew it!" said Horace, his pride and egotistical triumph returning, but just then his eyes grew moist and his voice thickened. "I knew it," he continued, "but I just didn't want her to value you, noble Arsène! It was an open wound for me, the way she could compare us in her heart of hearts. So you see, my friends, behind my vanity was remorse and shame."

"But in the end," Arsène said, "she didn't miss me enough, she didn't think enough about me, and it didn't cost her that much to forget me completely."

"She defended you for a long time," answered Horace, "with an energy that infuriated me. And then suddenly she stopped talking about you; she had resigned herself with a calm that seemed to defy and scorn me inwardly. It was during this time that poverty compelled me to let her resume working, and, although I appeared to have conquered my jealousy, I never could watch her go out alone without harboring a suspicion that tortured me. But I fought it, Arsène; I swear to you that I very rarely expressed it. Just a few times, in an angry tone I let an indirect reference escape my lips, that seemed to offend her and wound her mortally. She couldn't bear to be suspected of a lie, of a dissimulation as slight as it might be in my thoughts. Her pride rebelled against me more every day in a way that made me fear that her feeling would change or she would leave me. But for several weeks I succeeded in mastering my emotions, and, unjust as she was! she mistook my virtue for indifference.

"Suddenly an unhappy event stirred up the storm again. I believed that Marthe was pregnant; Théophile had put the idea into my head, and I was disheartened by it. Spare me the humiliation of telling you to what extent paternal feelings are undeveloped in me. Am I at the age where that instinct awakens in a man's heart? And then doesn't the horror of poverty make a calamity out of what could be a happy event in other circumstances? To make a long story short, I rushed back to my apartment about two weeks ago, when I left Théophile, and I interrogated Marthe, with more terror than hope, I confess. She left me in doubt; and then, irritated by the gloomy fears I was betraying, she declared that if she were lucky enough to become a mother, she wouldn't go and beg for support for her baby from a man of *my* station, who so poorly understood and accepted fatherhood. I saw in that a tacit appeal to you, Arsène. I flew off the handle; she treated me with crushing contempt.

"Since that day two weeks ago, our life has been a constant storm, and I haven't been able to clear up the aching doubt that started it. First she would say that she was six months along, then that she was not, and finally she told me that if she were, she would hide it from me, and would go and raise her child far away from me. I behaved atrociously in these arguments, I confess it, with tears of blood. When she denied that she was expecting, I provoked her into admitting it with a perfidious tenderness, and when she confessed, I broke her heart with my discouragement, my curses, and why shouldn't I tell you everything? with insulting doubts about her fidelity and bitter sarcasm about what happiness she expected for the heir to my debts, my laziness, and my despair. Yet there were moments of enthusiasm and repentance when I accepted this destiny with openness and a sort of feverish courage; but soon I reverted to the opposite extreme, when Marthe, with glacial disdain, said to me: 'You can calm down; I fooled you to see what kind of man you were. Now that I've taken the measure of your love and your courage, I can tell you that I'm not pregnant, and I assure you that if I were, I wouldn't claim to associate you with what I look upon as my one happiness in this world.'

"What can I tell you? Every day the wound became more inflamed. The day before yesterday our disagreement was more profound than the previous night, and then yesterday it became so excessive that it seemed a catastrophe was inevitable, if both of us hadn't become so blasé about such suffering. At midnight, after a quarrel that had lasted two endless hours, I was so scared by her pallor and despondency that I dissolved into tears. I went down on my knees, I kissed her feet, I suggested to her that she kill herself with me to put an end to our torturous love, instead of soiling it with a break. She answered me only with a piercing smile, raised her eyes to heaven, and remained for several moments in a sort of ecstasy. Then she threw her arms around my neck and pressed my forehead with her lips, parched from a slow fever. 'Let's not talk about that anymore,' she said to me then as she was getting up. 'What you're so afraid of won't happen. You must be very tired. Go to bed; I still have a little sewing to do. Sleep in peace; *I* have it, see for yourself!'

"In fact, she was very much at peace! And me, stupid and thick in my trust, I didn't understand it was the peace of death that was spreading over my life. I went to bed spent, and I didn't wake up till broad daylight. My first inclination was to look for Marthe, to thank her on my knees for her mercy. Instead of her, I found the fatal note. In her room, nothing spoke of a sudden departure. All was arranged as usual; only the chest of drawers that contained her threadbare apparel was empty. Her bed had not been mussed: she hadn't gone to sleep. The concierge had been woken up around three in the morning by the inside bell; he pulled the cord, as he does automatically in this time of cholera, when, at every hour, people go out to find or give aid. He didn't see anyone leave, he heard the door shut again. And I heard nothing. I was there, stretched out like a cadaver, while she carried out her escape, and tore the heart out of my chest, leaving me forever empty of love and happiness."

After the painful silence into which this narrative plunged us, we indulged in various conjectures. Horace was convinced that Marthe couldn't survive this separation and that if she had taken her clothes with her, it was to give her departure the appearance of a trip, the better to hide her suicidal intentions. I no longer shared his terror. I thought I could see in all of Marthe's conduct a feeling of duty and an instinct of maternal love that should have reassured us. As for Arsène, after we'd spent the day racing around and engaging in investigations as meticulous as they were fruitless, he parted ways with Horace, pressing his hand with an uneasy but solemn expression. Horace was despondent. "We must," Arsène said to him, "have more faith in God. Something tells me in the bottom of my soul that He has not abandoned the most perfect of his creatures, and that He's watching over her."

Horace pleaded with me not to leave him alone. Obliged to perform my duties for the victims of the epidemic, I could only spend part of the night with him. Laravinière, for his part, had been dashing around all day long looking for some sign of Marthe. We waited impatiently for his return. He came back at one in the morning having had no more luck than we did; but he found in his apartment a few lines from

Marthe, which the post had brought that evening. "You have showed so much interest in me and friendship for me," she said to him, "that I don't want to leave without bidding you farewell. I ask one last favor of you: reassure Horace on my account, and swear to him that nothing in my physical or mental situation should cause him to worry. I believe in God, that's the best I can say. Also tell *my brother* Paul. He will understand."

This note, while providing Horace with a certain tranquillity, revived his uneasiness on another point. Jealousy seized hold of him again. He found in the final words that Marthe had scribbled a warning, but also something like an indirect promise to Paul Arsène. "She had, while uniting with me," he said, "second thoughts that she always kept and that came back to her with every dissatisfaction I caused her. That's the thought that gave her the strength to leave me. She's counting on Paul, you can be sure of that! She maintains a certain respect for our relationship that prevents her from entrusting herself to another right away. I like to believe, besides, that Paul was not just play-acting with me today, and that in helping me search for Marthe even at the morgue, he didn't have in his heart the egotistical joy of knowing that she was alive but was already resigned to her loss."

"You shouldn't doubt him," I answered with spirit. "Arsène was suffering like a martyr, and I'm going right now, on my way home, to let him know about this last letter, so he may rest peacefully, even if only for an hour or two."

"I'll go myself," said Laravinière, "since his sorrow concerns me more than all the rest." And without paying attention to the irritated look Horace threw him, he took the note back out of his hands and left.

"You can see perfectly well that they're all in league against me!" exclaimed Horace furiously. "Jean is Paul's right hand and the emotional go-between of this chaste intrigue. Paul, who should understand full well, according to what Marthe says, how and why she *believes in God* (password that I also understand quite well, come on! . . .), Paul is running off to some prearranged spot where he will find her; either that or he will sleep like a log, knowing that, in two or three days consecrated to the tears that she thinks she owes me, the proud infidel will allow him to offer his consolations. All this is absolutely clear to me, although arranged with a certain artfulness. For a long time they have been hunting for a pretext to renounce me, and they had to put the blame on me. They had to be able to accuse me in front of my friends, and to bolster themselves against the reproaches of their consciences. Now they have it; they lured me into a trap by pretending, that is, *pretending to pretend*, that she is pregnant. You've innocently been the accomplice of this pretty machination; they knew my Achilles' heel: they knew that this possibility always made me tremble. They gave me the opportunity to be cowardly, ungrateful, criminal . . . And when they succeeded in making me hateful to others and to myself, they abandon me, all the while acting the merciful victim! Very clever! But I was the only one who was not fooled by it, since I remember how they abandoned the *Minotaur,* and how they remained hidden until the first squalls of anger and sorrow had passed. He, too, the poor imbecile, believed it was a suicide! He, too, went to the police and the morgue! He, too, no doubt, found a farewell note and pretty words of forgiveness at the end of a betrayal consummated with Paul Arsène! I think it's a note just like mine; the same one can work in all such circumstances! . . ."

Horace spoke for a long time in this extraordinarily acrimonious tone. I found him at this moment so absurd and unjust that, not having the courage to blame him openly, but not sharing his suspicions in the least, I kept silent. After all, I had to leave him on his own until the next day, so I preferred to see him revived by his bitterness than crushed by the unbearable anxiety of that day. I left him without saying anything that could influence his judgment.

When I came back to see him that afternoon, I found him in bed with a touch of fever and his nerves violently agitated. I tried to calm him down with fairly severe remonstrances; but I soon stopped, seeing that he wanted to be contradicted so he could vent his resentment. I rebuked him for having more spite than grief. Then he maintained that he was in despair, and speaking of his sorrow sent him into violent fits again; anger gave way to sobs. Right then Arsène came in. That generous young man, without a thought of Horace's insulting suspicions, which Laravinière hadn't hidden from him, came to try to do a little bit of good for him while dispelling them. He displayed such stature and dignity that Horace threw himself against his bosom, thanked him enthusiastically, and, switching from the most infantile aversion to the most exalted tenderness, begged him to be "his brother, his comforter, his best friend, the doctor of his sick soul and his delirious brain."

Although Arsène and I both felt strongly that all this was somewhat exaggerated, our hearts were softened by the eloquent words he knew how to choose to interest us in his misfortune, and we wanted to spend the rest of the day with him. Since his fever was gone, and since he had eaten nothing the night before, I brought him with Arsène to have dinner at my good man Pinson's. We ran into Laravinière on the way, and I invited him along, too.

At first our meal was silent and melancholy, as circumstances dictated; but little by little Horace became animated. I made him drink a little wine to restore his strength and to reestablish the equilibrium between his sanguine and nervous elements. Since he was normally a teetotaler, he felt the effects of two or three glasses of Bordeaux more readily than I had expected, and then he opened up and became full of energy. He seemed to redouble his friendship for all three of us, which at first we accepted warmly, but which soon upset Paul a little, and Laravinière quite a lot. Horace didn't catch on, and continued to enthuse, to sermonize first to one and then the other, hardly aware of what he was saying. With the memory of Marthe beginning to mix itself imperceptibly into his effusiveness, he indulged in the hope of finding her again, tossed this burning challenge in the face of heaven, boasted of how he could please her, make her happy, and, to let us in on his secrets, he regaled us with stories of the passion that he had inspired in her and depicted for us her ardor and devotion with a pride that was hardly decent. Arsène turned pale several times hearing Marthe's beauty and ineffable graces spoken of in such a novelistic fashion, with a warmth pumped up by vanity.

The fact is that Horace, restrained until then by our lack of encouragement and approval for his triumph over Marthe, had suffered from always savoring it in silence. Now that a common interest had fortuitously led us to speak to him openly, to question him, to listen to him, and to discuss with him this delicate subject, now that he saw all the respect and affection that we had for her whom he had so little appreciated, he experienced fresh satisfaction from the self-respect he gained from talking to us about her, and in recalling to himself the value of the treasure he had just lost. It was a pretext to make this treasure shine for us without his being guilty of fatuousness, and it was easy to see that he was half-consoled for his disaster by the right he claimed to recall his happiness. Although it tortured Arsène, he listened and even assisted Horace in this imprudent outpouring with a strange courage. Although the blood rose higher and higher in his face every moment, he seemed to have resigned himself to studying Marthe in Horace's imagination, as in a mirror that revealed her to him under a different light. He wanted to catch the secret of the love that his rival had had the good fortune to inspire. He knew very well how he had lost her, since he knew the serious side of Marthe's personality, but in his thoughts Arsène analyzed and commented on her romantic side, dominated as it had been by the passion of a senseless man, while hearing it portrayed by this senseless man himself. Several times he squeezed Laravinière's arm to keep him' from interrupting Horace, and when he had learned enough, he bade him farewell without bitterness or contempt, although that much levity and boasting certainly inspired in him a secret feeling of pity.

He had just left us when Laravinière, giving in to an indignation he'd kept under wraps for a long time, made several observations to Horace with a frankness that was a trifle harsh. Horace fumed, as they say. He gulped down coffee mixed with rum, though I objected to this excessive zeal, which went beyond the bounds of my prescription. He raised his head in surprise when he saw Laravinière's mute attention transformed into dry criticisms. But he was no longer in a mood to humbly tolerate a reproach: the fit of repentance and modesty had passed, vainglory had gained the upper hand. He answered Laravinière's cool disdain with bitter sarcasm about the ridiculous and ill-advised love that Laravinière imagined he felt for Marthe. Horace was witty; he succeeded in intoxicating himself on the verve of his responses and attacks. His remarks started to draw blood; he became angry while attempting to laugh and disparage. The dinner would have ended very badly if I hadn't intervened to cut short this extremely venomous discussion.

"You're right," Laravinière said to me, getting up, "I forgot I was speaking to a madman."

And after squeezing my hand, Laravinière turned his back on him. I took Horace home: he was completely pickled, his nerves more on edge than before. He had a new bout of fever, and since I still had to go visit my patients, I was afraid to leave him alone. I went downstairs to Laravinière's, who himself had just come in, and begged him to go up to Horace's.

"I'd like to," he said; "I'd do it for you, and also for Marthe, who charged me to do so if she knew him to be even the least bit sick. As for him, you see, he doesn't inspire the least interest on my part, I tell you. He's a fop who wraps himself in his pain, and who has infinitely less of it than you or I."

As soon as I left, Jean settled in by the bedside of his patient and watched him attentively for ten minutes. Horace cried out, shrieked, sighed, sat halfway up, declaimed, called Marthe first tenderly, then furiously. He wrung his hands, tore up his covers and practically ripped out his hair. Jean looked at him without saying anything and without budging, ready to counter any seriously delirious action, but resolved not to be duped by these dramas that he attributed to Horace's ability to act coldly in the midst of real misfortune.

In my eyes (and I believe I knew him as well as anyone could), Horace was not, as Jean supposed, a cold egotist. It's true he was cold; but he was also passionate. It's true that he had his share of ego; but at the same time he had a need for friendship, care, and sympathy that betokened a love of his fellow creatures. This need was so powerful in him that he was driven to childish ends, to a morbid sensitivity, to jealous domination. The egotist lives alone; Horace could not live a quarter of an hour without company. He had individuality, which doesn't at all translate as egotism. He loved others in proportion to himself; but he did love them, that's certain, and one could say without much sophistry that, not being able to abide solitude, he preferred the conversation of whoever came along to his own thoughts, and that, consequently, in a sense he preferred others to himself.

When Horace was sad, he had only one way to divert himself, and it was equally effective in regaining the hearts he'd wounded and in dispelling his own suffering: he got tired. This highly unusual fatigue, which occurred on the mental as well as the physical plane, consisted of giving his sorrow a violent external impetus, with words, tears, shouts, sobs, even with convulsions and delirium. It was not an act, as Laravinière thought; it was a truly severe and painful crisis that he entered into voluntarily. One can't say that he extricated himself from it the same way. Sometimes it prolonged itself beyond the moment when he felt it to be ridiculous or tiresome; but even the slightest external event could put a stop to it. A firm rebuke, a threat from the person whom he took as comforter or victim, the sudden offer of a diversion, any surprise whatsoever, a minor bruise or slight scratch incurred while gesticulating or in falling down: that was enough to lead him from the most violent overexcitement to the most docile tranquillity, and that for me was the surest proof that his emotions were not play-acting; since if he were as great an actor as Jean claimed, he would have managed more adroitly the transition from pretense to reality.

Laravinière was merciless with him, as those who control themselves and keep their self-possession are with those who become excited and throw off all restraint. If he had performed the duties of a doctor or nurse, he would soon have learned that between children and madmen there is a type of individual who is simultaneously fervent and weak, irritable and docile, energetic and indolent, affected and naive, in a word, cold and passionate, as I said above, and I repeat it to establish a fact that is widely enough observed, although it is generally regarded as improbable. Men like that are often mediocre, though they're sometimes of superior intelligence. In general it's the emotional and complicated temperament of artists that exhibits more or less these phenomena. Although they exhaust themselves with these frequent abuses of their capacity for exuberance, one sees them seeking, with a sort of fatal greediness, every possible means of excitement, and willingly provoking those storms that have only too much real violence in them. That's how Horace used his delirium and despair, as others use opium and strong liquor.

"He just has to shake himself up a bit," said Jean, "and right away his fury comes as if by magic, and you would think him possessed by a thousand passions and ten thousand devils. But threaten to leave him, and you will see him calm down suddenly like a child whose nursemaid threatens to leave him without a candle."

Jean didn't realize that in Bicêtre there are furious madmen who would kill themselves if left to their own devices, and that the threat of a little cold water on their heads immediately makes them fearful and silent.

"But," he said, "Horace makes all that racket so he will be heard, and when no one bothers about him, he decides to sleep or go for a walk." Unfortunately, Jean was right, and, in this regard, the poor child was inexcusable. His crises did him good: they attracted interest, care, devotion; and then those who were attached to him made a thousand attempts and found a thousand ways to distract and console him. One flattered him, and picked up his wounded pride; another complained about him, and made him more interesting in his own eyes; a third took him to the theater despite himself, and cured for the price of the entertainment the boredom that Horace's destitution imposed on him. In short, he enjoyed being ill, like a little schoolboy who goes to the infirmary to get some rest and treats, and, like a conscript who mutilates himself to avoid the army, he made himself very sick to escape a painful duty.

Unfortunately for him, he had to deal that night with the strictest of his guardians. He knew it, but he flattered himself that he could conquer and dominate him with a major deployment of suffering. He purposely raised his temperature and made himself as sick as he could. Laravinière was cruel.

"Listen," Laravinière told him in a glacial voice, "I have no pity for you. You deserve to suffer, and you're not even suffering as much as you deserve. I find your whole conduct blameworthy, and I despise regret after the fact. You've got flatterers, blind followers, I know; but I also know that if they had seen you as close up as I have, instead of spending the night keeping vigil over you, as I'm doing, they would be crowing over you. By treating you roughly while keeping the secret of your misery, I'm doing you a greater service than all of the ninnies who spoil you with their admiration. But listen well to this last bit of advice. Those flatterers will get to know you, and they will despise you; and you'll be the butt of their jeers if you don't start soon to be a man and to behave accordingly; because it isn't becoming to a man to cry and bite his knuckles for a woman who leaves him. You have other things to do, and you're not even thinking of them. A revolution is brewing, and if you're weary of life, as you claim, there's a very simple means of dying fruitfully and with honor for other men. Decide if you want to asphyxiate yourself like a cast-off grisette, or fight like a generous patriot."

That was the only consolation that Horace received from the President of the Bousingots, and he had to accept it. It was too late to deny how logical and advisable it sounded; since, before Marthe's flight, before the onset of this great despair he was feeling, he had committed himself, whether out of vanity, or boredom, or ambition, to take part in the first engagement. If Jean were to be believed, this opportunity would not be long in presenting itself. Horace boldly called for it in his prayers; and Jean, whose weak point was to forgive all, just as long as a rifle was the means of expiation, promptly gave Horace his respect again, his trust, and his devotion. He agreed to care for him for several days, to walk with him, and to excite him with preparations for the great day that he promised each day would come tomorrow, and Horace, resuming the preparations for his death, stopped crying over Marthe and no longer dared speak of her.

A month had gone by since that young woman had disappeared. None of us had been able to find out anything about her; and this profound silence on her part, to which Eugénie and Arsène flattered themselves to have been the exceptions, threw us into a mournful dismay. I began to believe that she had gone far from Paris to hide her suicide, or at least a serious illness, a melancholy death, and I did not dare divulge to friends the comments I was making to myself. I think the same discouragement took hold of the others. I hardly ever saw Arsène anymore. Horace no longer uttered the name of that ill-fated one, and he seemed to be nourishing sinister projects that he gave me glimpses of in a tragic and somber way. Eugénie often cried in secret. Laravinière was more conspiratorial than ever, and politics completely absorbed him.

In the meantime, the elder Madame de Chailly wrote to me that cholera had just broken out in the little town neighboring her lands. She trembled, not for herself (of whom she quite simply never thought), but for her friends, for her family, for her peasants, and invited me in the most urgent and affectionate manner to come and spend this sad period in her region. There were no doctors in our countryside; cholera had run its course in Paris. I saw I had a duty to fulfill, out of both humanity and friendship, since all of my father's former friends were in danger. I prepared to leave, and to take Eugénie with me.

Horace came several times to say goodbye. He congratulated me on being able to leave "this awful Babylon." He envied my fate in every way, he said, and would very much have liked to get away with me. Finally, I saw that he needed to unburden himself, and, postponing for a few hours my preparations for departure, I took him to the Luxembourg Garden and entreated him to explain himself. He let himself be coaxed quite a while, although he was dying to speak. Finally he said:

"Well, I have to open my heart to you, even though I'm bound by a frightful oath. I can't act blindly in such a serious matter; I need good advice, and only you can give it to me. Let's see! Put yourself in my shoes: if you had sworn on your life, on your honor, on everything sacred, to share the convictions and to further the efforts of a man in political matters, and if suddenly you understood that this man was mistaken, that he was going to commit an error, compromise his cause . . . I'll go one step further: if your ideas had surpassed his own, and if his principles had become absurd in your now open eyes, do you think he'd have the right to despise you? Do you think anyone in the world could blame you for abandoning the cause and for breaking with his motives on the eve of plunging in? Tell me, Théophile; this is very serious. My reputation is at stake, my conscience, my whole future."

"In the first place," I said to him, "I'm pleased to hear you speak of your future, since for the last month your gloomy ideas and continual thoughts of death have had me scared. Now you take me for the arbiter of a political fact or feeling. I'm quite embarrassed; you know how equivocal my position is on this ground. Son of a gentleman, friend and relative of Legitimists, I have a certain exterior dignity that's fairly delicate to maintain. Although my principles, my certainties, my faith, my sympathies may be even more democratic than those of Laravinière and his confederates, I cannot (how strange and painful!) give them my hand to take a single step in their ranks. I'd look like a deserter; I'd be scorned in the camp where I was brought up; I'd be rebuffed and mistrusted by the camp to which I would offer myself. My fate is that of a number of sincere young people who can't repudiate overnight the religion of their fathers, yet who still have a warm heart and a reliable hand. They sense that the cause of the past is lost, that it doesn't deserve to be fought for any longer, that the victory of the innovators is just and holy. They would like to be able to raise the new colors of equality, a principle that they love and practice. But there is the question of conventions that they are not permitted to violate and that, in every way, they are forced to respect, although, in every way, they know how arbitrary, hollow, and unjust those conventions are.

"So I'm forced to withdraw from any participation in political action; and when I'm an elector, I absolutely don't know if it will be possible for me to vote with the impartiality and discernment that I'd wish to bring to that noble function. In a word, I'm refraining until further notice, and who knows for how many years, from making a philosophical judgment on the men and things of my time. It's sometimes very painful, when I remember that I'm twenty-five and that I have the fervor and courage of my youth; it's also an infinite pleasure when I consider that political passions, with their errors, their strayings, their involuntary crimes, are forbidden to me for a long time, and that without being cowardly I can preserve my social creed in all its candor. But how can a man so separate from your movements and isolated from your agitating show you the way you should take, you, republican by nature, by status, and, so to speak, by birth."

"What you're saying," Horace replied, "gives me a lot to think about. So there's a way of loving the republic, and practicing its principles, other than blindly throwing oneself headlong into the flawed movements that are preparing its advent? Yes, certainly, I knew it, I felt it, and I've been thinking about it for a long time now! There's a domain of philosophical perseverance and action above these passing storms! It's a truer, purer, loftier point of view than all the speechifying and riotous conspiracies."

"I only settled the matter," I answered, "for myself and because of my situation, which you might call the exception in the current movement. I don't know what I'd do in your shoes; meanwhile, I can tell you that if I were royalist, Legitimist, and Catholic, like the majority of young people of my caste, I wouldn't hesitate to follow the Duchess of Berry, as I would any true principle."

"You would take part in a civil war?" said Horace. "Well, that's exactly what they're suggesting to me, that's where they want to lead me. And I loathe such means. I expect better from Providence."

"Indeed! In that case, you're renouncing any active role, since a parliamentary revolution would take at least a century, the way things are at present."

"A century! The people won't wait a century!" exclaimed Horace, forgetting the personal question in the general question.

"Then just be at peace with yourself," I said to him: "either there will be violent revolutions, and consequently speedy and fierce conflicts among our citizens, or there will be long debates with words, a patient struggle of principles, progress that's certain, but slow, where we'll have nothing to do, you and me, except to profit, for our benefit, from the lessons of history. That's already quite a bit, and I'm content with it."

"It will come sooner than you think; and as for me, I'm definitely counting on helping with the work, either with spoken words or with the pen, if I can find a tribune or a newspaper."

"In that case, you won't hesitate to decline to take part in any riot, and I approve of your courageous steadfastness, since temptation is strong, and I myself, who can't take part in them, often have a hard time resisting them."

"Yes, undoubtedly, that would take great courage," said Horace emphatically, "but I *will* have it, since I *must* have it. My conscience is bitterly reproaching me for having let myself be dragged into these incendiary projects; I obey it. You've done me a great service, Théophile, in explaining me to myself. I thank you for it."

I didn't see in what way I had enlightened Horace on a point that he had posed quite clearly since he'd begun to explain it; and, finding him so much in accord with himself, I was going to leave him, when he detained me.

"You haven't answered my question," he said to me.

"You haven't asked me one that I know of," I responded.

"By God!" he resumed, "I asked you if any of my friends or those who supposedly think as I do, if Jean the Bousingot, for instance, could presume to blame me, seeing me renounce the folly of violent conspiracy, to return to the wider and more moral path from which I should never have strayed."

"From what you've said to me," I answered, "I see that you're at fault. You swore a certain allegiance . . ."

"That's my secret," he said suddenly. Then he added: "I know of no allegiance, nor conspiracy, but Laravinière is a madman, a fanatic, as you very well know. He makes no secret of it among his friends, and no one is unaware that he's in the front ranks of any scuffle in the neighborhood. You certainly must have foreseen that we wouldn't live in the same building for several months without his speaking to me of his revolutionary dreams. In a moment of despair for all things and of complete surrender of myself, I desired emotion, battle, danger, and (why shouldn't I admit it?) a tragic death, to which some glory would be attached. Like a child I let myself go, and, if I'm quitting as of today, he won't fail to say I'm retreating. With his rough heroism, he will accuse me of being afraid, and I'll be forced to fight him to prove to him that I'm not a coward at all."

"God save us from such an event!" I exclaimed. "At all costs, avoid having your throat slit by one of your best friends. But I don't think he will respond with the violence and brutality that you imagine. A frank and loyal explanation of your thinking, of your principles and your resolutions, would help him judge your character more soundly."

"Unfortunately," Horace responded, "Jean has neither ideas nor principles. His ardent resolutions are the result of his bellicose instincts, of his sanguine humor, as you would say. He won't understand me, and he will make allegations against me; and then there's a much more serious danger than that of irritating him and crossing swords with him: it's the noise he will make about my supposed defection among his companions, Bousingots, brawlers and mischief-makers, who only know how to speechify in the taverns, sing the "Marseillaise" out of tune, trade a few punches with the coppers, and vanish with the smoke of the first gunshot. Supposing that their mad undertakings succeed, that the people choose sides for them and with them one fine day, that the bourgeois government is sent packing, and that an attempt at a republic begins; those people, who are nothing more than busybodies, will pass themselves off as heroes. There's so much charlatanism in this world, and revolutionary movements are so good at favoring that nasty quality, that they might be proclaimed the saviors of the nation. Then they will already have one foot in the door, and I'll be tossed aside and blamed by them for having hidden my head in the sand on the day of danger. Look! The most ridiculous things sometimes have serious consequences. Do you know that the main leaders of the opposition in 1830 lost much of their influence with the masses for having disavowed the riot of July 27th, and for having barely understood, on the 28th, that it was a revolution? All the more reason why I, an obscure young man, who up till now have only had this wretched nucleus of Bousingot students with which to bolster and develop myself, will be tarnished and blemished at the outset of my career, by the arrogant memories and the stupid accusations of those people. What do you think of that? That's what I'm asking you."

"I'll answer you, my dear Horace, by saying that anything is possible, but that there's one sure way of escaping such accusations: that is to be logical, and not to take part in any violent action, tomorrow even less so than yesterday. Either you're philosophical, like me; or you're revolutionary, like our friend Jean. There's no middle ground. If you keep your ambitious dreams, you need the opinion of the masses on your side. You still have no other circle than a small coterie; you must please this coterie, march with it, and obey it in order to convince it, and then dazzle it and dominate it later on. If you think as I do, that the moment has not yet come for serious men to see their principles realized; if you believe (as you said at the beginning of this conversation) that the undertakings you're being pushed into compromise the cause of freedom, you must be firmly resolved in advance not to seek personal advancement from an unexpected outcome. You must postpone your political career to a more distant hour. You're young; you may see the triumph of civilization by means that conform to your moral principles."

Horace didn't answer me, but walked home with me, dreamy and sad. Arriving at my door, he thanked me for my advice, declared it logical and rational, and left me without saying a word about what decision he had reached. I was going to leave the next morning.

That evening, worried about the manner in which we had parted, and fearing that he might have resorted to some dangerous resolve, I went to his apartment, but I didn't find him in, and Monsieur Chaignard told me in the most gracious manner:

"Monsieur Dumontet left for the provinces an hour ago. He received a letter from his parents; his mother is at death's door. The poor young man left very upset. He entrusted half his belongings to me as a deposit. No doubt he will return in a few days."

I went up to Laravinière's. "Have you seen Horace?" I asked him.

"No," he said to me, "but Louvet saw him get into a stagecoach with a look that showed so little affliction that it seemed he was going to inherit his uncle's fortune rather than bury his mother."

"Really, you hate him too much," I exclaimed, "you're cruel to him: Horace is a good son, he adores his mother."

"His mother!" answered Jean, shrugging. "She's no more sick than you or I."

He didn't choose to elaborate.

Cholera ravaged the town next to our land; but it didn't cross the river, and the inhabitants of our left bank were spared. While waiting for another possible outbreak, I remained on my small estate, visiting the Chailly family each day. Their chateau was situated a quarter of a league away, and I carefully watched over my old friend the Countess, and over her grandchildren, who occupied her attention more than they did that of their mother, the marvelous Viscountess Léonie.

The latter, although kind to me in her manners, met more and more with my displeasure. It was not a question of her lacking wit, or personality. She had certain shining qualities on the surface that had an equal attraction for the very affected and the very ingenuous: the latter taking her in good faith for the superior woman she wanted to be; and the former subscribing to her pretensions, provided that she honor their tacit pact that she acknowledge *them* as superior men. In Chailly, as in Paris, she had a small court, fairly ridiculous, even more ridiculous than its Parisian counterpart, since she recruited it from among several rustic squires, persons of adulterated elegance whom she mocked cruelly with the elegant beings of finer alloy she had brought from Paris. These young people of local vintage put on airs to attain the stature of her high wit, only rendering themselves more foolish; but they rode with her, followed her in the hunt, buzzed along her bridle path, or flitted around her stirrups, not realizing that they were welcome only to add numbers to her cortege and to make the women in the province say, spitefully, that the Viscountess monopolized all the men in the county.

The Countess, accustomed to the luxury of good company, kept to herself in the chateau. She supervised the children, the tutors, and the governesses, tillage of the land, and household order. Alert and vigilant despite her advanced age, she was so essential to the indolent Léonie that the Countess received her respect and gratitude, even though nothing could induce affection to enter the picture. The Viscount, her son, was at most a nonentity, carelessly indulgent and disposed to permit his wife anything provided she didn't trouble him in any way. Rich and narrow-minded, he was more concerned with spending his fortune on the young ladies of the Opera than in increasing it with his mother's help. He was almost always in Paris, and, to excuse his somewhat questionable absences, he scrupulously performed the shopping errands his wife the Viscountess entrusted to him for her toilette. That was their true conjugal bond, and the secret of their mutual understanding. The poor man loved his children instinctively, and his mother with more tenderness than he'd ever had for another; but he didn't understand her, and he was incapable of giving his children guidance. To an outsider, everything about this family breathed union and harmony, while in reality this was not a family at all, and without the absolute and indefatigable devotion of that elderly woman who was its head and providence it would not have been possible for the others to live together twenty-four hours under the same roof.

I had been in the area only a handful of days when I received a note from Horace, postmarked from his hometown. "My mother is saved," he informed me. "I return to Paris next week; I'll pass within twenty leagues of your house. If you're still there, I could make a detour and come and chat with you for a few hours under the linden trees of your birthplace. A word, and I change my itinerary to accommodate you."

Eugénie pouted when I told her I had responded to this note with an eager invitation; but as soon as Horace arrived she accorded him the hospitality of our humble manor with the dignified graciousness that was second nature to her.

Madame Dumontet had not been as gravely ill as her husband had initially feared when he had written to Horace. Cholera hadn't touched that area, and Horace had found his mother practically recovered; but he was not able to extricate himself immediately from his parents' embrace, and had he yielded to their desire, he would have spent the entire summer with them.

"You know, that little town has become *intolerable* to me," he said, "and I felt a hundred times more strongly than ever that I'm through with my poor region. What a life, my friend, that sordid penny-pinching that they use as a pretext to vegetate without honor, joy, or usefulness! What people these provincials are: envious, ignorant, bigoted, and vain! If I had to stay three full months among them, I swear to you I'd shove a pistol in my mouth!"

The fact is that modest habits, the mildly teasing sense of control, and the compulsory obscurity of small towns were irreconcilable with the tastes and needs that education had instilled in Horace. His good parents had done everything to make sure he would be that way, and yet they were naively stupefied by the results of their ambition. They understood nothing of the enormous expenses incurred by this young man who seemed to them so disdainful of the pleasures of their town, the public dancehall, the café, traveling actresses, hunting, etc. They grieved at the mortal boredom that overcame him around them, which he didn't have the strength to hide. His intolerance for their prudence in political matters; his sour contempt for their old friends; his disgust for the caresses and attentions of his rustic relatives; his melancholy with no avowed cause; his proclamations against the century of money (coupled with his own great need for currency); his somber and uneven disposition; his mysterious reticence on the subject of women, love, and marriage; these made up so many profound and devouring sorrows for his parents, and above all for his poor mother, who thought she detected in him a case of exceptional, unheard-of unhappiness, not seeing that the other offspring of the province, raised as he had been, also cursed their fate as he did.

A few hours of discussion with Horace apprised me fully of his family's anxiety, all the boredom he had felt as a result of it, all the ways he'd been wrong—although these he didn't admit to me except by presenting them as the inevitable consequence of his position. He was *obsessed* by the worried questions his father had permitted himself to ask about his studies and his plans. He was *tortured* by his mother's suggestions and entreaties about his work and expenses. Finally, after his recriminations, proclamations, and tears of rage and tenderness while painting a picture for me of the blind and unintelligent love of the dear and unbearable authors of his being, he ended by telling me that he had an immoderate need to be distracted so that he could shake off his disgust, and he asked me to take him to the chateau of the Chailly family, where he had heard that a fine hunting party was being organized.

One hour later he was invited by the Countess herself, who interrupted her walk to rest a moment at my house, as was her wont. She had understood Eugénie at first glance and had developed a benevolent sympathy for her. Horace was struck by the friendly familiarity with which this great lady sat next to this daughter of the people, the medical student's mistress, the simple and affectionate way she spoke to her. He also took note of the good sense and dignity that Eugénie brought to this conversation with the Countess. From that day on he had a respect for her which rarely flagged, and forswore almost all of his former biases.

Horace's arrival at the chateau was a stroke of good luck for the Viscountess, who was beginning to be bored by her entourage and who remembered having found this young man witty and original. She reproached him good-naturedly for having neglected her in Paris.

"You must have found our home boring," she said to him in that tone in which flattery and mockery are so close it's difficult to tell which of the two is being conveyed. "Perhaps we will be less so here; and besides, in the country, one is less particular."

"It's just for that reason that I summoned the courage to present myself to you, Madame," replied Horace with an impertinent humility that was not badly received.

The Viscountess was no better connoisseur of true intellect than she was of true merit. In a man she looked for one ability, and one ability alone: knowing how to praise and flatter a woman. With a glance she sized up the effect she would have on the mind of a new arrival; and if she had no hold over that mind, she took no unnecessary pains, she treated him immediately as an enemy. Therein lay her tact. She made herself vulnerable to no one, and no enmity caused her to retreat. She knew how to acquire enough partisans not to fear adversaries. To judge the men who approached her she had, therefore, but one yardstick: whoever did not value her was considered, with no turning back and no appeal, as a lout, a cad, or a fool; whoever paid attention to her and sought her attentions was noticed and enrolled in advance among the ranks of her favorites or her protégés. She liked timid manners, the emotion of a young adorer; but she liked the audacity of an enterprising fop even more.

Cold and sickly, the Viscountess couldn't be completely wanton; but she was flirtatious and licentious in her own way, and bestowed the apparent rights to her heart, all sorts of hopes, and small favors on several men at the same time, while managing to make each of them think that he was the first and last she had loved or would love. As there is no bad character that does not derive, as they say, some good qualities from its faults, one could add in her praise that she was not hypocritical and that she did not affect principles which she did not have. She showed a good deal of independence in her ideas, and eccentricity in her conduct. She believed in no virtue; but, blaming no vice, she spoke of other women more fairly than women in society normally do. She did it without inhibition or ill will, not priding herself on feminine modesty in this regard, having no more of it than she had passion.

Horace didn't even think of doubting that feminine superiority which sought out his veneration. He accepted her from the outset, not only because she was rich, patrician, courted, and well adorned, and because all of that was new and seductive to him, but also because he judged people and responded to them absolutely the same way she did, with affection or antipathy according to whether he was liked or disdained. From the very first day that he and the Viscountess traded glances, this mutual need for the admiration of others, which possessed them, had been evident. Their reciprocal vanities grappled with each other hand to hand, challenging and attracting each other like two champions greedy to measure their strength and win glory at the other's expense.

All night long the Viscountess thought about the three outfits she would wear the next day. First she appeared in the morning on the steps of the front entrance in a robe so white, so fine, so flowing that it recalled Desdemona singing the willow song. Then, while her hair was being done, she dressed in a riding habit from the time of Louis XIII, hazarding a black feather over her ear, which would have been in bad taste in the woods of the Bois de Boulogne, but which looked extremely smart and graceful in the middle of the forest of Chailly. Returning from the hunt, she put on a rustic outfit of exquisite taste, and covered herself in so many perfumes that it gave Horace a migraine.

As for him, he woke up before dawn to rig himself out as a proper hunter; thanks to my wardrobe, he succeeded in improvising for himself a costume that was not too redolent of a Paris law student. I warned him that my horse was a trifle high-spirited, and obtained a promise to treat him gently. They left on reasonably good terms; but when the horseman was caught in the crossfire of the Viscountess's glances, he forgot my advice entirely and had some nasty dealings with his mount. The spectators remarked that he had no idea how to rein a horse.

"You're riding like a daredevil, my dear boy," shouted the Count de Melleraie in a familiar tone. The Count was the Viscountess's principal adorer. "You will be crushed against the rampart."

Horace found this lesson to be in bad taste, and, to show his contempt for it, he made his horse rear up in anger. He was fearless and strong, and though he'd had few lessons in horsemanship, and knew quite well that he couldn't struggle with art and science against the seasoned and pedantic riders who surrounded the Viscountess, he at least desired to eclipse them in boldness. He succeeded in frightening the woman of his dreams so much that she went pale and pleaded with him to be more careful. The desired effect had been produced, and Horace's triumph over his rivals was assured. Women prize courage over dexterity. The men maintained that he was a detestable sort. All of them declared they would not lend a horse to such a madman; but the Viscountess told them that not one of them would dare commit such wild excesses and risk his life in such a carefree manner. As she saw quite clearly that all of Horace's swagger was in her honor, she was infinitely grateful to him, and she paid attention to him alone during the hunt. Horace helped her along wonderfully by barely leaving her side, and by showing for the hunt itself all the indifference he could muster. He knew as little about hunting as he knew about riding, and since he only made mistakes at it, he affected a profound contempt for such a boorish passion.

"Why, then, did you come?" Madame de Chailly said to him, hoping to elicit a gallant response.

"I came to be near you," said he without ceremony.

That was more than the Viscountess had expected. But circumstances were in Horace's favor, since this abrupt declaration which he had thrown out, and which better breeding would have made him express more delicately, seemed to the one who received it the product of a violent passion, ready to dare anything. This woman, of debatable beauty and dubious heart, had never been loved. She had been besieged and pursued out of curiosity or vanity. Never had she been desired, and she herself desired nothing so much as to inspire a runaway love, even if it were to compromise the reputation for delicacy, taste, and pride that she had painstakingly fashioned for herself. Perhaps she hoped that such a love would awaken in her an enthusiasm she had never known. But certainly her imagination was sated in all other respects; her vanity had been jaded by her witty and coquettish triumphs, and she had never experienced the transports that beauty kindles and passion feeds. She was weary of sycophancy, solicitude, and insipidness. She wanted to see mad acts committed for her; she wanted not just excitement, but intoxication. And Horace seemed completely disposed to this role of furious and bold lover, the novelty of which would put a stop to the languidness and the boredom of vulgar loves.

And yet this poor woman had had a friend in her life, she had even kept him. It was the Marquis de Vernes, who, when he was fifty years old, had been her first lover. This had all transpired roughly twenty years earlier and the world had never learned of it, or was never certain of it. Friend of the family, this skillful rake had taken advantage of the first grounds for resentment the unfaithful Viscount de Chailly had given to his wife. The Marquis had been the confidant for Léonie's sorrows, and he had abused this privilege to seduce an inexperienced child, who looked up to him and trusted him as a father. Until that time this unfortunate girl had had no other fault than vanity; this frightful start in life, with an old libertine, developed vices in her heart and her intellect. She was horrified by her fall, felt herself debased, and thought herself lost forever, if, by skill and flirtation, she couldn't succeed in recovering from it. The Marquis helped her—not because he was subject to remorse, but because, in the sort of morality he had constructed out of his vices, he made it a point of honor not to stain a woman in her own eyes and those of society.

He was a peculiar man, mysterious, profoundly cunning, and coldly dissembling, in the midst of which a certain loyalty reigned. Born to be a diplomat, but estranged from that career by the events of his life, he put his secret power to work to satisfy his passions, not without vanity, but at least without scandal. Indeed, he took pride in being what society women refer to as a "safe man"; and although from his sweetly cynical glance, his delicately obscene manner of speaking, his finely dogmatic tone concerning the intrigues of love, one recognized a superior type of libertine, a debauchee of the highest order, never did the name of one of his mistresses, though she be dead for forty years and have acquired an odor of saintliness, escape from his lips; never was a woman compromised by him. Rejected, he never complained; betrayed, he never sought revenge. And the number of his conquests was legendary, even though he had always been quite ugly. Not loving at all with his heart, and well knowing that he owed his triumphs only to his cleverness, he had never been loved; but he made himself necessary everywhere, and he had kept his rights longer than men who, though loved, detract from one's reputation and repose. When he desired someone, he was the most dangerous persecutor in the world, fascinating for his perseverance and icy boldness. As soon as he possessed, however, he became once more not merely inoffensive, but even useful and precious. He conducted himself generously, performed the most delicate acts of devotion, worked to repair the lives of the women he had sullied, in a word, improved in public, by his manner, speech, and conduct, the reputation of her whom he had dishonored in private. He did all of this coldly, systematically, molding all his intrigues into three distinct phases: trick, subjugate, and keep. During the first act, he inspired confidence and friendship; during the second, shame and fear; during the third, gratitude and even a sort of respect: bizarre result of a love that was simultaneously the most disloyal and the most chivalrous that ever crossed the human brain.

Viscountess Léonie was one of the Marquis's last victims. From then on, she was the woman to whom he was most devoted. With her, the unspeakable drama of seduction had been more serious for him than with most others. She was not in the slightest bit carried away by him, and he had been forced to attack and to flatter her vanity, perhaps more ingeniously and more patiently than he ever had in his life. His sad victory aroused a profound disgust in Léonie, a bitter resentment, neighbor to hatred and fury. She had threatened to unmask his conduct to her family, to demand that her husband seek revenge, even to obtain justice on her own by stabbing him. This violent reaction on her part was not the result of outraged virtue, but of wounded and humiliated pride. For her, so lofty, so smitten with herself, to belong to an old man, ugly and cold! She almost died, and it was the worst sorrow of her life. For the first time the Marquis felt scared, and he labored to reassure her and to raise her up in her own eyes with a care and a zeal that surpassed all his previous miracles in this realm. The last thing he wanted was to leave a disdainful and vindictive soul with such a hateful memory. He went to the extent of pretending remorse, despair, and passion, and he did it so well that the Viscountess thought herself the first love of this blasé old man.

The Marquis's first act of healing was to find and give to her a lover who could console her ego, and he succeeded in this without that man ever suspecting his intentions or discovering his conquest. Léonie didn't know that the Marquis acted in this manner with all the women with whom he wished to remain friends; and then he did one thing differently in her case: with the others he had spoken like an eighteenth-century philosopher, but with her he spoke like a hero of the nineteenth. He pretended that he was sacrificing himself, that it tore his heart out to create a rival; and since she loved believing that she was capable of inspiring sublime feeling, she accepted the new role that he had created for her. For his part, he tasted the pleasure of inspiring impassioned gratitude; together they acted out this comedy the rest of their lives. He was the resigned confidant of all her whims and the emotional go-between for all her intrigues. Now too old to lay claim to his share of the spoils, he consoled himself by seeing himself openly praised and cajoled by a woman who would have blushed to confess the roots of their intimacy, but who declared him the most remarkable man, the greatest intellect, the most shining character she had ever encountered. Women in their second and third childhoods, who had paid dearly for knowing the Marquis, were not fooled by this sisterly friendship; but they didn't brag that they guessed its real cause. And when one of them happened to say amen to an encomium Léonie bestowed on the Marquis, it was rather curious to observe the chaste and calm countenances of these two women who hoped to fool one another, yet they knew very well each other's bitter secret.

One day sufficed to reveal to the Marquis the Viscountess's penchant for Horace. Since, from the standpoint of prudence, which is all that the world knows of morality, the Marquis had never given her anything but good advice, he looked askance on this inclination. He couldn't take part in the hunt; but he read on the face of the young commoner, when Horace helped the Viscountess down from her horse at the end, that his hopes were now at a full gallop. The Marquis entered Léonie's apartments while she was having her hair done by one of her maids, one of the few servants left in whose discreet presence one could comfortably talk. To attend the toilette of ladies was one of the privileges of the old regime of which the Marquis's age still permitted him to partake.

"Now, then, my dear child," he said to Léonie, "I hope that if you are having your hair done for that handsome brown-haired man who has fallen out of the blue, at least you have not fallen for *him*. He is an appetizing young man who chats nicely, I readily agree, but he does not suit you at all."

"Since I am accustomed to your jokes, I will not bother to defend myself against your conjectures," the Viscountess replied, laughing; "but do tell me why he would not suit me."

"You know very well—you, the world's most clear-sighted and perspicacious woman."

"My perspicacity has told me nothing, since I have not paid him the slightest attention."

"In that case, I will tell you," resumed the Marquis, who was not the least bit taken in by this falsehood. "That gentleman is a nothing, a common being, in a word, a cad."

"My dear friend, that has no meaning for me," said the Viscountess. "You always forget that my opinions and ideas date from after the Revolution."

"And mine before, and yet I do not have more prejudices than you, my dear Viscountess; but there are facts, and I observe them. People of a certain class are capable of having qualities that we lack; but they also have faults that are not ours, and that cannot harmonize with ours. I deny them neither talent, nor learning, nor energy; but I absolutely will not concede to them good manners."

"Was that young man lacking in them?" said the Viscountess distractedly. "I hadn't noticed."

"He has not lacked them yet; he will not lack them as long as it is only a question of being your humble servant. In that situation, he could only lack good breeding, and you know how little importance I attach to such trifles. But if you elevate him to a height for which he was not at all intended, you will soon see him—as with all his equals given equal chances—lacking in tact, modesty, taste, and good behavior, and he will soon give you reason to blush."

"Really!" cried the Viscountess with a forced laugh. "You speak of him as if I already had my mind set on him, when I have only begun to consider whether I fancy the line of his nose."

Horace had a dangerous adversary in the Marquis, and, if he had surmised this, his own haughtiness and bravado would certainly have set the Marquis even more strongly against him. But the poor boy was too ingenuous to suspect the hold the old rake had on the mind of his beautiful Viscountess. Horace mistrusted him so little that he gave in to that benevolent admiration that titles inspired in him. Despite all his republicanism, Horace's soul was aristocratic. To him might apply the picturesque expression from *The Misanthrope:* "Titles just make him giddy." For that world he felt a political tolerance without bounds, a natural sympathy. He could see no crime in habits of loftiness and grandeur, he who was devoured by the need for such things and who felt himself born to play a role in them. He admired those of high society without respecting them; he wanted his manners to be in unison with theirs, and he tried his hand at it with complete confidence that he would succeed in no time at all.

This facility for self-transformation, this absence of rigidity or fear, truly made him charming. He committed twenty blunders, and not one was displeasing, since he was the first to recognize them and he laughed about them gracefully, without begging forgiveness for being ignorant of what he'd never been taught, declaring to all who would hear him that he had never been in society and showing neither false shame nor foolish pride. The laxity of the country came to his rescue. The Viscountess managed to push this free and easy atmosphere as far as possible, and always skirted a negative tone in her playfulness with exquisite dexterity. With all her heart she laughed at the newcomer's awkward ways, after having provoked them herself; but she only laughed at them in front of him and with him; and on his side he mustered so much good nature and heartfelt openness, that, despite all the biases of her entourage, in one day he won everyone's sympathy, even that of the Count de Melleraie, who took no umbrage with him, relying on the superiority of his own beautiful manners. Unfortunately for him, the Count attributed to his manners an importance that the Viscountess no longer concurred in as of twelve hours before. Horace was a hundred times more likable, with his madcap and offhand manner, than the Count, with his dandyism and duncery. She used the latter word in an explanation to Horace, who naively asked her what the literal meaning was of the first one.

Despite the fatiguing ride, they stayed up late in the parlor; at midnight they drank tea, and at two in the morning they were still having a lively chat around a table laden with fruits and dainties, which Horace readily plundered. The Count de Melleraie, who knew how romantic Léonie was (to the point of declaring that Lord Byron, whom she had never seen, was the only man she had ever loved), rejoiced to see the man who had worried him so much that morning acting in such a prosaic manner. He crammed Horace with pastries and marmalades, enchanted to see the Viscountess burst out laughing at his schoolboy voracity, and was full of friendly gratitude for Horace, who took on so easily the role of a man of no consequence. But the Viscountess was laughing for the first time in her life without irony; she understood that Horace was offering himself up to amuse her in order to become, no matter what the price, her intimate. She had heard him speak better than any of the men whom he now let make fun of him; during the hunt she had seen him leap over ditches and barriers that all the others had recoiled from, since the odds were in fact ten to one that they would be dashed to pieces. She knew then that he was superior to all of them in both intellect and courage. With those advantages, his willingness to accept the only part left in order to amuse her was, from her point of view, an admirable act of devotion and proof of a boundless love.

But the one who, after her, was most won over by Horace's apparent good nature was his declared opponent, the old Marquis de Vernes. With the latter, Horace didn't play a role; he became immediately infatuated with that character of a great lord: with his princely, smutty anecdotes and with that improper and shining insolence that conveyed a glimmer of the mores of an earlier era. For those who have never seen a marquis of the good old days except on the stage, to witness a specimen of that lost race in real life is a true stroke of luck. Horace, without knowing that the courtiers of the absolute monarchy had degenerated, just as the gallant knights of the feudal era, thought he saw a Lauzun or a Créqui in the Marquis de Vernes. He almost saw in him, at other moments, a Duke de Saint-Simon. Certainly Horace was taken with a respect and admiration for him that was summed up by his desire to equal and copy him as much as possible. Horace's mind was so fickle, he was so impressionable, that he could not keep himself from imitating the Marquis.

He hadn't been going to the chateau for three days before he tried to speak to us out of the corner of his mouth, the way the Marquis did, and implored me to give him one of my father's snuff boxes so that he could practice elegantly sprinkling snuff onto his shirt, copying the old man's graceful indolence as well as a sophomore could, that is, in the most ridiculous manner imaginable. Eugénie informed him how he looked, and he was quite mortified: he had forgotten that his model was sufficiently close at hand to deprive his plagiarism of all appearance of originality. But that made him no less determined to ape the Marquis in front of all those who could not compare, as we could, the teacher and the pupil.

Thanks to one of his numerous character anomalies, while he made us witness his attempts at affectation, a quarter of a league away, under the eyes of the Viscountess, he deployed all the charms of artlessness. Who could have guessed that it, too, was a role, and even a way of composing himself for effect? Horace most certainly had a real ingenuousness about him; but he used it or shed it depending on the situation. When it worked for him, he let it be, and he was *himself*, that is, adorable. When it harmed him, he took on another role with inconceivable ease, and he dominated when there was no more powerful opponent in the field. This game was very dangerous with the old Marquis, who knew it better than he, and even more so with the Viscountess, educated by the old rake and capable in her own right of competing successfully against her teacher.

So Horace, having decided to be natural, seduced them both. The Marquis didn't like young people, although, in the company of the women to whom he had devoted himself, he was forced to live perpetually surrounded by them; but Horace was so friendly to him, listened to him so avidly, enjoyed his old anecdotes so heartily, asked him so many questions, consulted his expertise so many times—in a word, took him so blindly for his guide and arbiter—that the old man, more vain than suspicious, also became infatuated with Horace and declared, even to the Viscountess, that Horace was the most amiable, the wittiest and the best of the entire younger generation.

Horace, seeing that he was appreciated, surrendered completely. He made the Marquis his confidant, and implored him to teach him how to please the Viscountess. Then something strange happened to the master's mind; he became pensive, serious, almost melancholy; and clapping his hand down on his student's shoulder, he said to him, "Young man, you put me in a very delicate situation. Give me a few hours to ponder it, and I will give you my answer tonight."

The Marquis's solemn tone, which was far from expected, kindled Horace's curiosity. How did it happen that this man, who in the commerce of jests sold all morality so cheaply, was taking on such a grave demeanor when it came to Léonie? Was she, then, a singular woman, even in the eyes of this skeptical surveyor of all human modesty? Up until then she had seemed to him free of all prejudices (that was her term for what others called principles), and Horace, who had none when it came to love, found this way of seeing things very much to his liking. But since she was not putting any brakes on his inclinations, was she saying she might have strong enough ones of her own to favor a new arrival in the midst of a phalanx of hopefuls with stronger claims? Had she made no choice among them? Was not the Count de Melleraie her lover? Was it possible to supplant him; and all those advances that seemed to be made to Horace, were they not just a trap set to force him to fall into line as soon as possible among the rejected suitors?

While Horace was questioning his fate along these lines, the Marquis, for his part, was daydreaming of the path of conduct he would mark out for his young friend. At that point, the old diplomat had been completely duped by his disciple. He judged him to be so candid, so passionate, so generous, that he was scared of the consequence of his loving a woman as skillful, as cold, as self-interested as the Viscountess. The Marquis feared storms that he could no longer ward off; and since all the tactics he had taught Léonie consisted in always keeping oneself free of scandal, he didn't know how to reconcile the sort of affection he truly felt for her with the lively sympathy that his flattered vanity made him feel for Horace.

Perhaps for the very first time in his life, he decided to be sincere, as if Horace's openness had exercised upon him the same magnetism that his own rakishness had exercised on that young man.

"Look here," he said to him while they wandered, by moonlight, the deserted lanes of the English garden, "I will speak plainly to you. I believe, with all my soul, that you are smitten with the Viscountess, and I believe it is not impossible that she will come around to hearing your pleas. But if, despite your agitation (and your hopes, which I guess quite clearly), you are still capable of listening to good advice, you will renounce your attempt to pierce her heart."

"I will renounce it if you give me good reasons," Horace responded;

"and you can't lack them, Monsieur le Marquis, since you have been weighing them all day long."

"You won't take my word for it, and abstain, until my reasons become clear later on?"

"How could you ask me such a thing, you who know the human heart so well? With all the faith I have in you, it would be useless to promise you what I couldn't fulfill."

"Then I shall attempt to convince you. Have you ever loved?"

"Yes."

"What sort of woman?"

"A woman of humble birth, like me, but beautiful, intelligent, and devoted."

"Faithful?"

"I believe so."

"Were you jealous?"

"Madly, or to put it better, foolishly."

"How did you come to leave her?"

"Don't ask me that; I was ridiculous or hateful, I'm not sure which."

"But is it over with her?"

"You're trying to force me to tell you something that breaks my heart to remember, and that you wouldn't advise me to laugh about, I'm sure: she committed suicide."

"Oh, now, that's good, that's really good!" said the Marquis, quite seriously. "I congratulate you. That's never happened to me. A suicide! Truly superb, my dear boy, and at your age! If this gets out, every woman is yours. Yes, indeed! You have a calling, a fine career ahead of you! Since that's how things stand, I advise you to take your time and choose. Tell me: how did you take this suicide? Was it a terrible shock?"

"Monsieur le Marquis," said Horace, "this goes beyond pleasantries. I fail to comprehend how you can ask me questions about such a delicate matter; but even if you should despise me for my weakness, I'll tell you that I was quite ready to blow my brains out. Laugh, now, if you like."

"But you didn't do it?" continued the Marquis, still following his line of questioning with absolute composure. "You didn't obtain a pistol? You didn't wound yourself? Come on, tell me, you didn't indulge in such foolishness?"

Horace remained dumbfounded, divided between the indignation that his teacher's calm cynicism inspired in him and the need to excuse his own levity.

The Marquis resumed in the same offhand manner: "You were really in love, then?"

"On the contrary," Horace answered, "not enough. She was too perfect: my life with her bored me."

"And she killed herself to reconnect you with life? How very sweet of her. Now then! Will you insist that all your future lovers also kill themselves for you?"

Horace, who had only made this exaggerated confession about Marthe's suicide on an impulse of vanity, felt that he had done something foolish; the Marquis was warning him of this with his bantering. Confused and irritated, he remained silent for a few minutes, overcome. Finally, no longer able to stand it, "Monsieur le Marquis," he said, "I'd hoped for more from someone of your elevated position. There's no glory in crushing a poor devil when one is a great lord, and a child when one's hair is white. You find me fatuous and ridiculous to aspire after the Viscountess. Well, if you've been appointed to poke fun at me . . ."

"What would you do in that case?" asked the Marquis eagerly.

"What could I do with respect to a woman and an . . ."

"And an old man?" said the Marquis, calmly finishing Horace's sentence. "Well, let's see! Would you withdraw, completely crestfallen?"

"Perhaps not, Monsieur le Marquis," answered Horace energetically. "Perhaps I'd accept the challenge, until forced to retreat; but at the very least I wouldn't give up without a fight."

"Good man," said the Marquis, extending his hand to him. "That's what I like to hear. Now, listen to me. I'm not making fun of you, I respect you, and I pity you, since you still have too many illusions and too much fire not to play out, to your detriment, the comedy: or, if you wish me to speak in a more modern way, the *drama* of the passions. You have no experience, dear boy."

"I know. That's the reason I sought your advice."

"Well, then, I advise you to limit yourself for the next five or six years to enthusiastic and mad women who kill themselves for love or out of spite. When you have destroyed or laid waste a dozen of them, you will be ripe for the great undertaking you rashly contemplate today, attacking a woman of the world."

"Is this a lesson? I accept it; but I want it to be complete and serious in order to be able to benefit from it. Now, without disdain, without spite, Monsieur, a woman of the world is quite strong, then, quite invincible for a man who is not of that world?"

"Just the opposite. Nothing could be simpler than to conquer, as you understand it, the strongest of those women. You see that I am being neither disdainful nor spiteful to you."

"In that case . . . finish what you were saying."

"Do you want me to? Then you should know that it is easy to win over the desire and curiosity of a woman. Nothing to it. Without youth, without looks, with just a little wit, it's done every day. But to not be thrown down the very next day by that unmanageable steed they call *reflection*: that is what is not given to everyone, and what requires some art. You might as of tonight, by surprise, obtain what is called victory. But you might very well be shown the door tomorrow night, and meet your conquest the day after tomorrow without her so much as nodding hello."

"So that's how it is! That's the way they act?"

"That is their right; what's wrong with it? We besiege them; we force ourselves into their thoughts, their imaginations, their consciences; with ruses and boldness we wrest their consent from them, and they can't change their minds when our desire loses its intensity with its potency! They can't seek revenge for having been beaten in the game, and get even as soon as they have a chance? Come, now! Are we Moslems, that we should forbid them their judgment and freedom?"

"You're right. I'm beginning to understand. But then what's that mysterious science without which we can't please them for more than a day?"

"Why, it's the science of never displeasing! It's a great science, believe me."

"Teach it to me, I want to learn it," said Horace.

Then the old Marquis, with an inner satisfaction he had kept even from himself, and with the pedantry of his vanity, fed by the humiliating sacrifices and puerile plottings of a half century of intrigues, laid out at length his designs and his doctrine for Horace. He brought the same solemnity to it as if he had been initiating a young follower into a profound science, a secret vital to the future of mankind. Horace listened in a stupor, and left so upset and broken by what he had heard that he was sick from it all night long. He persisted in admiring the Marquis; but, despite himself, he had been seized with such disgust by the depiction of these profanations of love, and by the idea of these cold machinations, that he couldn't bring himself to return to the chateau the next day. He remained for three days under the influence of these deadly revelations, not believing in anything anymore, bitterly regretting his illusions, blushing first for this world into which he had thrown himself with such ardor, and then for himself, whom he thought so inferior in the art of lying, no longer thinking of the Viscountess, whom he saw from then on through the Marquis's dry and repulsive analysis, like a corpse distilled to a formless essence.

This unpremeditated absence allowed him, without his even knowing, to make a great deal of headway in the Viscountess's heart. She had composed a novel in her head that she didn't want to leave in the first chapter. Through a spyglass mounted on the upper perron of the chateau, she could distinctly see our little house and the surrounding meadows. She could make out Horace walking some distance away in an unwooded area touching the border of the Chailly park. She went out walking there as if by chance, ran into him, strolled with him for a long time, displayed all the grace of her wit, and yet couldn't coax him to declare himself to her.

Horace had been so astonished by the Marquis's instructions, so horrified by the science he had taught him, that, despite the intoxication of vanity that Léonie's advances had plunged him into, he felt he had the strength to resist. He had this strength for a very long time, that is, about three weeks, an immense period for two beings who mutually desire one another, and who are not restrained by any moral consideration. Perhaps this young man's courage would have offended and repulsed the Viscountess had it persisted any longer. But the Marquis de Vernes (who feared cholera while pretending to brave it), having hearsay evidence that a case had appeared on the right bank of the river, claimed that a letter from his banker compelled him to return to Paris, and left the very same day.

Deprived of his mentor, Horace lost his strength. The Viscountess, cut to the quick, seeing herself desired and not being able to understand how a child with no experience could have the energy to defer an interest that was initially so lively, resolved to conquer, and every day she devised new seductions. One hundred times she saw him ready to melt, and then suddenly he would tear himself away from her, moved, overwhelmed, but without having uttered a word of love. They contented themselves with affection, with friendship. The Viscountess, in the midst of the most delicious surrender, was able to regain her composure in time and to pull back, with an admirable presence of mind, from the missteps she had risked. Horace saw clearly that, while throwing herself at his feet, she maintained the upper hand. He waited in vain for her to foreclose the possibility of an afterthought; and yet, whatever he did, at the end of three weeks of unbridled flirtation, she hadn't uttered a syllable to him that she could not take back and interpret with the opposite meaning, at the first whim of resistance that might cross her mind. This miserable struggle made him suffer horribly, but he could not extricate himself from it. He forgot everything: he no longer thought about returning to Paris; he didn't dare let his parents know that he had left them only to stop in mid-route, and, in order not to inflict on them this proof of his indifference, he let them worry, waiting in vain for news from him, not knowing what had become of him.

As for Marthe, it seemed she had never existed for him. With only one thought in mind, stoically playing his role as a carefree member of the Viscountess's circle, surrounding himself with somber and bizarre mystery in his tête-à-têtes with her, and returning to our house at night, bitter and taciturn, he was devoured by a thousand furies, and he pursued, weakening little by little, his apprenticeship as a rake, to which he had sentenced himself in order to resemble the Marquis de Vernes.

After having searched long and hard for the weak spot in this marvelous armor, the Viscountess finally found the seam: his literary vanity.

She managed to get him to admit that he was a poet, and asked to see his fledglings. Horace, who had never finished anything, would have been very embarrassed to satisfy her request; but she showed so much enthusiasm for writing talent that he keenly wished to taste the poison of this new sort of flattery, and so he set to work. It had been a good three months since he had dipped his pen in an inkwell to stitch together two or three verses. When he rummaged through the limbo of his brain, he could find only one impression, however little life and completeness it had: Marthe's disappearance and presumed suicide. We mustn't forget that this presumption had become a certainty for Horace, once he had used it to effect on two or three people while confiding in them the tragic secret that was reputed to have shattered his soul and disenchanted him with life. The subject was dramatic; he drew his inspiration from it happily. He crafted some fairly nice verses, and read them to me with an emotion that gave them merit. I, myself, was deeply moved. I didn't know that this was the first time in six weeks that he had thought of Marthe; he hadn't confided in me his affairs of the heart with the Viscountess. In a word, I was far from guessing that the tears that ran from his eyes during his elegy were only a rehearsal for the scene that he was planning for Léonie.

The next day marked his literary triumph and his diplomatic defeat with the Viscountess. He recited his verses to her, which he claimed to have written two years earlier. I should tell you that he had padded his age with a few extra years in order not to appear too much the child in that world; besides, this antedated suffering gave him a more Byronic quality. He declaimed with even more talent than he'd displayed to me, the sobs choking off his voice at the last hemistich. The Viscountess tried so hard to cry that she nearly fainted! To her credit, she did manage it, and poured forth tears—real tears. Alas! Yes, one can cry just as well from affectation as from real emotion. It happens every day, and it's also a physiological-psychological discovery belonging to nineteenth-century science, a discovery I refused to believe for a long time, but of which I've seen the proof, dazzling, incontestable, atrocious.

What's odd about individuals gifted with this ability is that they are easily duped when they encounter analogous natures. Horace knew very well that he was crying for Marthe without missing her; he did not see that he was making the Viscountess cry without softening her heart. When he admired the effect he had just had on her, it turned his head: he forgot all of his resolutions, all of the Marquis's lessons. He threw himself at Léonie's feet and expressed his passion to her with great eloquence, since he was already in top form: all the resources of his intellect were stretched taut. He still had moist eyes, a hoarse voice, tousled hair, and pale lips. The Viscountess believed that she was adored, and the joy of triumph made her beautiful and young for a few moments. But she was not a woman to yield a day too soon. She wanted, after taking such pains to be attacked, to make him feel the cost of her supposed defeat, and to prolong the greatest pleasure known to flirts: that of being implored.

Suddenly she seemed to undergo a powerful struggle with herself, and, tearing herself out of Horace's arms while perfectly mimicking fear, surprise, and shame, she left him amazed in her boudoir, where this scene had just been acted out, and ran and shut herself in her room. Perhaps she thought Horace would force the door. He had neither the wit nor the foolishness to do so. He left the chateau, mortally wounded —believing he had been toyed with, insulted—and in the throes of a sort of fury. The Viscountess did not take this susceptibility for any sort of awkwardness: not at all. She looked on it as proof of an immense pride, and was hardly mistaken. Thus she congratulated herself on her inspiration, seeing clearly that this pride had to be broken bit by bit, if she did not want to expose her own to serious damage.

This game, egotistical and in bad faith, went on for several more days. Horace had by now lost whatever advantage he had gained. He sulked; he was always revived in the name of friendship. He was forced to speak, but then his listener barely deigned to pay attention to him. Silence was imposed on him once he had said all she desired to hear. He lived on a diet of rejection and hope. The game was that her candid and fraternal friendship had been caught unawares, turned topsy-turvy by astonishment, worry, tender compassion, the generous and timid desire to close a wound that appeared to have been inflicted involuntarily. Léonie indulged herself to her heart's content; but, caught in her own net, she was as ridiculously fooled as she was perfidiously hypocritical. She imagined that she was struggling with a serious love, fighting against a still-bloodied remorse, triumphing over a terrible past. Poor Marthe served as the stakes in this game. The Viscountess believed she was erasing that memory, never suspecting that it was only a fiction to lure her into the trap. Who was fooled—Horace or Léonie? They both were; and the day they both succumbed to each other, their love, if they indeed felt fires worthy of such a beautiful name, was already spent by the fatigue and vexations of war.

That *happy* day, the most memorable and disastrous in Horace's life, went down in history in a more serious and solemn manner. It was the fifth of June, 1832; and although I spent that day and the one after in complete ignorance of the unforeseen tragedy for which Paris was the stage, and in which several of my friends acted roles, I will interrupt the narrative of Horace's good fortune to follow Arsène and Laravinière in the midst of this bloody drama of an abortive revolution. My purpose is not to recall the events, the very memory of which still bleeds in so many hearts. I have no special knowledge of those events, other than the part my friends played. I don't even know how Laravinière was involved in them, if he had foreseen them, or if he threw himself into them in the heat of the moment, pushed by the provocation of military force at the funeral of the illustrious Lamarque and by the disorder, still poorly understood, of that deplorable day. Whatever may have been the case, that struggle could not have passed before his eyes without pulling him into it. It also pulled in Arsène, who had no hope that it would succeed, but who, desiring death, and seeing his dear Jean seeking it behind the barricades, shadowed him everywhere, shared his dangers, and experienced the heroic and somber intoxication that seized the desperate defenders of these new Thermopylæs. At the final hour for these martyrs, as the troops overran the Saint-Merry cloister, Laravinière, already riddled with wounds, fell with the impact of one last shot.

"I'm done for," he said to Arsène, "and we've lost this game. But you can still escape. Run!"

"Never," said Arsène, throwing himself over him. "They will have to kill me over your body."

"What about Marthe?" Laravinière answered. "Marthe, who may still be alive, and who has only you on this earth! The last wish of a dying man is sacred. I leave you Marthe's future, and I command you to save your life for her sake. Since there's nothing left to do here, you can and you must escape these executioners, who are coming to get us, drunk on revenge and wine; poor soldiers who think themselves victors when they outnumber us a hundred to one!"

Two minutes later, the intrepid Jean fell lifeless onto Arsène's bosom. The house, the last refuge of the insurgents, had been overrun. Arsène was one of the few who got away along the rooftops. This escape was something of a miracle and unfortunately wrested only a few of the brave from the fury of the assailants. Hiding several times in chimneys, in dormer windows; twenty times spotted and pursued, twenty times avoiding the search with a luck that seemed to proclaim the intervention of divine providence, Arsène, covered with wounds, broken by several falls, feeling at the end of his strength and courage, attempted one last effort to fight for a life to which he was barely attached by a weak hope. He had to jump from one roof to another to enter a garret through a slanted window he could see from several feet away. It required only one step, one moment of resolve and composure; but Arsène was dying and half mad. Laravinière's blood, mixed with his own, was still warm on his chest, on his benumbed hands, on his inflamed forehead. He had vertigo. His emotional suffering was so violent that it didn't allow him to feel the physical suffering; and yet his survival instinct still guided him, without his noticing how rapidly his exhaustion was increasing, without his being aware of the agony that was beginning. "My God," he thought, approaching the gap between the two roofs, "if my life is still good for something, save it; if not, let it leave me as quickly as possible!" And, leaning his body forward, he more let himself fall than leapt toward the opposite edge. Then, dragging himself on his knees and elbows, since his feet and hands refused to do his bidding, he arrived at the window he was looking for, pushed it in by placing his two knees against the glass, and, bringing the whole weight of his body to bear against this last obstacle and abandoning himself with indifference to the generosity or cowardice of those he would surprise in this wretched dwelling, he rolled in a dead faint onto the garret floor. Receiving this last shock, which he didn't feel, he experienced a lucid reaction that lasted barely a few seconds. His eyes saw objects; his brain hardly understood them, but his heart experienced a sort of swelling with joy that brightened his face at the moment he lost consciousness.

What had he seen in that garret? A pale woman, thin and miserably clothed, seated on a straw pallet and holding in her hands a newborn infant, whom she hid in terror behind her when she saw a man fall from the roof to her feet. Arsène had recognized this woman. In an instant as brief as lightning, but as complete as an eternity in his thoughts, he had contemplated her; and forgetting all he had suffered as well as all he'd lost, he had tasted a happiness that twenty centuries of suffering could not have erased. That's how he later explained that ineffable moment in his life, which opened up for him a new source of reflections on the fiction of time as created by man, and on the permanence of the divine abstraction.

Marthe hadn't recognized him. She, too, had been broken by suffering, poverty, and pain; she was not to be buoyed by a feverish exaltation that could suddenly revive her and make her feel the joy at the heart of despair. First she felt afraid; but she didn't have to look long for an explanation for such a bizarre visit. The whole day, the whole of the previous night, the whole of the preceding day, attentive to the sinister sounds of the battle, whose theater was near to her dwelling, she had had only one thought: "Horace is there," she said to herself, "and each one of those gunshots I hear might be bound for his chest." Horace had given her a hundred hints that he would throw himself into the first riot that occurred; she believed he was capable of persisting in such a resolution. She had also thought about Laravinière, whom she knew to be ardent and prepared for any struggle. But she had heard Arsène so many times speak of detesting his tragic memories of the days of 1830 that she never imagined he was involved in these.

When she saw a man fall down, expiring before her eyes, she understood that he was a fugitive, one of the vanquished, and, whatever side he may have been on, she got up to help him. It was only when she brought her lamp close to this face, blackened by powder and stained with blood, that she thought of Arsène; but she didn't believe her eyes. She took her apron to stanch that blood and to wipe away that powder, without fear or disgust: the unfortunate are hardly susceptible to such weakness. She leaned over that bruised and disfigured head, which she had just placed on her trembling knees; and only then was she sure that it was her devoted brother, her best friend. She thought he was dead, and, letting her face fall onto that livid visage that still smiled with a contracted mouth and blank eyes, she kissed him several times and remained, without dropping a tear, without exhaling a moan, plunged into a mournful despair, close to idiocy.

When she had recovered some presence of mind, she sought for signs of life in the beating of his arteries. It seemed to her that his pulse was still beating; but her own was so distended that she couldn't sense things clearly and she couldn't be sure of the truth. She headed toward the door to summon a few neighbors to help her, but, remembering that among these people, whom she did not yet know, some scoundrel or coward could give the fugitive up to the vengeance of the law, she bolted the door instead, came back to Arsène, joined her hands together, and asked out loud what God, her only refuge, would have her do. Then, obeying a sudden instinct, she tried to lift up his inert body. Twice she fell down next to him without succeeding in budging him; then, all at once, filled with a supernatural strength, she picked him up as she would an infant, and deposited him on her cot, next to another unlucky one, a real infant who was sleeping there, unaware of his mother's terrors and anxieties. "Look, my son," she said to him in a frenzy, "look how your life is starting out; here's some blood for your baptism, and a corpse for your pillow." Then she ripped up the linens to wipe and bandage Arsène's wounds. She washed out the clotted blood that was sticking to his hair, she stoppered his torn veins with her fingers, she warmed his hands with her breath, she prayed to God fervently from the bottom of her grieving soul. She had nothing, and could do no more.

God came to her aid, and Arsène regained consciousness. He made a violent effort to speak.

"Don't trouble yourself," he said to her. "If my wounds are mortal, there's no point in caring for them; if they are not, it matters little if my pain is relieved a little sooner. Besides, I'm not suffering; sit there, give me just a little water to drink, and then leave me that handkerchief, I can stop the blood myself that's flowing from my chest. Leave your hand on my temple, I don't need any other dressing. Tell me I'm not dreaming, since I'm happy!. . . *Happy?*" he added with dread, changing his mind, since the memory of Laravinière had just been reawakened. But thinking that Marthe had quite enough to suffer for, he hid this horrible thought from her and kept his silence. He drank the water with a greed that he soon repressed. "Take this glass away from me," he said to her. "When the wounded drink, they die soon after. I don't want to die, Marthe; because of you, it seems I shouldn't die."

Yet that entire night he dangled between death and life. Devoured by a furious thirst, he had the courage to abstain. Marthe managed to stop the bleeding. The wounds, though deep, were not the immediate danger; but exaltation, sorrow, and fatigue lit in him a delirious fever, and he felt fire moving through his arteries. If he had given in to the transports that were seizing him, he would have lost hold of his life, since he felt the destructive rage that had possessed him for two days turning against him. In that violent state he still conserved enough energy to fight his illness: his soul was not defeated. This powerful soul, on the verge of the disintegration of physical life, experienced such cruel turmoil, but stiffened itself against its own distress, and, with almost superhuman effort, it knocked down the ghosts of the fever and the suggestions of despair.

Twenty times he got up, ready to tear open his wounds; to push Marthe away, whom at moments he no longer recognized and took for his enemy; to betray his secret hiding place by screaming in a fury; to smash his head against the walls. But then miracles of willpower occurred in him. His mind, profoundly religious, preserved, even in a frenzy, an instinct for prayer and hope; and he joined his hands together and cried, "My God! What is this? Where am I? What's going on within me and without? Would you abandon me, my God? Won't you at least give me an end with piety and resignation?" Then, turning to Marthe: "I'm a man, isn't that right?" he said to her; "I'm not a murderer, I never shed innocent blood on purpose! I have not lost the right to call on Him. Tell me it's really you, Marthe! Tell me that you hope, that you believe! Pray, Marthe, pray for me and with me, that I may live, or at least die like a man and not like a dog."

Then he buried his head in the bolster to stifle the roars that escaped from his chest; he bit the sheets, to keep his teeth from grinding against each other; and when objects took on chimerical forms in his eyes, when Marthe was transformed in his imagination into a frightening vision, he closed his eyes, he regrouped his ideas, he forced the hallucinations to yield to his reason; and with his hand parting the specters, he exorcised them in the name of faith and love.

This frightful struggle went on for almost twelve hours. Marthe had taken her baby in her arms; and when Paul lost his courage and cried out sadly, "My God, my God! You're forsaking me again!" she fell prostrate and offered Arsène this innocent creature, the sight of whom seemed to impose a sort of fearful respect on him. Arsène hadn't yet expressed a single thought on the subject of this child. He saw it, he looked on it calmly, he asked no questions; but as soon as he had, despite himself, let out a groan or a sob, he turned quickly to see if he hadn't woken him up. Once, after a long silence and a stillness that resembled ecstasy, he suddenly said:

"Is he dead?"

"Who's that?" asked Marthe.

"The *child,*" he answered, "the child isn't crying anymore! We must hide the child, the thieves are winning, they'll kill him. Give me the child so I can rescue him; I'll carry him on the roofs, and they won't find him. Let's rescue the child: don't you see, all the rest is nothing, but a child—that's sacred."

And caught in a delirium where the idea of duty and devotion still dominated, he repeated one hundred times: "The *child,* the child has been rescued, hasn't it? . . . Oh! Don't worry about the child, we'll definitely save him."

When he had come to his senses again, he looked at the baby, and said nothing more. Finally he became calmer and less agitated, and slept for an hour. Marthe, drained, had put the infant back onto the bed, next to the moribund man. Seated in a chair, with one of her arms she encircled her son to keep him safe, with the other she supported Paul's head. Her own had fallen onto the same cushion, and these three ill-starred souls reposed that way under the gaze of God, their only refuge, isolated from the rest of humanity by danger, poverty, and agony.

But they were soon awakened by a muffled clamor all around them. Marthe heard voices she didn't recognize, heavy and rushed footsteps that froze her heart with terror. Policemen were making the rounds of the garrets, searching for victims. They were approaching her own. She threw the covers over Arsène, made the bed level by hiding her worn clothes under the sheets, and, placing her infant on top of Arsène, she went to open the door with the resolution and strength that extreme peril provides. The debris of the window frame had been hidden away in a corner of the room, and she had attached her apron to look like a curtain in front of the broken window to veil the damage. A charitable neighbor, whose apartment had just been investigated, followed the sbirros right to Marthe's threshold.

"And here, good sirs," she said to them, "lives only a poor woman barely recovered from her lying-in, and still quite ill. Don't frighten her, good sirs, it would kill her."

This plea hardly touched the heartless and pitiless beings to whom it was addressed; but the composure with which Marthe presented herself removed any suspicions they may have had. A glance around the room, too tiny and too poorly furnished to conceal a hiding place, persuaded them of the futility of a more exacting search. They went away without noticing the traces of blood poorly wiped off the floor: and this was yet another of the miracles that contributed to Arsène's salvation. The elderly neighbor was a worthy and generous creature who had assisted Marthe through her delivery pains. She helped her hide the outlaw, took responsibility for bringing him food and medicine; but, not knowing any doctor whose opinions would guarantee his silence, and terrified of the truly inquisitorial harshness that was shown to the victims of the Saint-Merry cloister, she limited herself to the modest help that she herself could provide. Marthe didn't dare take even one step outside her room for fear someone might come and search it again in her absence. Besides, Arsène had become so calm that her worry had dissolved, and she was counting on his speedy recovery.

It was not to be. His weakness continued and for over a month he couldn't get out of bed. Marthe slept this entire time on a bundle of straw that she had procured on the pretext of making herself a mattress; but she didn't have the means to purchase the linen for it. The elderly neighbor was absolutely penniless. The state of the patient and his own prostration didn't allow Marthe to work, much less go out and look for employment. During the two months since her separation from Horace, resolved not to be a burden to anyone when she became a mother, she had lived on what her last belongings could bring in when sold or pawned; since her delivery had been longer and more painful than she could have foreseen, she had exhausted this meager resource and now found herself in a state of total destitution. Arsène was no more fortunate. For some time, anticipating, based on Laravinière's statements, an upheaval in Paris, and wanting to be free to throw himself into it, he had given his small savings to his sisters and had sent them back to the provinces. Believing there was nothing else for him but to die, he had kept nothing. So the situation of these two abandoned creatures was dreadful. Both sick, both broken; one nailed to a bed of pain, the other nursing an infant; living only on bread and sleeping on straw, not even sheltered by this garret whose window she didn't dare have fixed, since a deadly secret could be traced to the breakage, not to mention the fact that she was too weak to take a step. And then, add to these impediments a sort of apathy and mental impotence, caused by privation, exhaustion, a habit of excessive pride, and isolation that paralyzes all of one's faculties: and you will understand how, although they would have been able to warn Eugénie and me with a few precautions and a little less pride, they let themselves waste away silently for several weeks.

The baby was the only one who didn't suffer too much from this distress. His mother had little milk, but the neighbor shared with the nursling the milk from her lunch, and every day she took him for a walk in her arms in the sunshine of the flower market by the Seine. A child of Paris needs no more than this to spring up like a fragile but tenacious plant along these damp walls where life flourishes in spite of it all, more sickly, more delicate, and yet more intense than in the pure air of the fields.

During this difficult test, Arsène's patience never flagged; he didn't complain even once, although he suffered a good deal—not from his wounds, which were no longer festering and were healing little by little without alarming symptoms, but from a violent irritation of the brain that occurred repeatedly and gave way to periods of deep dejection. Between exaltation and depression, he had few gaps when he could talk with Marthe. During his fever, he imposed absolute silence on himself, so Marthe didn't know how sick he really was. In his moments of calm, he set his mind to mustering his forces, in order to be able to fight when the crisis recurred. The result of this stoic resolution was a recovery whose slowness surprised Marthe, since she didn't understand the seriousness of the illness, and whose speed seemed inexplicable to me when, later on, I heard from Arsène's own lips the details of how he suffered. At moments, despite the confidence he had been able to instill in her, Marthe still was scared by the indifference with which he seemed to await his recovery without desiring it. At those times she felt that his mental faculties had received a serious blow, and feared that he would never completely regain his vigor. But while she was giving in to this gloomy conjecture, Arsène, full of persistence and determination, was counting the days and the hours; and, feeling the attacks of his illness slowly diminish, he rightly concluded that a grave relapse was imminent if he didn't hold the reins of his will as taut as ever. So, wanting to abstain from any violent emotion, from any puerile discouragement, he seemed not to see the horror of the predicament Marthe was sharing with him.

One day when he had closed his eyes and appeared to be sleeping, he overheard the old neighbor, who was taking an interest in Marthe, in keeping with the scope of her ideas and sentiments, no doubt good and humane, but limited and a bit coarse. "Do you know, my dear," she said to her, "it's a great misfortune for you to have to harbor that man. You were already fairly destitute, and here you are forced to share with him your daily bread, which would make some milk for your baby!"

"If I could only share it, my good friend!" answered Marthe with a sad smile. "But he only eats an ounce of bread a day in his soup. And what a soup! A drop of milk in a pint of water; I don't understand how he can live like that."

"Then his illness will drag on for eternity!" answered the old woman. "He can never regain his strength with that sort of diet. Your effort will be in vain; you will wear yourself out without being able to save him."

"I'd rather die with him than abandon him," said Marthe.

"But if you cause your own child's death?" said the old woman.

"God wouldn't permit it!" cried Marthe, horrified.

"I'm not saying it's going to happen," resumed the old woman sweetly. "Nor do I say that you've pushed your devotion for this refugee too far. I know what one's duty is to one's next of kin; but he should understand that he will only be saved from the scaffold at the price of taking you along with him to the hospital. That poor young man can't know how much harm he's doing you. He doesn't see that, sleeping on straw as you do, with an open window at your back, you can't last long. Sickness is depriving him of his ability to think, it's that simple; if you would only allow me to speak to him, I assure you that the very same day he will decide to drag himself outside as best he can. Look, with the two of us to hold him upright, we could get him to the hospital; he'd be better off there."

"To the hospital!" exclaimed Marthe, turning pale. "Haven't you heard (and haven't you repeated to me) that doctors are forbidden to release the wounded who entrust themselves to their care, and that each sick person admitted to a hospital is designated for a police investigation according to a sign placed above his bed? What! The men with the most holy of functions are forced to be informants (on pain of being accused of complicity); and you want me to abandon this victim to the vengeance of a society where such orders are universally accepted without revolt, and perhaps even without horror by many? No, no, if the world has become so cutthroat, at least one can still find in the hearts of poor women, and under our garret rooftiles, a little religion and humanity, isn't that so, good neighbor?"

"Enough!" answered the neighbor, wiping her eyes with the corner of her apron, "here you go molding me any way you please. I don't know where you pick up what you say, my child; but you speak according to God and to my heart. I'll go get you a bit of milk and sugar for your sick one, and also for that little treasure," she added, kissing the infant clinging to its mother's breast.

"No, my dear friend," said Marthe, "don't strip your cupboard bare for us; you've already done enough. It's not right that at your age you should condemn yourself to suffer. We're young, all of us here, and we have enough strength to do without for a while."

"And what if *I* want to do without, what if *I* want to suffer!" exclaimed the good woman angrily. "Do you take me for a wicked soul, a miser, an egotist? Besides, what gives you the right to refuse me when it's a question of the *love for a child* like yours, and of an unfortunate whom the good Lord entrusts to us?"

"Well, then, I accept," said Marthe, throwing her emaciated arms covered with tatters around the neck of the old woman. "I accept with joy. The day will come, in the not too distant future perhaps, when we will reciprocate all the good that you're doing for us now, since God will give us strength and freedom!"

"You're right, Marthe," said Arsène in a weak and measured voice, when the neighbor had left. "Freedom will be given to us, and our strength will return. Your pity is saving me, and I'll have my chance. Go, my poor Marthe, save your courage, as I maintain my own in silence and submission. I need more of it than you to see you suffer as you do, and to think without despairing that not only can I not lighten your load, but I'm actually increasing your misery. During the first few days, I often asked myself if it wouldn't be better for me to go back out on the ledge and die in some roof gutter, like a poor bird with a broken wing; but I felt, in my tenderness for you, that I would overcome this sickness, that by wanting to live I *will* live, and that in accepting your support I would assure you of my own in the future. You see, Marthe, God knows just what he's doing! In your pride, you were distant and hidden from me. You wanted to spend your life in isolation, sorrow, and need, rather than accept my devotion. Now that destiny has sent me here to profit from your devotion, you will no longer be able to spurn me, you will no longer have the right to refuse my support. I offer you only my heart and my hands, Marthe, since I have neither gold, nor silver, nor clothing, nor refuge, nor talent, nor protection; but my heart cherishes you, and my hands will be able to nourish you, you and your 'little treasure,' as our neighbor says."

While saying all this, Paul picked up the baby and kissed it; that was the first sign of affection he had given him. Up until that day, Paul had often held him and cradled him on his lap to relieve the mother; he had lulled him to sleep several times every night in his arms, warming him against his chest. But in caring for him, he had never caressed him. At that instant, a tear of tenderness flowed from his eyes onto the baby's face, and Marthe gathered it in with her lips. "Oh, my Paul, oh, my brother!" she cried, "if you could only love him, this dear, sad, little treasure!"

"Quiet, Marthe, let's not talk about that," he answered, giving her back her son. "I'm still too weak; I haven't yet said a word to you about it. We'll talk, and you will be happy with what I have to say, I hope. In the meantime, we must continue to suffer, since that's God's will. I see very clearly how you're going hungry, how you sleep on the floorboards with only a bundle of straw for your head, and I hardly dare say to you: Take back your bed, and let me lie on that pallet; since that idea shocks you, and you overwhelm me with a goodness that does me too much good and too much harm. I need to remain here so I can endure the sight of your fatigue, so I can be calm and say to you *All's well!* Alas, my God, may I win this victory completely!"

"I certainly hope, Marthe," he said to her in another moment of calm the next day, "that you won't forget what you're doing for me, and that you won't come and say to me one day, when I remind you of it, that you didn't suffer as much as I claim! Oh, I know you, Marthe: you're capable of such treachery."

A pale smile glided over their lips; and Marthe, leaning over him, pressed a chaste kiss on her friend's forehead. That was the first caress she had dared to give him during the five weeks they had been shut in together, just the two of them, day and night. All that time, whenever Marthe, in an outpouring of pain and fear for his life, came near him to embrace him as if to bid him farewell, he had quickly pushed her away, saying with a sort of anger: "Leave me alone. Do you want to kill me?" Those were the only moments when the memory of his passion had seemed to reawaken. Besides these fleeting and rare emotions that Marthe had realized she had to stop provoking from his fraternal impulses, they hadn't exchanged a word that alluded to the earlier unhappiness. One would have said that between the peaceful friendship of their youth and that tragic day at the Saint-Merry cloister nothing had happened, since one of them showed such delicacy in diverting memories away from the intervening time, and the other felt such shame and anguish when they were recalled! Only on that day both of them thought of those times simultaneously and without turmoil, and both of them understood that the thought could cease to be bitter. Paul, far from spurning her kiss, returned it to her child with even more tenderness than he had shown the day before, and he added with a sort of melancholy gaiety: "Do you know, Marthe, how charming this child is? They say that these little creatures are all ugly at this age; but those who say that never looked on one with a father's eyes."

CHAPTER

28

Horace had given us an inkling, since he had first become a regular at the Chailly chateau, that he had set his sights on the Viscountess and formed hopes about her. Eugénie had made fun of his conceit; and I, who did not at all think it impossible that he should succeed, did not congratulate him on this undertaking. Far from it: I told him very bluntly how little value I placed on Léonie's character. He didn't like the way we received his confidences, and he had stopped letting us in on them for quite some time, until the day of his victory arrived and filled him with a pride that he found impossible to repress. On that day, dining with us, he couldn't keep himself from pulling the conversation at every turn back to her imposing graces, her superior mind, her exquisite tact, all the seductive qualities that he wanted us to admire in the Viscountess. Eugénie, who had been her dressmaker, and who had witnessed her beauty, her fine manners, and her great wit without their petticoats, persisted in not sharing this enthusiasm and in declaring that this woman was haughty when familiar, and dry and cutting even when being protective. The memory of Marthe, the indignation that Eugénie felt in seeing her so briskly forgotten, gave her opposition a bitter flavor. Horace got carried away and treated Eugénie like a silly half-wit who owed some respect to Madame de Chailly, and who was forgetting her place. He took it upon himself to tell her that she couldn't under-stand the charm of a woman of the Viscountess's station and merit.

"My dear Horace," Eugénie answered with the most perfect sweet-ness, "what you're saying doesn't anger me. I've never presumed to fight for your respect. If, in giving you my frank opinion, I've wound-ed you, my only excuse is the interest I take in you and the fear I have of seeing you tormented and humiliated by that beautiful lady, who has toyed with many men as fine as you, and who even brags about them in front of her dressers; which I, personally, consider in bad taste and bad form."

Horace became more and more irritated. I tried to calm him down by insisting on the truth of Eugénie's assertions, begging him for the last time to reflect carefully before exposing himself to the Viscountess's mockery. It was then that, wounded by this notion and no longer able to contain himself, he shut our mouths by announcing to us in the clearest terms that he no longer ran the risk of being shamefully shown the door, and if the Viscountess fancied adding another notch to the brooch of victims she fastened to her shawl, he, too, could certainly display her colors in the buttonhole of his coat.

"You wouldn't do it," replied Eugénie coldly, "because a man of honor doesn't boast of his good fortune."

Horace bit his lip, then added after a moment's thought: "A man of honor doesn't boast of his good fortune so long as he's proud of it; but sometimes he criticizes himself for it, when he's made to blush. That's what I'd do, believe me, to a woman who backs me into a corner."

"That's not the system of your friend, the Marquis de Vernes," I answered him.

"The Marquis's system," responded Horace, "(and he's someone who knows more on this score than either you or I) is to prevent anyone from ever mocking him. I don't claim to imitate his example by adopt-ing the same means. To each his own, and all means are good that bring about the same end."

"I'm not sure what the Marquis de Vernes thinks about this," said Eugénie; "but as for me, I'm sure I know what *you* would think if you ever found yourself in such a situation."

"And would you be so kind as to tell me?" asked Horace.

"Here it is," she answered. "You would weigh, in a spirit of reason and justice, the wrongs that were done to you, and those you would be tempted to do. You would compare the wrong a woman could do to you in bragging that she had rejected you, and the wrong you would unavoidably do to her in bragging that you had conquered her; and you would see that you would be committing an outrage to avenge yourself for what is, at most, a little ridicule. The world (yes, I'm sure of it, the world at large as well as popular opinion) respects a woman who is respected by her lover, and scorns her whom her lover scorns. Her mistakes are considered crimes; and it's important to recognize that, in this regard, women are much to be pitied, since the most prudent and skillful of them are still vulnerable to being insulted by the man who implored them the night before. Look, isn't that the way it stands, Horace? Don't laugh; answer me! To have your pleas heard by the Viscountess herself, which I don't think is so outlandish, wouldn't it behoove you to be very constant, very humble, very supplicating for a period of time? Shouldn't you show some love for her, or at least the pretense of it? What do you say!"

"Eugénie, my dear," replied Horace, half disturbed, half satisfied by what he took to be a roundabout interrogation, "you're asking extremely indiscreet questions; and I'm not obliged to account to you for what has occurred, or might occur, between the Viscountess and me."

"I'm only asking questions to which you can respond without compromising anyone, and I'm only asking a rhetorical question. Isn't it true that you would not court a woman who would yield without putting up a fight?"

"You know very well, I can't imagine making an appeal to a woman other than one who defends herself, one whom it is perilous and difficult to conquer."

"I know your pride in this matter, and I say in that case you will never have the right to betray any woman, because you will never possess any to whom you have not sworn respect, devotion, and discretion. To defame her afterward would be cowardice and perjury."

"My dear friend," resumed Horace, "I know that you've studied the debates at Taitbout Hall; consequently, I know that all your conclusions will always favor the rights of women. But no matter how subtle your arguments, I'll answer you that I don't go along with your notion that women must assume the dominant role. Nor do I find it just that you should have the right to make us out to be fools, to be upstarts or slaves, without our being able to appeal on the basis of equality. What! A flirt should bring me to my knees, entice me for weeks on end, overcome my prudence, finally give me, in exchange for her victory, the rights of a spouse and master, and then start up the very next day with another, and flick me away while telling my successor, her friends, her chamber-maids: 'You see that nobody? He pursued me obsessively; but I put him in his place; I brought down his foolish pride!' That would be too much, and, by my faith, I'm not inclined to let myself be toyed with in that way. To my mind, ridicule is just as serious as any other disgrace. In France, it might well be, at present, the worst of all; and the woman who inflicts it on me can expect reprisals that she will remember her whole life. 'An eye for an eye' governs our laws."

"If you accept that punishment as just and humane," answered Eugénie, "I have nothing more to say to you. In that case you subscribe to capital punishment and all the other barbaric institutions that I thought your heart had risen above. At least, I've heard you claim that; and I'd thought that, in matters of personal conduct where we can all correct the ineptitude and cruelty of the law, in comparison to public opinion, for instance, you would seek more grandeur and nobility than you profess at this moment. But," she added, getting up from the table, "I hope that all this is, as we say among my class of good folk, *just talk,* and that when the opportunity arises your actions will be worth more than your words."

Despite Horace's resistance, Eugénie's noble sentiments made an impression on him. When she left, he said to me with a good deal of enthusiasm: "Your Eugénie is a superior creature, and I believe she has, if not as much wit, at least more ideas than my Viscountess."

"Then she's definitely *yours,* my poor Horace?" I said to him, taking his hand. "Well! I'm genuinely distressed, I must confess."

"But why?" he exclaimed with a superb laugh. "Really, you astonish me, you and Eugénie, with your condolences. One would think I was the unluckiest of men, because I possess the most adorable and seduc-tive of women! I don't know if she's a perfect heroine for a novel, as you seem to want; but for me, since I'm more modest, she's a pretty conquest, a rapturous mistress."

"Do you love her?" I asked him.

"The devil if I know," he answered giddily. "You're asking too much of this. I've loved, and I think that it will be for the first and last time in my life. From now on, I can only look to women for a distraction from my weariness, some excitement for my half-extinguished heart. I go into love as one goes into war, with precious little human feeling, no concept of virtue, much ambition, and not a little pride. I admit that this victory has stroked my vanity, since it cost me time and effort. What harm is there in that? Are you going to play the pedant with me? Are you forgetting that I'm twenty years old, and if my emotions are already dead, my passions are still at their most violent?"

"It's just that all this seems to me false and strained," I said to him. "I'm speaking to you out of the sincerity of my heart, Horace, without any regard for the vanity you hide behind, which seems too petty an emotion for you. No, great emotion, great love, isn't dead in your heart; I even believe that it hasn't begun to blossom there yet, and that you have not loved at all up till now. I believe that noble passions, stifled for a long time by ignorance and pride, are fermenting in you, and will prove to be your torment—or your happiness. Oh! my dear Horace, you're not, you can't be, the Don Juan that Hoffman describes, still less Byron's. Those poetic creations are crowding your brain too much, and you become affected when you make them part of the reality of your life. But you're younger and more powerful than those phantoms. You were not broken by the loss of your first love; it was only an unfortunate first try. Make sure that the second one, despite the frivolity you want to surround it with, doesn't become the fatal and grave love of your life."

"Well, if that's how things stand," answered Horace, whose pride easily accepted my assumptions, "let the chips fall where they may! Léonie is well suited to inspire a true passion, since *she* feels one—that I can't doubt. Yes, Théophile, I'm ardently loved, and that woman is ready to make the greatest sacrifices for me, to commit the greatest follies. Perhaps her love will awaken my own, and we'll spend stirring days together. That's all I ask from destiny, to escape from this hateful torpor in which I've felt myself immersed lately."

"Horace," I exclaimed, "she doesn't love you. She has never loved anything, and she will never love anyone—she doesn't even love her own children."

"Absurdities, mere pedagogy!" he answered crossly. "I'm delighted that she loves nothing, and that she's surrendering to me a heart that's still virgin. It's more than I hoped for, and what you're saying only inflames my interest instead of cooling me off. My God! If she were a good spouse and mother, she couldn't be a passionate lover. You take me for a child. Do you think I can have illusions about her, and that I didn't feel her rapture today? Ah! How different her frenzy is from Marthe's chaste abandon! Marthe is a nun, a saint; love and respect to her memory, forever sacred! But Léonie! Now, that's a woman, a tigress, a demon!"

"She's an actress," I resumed sadly. "Woe to you, when you make your entrance with her behind the scenes."

If the Viscountess had had a true friend by her side at that moment, he would have told her the same things about Horace that I told him about her; but having surrendered to her feverish desire to be loved with all the romantic fury that she found in books, and that no man of her caste had yet expressed for her, she would not have accepted good advice any more than Horace had listened to mine. She surrendered to him, believing that she was inspiring a violent passion, pulled in only by her vanity and her curiosity. So, as one might say, the game was tied at deuce.

I myself have never understood how so penetrating a woman, shaped early on by the Marquis de Vernes's lessons on the wiles to use on men and on the ways to predict events, could so deceive herself when it came to Horace, as the Viscountess did. She flattered herself that she had found in him a romantic devotion that nothing could shake, an admiration that would not look at things too closely, a sort of modest vanity that would always make him feel honored to possess a woman such as she. She was very much mistaken: Horace, intoxicated for a few days, suddenly woke up despite his inexperience in order to salvage his pride, and he soon had to pit his own against that of Léonie. I can't explain that woman's mistake except by recalling that she was venturing onto completely unknown terrain by choosing the object of her love from the ranks of the bourgeoisie. She certainly had no aristocratic prejudice. She pretended to have a sort of intellectual superiority, and she dreamed him onto a lowly rung of society in order to make him more exotic, mysterious, and poetic. Don't forget, her imagination was as lively as her heart was cold. Bored by all that was familiar to her, and knowing in advance and by heart all the standard phrases as soon as her noble worshippers pronounced their first syllables, she found, in Horace's original bluntness, the novelty for which she thirsted. But, in guessing the merit of this man without birth, she didn't ascertain the defects of a man without practice, without *savoir-vivre,* as the old Marquis put it with just the right turn of phrase. In a society without principles, the point of honor that takes their place, and the upbringing that allows one to affect the appearance of them, are more real advantages than one would think.

Horace felt the sort of superiority of those who are termed well bred. In love with all that could elevate and exalt him, he would have liked to catch it from them. But if he succeeded in the little things, he couldn't manage the large ones. Nature and habit can be defeated where etiquette requires only small sacrifices; but when it demands that vanity be sacrificed, it's impotent, and the slightly coarse conceit, the slightly improper presumptuousness, the slightly rough personality of the man of the lower ranks dominate once more. It was the opposite of what the Viscountess had hoped. She loved Horace's witty and gracious awkwardness; she felt he lost it too quickly. She hoped for a great abnegation on his part, a sort of heroism of love; she found not the least impulse for it in him.

Yet since this young man's heart had not been corrupted, but simply warped, he felt, for the first few days, truly grateful to the Viscountess. He expressed this to her with talent, and she believed that she was finally adored, as it was her ambition to be. There was even a sort of magnificence in the way Horace accepted without mistrust, without curiosity, and without worry his new mistress's past. She told him he was the first man she had ever loved. She was telling the truth in the sense that he was the first man she had loved in this way. Horace didn't hesitate to take her at her word. He accepted without difficulty the idea that no other man had deserved the love that he inspired; and as for the peccadilloes which he certainly thought that Léonie's life was not exempt from, they mattered so little to him that he posed not a single indiscreet question. With her, he hardly experienced that retroactive jealousy which had made his love affair with Marthe a double torture. On the one hand, his ideas on the merits of women had been changed a good deal by the Viscountess's society and the old Marquis's schooling. He no longer sought the bourgeois chastity that had been his ideal for so long, but rather the breezy and elegant offhandedness of a fashionable woman. On the other hand, he was not humbled by taking his place among his predecessors with the Viscountess, as he had been when it came to succeeding in Marthe's heart Monsieur Poisson, the café owner, and (according to his suspicions) Paul Arsène, the café waiter. With Léonie, it was no doubt great lords, dukes, even princes perhaps, whom he was following; and that brilliant advanced guard, who had commenced and preceded his triumphant march, seemed to him a retinue not to make one blush. Poor Marthe, who for accepting with sweetness and repentance all his reproaches for a single error, had been crushed by Horace's skittish pride. The haughty Viscountess, ready to brag of a long series of faults, was respected, thanks to this same pride.

If he had interrogated her as he had Marthe, the Viscountess would not have deigned to respond. But had she done so, she would not have concealed any of her deeds. She was not hypocritical about principles. Quite the contrary, in this regard she had a certain Voltairian cynicism that expressly contradicted her emotional hypocrisies. She didn't pretend to be a virtuous woman, but rather to be a young, ardent soul, open to whatever passions could be inspired in her. It was a sort of prostitution of the heart, since she gave into every desire, commanding respect with this watchword: "I cannot love"; leaving herself open to attack by this other one, which she added for certain men: "I would like to be able to love."

When Horace became her lover, she was nearly alone with him in a sort of intimacy at the chateau of Chailly. The Count de Melleraie had gone off; the usual adorers had dispersed, cholera scaring some off and bringing to others precious inheritances or acute losses. In the meantime, the plague withdrew from our district, and Léonie did not call her court back around her. Absorbed by her new love, and perhaps embarrassed to make her friends accept it, she turned away visitors by writing in all her letters that she was on the verge of returning to Paris.

Meanwhile, one week followed another, and Horace exulted secretly (too secretly for his taste) over the absence of his rivals.

Despite her pretense that this was her ordinary degree of candor, the Viscountess, because of her mother-in-law and her children, demanded from Horace the deepest secrecy. Thanks more to Léonie's aplomb than to the closeness of their respective dwellings and to the precautions taken, not a word was breathed of this liaison. Léonie's habits, her language, her pretensions, her reticences, her half-vows, her entire blend of openness and falseness, had made her external life an enigma, which her fortunate lovers were pleased to veil in order to make their glory more pointed and the rejected lovers respected to soften the shame of their position. Horace passed for just one more intimate, for one of those regulars of whom it is said: They're all fortunate; either that, or none of them is; all of them are equally favored or else kept at a distance. That was not the way Horace would have designed his role, if the choice had been left up to him. His principal emotion with regard to Léonie had been the desire to crush all his rivals, in appearance, if not in reality, and to have it said of him: "That's the one she favors; she won't hear of anyone else." Soon he began to suffer from the obscurity of his position—he wanted his victory to resound. Horace consoled himself by confiding it under the seal of secrecy, not only to me, but to a few others whom he didn't know well enough to treat with such candor, and who, judging him extremely conceited, did not want to believe in his success.

These indiscretions served to shame Horace and glorify the Viscountess, who learned of them and denied them by saying, with admirable self-possession and angelic sweetness, that it was impossible, since Horace was a man of honor, incapable of inventing and spreading a story contrary to the truth. But the next time they were alone together she made him feel how much at fault he was, with her thoughtfulness that was so cruel and her indulgence that was so biting. He was forced, while suffocating with rage, to fling at her a patchwork of denials and lies in order to reconquer her trust and respect. But the damage could not be undone. Léonie's curiosity had been satisfied; her vanity had been assuaged by all the bombastic praise that Horace had squandered on her, instead of ardor, in his outpourings and, instead of affection, in his epistles in prose and verse. He had exhausted for her his entire breathtaking vocabulary of fashionable love; he had saturated it with rapturous epithets, and his love notes were riddled with exclamation points. Léonie had had enough. As a woman of wit, she soon grew weary of all this poetic bad taste. As an astute diplomat, she recognized that this love only differed from the other ones she had known in its manner of expression, and that it was not worth the trouble to expose herself to public ridicule in order to hear what amounted to no more than the jargon of love. After a month of this, each day colder and sadder than the last, Léonie resolved to rid herself little by little of this intrigue, in order, while waiting for something better to come along, to return to the Count de Melleraie, who had the most excellent manners.

The Viscountess, who never blushed at her own errors, blushed quite often at those of the men who made her commit them; and from that stemmed the fact that, while sometimes confessing with great candor, she had never named anyone. She had begun to nourish this painful and mysterious shame when she had fallen prey to the old Marquis. With him she maintained only filial relations; but she hadn't garnered enough pride from her other loves to be able to erase that wound and to wash out that stain in her own eyes. Because of it she had retained a hatred and profound contempt for men whom she didn't like, or whom she no longer liked; and even for those who were able to please her she nourished a continual suspicion. She had never ratified their power over her by confiding in her friends (with the exception of the Marquis, to whom she told almost everything), even less so by taking compromising measures. In general, she had been backed up by the delicacy of their conduct and the coolness of their rupture, since these were men of the world, equally incapable of a regret or a vendetta. Horace, for whom she had almost cast off all her prudence; Horace, whom she had judged to be so pure, so smitten with her, so naive; Horace, whom she hadn't distrusted, seemed to her the most wretched of them all, when he tried to force her to recognize him as her lover in the eyes of others. She rebelled so strongly against this that she not only swore that she would show him the door as soon as possible, but also that she would avenge herself on him by not leaving behind the slightest trace of her kindness to him. "You will be punished as you have sinned," she said to him in her ulcerated soul. "You wanted to be recognized as my master, but as soon as I have the chance, I will see that you are recognized as my clown. Your conceit will fall on your own head; and wherever you have sown tales of your glory, you will reap only shame and ridicule."

Horace had a foreboding of this vengeance, and a new struggle began between them: not just to dominate each other, but to destroy each other.

In the meantime, we knew absolutely nothing about the fate of three people who acutely interested us: Marthe, whom we had already grown accustomed to thinking of as lost forever to us; Laravinière, whose friends were searching for him without success; and Arsène, who had promised to write to us, and from whom we had received no more news than from those other two. Jean's disappearance was complete. It was presumed that he had died in the Saint-Merry cloister. Although the bravest Bousingots had followed him throughout the day of June 5th, that night they had dispersed to hunt for arms, ammunition, and reinforcements. The morning of the 6th, the insurgents were unable to regroup, since the troops, deployed at every point, had penned them up in their last retreat. I'm not clear on whether all the students persevered boldly in their next effort, but it's clear that several of them did attempt it, and that while the house where their leader was entrenched was overrun, they took advantage of the confusion to try to find him, in order to help him escape or at least to recover his body. This final consolation was denied them. Louvet found only his red cap, which he kept as a relic, and he was not able to find out if his friend was among the prisoners. Later on, the judicial proceeding brought against the victims revealed nothing new, since Laravinière was not mentioned. His friends wept for him, and gathered to honor his memory with speeches and songs of mourning, one of his friends writing the words and another the music.

They wrote to me on this occasion to ask me if I hadn't had any news of Paul Arsène, and that's how I learned that he, too, had disappeared. I wrote to his sisters, who were no better informed than I. Louison replied with a letter of lamentation in which she expressed fairly ingenuously her concern and tenderness for her brother. She closed by saying: "We have lost our sole support, and now we are forced to work without respite to keep from falling into destitution."

While we were all preoccupied with these perplexities—in which Horace hardly had the time to take part, although he expressed sincere regrets about Jean and Paul when he was made to think about them— Paul began convalescing in poor Marthe's obscure garret. The latter started to go out again, once she was confident that tranquillity finally reigned over the neighborhood. Although those in the adjacent garrets had some suspicions that a *patriot* had taken refuge with her, this secret was faithfully kept, and the police didn't watch her comings and goings. Still, for Arsène, once he was ready to go outside, it became crucial that he change neighborhoods, to put a distance between himself and the place where his face had certainly been noticed behind the barricades and in that house that had been riddled with gunfire. He couldn't show his face three times in nearby streets without malevolent or blundering witnesses making remarks about him that a spy's ear might catch in passing. He resolved to go and live at the opposite end of Paris. The difficulty was not in getting out of his refuge: he had begun to walk, and, going out cautiously at night, it would be easy for him to steal away without being seen. But he didn't dare abandon Marthe, in her current state of poverty, to the persecution of a landlord she couldn't pay, and who, in checking the condition of the premises, would certainly notice the broken window; then this incensed creditor might turn Marthe over to the police. Finally, since by sitting on his hands he couldn't avert this danger, Paul decided to leave the house before the day when payment was due and entrust his fate to Louvet, who right then and there bundled him into a cab, moved him to Belleville, and brought the elderly neighbor enough money to extricate Marthe from her difficulties. Then they looked for a worker dedicated to the republican cause; such a man proved not hard to find, and silently he repaired the garret window. Meanwhile, Louvet brought Marthe, the baby, and the neighbor, who didn't want to leave them, to the rundown quarters

where he had set up house for Arsène under his own name, lending
him his passport. This Louvet was an excellent young man, the poorest
and thus the most generous of all those whom Arsène knew among
Laravinière's intimates. It grieved Paul not to be able to repay him
immediately for the advances he so promptly made to him; but, for
Marthe's sake, he was forced to accept them. Louvet had not even given
him a chance to ask for them. On the way he promised secrecy in all
matters, and kept his pledge so faithfully that this change of address left
me as much in the dark as ever with regard to Marthe and Arsène.

Paul had barely moved into Belleville when he began to look for
employment; but he was still so weak that he became easily fatigued,
and he was discharged. He rested two or three days, regained his
courage, and offered his services as a day laborer to a master paver.
Arsène had no time to lose, and no choice: they were beginning to
want bread. But he understood nothing of the duties assigned to him;
once more he was discharged. He was then, in turn, waiter in a wine
shop, plaster mixer, messenger, machinist in the Belleville Theater,
shoemaker, ditchdigger, brewer, mortar mixer, baker's man, and who
knows what else. Wherever he might earn a morsel of bread he offered
his arms and his sweat. He couldn't take hold anywhere, since he hadn't
recovered his health, and, despite his zeal, he did less work than the
next man. Their poverty became more horrific with each passing day.
Their garments went all to shreds. Their neighbor tried knitting, in
vain: she earned hardly anything. Marthe couldn't find work; her pallor, her tatters, and her having to nurse, damaged her prospects everywhere. She went to work cleaning houses for six francs a month. And
then she succeeded in getting hired as dressmaker for actresses with
minor roles at the Belleville Theater, and since those women often did
not pay her, she decided to ask that theater for employment as an usher
for the private boxes. They objected that this was too ambitious, that it
was an important position; but they took pity on her and gave her a job
as a dresser, and the leading ladies of the day were pleased with her skill
and promptness.

That was when Paul, during his brief stint as a machinist, once he
had heard the plays and observed the actors carefully, thought of trying
his hand at the theater. He had a prodigious memory. If he heard only

two rehearsals, he knew all the roles by heart. He was tested: they found that he didn't lack the proper disposition for serious plays; but all the parts for this genre were already oversubscribed, and the only opening was for a comic actor, who would make his debut in the role of a beaten, rascally servant. Arsène dragged himself across the stage, dying inside, his knees shaking with shame and repugnance, his stomach growling, his teeth clenched in anger, fever, and emotion. He acted sadly, coldly—and was booed outrageously. He bore this affront with stoic indifference. He hadn't braved the audience to satisfy any foolish conceit: it was a desperate attempt, among twenty others, to obtain nourishment for his wife and child; since he had married Marthe in his heart, and adopted Horace's son before God. The director, a man used to this sort of disaster, laughed at his novice's misadventures and persuaded him not to take the risk again; but he took note of the composure and the presence of mind that Paul had demonstrated in the midst of the storm, his clear enunciation, his pure diction, his infallible memory, and his comprehension of the dialogue. He expressed hope for his future, and, to give him the means to improve himself without irritating the Belleville public, he gave him work as a prompter, at which he acquitted himself wonderfully. Soon Arsène showed that he also had a way with costumes and scenery, which he sketched quickly and well, that he had taste and knowledge. What he had observed and copied at Monsieur Dusommerard's served him well on this occasion. His lack of pretension, his probity, his active nature, his mind for order and administration, succeeded in making him valuable, and in the end he became, after several months of despair, worry, suffering, and last resorts, a sort of factotum of the theater, with earnings of several hundred francs assured and very welcome.

Marthe, while dressing the actresses and helping in the wings during performances, became familiar with the stage. Her lively intellect quickly grasped the weak and strong points of the trade. She retained, it seemed in spite of herself, entire scenes, and when she had gone home to her garret, she chatted with Arsène about them, analyzed the play masterfully, skillfully critiqued the performances, and, after having counterfeited maliciously and playfully the unbecoming mannerisms of the actresses, she spoke their roles as she felt them, naturally, with distinction, and with piercing emotion, which several times moistened Arsène's eyelids and made the old neighbor sob, while the baby, astonished by his mother's gestures and the inflections of her voice, threw himself screaming into the bosom of old Olympe. One day, Arsène exclaimed: "Marthe, if you wanted to, you could be a great actress."

"I'd try," she answered, "if I could be sure of keeping your respect."

"And why would that make you lose it?" he answered. "After all, I'm an ex–bad actor myself!"

Thus Marthe, promoted by the leading lady, who wanted to play a trick on an ingenue, her rival and enemy, made her acting debut, and she had a sparkling success. She was hired two weeks later, at a salary of five hundred francs, her costumes paid for and three months' vacation included. It was a fortune; ease and security rescued that poor household. Mother Olympe partook of their well-being, and, all puffed up with the brilliant prospects of her young friends, she took the baby for strolls down the picturesque streets of Belleville, seeking out pedestrians or gossips to whom she could say triumphantly, holding him up in her arms: "This is Madame Arsène's son!"

While bearing her friend's name, living under the same roof, and letting those around her believe she was united with him, Marthe was nevertheless neither the wife nor the mistress of Paul Arsène. There are circumstances under which such a lie is an act of impudence or hypocrisy. In the situation in which Marthe found herself, however, it was an act of prudence and dignity, without which she would not have escaped the malign questions and insulting pretensions of her surroundings. The modest and resigned couple had recognized that it was impossible, the way things stood, to sustain themselves in the hard but honorable class of workers. It would certainly not have been repugnant to either one of them to persevere down the painful road traced by their fathers; certainly neither of them felt drawn by taste or ambition to the vagabond vocation of the bohemian artist. But clearly the domain of art was the only one where they could find a refuge while providing for their material existence, and where their intellectual lives could develop.

In the social hierarchy, all positions are still acquired through hereditary rights. Those who rise by right of conquest are the exceptions. In the proletariat, as in the other classes, certain specific talents are required that Arsène didn't and couldn't have. Forgetful of his own future and only occupied with securing the well-being of the objects of his affection, he hadn't thought to master any particular trade. If he had been alone in the world, he would gladly have undergone any hard and tedious apprenticeship; but now, encumbered with a family, he was in a great hurry to accept any task, provided it was lucrative enough to meet the generous goal he had proposed for himself. To make matters worse, he lacked physical strength right when he needed it the most. So he had to swell the numbers, already enormous, of the lost children of this egotistical civilization that has forgotten to find a place for the sickly and intelligent poor. To them the theater, literature, art, with all their shining or wretched details, offer at least a career, where, unfortunately, many rush in because of laxity, vanity, or a love of disorder, but where, in general, talent and zeal have a chance for a future.

Arsène had aptitude, and one might even say genius, for everything. But everything was forbidden to him, since he had neither money nor credit. To be a painter, he would have had to study too long, and he didn't have an opportunity to devote himself to it. To become an administrator, he would have needed well-placed patrons, and he had none. The smallest bureaucratic niche is coveted by fifty aspirants. He who obtains it owes it not to respect for his personal merit, nor to the interest his needs inspire, but to nepotism. So Arsène could knock on only one door, the keys to which are chance and fantasy, the door that opens for boldness and talent: the door to the theater. It is sometimes the refuge for what is greatest in society, although society often forces it to be what is most vile. That's where the most beautiful and the most intelligent women end up, that's where men end up who have received, perhaps from on high, the gift of preaching. But the man who, in a century of faith, could have worked miracles with words; the woman who, in a religious and poetic society, should have been a priestess and initiator—if they have to descend to the role of histrion to amuse an audience that's often coarse and unfair, sometimes impious and obscene, what grandeur, what conscience, what elevated ideas and sentiments can we expect from them, driven as they are from their path and twisted as their motives become? And yet, the more the horror of prejudice is erased and ceases to add discouragement, revolt, and isolation to the causes of their demoralization, already so powerful, the more we see in so many cases that if honor and dignity are not easy, at least they're possible in the class of artists. I'm not speaking only of the great celebrities, those lives that have reached the social summit; but among the most humble and obscure, there are lives that are chaste, industrious, and respectable.

Marthe's was further proof of this. Delicate in body and mind, given to enthusiasm, endowed with an intellect more striking than creative; too little educated to pull works of art out of her own depths, but capable of understanding the most elevated feelings and quick to express them well; a person of extreme charm, of beauty accompanied by innate grace and distinction: she couldn't, without suffering, smother all these abilities, annihilate all that power. Yet she had done it without bitterness or regret since her arrival in the world; she herself didn't know the cause of her languors and of her sudden exaltations, of her deep dejections, and of the continual need for enthusiasm and admiration that she experienced. Her love for Horace had been the result of these propensities, excited but not satisfied by reading and reverie. The theater opened up a career of necessary fatigue, of continual study, and of invigorating emotions.

Arsène understood that this tender and restless soul needed nourishment, and he encouraged her attempts. He didn't mislead himself about the possible dangers, but he hardly feared them at all. He felt that a great calm had entered Marthe's heart, and that a great power had revived his own, ever since both had found a definite goal. Marthe's was to make sure, through her work, that her child had all the benefits of education; Arsène's was to help her attain this end, without thwarting her independence, and without compromising her dignity. In effect, Marthe's dignity *had* suffered from the position of being in debt and protected, which makes most women the inferiors of their husbands or lovers. Ever since, instead of submitting to another's help, she had felt herself to be an effective and active mother and protector of a being weaker than she was, she felt a sweet pride and held her head up, which had for a long time been bowed and humiliated under man's domination.

This new sense of well-being removed whatever pain the idea of being protected again might have had for her at the outset of her union with Arsène. She got used to not fearing his devotion, and to accepting it without remorse, now that she could do without it. She no longer saw him as the husband she had to accept to support her child, the lover whose pleas she had to entertain to pay off her debt of gratitude. Arsène was in her eyes a brother, who linked himself through pure affection, and not through the generosity of his pity, to her fate and to that of her son. She understood that he was not a benefactor who had come to forgive her for her past, but a friend who asked her, as a favor, for the happiness of living by her side. This unexpected situation assuaged her fearful heart and satisfied her justifiable pride. She felt it even more since Arsène had not addressed a single word of love since the miraculous meeting of June 6th. Each day, she had waited with trepidation for the explosion of this long subdued tenderness, and yet, instead of giving in to it, Arsène seemed to have conquered it: he was calm and respectful in his familiarity, playful in his melancholy. There had been no explanation between them other than Arsène's reiterated request that he not be exiled from her during her bad times.

Once prosperity was assured on both sides, Arsène finally spoke, but with so much nobility, strength, and simplicity that Marthe's entire response was to throw herself into his arms, crying: "Yours, yours completely and forever! My mind has been made up for a long time now, and I feared that you had renounced me."

"My God, you finally took pity on me!" said Arsène effusively, raising his arms to heaven.

"But what about my child?" added Marthe, throwing herself on her son's cradle. "Keep in mind, Arsène, that you have to love my child as you love me."

"Your child and you are the same to me," answered Arsène. "How could I separate the two of you in my heart and thoughts? While we're on this subject, listen, Marthe, I have an important question to ask you. You have to resign yourself to uttering a name that has not even crossed our lips for a long time. Now that you will be mine, and I will be yours, this child must be ours, and another can't have rights over what's dearest to us in all the world. Since you separated from Horace, have you had any contact with him?"

"None," answered Marthe, "I've never even known where he was, what he was thinking about. Sometimes I've wanted to know, I admit; although I no longer feel any affection for him, I've felt despite myself some stirrings of pity and interest. But I've always stifled them, and I've resisted the desire to ask you even a single question about him."

"What do you want to do? Have you decided how to act toward him?"

"I've decided nothing. I don't want to ever see him again, and I hope it won't happen."

"But if he came one day to reclaim his child, how would you answer him?"

"*His* child! *His* child!" exclaimed Marthe, horrified. "A child he doesn't know, whose existence he's unaware of? A child he didn't want, whom he engendered despite himself, and detested my hope for? A child he would have forbidden me from bringing into the world if it had been in our power? No, it isn't his child, and it never will be! Oh, Paul! How could you not understand that I could forgive Horace for humiliating me, for shattering me, for hating me; but that for having hated and cursed the child of my heart, he will never be forgiven? No, no! This child is ours, Arsène, and not Horace's. Love, devotion, and care are the true paternity. In this frightful world, where a man is allowed to abandon the fruit of his love without being considered a monster, the ties of blood count for almost nothing. And as for me, I've already taken advantage of the power that the law grants me to break completely the connection that unites my son with Horace. Mother Olympe took him to the city hall under my name, and for the father's name she wrote *Unknown.* That's the only revenge I've had on Horace: it would cut him to the bone, if he had the heart to feel it."

"My friend," said Arsène, "let's speak without bitterness and resentment of a man more weak than evil, and more sad than guilty. Your revenge was harsh, and you might regret it later. Horace is only a child, and he may continue to be one for several years; but in the end he will become a man, and he will perhaps forswear the errors of his heart and his mind. He will repent of the harm he did without understanding, and you will cause a piercing remorse in his life. If one day he sees this beautiful child, who, thanks to you, will no doubt be adorable, and if you refuse him the right to press it to his heart . . ."

"Arsène, your generosity is getting the better of you," interrupted Marthe with a wistful energy. "Horace will never love his child. He didn't feel this love at the age when the heart is at its full strength; how could he experience it at the age of egotism and self-interest? If his son had something that tickled his vanity, it would perhaps amuse him for a few days; but you can be sure that he wouldn't provide him with the lessons and examples my heart would desire. So I don't want him to belong to him. Oh, never! By no means!"

"Well," said Arsène, "have you definitely decided that? And do you want to stick to this choice without turning back?"

"Yes, I do," Marthe answered.

"In that case," he resumed, "there's a very simple solution. This child will pass for my son, because no one in our current circle knows our past or present relationship. They believe we're spouses or lovers. It would hardly enter into the morality of the theater to demand of any couple legal proof of their association. We've let them form this opinion; we deemed it necessary for our safety. Only Mother Olympe could say that the child doesn't belong to me, and she's too discreet and devoted to betray our plan. So far, nothing could be simpler: all we have to do is let stand an already established fact. But when we're reunited with our old friends (since even if we try to avoid them, it would be impossible for us not to run into someone; one day or another it's bound to happen), tell me, Marthe, what should we say to them?"

Marthe, dumbfounded and as if mortified, reflected a moment; then, making her decision, she answered firmly: "We shall tell them what we told the others, that this child is yours."

"Are you thinking of the consequences of that lie, my poor Marthe? Remember that Horace's jealousy was fairly well known among his friends: not all of them knew you well enough to be sure that it was not well grounded. . . They will all believe then that you deceived him; and that unjust accusation, which you didn't allow from Horace's lips, will be on everyone's lips, even those of the friends who never doubted you, like Théophile, Eugénie, and a few others!"

Marthe turned pale.

"That would hurt me very much," she answered. "I was so proud! I became so indignant when he suspected me! Now they will think that I was impudent and that I lied shamelessly. But in the end, what difference does it make? They can only accuse me of foolishness and vainglory; since they will know very well that I didn't present this child to Horace as his own, and that I distanced myself from him at the moment when I became a mother."

"They will say he turned you out, that you tried to deceive him, but that he perceived your infidelity; and he will be completely justified in the eyes of others and in his own."

"In his own eyes!" cried Marthe, struck by an idea that hadn't occurred to her before. "Oh! That's exactly right! That would be saving him from the punishment that God's justice has reserved for him! That would remove the shame that he *must* feel when he sees how you've taken on the duties he neglected. No! I don't want him to be ignorant of your greatness and the purity of your love! I want him to be humiliated by it to the depths of his soul, and I want him to be forced to say to himself: 'Marthe was quite right to take refuge in Arsène's arms!' "

"That's not important," said Arsène; "but what is important to *me* is that that blind and arrogant man does not claim for himself the right to scorn you and to go crying to your true friends: 'You see! I was absolutely right to mistrust Marthe. She was Arsène's mistress at the same time she was mine. I was right to curse her for getting big with child. The child she wanted to give me had two fathers, and I don't know to which of the two it belongs.' "

"You're right," answered Marthe. "Well then, we won't lie to our old friends; and if I ever have the misfortune to encounter Horace, I'll have the courage to tell him face to face: 'You didn't want to have anything to do with your child; someone else is proud to take responsibility for him, and so he deserved to be my spouse, my lover, my eternal brother.' "

Marthe, speaking these words, rushed into Arsène's arms and covered his face with kisses and tears. Then she took the infant from his cradle and solemnly presented him to Paul. Paul held him up in his hands, called on God as his witness, and consecrated this adoption in the eyes of heaven, holier and more trustworthy than any of those ratified by law in the eyes of men.

At the end of the summer, the Viscountess sped up her departure from the country on the pretext of attending to pressing business, but in reality it was to flee Horace, whom she no longer loved, and whom she had even begun to detest. In order to rid herself of this dangerous lover, she had written to her old friend, the Marquis de Vernes, and asked his advice, as was her habit when she needed him. She confessed her former gusto for Horace, and the disgust that followed, the contempt and resentment that his indiscretions had unleashed in her, and her fear that he might commit others. She recounted to the Marquis how, when she had tried to deal with Horace from a slightly elevated position to teach him some respect, her tactic had failed: Horace had wanted to impress everyone with his rights, and, to make himself feared without making himself hateful, he had spoken of jealousy and revenge like a Calderón hero. Léonie, terrified, asked the Marquis if he would do her the favor of rescuing her from this madman.

"Just as I predicted," the Marquis answered. "I liked this young man, and so did you, even more than I. He has the good qualities of the talented and the oddities of a *nobody*. He loves you, and he will soon hate you, since you can neither hate nor love him as he understands those words. His hatred or his love will be equally deadly for you. There is only one way to defend yourself against them, and that is to strive to make him indifferent to you. For that, you must at all costs avoid showing any indifference to *him*. That would reignite his desires, awaken his resentment, and push him to terrible extremes. On the contrary, be passionate; outdo his jealous fits, his injustices, his threats. Frighten him, wear him out with emotion. Try to irritate him with the strength of your unreasonableness. Take your turn at playing the Spanish lover, and make him so unhappy that he wants to leave you. Try to get him to take the first step toward a break, and make it a violent one; then you will be saved: he will have committed the first offense. The alacrity with which you take advantage of this to leave him will be a source of legitimate pride, the mark of a great personality, the implacable anger of a great love! I will vouch for the rest. I shall get hold of him when the opportunity presents itself; I shall hear his complaints, I shall prove to him that he alone is at fault, and, though he will hate you, he will be forced to respect you. He might pester you, he will commit acts of folly to reach you. Be merciless. He may blow his brains out, but only a bit; he has too much wit to wish to renounce the beautiful novels with which his future is rife. Then all the extravagant acts he will commit for you, far from compromising you, will turn into a triumph for your pride. Perhaps everyone will know that this young man adores you; but everyone will also know that you are driving him to despair; and if it so happens that, in his anger, he brags of his past, he will be looked on as a fop or a fool. From all of this, my beauteous friend, an excess of glory will accrue to you. Your power will be more envied than ever by women, and men will come to prostrate themselves by the hundreds at your knees."

The Viscountess faithfully followed her mentor's advice. She played the passionate role so well that Horace was terrified by it. As soon as she saw him recoil, she advanced and didn't balk at demanding that he spirit her away. This idea made Horace smile at first, because of the reverberations such an adventure would have, and because of the honor it would do him in his province and even in society, the *extravagant* passion of a lady of such rank and wit. The Viscountess shuddered to see him waver; but, twenty-four hours later, Horace got scared of the idea of living with so jealous and imperious a mistress. He thought of how he would suffer when the curiosity seekers would run after him to see him pass with his conquest, one saying: "Look! She's no more beautiful than that?" and another: "Lord knows she's not young!" And, having considered all sides, he refused the sacrifice she offered him on the pretext that he was poor, and that he couldn't resign himself to sharing his poverty with a woman like her, cradled in opulence. In fact, this pretext was fairly well grounded. The Viscountess made a show of not taking it into account, of disdaining riches, of wanting to defy society, which she pretended to hate and scorn. But as soon as she was sure of the sincere repugnance that Horace felt for this course of action, she accused him of not loving her at all; she shammed being jealous of Eugénie; she invented who knows what absurd grounds for suspicion and resentment. She even cried, and tore out a few strands from her hairpiece. Then she suddenly chased Horace out of her boudoir, prepared for her departure, refused to receive his excuses and farewells, and returned to Paris, exhausted by the drama she had just acted, satisfied to be finally delivered from the object of her terror.

From this moment on, just as the Marquis had predicted, her victory was assured; and Horace, while complaining of his supposed sorrow, and rejoicing that he no longer had to endure such violent emotions, felt himself to be the weaker party, since he believed himself to be colder.

In the autumn, the young nobles of the country who made up Léonie's usual court remained at their chateaux to devote themselves to the pleasures of the hunt; and one of them, who had befriended Horace and who seriously considered him a great man, invited him to come and finish out the season on his estate. Horace accepted this offer with pleasure. His host was a rich young fellow. He had little wit, no education, was goodhearted, and had good manners. He was a man Horace could dazzle with his erudition and charm with the brilliance of his mind, at the same time taking advantage of his company to mold himself according to aristocratic customs, with which he was then more than ever infatuated.

His first need was to forget the weeks of painful tumult he had just endured, and Louis de Méran's home was a delight for him. To have handsome horses to ride, a Tilbury at his disposal, magnificent arms and excellent dogs for hunting, a fine table, gay companions, and indeed, several other distractions which he didn't boast about to me after all the contempt he had shown for this sort of pleasure, but to which he abandoned himself when the dandies he was imitating boasted of, and cultivated, debauchery: it was enough to astound and intoxicate him until the first signs of winter. Since he actually was the superior of his new friends from an intellectual standpoint, with the power of his wits he made up for his lack of birth, wealth, and manners; for which, moreover, they would not have faulted him unless he paraded it, but he carefully refrained. He was so afraid of seeing the pride of these young people raised above his own that he led them to believe that he came from a good family in the legal profession and was comfortably well off. The slenderness of his valise certainly contradicted his braggadocio: but he was traveling; it was mere chance that he had stopped in this area, where he had come with the intention of staying only a few days; and, to make the all-too-obvious lightness of his wallet excusable in the eyes of Louis de Méran, he pretended several times that he wanted to leave, in order, he claimed, to go and fetch the money he needed *from his banker,* no less.

"Never mind about that!" said his host, who had the misfortune to become bored when left alone in his chateau, and who found Horace's company most pleasant. "My wallet is at your disposal. How much do you need? Do you want a hundred louis?"

"A hundred francs would do just fine," exclaimed Horace. Such a magnificent offer made him open his eyes wide, since up till then he had been tormented by the thought of how he could even manage a *tip* for the servants of the house when he left.

"Don't even think of it!" said his friend. "A lot of young people are going to get together on the occasion of a sort of country fair that we all attend, and where we sometimes spend a week in parties. We play a ruinous game there. Being new to the province, you have to be able to throw a few handfuls of gold on the table, if you don't want people to think you're a *cad.*"

Although Horace knew perfectly well that he could never repay this money unless he got lucky at the gaming table, no sooner did he glimpse this chance for success than he blindly trusted in it, and accepted his friend's offer. He had never wagered in his life, since he had never been in a position to, and he knew no game except billiards, at which he was a first-rate player, earning him the respect of several of the august personages in whose midst he had thrown himself. He soon got the knack of pair-royal, after seeing it in practice, and the day of the fair he made a passionate debut in this new career of emotions and dangers. He had, much to his later misfortune, insolent good luck that day. With a hundred louis he won a thousand. He hastened to reimburse Louis de Méran for his stake, put aside four hundred louis, and continued to play the following days with the remaining five hundred. He lost, won them back, and, after a few further fluctuations in his luck, returned to the chateau of Méran with seventeen thousand francs in gold and bank notes in his valise. For a young man with an enormous need for money, and who had led such a precarious existence, it was a fortune. He thought he would go mad with joy, and I think that after that he did, actually, a bit. He came to see us to inform us of his good luck, and never thought of repaying the hundred and fifty louis he owed me. I didn't venture to remind him, even though it bothered me a good deal; I considered it impossible that he could forget. Yet he never remembered, and I forgive him wholeheartedly, certain that his will played no role in this oversight. The dispatch with which he came to announce his wealth to me is the best proof. His first thought was to send one hundred louis to his mother, but he didn't dare tell her he had won the money gambling: the good woman would have been more frightened by it than gladdened. He wrote her that it was the fee for the literary work to which he had devoted himself during his hermitage, and which he was sending to a publisher in Paris.

"I intend," he said to me, laughing, "to reconcile her to the profession of a man of letters. She had so many regrets about my embracing it, but from now on she will look on it as terribly honorable. In a few months I'll send her another thousand francs or so, and so on, as long as I have the money. If only I could send her the whole sum today! I'd be so happy to be able to pay her back in one instant for the sacrifices she has made for me my whole life! But she would understand so little of what's happening to me that she would demand impossible explanations; and the people in my province, who are about as judicious as they are charitable, seeing Mother Dumontet stocking up on dishes and buying dresses for her daughter, would certainly conclude that, to secure such opulence for my family, I would have to have murdered someone. It's true that my good father, who prides himself a bit on belles-lettres, will want to read my prose in print. I'll tell him I'm writing under a pen name, and I'll cut a hundred pages out of a new volume by some mystical German poet, newly translated, and send them to him, telling him they're mine. He will be completely taken in and show it to all the fine wits of his little town, who, not understanding it in the least, will finally recognize that I'm a superior man."

When he recited these follies to me, Horace, who sometimes made fun of himself quite readily, burst out laughing. It was true he would have sent all the money to his mother at that very instant if he had been able to without frightening her. He had a generous heart; and if he rejoiced in his wealth, it was not so much because he possessed it, but because he had scored a certain triumph over what he called his evil fate.

Unfortunately, he forgot his resolution the very next day. His mother received nothing more from him, and all his Paris creditors were equally ignored. The only thing remaining of this moment of enthusiastic devotion was a sort of senseless and bizarre pride, which consisted of his believing in his lucky star when it came to monetary success, just as Napoleon believed in his when it came to military glory. This absurd trust in a providence preoccupied with favoring his whims, and in a God disposed to intervene in his undertakings, made him vain and reckless. He began to act the part of a young man for whom fifteen thousand francs was merely half of an annual allowance of thirty thousand. He bought a horse, scattered gold pieces among all his host's valets, wrote to his tailor in Paris that he had come into an inheritance and that he must send him the latest fashions. Two weeks later, he appeared decked out in the most ridiculous manner. His friends mocked the bad taste of his attire, and advised him to discharge his Latin Quarter tailor in favor of one who was a celebrity in the world of fashion. He immediately gave away his new wardrobe to the grooms of these gentlemen and ordered another from Humann, who outfitted Louis de Méran. Recommended by this elegant and rich young man, he had an open line of credit with this prince of tailors, about which he never had to concern himself, and which opened up underneath him an invisible abyss.

As soon as the joyful companions who surrounded him saw him being impudently wasteful and clothed in the outfit of a dandy (disguising his plebeian origins amazingly), they adopted him completely, and had the greatest esteem for him. It's no longer time but money that is the great teacher. Horace, held back and vexed by poverty no more, gave himself up to all the flights of his shining gaiety and his bold imagination. Money worked miracles on him; since it gave him, with trust in the future and enjoyment in the present, the capacity for work, which he had seemed to have lost forever. He recovered all his abilities, blunted by the sorrows and worries of the previous winter. His mood became again even-tempered and playful. His ideas, without becoming more sound, worked together, acted in concert. His style suddenly crystallized. He wrote quite a remarkable short novel with poor, sad Marthe as the heroine, and his loves as the subject. He gave himself a prettier role in it than he'd had in reality; but he justified and poeticized his faults very skillfully. One might say that his book, if it had caused more of a stir, would have been the most pernicious work of the Romantic era. It was not only an apology for, but an apotheosis of egotism. Certainly Horace was worth more than his book; but he had put enough talent into it to give this work some real value. Since he was rich then, he easily found a publisher, and the novel, printed at his expense and published shortly after his return to Paris, enjoyed a sort of success, particularly in elegant society.

This life of luxury mixed with intellectual labor and physical activity was Horace's ideal, his true element. I noticed that his speech and his manners, at first ridiculous when he tried to transform them from bourgeois to patrician, became gracious and dignified, as soon as, strengthened by his own merit and rich from his own money, he no longer sought to imitate others while reshaping himself. In Paris, his new friends introduced him in various rich and noble houses, where he saw the old high society and the new. He witnessed parties of Israelite bankers, and the less sumptuous and purer soirées of a few duchesses. He went everywhere with aplomb, certain of never being out of place, after having been the lover and pupil of the precious Viscountess de Chailly.

After two months of this life, Horace was completely transfigured. He stopped by to see us one morning in his Tilbury, his groom holding his lovely horse. He walked up our five flights as if he had never done otherwise in his life, and he had the good taste not to seem winded. His appearance was beyond reproach: his overgrown hair had finally been mastered by Boucherot, Michalon's successor. His hands were as white as a woman's, his nails trimmed to a bevel, his boots varnished, and he sported a Verdier cane. But the most extraordinary thing was that he had assumed a completely natural tone of voice, and it was impossible to guess that all this was the result of study. Only one detail betrayed how new this metamorphosis was: the triumphant joy that illuminated his forehead like a halo. Eugénie, whose hand he kissed (for the first time in his life) when he came in, had some difficulty at first in taking him seriously, and ended up being as astonished as I was by how easily this young butterfly had shed his chrysalis. He had gone to such a good school that he had learned not only the correct bearing, but how to make conversation. He no longer talked about himself; he questioned us about everything that might interest us personally, and he seemed to be interested in it himself. We had witnessed his first efforts to attain the style he finally mastered, and we were amazed that he had already lost the bombast and arrogance of the upstart.

"So, tell me a little about yourself," I said to him. "Business seems to be flourishing. I hope your new fortune isn't based only on cards, but of course on literature, where you have made such a fine debut."

"The money from gaming is coming to an end," he answered, naively: "I hope to renew it by drawing from the same source, and so far my attempts have not been unlucky; but since one must be prepared to lose, I thought of literature as a more solid foundation. Just the other day my publisher advanced me three thousand francs for a slim volume that I shall dash off in a fortnight; and if the public receives it with as much indulgence as the other book, I hope I shall no longer find myself short of funds." Three thousand francs for a slim volume, I thought, is a bit much; but it all depends on the terms.

"I must," I said to him, "speak to you about this novel you just published."

"Oh, please!" he exclaimed, "don't mention it to me. It's so bad that I'd rather never hear it spoken of again."

"It's not in the least bit bad," I said. "One might even say, from an artistic point of view, that it's a paraphrasing of the remarkable *Adolphe,* the little literary masterpiece of Benjamin Constant, which you seem to have modeled it on."

This compliment didn't please Horace much; his countenance suddenly changed.

"You think," he said to me, forcing himself to maintain his nonchalant air, "that my book is an imitation? That's quite possible: but it never occurred to me, the less so since I never read *Adolphe*."

"But I loaned it to you last year."

"You think so?"

"I'm certain of it."

"Oh! I don't remember. Then my book is a reminiscence."

"It's impossible," I resumed, "for the first work of a twenty-year-old author to be anything else; but since yours is well done, well written, and interesting, no one will complain of that. Yet, at the risk of sounding pedantic, I want to scold you a bit. You have, it seems to me, rehabilitated egotism . . ."

"Oh! my dear boy, drop that, I beg of you," said Horace with a touch of irony. "You're talking like a journalist. I catch your drift already! You're going to tell me that *my book is an evil deed*. This month alone I've read at least fifteen feuilletons that closed with the same statement."

I insisted. I fought a little battle with him; I countered his theories on "art for art's sake" with a sort of obstinacy that I felt was my duty as his friend, but against which he didn't maintain for long the veneer of playful modesty with which the study of good taste had provided him.

He grew impatient, defended himself crossly, bitterly attacked my ideas, and, losing little by little all his borrowed grace and calm as he returned to his former declamatory style—the vocal outbursts, theatrical gestures, even some of his old expressions from Latin Quarter café billiard tables—he let the old man out of the poorly whited sepulcher in which he claimed to have sealed him. When he realized what had happened, he was so ashamed and so incensed that he suddenly became gloomy and taciturn. But this was no newer to us than his noisy anger: we had seen him slip from speechifying to sulking so many times!

"Look, Horace," Eugénie said to him, familiarly placing her two hands on his shoulders, "as charming as you were at the beginning of your visit, and as sullen as you are right now, I love you more this way. At least it's you, with all your faults, which we know by heart, and which don't stop us from loving you. The other way, when you want to seem accomplished, we no longer recognize you, and don't know what to think."

"Thank you so much, my beauty," said Horace, trying to kiss her cavalierly to punish her for her impertinence. But she defended herself by threatening to give his face a little slash with her needle, which would have prevented him from going out in society that evening, and he *certainly* didn't want to expose himself to that danger. He tried to regain his ease and his distinguished manners before leaving us; but he couldn't quite get there, and, feeling awkward and unnatural, he cut short his visit.

"I'm afraid we got him angry and that he won't return in a hurry," I said to Eugénie when he had left.

"We'll see him again when he's earned more money and has a two-horse brougham he wants us to see," she answered.

"For a quarter of an hour I thought he'd corrected all his flaws," I continued, "and it delighted me."

"But it grieved me," said Eugénie, "since he seemed full of impudence, which is the worst of all vices. It's fortunate, don't you see, that he can never prevent himself from being ridiculous, because in spite of all his affectation, he has a core of naiveté that always gets the better of him."

That same day, we were surprised and thrown into confusion by a visit that was in all other respects pleasant. While we were still leaning over our balcony, our eyes following Horace's fleet Tilbury, we noticed that he almost ran over, at the turn for the bridge, a man and a woman who came toward him with linked arms, talking with their heads down, paying no attention to what was going on around them. Horace yelled, "Watch out!" in a resounding voice that rose above all the noise in the street as far as our ears, and we saw him whipping his fiery horse with the intention of scaring those ill-bred people who had forced him to stop for a second. Our eyes involuntarily followed that unassuming couple who kept coming toward us, and who seemed to have noticed neither the dandy nor his carriage. They walked pressed against each other, and more slowly than all the busy people along the sidewalk.

"Have you ever noticed," Eugénie said to me, "that one can guess, from the demeanor of two people of the opposite sex walking arm in arm, the feelings they have for each other? There's a couple who adore one another, I'll bet! They're both young, I see that from their shape and their bearing. The woman must be pretty, at least she has a charming figure; and from the way she's leaning on the arm of that young husband or new lover, I see she's happy to belong to him."

"It's a novel in and of itself and those two passing by may hardly even imagine they are in it," I answered. "But look, Eugénie! The closer that man gets, the more I seem to recognize him. He made a gesture like Arsène; he raised his eyes to our balcony. My God! If it could only be!"

"I can't see his features from this high up," said Eugénie; "but who could that woman be he's accompanying? It's definitely not Suzanne or Louison."

"It's Marthe!" I exclaimed. "I have good eyesight; she looked at us, she's coming in here . . . Yes, Eugénie, it's Marthe with Paul Arsène!"

"Don't tell me such stories!" said Eugénie, terribly moved, tearing herself away from the balcony. "You're giving me false hopes."

I was so sure of what I had seen that I flew down the staircase to meet these two ghosts, who, a minute later, were hugging Eugénie in their entwined arms. Eugénie, who had thought both of them dead, and who had cried bitterly for them, almost fainted when she saw them again, and only regained the strength to embrace them when she had showered them with tears. This greeting touched them keenly, and they spent several hours with us, during which they obligingly informed us of the most minute details of their story and their current situation. When Eugénie found out that her friend had become an actress, she looked at her in amazement, and said to me while facing her toward me:

"You see how she's still the same! She has become more beautiful, she dresses more elegantly, but her voice, her intonation, her manners—nothing has changed. All of that is as simple, as true, as lovable as in the past. Not like . . ." And she stopped herself in order not to utter a name that Marthe, in her narrative, had repeated several times without show-ing signs of pain. But at every moment, Eugénie, watching Paul and Marthe, and inwardly pursuing the comparison with Horace, couldn't keep herself from exclaiming:

"There they are! They haven't changed! It seems as if I left them just yesterday."

Marthe wanted an explanation for this reticence, and it seemed to me that it was better to speak openly and naturally about Horace than to force her to ask us about him. I recounted the story of the visit he had just paid us, and the entire tale of his sudden opulence. I even spoke to her about his relationship with the Viscountess de Chailly. I believed I had to do it to put the final touches, if they were needed, on the curing of this saved soul. She smiled out of pity, trembled slightly, and, throwing herself on her spouse's bosom, she said to him with a sweet, sad smile:

"You see how well I knew Horace!"

They had to leave at four o'clock. Marthe was to go on stage that very night. We went to see her, and we returned moved and over-whelmed with her talent, crying joyful tears at having found again these two cherished beings, finally united and making one another happy.

Horace, launched in society with a handsome face, good manners, witty conversation, the beginnings of a literary reputation, the appearance of having some wealth, and a name he signed *Du Montet,* could not help but be noticed; and there came a moment when, without too many illusions, he could flatter himself that he was destined for great success with those beautiful salon dolls called women of fashion. Two or three coquettes past their prime would have made him all the vogue, if he had let himself be promoted by them; but he had set his sights on a higher goal, and that was his downfall. He had gotten it into his head that these transitory love affairs were too easy, and that he should aspire to a brilliant marriage.

Ever since he had tasted wealth, he felt it was the only real and desirable thing. He no longer saw talent and glory as anything but means to achieve fortune, and he counted on the gifts he had received from nature to capture the heart of some rich heiress. With ability, time, and prudence, who knows if his dream wouldn't have come true? But he didn't know how to manage the resources of his position, and his excessive self-confidence led him astray. Quick to mistake the emotions he inspired, he plunged into an intrigue with a banker's daughter, a romantic schoolgirl who answered his letters, arranged trysts with him, and plotted with him an elopement and marriage at Gretna Green. Unfortunately, Horace didn't have enough money to pull off this escapade. The two or three thousand francs from his second novel had been eaten up before he ever got his hands on them, and he began to have as bad luck at gaming as he flattered himself he had good luck in love. He hurried matters, asked for the young lady's hand from her parents in a fairly imperative tone of voice, bragged to them of the passion she felt for him, and even let them know that it was too late for her to refuse him. This last point was a lover's trick that he hoped the young woman would go along with, since he had been, despite himself, more delicate than he would have liked to admit. He had respected the imprudent little heroine of his story, and their relationship had actually been so chaste that she didn't think he had put her in any danger. The parents, shrewd and prudent, as self-made people are, soon got to the heart of the matter. They won back their child with sweetness, depicting Horace to her as a fop, a heartless man, ready to compromise her to enrich himself by marrying her. They parleyed, cut off their correspondence and those shadowy rendezvous, bought time, talked of giving him her hand but not her dowry, and in only a few days were able to make these two lovers so disgusted with one another that Horace withdrew, furious with his beauty, who pushed him away with contempt and aversion. This sad adventure was kept secret: neither party was tempted to boast of it, and Horace, out of spite, rapidly turned his attention to a widow of good standing, who enjoyed an income of some twenty thousand pounds and was still young and beautiful.

Since she was devout, sentimental, and coquettish, he imagined that she would never belong to him except through marriage, and he was mistaken. Either because the widow only wanted to make him her *gallant,* who would serve with the best and most honorable intentions, or because she was less scrupulous and wanted to love without losing her freedom, he was welcomed gracefully, enticed artfully, and began to feel he was in love before he knew what to believe. I don't know whether—despite his extreme youth, which he concealed inside his thick beard; his roturier name, which he had made more suitable on his calling cards; and his poverty, which he could hide beneath his new clothes for a while—he could have satisfied his love and ambition. The hope of being a young man in politics had returned with that of becoming eligible to make a marriage. He nourished thoughts of even sweeter projects, and waited to confess his true circumstances until he had inspired a love violent enough to make them acceptable. But he had an enemy who was to block his path, and that was the Viscountess de Chailly.

Although she no longer felt any love for him, she had hoped to see him crawl at her feet, in accordance with the Marquis de Vernes's predictions, as soon as she left him; but the Marquis, judging Horace to be proud in love, had made a mistake. Horace was only vain, and his inconstancy, coupled with his natural goodness, prevented him from developing a serious grudge against her. He saw quite clearly that the Viscountess had gone back to the Count de Melleraie; but since she received Horace with apparent goodwill and continued to admit him to the ranks of her friends, Horace considered himself satisfied, and saw her without bitterness or pretension. That was the most desirable state of affairs for both of them; but Horace couldn't let a week go by without committing a grave error.

He loved to get intoxicated, perhaps to suffocate certain secret regrets. After a luncheon at the Café de Paris, he got drunk, became expansive, bragged, and let someone pry out of him the secret of his success with the Viscountess. One of those who perfidiously helped him in this confession hated the Viscountess, and was an intimate of the Count de Melleraie. The next day, the latter was informed of his mistress's infidelity. He didn't make a scene, since he didn't love her enough to get carried away, but he reproached her pointedly, wounding her deeply. From then on, Horace was the object of this woman's implacable hatred. She knew the widow he was courting fairly well, and she already sensed the direction this liaison was taking. She played up to her, won her trust, and turned her against Horace by uttering this simple phrase to her: "He's a man who *talks*." Horace was abruptly shown the door. The more he struggled, the more his defeat was shamefully confirmed.

This cruel mortification could not have come at a more inopportune moment. His second novel had just appeared, and it was not good. Horace had exhausted in his first the small sum of talent he had amassed, because he had spent in it the small sum of emotion he'd received. For him to produce a new work, his inner life would have had to renew itself quickly enough to warm and inspire him a second time. He had forced his brain into a childbirth that aborted. In trying to paint

Léonie and his love for her, he had been as cold and false as his model and his own feelings. Nevertheless, this bad work could have enjoyed a certain kind of success in a certain kind of world if he had deliberately served up the Viscountess to the wickedness of the salon public, and if he had fed these elegant readers the bait of a little scandal. But Horace had too noble a heart to seek this sort of vogue. He so poeticized his heroine that she wasn't true to life, and no one could recognize her. Incapable of keeping a romantic secret, he was equally incapable of revealing it coolly and out of vengeance.

The same day that he was dismissed by the prudent widow, he lost the last of his louis gambling and returned home in a fairly tragic state of mind. On his mantel he found a letter from his publisher, in response to a note he had written him the previous day requesting a new advance in return for the promise of a new novel. "Hateful profession!" he exclaimed, unsealing the letter. "So I'll have to write again, write forever, no matter what my state of mind; to be light in style when my brain is weighted down with fatigue, emotionally tender when my soul is withering with anger, fresh and blooming with metaphors when my imagination is blighted by disgust." He broke the seal convulsively, and, much to his surprise, read a point-blank rejection in the style of a dis-contented publisher, who calls a spade a spade and a missed chance at success a lemon. The worthy man was out of pocket for his expenses. In the two weeks since the work had been published, he had sold only thirty copies. And then, it was so short! Bookstores would only take this *wafer* at a discount. He made a point of telling Horace that he should have stretched out the ending. Two more folios, and the book would have earned fifty centimes a copy. And then, the title was not *thunderous* enough, the premise was not *moral,* there were *too many reflections;* and a thousand other causes for its lack of success that made the poor author hit the ceiling, beyond fury and full of despair.

When one's only wealth is beautiful words, boots with holes, and a threadbare outfit, one doesn't get discouraged by a publisher's rejection; one sets a campaign in motion and, despite snub after snub, finds another publisher with more confidence or money. But to run around in a Tilbury, followed by one's groom, from door to door begging for alms is not so easy. Still, beginning the very next day Horace tried it.

Everywhere he was received very politely, but with an incredulous smile for his literary future. His first novel had enjoyed a critical success, but not a financial one. The second was a complete fiasco. One asked him to get a preface by Eugène Sue, another a letter of recommendation from Monsieur de Lamartine, a third demanded that he be guaranteed one of Jules Janin's feuilletons. All agreed that they wouldn't pay for the publication, and not one of them offered to put up even the smallest advance. Horace cursed them all, the big fish as well as the little, and returned home sick at heart.

The next day he sold his horse to pay off his servants; the day after, he sold his watch to get a few gold coins so he could spend one more day in the role of the tycoon. He went to see Louis de Méran, who was playing whist with his friends. Horace won a few louis, lost them, won them back, and folded around three in the morning in debt five hundred francs, which, according to the laws of that world, he had to pay within three days to one of his best friends, a man endowed with an income of three thousand pounds, on pain of being despised and charged with beggary. After having tried his utmost to obtain the sum from a publisher, on the evening of the third day he decided to borrow the money from Louis de Méran, not without mortal unease; since he knew that without a new lucky streak in gaming he could not repay it, and the lack of care he had lately experienced had changed to lack of trust and to terror ever since he had known the harsh joys of possession and the bitter anxieties of financial ruin. This suffering became all the worse when it seemed to him he saw in his friend's glance and in his whole demeanor something cold and reserved that contrasted with his usual eagerness and trust. Up until then this young man had appeared, when lending him money, to be thanking him rather than putting him under an obligation, and so far, certainly, Horace had scrupulously reimbursed him. Ever since he had started passing himself off as rich, he had paid punctually, not his former debts, but those which he had incurred with his new entourage. That day it seemed to him that Louis de Méran gave him alms with a displeasure contained only by politeness. Did he guess that day that for the first time that Horace didn't have the means to repay him? But how? True, Horace had dismissed his retinue and moved out of the pretty, furnished apartment he had been occupying, on the pretext of an upcoming journey to Italy he had been announcing for some time, a plan for the sake of which he had ostensibly forgone buying furniture and setting up a house in keeping with his supposed ease. He pretended to be detained for a few more days on unforeseen business, in the hope that, during those few days, the luck of the draw, or even of love, would change in his favor, and permit him to postpone his trip indefinitely.

Nevertheless, the cold countenance of his noble friend, and a certain reluctance he thought he noticed in him to accompany him to the Opera, made him profoundly anxious. He feared that the worried expression he'd worn for several days had allowed others to suspect his troublesome position, and he resolved to erase those doubts by showing himself in public in the evening with his customary dandyism. In the heart of the Cité he went to find a dealer in secondhand items, with whom he had dealt before, and Horace sold him his diamond pin at a considerable loss; but now he had a hundred francs in his pocket. He rented a livery coach, put on the best suit he still owned, popped a magnificent rose into his buttonhole, and settled down at the front of the Opera, in one of those very visible stage boxes that are called today, I believe, "the lions' cage." At that time, the elegant denizens of the Café de Paris did not yet bear this strange name; but I think the same species of dandy was meant, or very close to it. Horace was enrolled in this variety of the human species, or professed to appear so. He had an entrée into a box where Louis de Méran paid a part of the cost and took him once or twice a week. He was always cordially welcomed there by the other occupants, since they liked him, and his wit livened these bored loafers. But that night they barely turned their heads in his direction when he entered, and no one bothered to make room for him. It's true that Nourrit was singing with Madame Damoreau the duet from *William Tell:*

Oh Matilda, idol of my life, . . .

Probably at that moment they were listening more attentively. Horace, afraid for a moment, was reassured; and he soon regained all of his usual aplomb when, at the end of the act one of these gentlemen enlisted him to dine at his house with the others after the show. Forcing himself to be playful, he managed to be enormously witty. And yet, from time to time, he thought he saw smirks being exchanged around him. Then a cloud would pass before his eyes, his ears would buzz, he could no longer hear the orchestra, the only thing he could see in the theater was an assembly of ghosts watching him, pointing their fingers at him, sneering horribly; and specters of women whispering strange words to each other behind their fans: *adventurer! adventurer! braggart, blusterer, a nobody! a nobody!* He would be on the verge of fainting when, collecting his wits about him again, he reassured himself that it was only a hallucination, and he made a violent effort to hide his anxiety. Once one of his companions asked him why he was so pale. Horace, particularly disconcerted by that remark, answered that he was in pain. *Perhaps you're hungry?* said another. Horace was mortified. He imagined he saw a horrible sarcasm in this insignificant phrase. He thought about retreating, hiding, never reappearing.

And then he thought that he shouldn't throw in the towel this way, that he should arrive at an explanation, confront the attack and boldly defend himself, and find out at all costs if he were the victim of some secret persecution, or just a bad dream. Following the merry band to the home of the Amphytrion of the night, Horace was in turn chilled and reassured by the alternately cool and benevolent manner of his fellow guests.

The woman of the house was a kept woman, extremely beautiful, extremely intelligent, extremely mocking, and excessively naughty. Horace had always hated and feared her, even though she had made advances to him. That day she was wearing a scarlet satin dress, her blond hair fell in waves, and she had a certain way about her that was more impertinent than usual. Her eyes shone with a diabolical luster: she was a true daughter of Lucifer. She welcomed Horace with feline grace, seated him next to her at the table, and poured for him with her beautiful hands the headiest wines of the Rhine. It was a very gay party. Horace was treated as well as usual; he was asked to recite his verses; he was applauded, flattered; and they succeeded in getting him drunk, not to the point of losing his reason, but to the point of regaining his self-confidence.

Then one of the guests said to him:

"Speaking of women, instruct us, my dear boy, why the Viscountess de Chailly bears such a grudge against you. Is it true that during a luncheon at the Café de Paris with B . . . and A . . . you compromised her honor?"

"The devil take me if I remember," answered Horace, "but I don't think I did."

"Then you must explain yourself regarding her, since she was told that you boasted of what a man of honor never boasts . . ."

"On an empty stomach!" added another. "But *in vino veritas*, isn't that right, Horace?"

"In that case," Horace replied, "as tipsy as I may have been, I should not have boasted of anything."

"What he means by that," observed Proserpine (that's what Horace called his host's mistress that night), "is that he had nothing to boast of, and I agree. Your Viscountess is dry, shiny, and angular as a seashell."

"She has a good deal of wit," another added. "Confess it, Horace, you were in love with her."

"Why not? But if I was, I don't remember any more than that."

"Yet they say that you remembered so much that you told them about some strange goings-on during your stay in the country last summer?"

"What is the meaning of all these questions?" said Horace, raising his head. "Am I before a jury?"

"Oh, no!" said Proserpine. "Small claims court, at most. So, my handsome poet, tell us about it among friends. The Viscountess wouldn't hate you so much if she hadn't loved you so much."

"And since when am I honored with her hatred?"

"Since you were unfaithful to her, my fickle friend!"

"And if I was not, it's your fault, my cruel friend," answered Horace in the same mocking voice.

"So you confess," she resumed, "that you had sworn to be faithful to her to the grave?"

"Will that be far off, then?" quipped Horace, laughing.

"Certainly," said someone, "you are making the Viscountess feel a violent resentment, and she speaks very ill of you."

"And what ill could she speak of me, pray?

"Are you eager to know?"

"A little."

"Well! She claims that you're poor, and that you pass yourself off as rich! That you're a child, and that you pretend to be a man; that every woman shows you the door, and yet you assume the pose of a conqueror."

Here it is, thought Horace; the time has come to weather the storm.

"If it amuses the Viscountess to pawn off impertinences of that sort," he answered firmly, "since I don't know how to avenge myself on a woman, I'll limit myself to saying that she is mistaken. But if a man were to repeat that charge with the slightest doubt about my honesty, I would answer him that he's lying."

The interlocutor to whom he addressed this answer made an angry gesture. His neighbor restrained him, and hastened to say in a fairly equivocal tone of voice:

"No one here doubts your honesty. If you betrayed the secret of your liaison with a woman during one of those moments after a few drinks where truly the truth escapes us without our being aware of it, the Viscountess is pushing her revenge too far in slandering you. But what if you were slandering her? If, despite your denials, you've lied, she must be excused for taking reprisals."

"But you yourself, Monsieur," said Horace, "you seem uncertain? I wish to know your opinion regarding me."

"My opinion is that you were her lover, that you recounted it to someone amidst the champagne bubbles, and that you committed a grave act of imprudence in doing so."

"What do you say?" asked Proserpine, filling Horace's glass. "Speak, gentlemen of the jury."

"It deserves at least two days' solitary confinement in the private chapel of Madame de ***."

Here the beautiful widow whom Horace had hoped to marry was named.

"Oh! Are charges being brought concerning her, too?" said Proserpine, eyeing Horace with a reproachful gaze aimed at intoxicating his vanity.

Although Horace was feeling a bit tipsy, he understood that he needed all his wits, and he abstained from emptying his glass; he sought to guess from the expressions of his fellow guests if this little war were a perfidious trap or a friendly tease. He believed there was nothing malevolent in it, and he endured all the interrogations in a playful spirit. Everything they said to him served to clarify a point that up until then had been a mystery to him: it was the Viscountess who had undermined him with the widow. He saw, what's more, that the Viscountess had tried to undermine him in his friends' eyes, and the way in which things were presented led one to believe that this civil war was the result of a wounded love. He found everyone inclined to judge him according to this light, and to absolve him, in this case, of the damaging suspicions leveled against him by an incensed and jealous woman. He could only justify his actions by confessing his intimacy with her; but he couldn't confess that without being accused of fatuousness, an imputation he had been staving off for a quarter of an hour. He had only one option, which was to get completely drunk, and he did it to the best of his ability, so that it would be acceptable for him to speak in spite of himself.

But by one of those flukes of human logic, which only leaves us when we want to hold on to it, and which insists on being faithful to us when we want to push it away, the more he drank, the less drunk he felt. He had a migraine, his eyelids were heavy, his tongue thick; but never in his life had his mind been so lucid. Yet he had to talk nonsense, alas! And so Horace talked nonsense. He admitted it to me later, after a severe interrogation: he played intoxicated, while not intoxicated, and, pretending to have lost his reason, he gave, with much discernment, the incontrovertible proof that he was telling the truth. He did it with a certain delight in the resentment he felt for the naughty creature who had wanted to dishonor him, and he thought he had savored the fatal pleasure of avenging himself; since he saw his convinced audience applauding his admissions, and registering them as if to unmask his enemy's conniving.

But suddenly his host, getting up from the table to accept the farewells of his guests, who were leaving, spoke to him in a cynical tone, coolly and scornfully: "Go to bed, Horace; since, although you're no more drunk than I am, you're as *plastered as a* . . ."

Horace didn't hear the last word, and I shall refrain from repeating it. He was astonished; and since his legs could no longer support him, his tongue could no longer articulate a single word, they pulled him along, and then they threw him, rather than setting him down at the door of Louis de Méran, at whose house, since the day he had left his lodgings, he had accepted temporary refuge.

What he suffered once he found himself alone could only be appreciated by those who have had faults that wretched for which to reproach themselves. Experiencing horrible physical pains, and unable to drag himself as far as his bed, he spent the rest of the night in an armchair, measuring the horror of his situation; since, to add to his torture, his reason had completely cleared, and he no longer had any illusions about the blame, suspicion, and scorn of those men whom he had wanted to dazzle and fool, and who, despite his superior mind, had just maneuvered him into a crude trap. Now he understood the test he had undergone, and the path of conduct he should have taken to escape vindicated. If he had confronted Léonie's charges with dignity, while persisting in respecting the secret of her vulnerability, and accepted their conjectures instead of shoving them aside for his own cowardly revenge—although his judges were not very enlightened, nor very delicate about such matters, they would have had enough instinctive generosity in their souls to forgive him everything. They would have respected the nobility and goodness of his heart, while blaming the vanity of his personality. These frivolous young people, who were worth no more than he in many ways, had at least absorbed from the fashionable world an education in chivalry that would have allowed them to act magnanimously, if Horace had set the example for them. When he lost the upper hand, he fell back lower than he deserved to be.

He could no longer have any doubts on this score. While bringing him home in their carriage, four or five young people, pretending to believe he was asleep, as he was pretending to be, let him overhear their terrible words, harsh and ironic. Yet he was condemned not to notice them, since he had condemned himself not to hear them. He wanted to scream; convulsions of fury shot through all his limbs, but, for the first time in his life, instead of giving in to his nervous exasperation, he had the strength to repress it, because he saw that they wouldn't believe it and they would be pitiless toward his delirium. It was truly too rough a punishment for a young man who was merely vain, flighty, and awkward.

When broad daylight came, Louis de Méran entered his room with a look so severe that Horace, unable to bear this unaccustomed greeting, hid his head in his hands to conceal his tears. Louis, disarmed by his pain, took a chair, sat down next to him, and, grabbing his hands with grave kindness, spoke to him with more reason and high-mindedness than he had seemed likely to display. He was a fairly ignorant young man, a spoiled child, but fundamentally good; tenderness of the heart brings out intelligence when the need arises. "Horace," he said to him, "I know what went on last night at that dinner, which I did not want to attend in order not to witness the humiliation they had arranged for you. Despite myself I would have taken your side, and that would have been a serious business to embark on with people whom, by right of seniority and through a long exchange of favors, I'm forced to prefer to you. I did my best to persuade you to stay home last night; you refused to catch my drift. Finally you betrayed yourself, and you made your situation worse. You committed errors that, according to the justice of my conscience, I find quite pardonable, but for which you will find no indulgence in that haughty and cold world that you wanted to brave without knowing. You have an implacable enemy, with whom you can exchange wound for wound, insult for insult. She is a wicked woman, whom I learned the hard way to avoid. But she is in society, and you're not. The laughter will be on your side, the influence on hers. She will have you chased out of every home, just as she got Madame de *** to dismiss you. Believe me, leave Paris, travel, go far from here, allow yourself to be forgotten; and if you insist on reappearing in what is called, quite arbitrarily no doubt, high society, don't return until you have a secure living and an honorable name in the world of letters. You made a serious mistake: you wanted to fool us. To what end? None of us would have considered it a crime for you to be poor and of obscure birth. With your wit and talents, you would have gotten us to accept you, perhaps a bit more slowly, but in a more solid manner. You wanted, beginning with a precarious existence, suddenly to enjoy the advantages of wealth and esteem that only your work and your pride and discretion could win. If I'd known that you were not twenty-five but twenty years old, I would have guided you a bit better. If I'd known that you were the son of a provincial clerk, and not the grandson of an attorney of the courts, I would have steered you away from the idea of falsifying your name. Finally, if I'd known that you had absolutely nothing, I would not have launched you on a way of life where you could only compromise your honor. The damage is done. Leave it to time, which erases scandal, and to my friendship, which will remain faithful to you, to repair it. You have talent and education. One day you may, with good sense, march alongside those shining personages whose free and easy manner seduced you, and whom you will perhaps look on then with pity. Promise me you will leave, and without concocting any schemes on how to avenge yourself for the suspicions that were formed about you. Fighting ten duels still wouldn't prove that you told the truth, and would produce an uproar about your adventure, which so far has been avoided. You need money to travel; here's some: too little, in truth, to lead the life abroad of a young man of good family, but enough to modestly await the fruits of your work. You will repay me when you can. You should hardly torment yourself about it; I'm wealthy, and I swear to you, Horace, that no favor I've done you has given me as much pleasure as the one I'm doing at this moment."

Horace, pierced with repentance and gratitude, squeezed Louis's hand firmly, obstinately refused the purse he was giving him, but very sweetly thanked him for his good advice, promised to follow it, and abruptly left his home. Louis de Méran wrote to me right after that, to bring me up to date on all these things, and to enlist me to get Horace to accept under my name the advance that he hadn't wanted to receive from him, but that he needed in order to begin his trip.

Unfortunately, this excellent young man's act of devotion was not as promptly efficacious as he would have wished. Horace didn't come to see me, and I looked for him for several days without succeeding in discovering his refuge.

So he spent three or fours days in solitude, anguished by his shame and poverty, not knowing how to hide from one or how to stop the progress of the other. His soul had experienced the most painful blow that it was prepared to absorb. The sorrows of love, the torment of remorse, even the worries of destitution hadn't seriously unsettled him; but the deep wound sustained by his vanity was more than enough to punish him. Unfortunately, it was not enough to correct him. Horace had no strength or hope to react to the sentence that had been slapped on him. Shut in a garret, wandering the streets alone at night, he wrung his hands and shed tears like a baby. So society, that is to say the life of pomp and dissipation, this elysium of his dreams, this haven against all the reproaches of his conscience, was closed to him forever! The consolations that Louis de Méran had tried to offer seemed illusory to him. He knew quite well that people who live on pretension, legitimate in their own eyes, are pitiless toward the poorly founded pretensions of others. He had enough pride not to want to get back into favor by seeking to justify his conduct; and even if he had been assured of victory in the eyes of society in his struggle against the Viscountess, the mere thought of braving humiliations such as those he had just endured made him shudder with pain and disgust.

He had showed off his fleeting prosperity, as much with his old friends as in his correspondence with his parents, so that he no longer dared, in his distress, appeal to anyone. And to tell the truth he couldn't decide on any one plan. He felt sure that the quickest and wisest way would be to return to his region and to write a literary work there, in order to pay off his last debts and to accumulate what he needed to set out on foot for Italy; but he didn't have the courage. He knew that his parents, deceived about his literary successes, hadn't failed to proclaim them from every rooftop in their little town, and he feared that one fine day some slander, gathered by chance from far away, might reach them and change their admiration to scorn. Six months earlier, he had gaily and heedlessly loaned a louis a week to several classmates. In that world, no one blushes at being poor, and students recount laughingly to one another how they didn't eat dinner the previous night, for want of nine sous to pay the check at Rousseau's. But when one has frequented the salons closed to the needy, when one has dazzled one's friends who travel on foot with one's coach and retinue, one hides one's indigence like a vice and one's hunger like an opprobrium.

And yet, one night, Horace made up his mind to come up to my place, though not without retracing his steps at least ten times. His countenance was heartrending to see: his face had withered, his cheeks were sunken, the fire in his eyes had flickered out. His hair in its disorder still bore the signs of curliness, and, seeking to regain its natural posture, stood up in stiff and twisted locks around his forehead. He no longer had the courage to conceal his poverty under a guise of tidiness. His whole neglected and disordered personage testified to the profound discouragement into which he had allowed himself to sink. His fine and stylishly pleated shirt was dirty and rumpled. His suit, so elegantly cut, had several buttons missing or broken, and no one had thought of brushing it for several days. His boots were covered with dried mud. He had no gloves, and for a cane he carried a large, lead-filled stick, as if he were constantly on guard against some ambush.

Fortunately Eugénie and I had been warned, and we tried not to act surprised when we saw how he had metamorphosed. We pretended not to notice, and, asking no questions, we suggested right away that he dine with us. In fact, we had already had dinner; but Eugénie, in less than a quarter of an hour, organized a new meal for us, which we made a semblance of nibbling, and which Horace craved too much to realize our deceit. He was so famished that, to our amazement, he became absolutely prostrate as soon as he was sated, and fell asleep in his chair before the tablecloth had been taken away. By chance the apartment that Marthe had occupied next to ours was vacant. We hastily brought a cot in there and a few chairs; then, gently approaching Horace, Eugénie said to him:

"You're suffering a great deal, Horace; you would do well just to lie down on the bed that we made available for the past few days to a friend from the provinces—it's still all made up. Take advantage of it till you feel better."

"It's true, I feel terribly ill," Horace answered; "and if it wouldn't be indiscreet of me, I'll accept your hospitality till tomorrow." He let himself be led into Marthe's room, where he seemed to be struck by no painful memories. He was as if stupefied, and this state, so contrary to his natural liveliness, had something frightening about it.

He was still sleeping the next day when Paul Arsène came to our apartment, bearing Marthe's baby in his arms. "I'm bringing you your godson," he said to Eugénie, who had grown fond of this strapping boy, and who had given him the name of Eugène. "His mother is overwhelmed with work today, and I am, too. She's making her debut tonight at the Gymnase, where I've been hired as a ticket seller, as you know. Mother Olympe is a bit sickly, and is going out of her mind. We're afraid our *treasure* will be poorly looked after. You must come to our rescue and watch him all day, if that's not too much trouble."

"Give me that treasure right away," exclaimed Eugénie, joyfully grabbing the kid, whom, with his enormous and naive tenderness, Arsène no longer called anything else.

"The treasure is adorable," I said to him; "but think of the inevitable encounter later on? . . ."

"Arsène," Eugénie added, "gather up all your courage and composure: Horace is here."

Arsène turned pale. "No matter," he said; "after what you've confided in me, I certainly should have expected to meet him here one of these days. The baby's name is hardly written on his forehead, and besides, thanks to him, the 'treasure' is anonymous. Poor angel!" he added, kissing Horace's son; "I entrust him to you, Eugénie; don't give him up to his lawful owner."

"He won't fight you for him, don't worry!" she answered with a sigh. "But warn your wife, so she stays away from here for the next few hours. Horace can't stay in Paris, and it would be easy to avoid that meeting."

"I would very much like that," said Arsène; "it seems to me that even that man's glance might do her harm. But if she wants to see him, so be it! Up till now she's said she doesn't desire that. Farewell. I'll come and fetch my child this evening."

"Oh, you have a child?" said Horace indifferently when he entered our apartment around ten o'clock to eat lunch.

"Yes, we have a child," answered Eugénie with a secret, harsh malice. "What do you think of him?"

Horace looked at him. "He doesn't look like you," he said with the same air of indifference. "It's true that those chubby babies don't look like anything, or rather they all look alike: I've never understood how one can tell one little child from another of the same age. How old is that one? One month? Two months?"

"It's easy to tell you've never even seen one before!" said Eugénie. "This one is eight months old, and he's superb for his age. Don't you think he's a beautiful baby?"

"I'm no judge of that. I'll say he's *ravishing* if that will make you happy . . . Wait, I'm thinking! You couldn't possibly be his mother. I saw you eight months ago . . . Come on! This baby isn't yours."

"No," said Eugénie brusquely. "I was poking fun at you. It's the child of our concierge, it's my godson."

"And is that fun for you, carrying him in your arms while you do your housework?"

"Do you want to hold him for a bit," she said, giving him to Horace, "while I serve lunch?"

"If it speeds lunch up a little, I'll do it gladly; but I assure you I don't know how to handle such a *thing,* and if he gets it into his head to scream, I won't know what else to do but set him on the ground. Fie! Since you're not his mother, I can safely say to you, Eugénie, that I find him very ugly with those puffy cheeks and round eyes!"

"He's handsomer than you," exclaimed Eugénie, frankly angry, "and you're not worthy of holding him."

"Look, he's squawking," said Horace. "Let me to return him to his dear parents' lodge."

The baby, scared by Horace's thick, black beard, had thrown himself, crying, back into Eugénie's bosom.

"And I," she said, caressing him to calm him down, "I'd be so happy to have a child like you, my poor little treasure!"

Horace smiled disdainfully, and, sinking into an armchair, he began to daydream. The past finally seemed to reawaken in his memory, and he said to me dejectedly when Eugénie, after depositing the baby on my lap, had gone into the next room: "Eugénie will never forgive me for not having understood the joys of fatherhood: women are so unjust and pitiless. I've thought a lot about it, since my *unhappiness;* and I've sought in vain for a way the delights of family life can be appreciated by a man of twenty. If a child could enter the world at the age of ten, when its beauty and intelligence start to develop (assuming, for the moment, that it's not ugly, or redheaded, or hunchbacked, or retarded), I would understand, up to a point, how one could take an interest in it. But to take care of that little unclean, crabby, stupid, and yet despotic entity, that is a woman's business, and for that God made them different from us."

"That's only true up to a point," I answered. "Women love them more tenderly, and understand better how to raise them during the early years; but I, personally, have never understood how, in the presence of such a weak and mysterious being who bears within it an unknown past and future, one could experience, of all feelings, repugnance. The men of the people are better than us, Horace. They love their little ones with admirable naiveté. Have you never been seized with respect and tenderness by the sight of a robust worker in the evening dandling his kid in the doorway in his bare arms, still all black from his labor, cheering it up to relieve its mother?"

"Such virtues are irreconcilable with cleanliness," answered Horace, bantering disdainfully, and not realizing that at that moment, he himself was quite unclean. Then, passing his hand over his forehead, as if to reassemble his thoughts: "Thank you for sheltering me last night," he said; "but I don't know if you put me in that fatal room to reawaken in me a beneficial remorse. I had horrible dreams there, and I must, since now I definitely am in the most sinister state of mind, ask you a painful and delicate question. Did you ever find out, Théophile, what became of the unfortunate woman whose heart I so horribly broke by committing the strange crime of not being enchanted with the idea of becoming a father at the age of twenty, when I was indigent?"

"Horace," I said to him, "are you posing this question with the emotion that you have, at this moment, written on your face, that is to say with a fairly lazy curiosity, or with the one you must have in your heart?"

"My face has turned to stone, my poor Théophile," he answered in a tone of voice that became increasingly declamatory, "and I don't know if I can ever cry or smile again. Don't ask me the cause; it's my secret. As for my heart, its destiny is to be misunderstood; but you who have always been better and more indulgent to me than all the others, how can you insult me now by not knowing that it will bleed forever from this wound? If I were certain that Marthe were alive and that she had found consolation, I might possibly be unburdened today of one of the mountains that bears down on all of my past, and perhaps my future as well!"

"In that case," I said, "I'll answer you with the truth: Marthe isn't dead; Marthe isn't unhappy; and you can forget her."

Horace didn't receive this news with the emotion I expected. He had more the look of a man who can breathe again when he throws down his bundle than of a guilty man who has regained heaven's grace.

"God be praised!" he said without thinking of God in the slightest; and he fell back into his reveries without asking another question.

Yet he came back to this thought later in the day, wanting to know where she was and how she was making a living.

"I'm not authorized to give you any sort of information on this matter," I answered him, "and I advise you for your peace of mind and hers not to seek her out; it would be too late to undo your past mistakes, and it would only pain you to learn that there is no need to undo them."

Horace looked at me bitterly: "From the moment Marthe left me without regrets and without the suicidal intentions that I was afraid she had; from the moment that she was no longer unhappy, and that she shook off her love out of weariness or inconstancy, I don't see how my mistakes were so serious that either she or another has the right to remind me of them."

"Enough on that subject," I said to him. "This is a very inopportune moment for explaining yourself."

That put him into an ill humor, and he left; but he came back at the dinner hour. Eugénie had not dared invite him, for fear of seeming to be aware of his predicament. I didn't want to tell him that I knew of it, since I was waiting for him to make a clean breast of it. He still didn't seem inclined to do so, and he said to me when he came back:

"It's me again: we left on rather cool terms earlier, Théophile, and I can't leave things that way with you." He held out his hand to me.

"That's fine," I said to him; "but to prove to me that you don't hold a grudge, you must dine with us tonight."

"Certainly," he answered, "if that's all it takes to erase my mistake . . ."

We sat down at the table, and we were still there when Mother Olympe came to reclaim the baby to put it to bed.

In the midst of the myriad activities of the day, Arsène and Marthe had forgotten to warn that good woman that if she encountered Horace at our apartment she should not chatter away in front of him. Unfortunately, she loved to talk. She was wholeheartedly and heatedly, as she herself put it, for her young friends; and that day, more than usual, overexcited by the splendor of their new situation in a theater that was in vogue, she felt a pressing need to become emotional when speaking of them. Eugénie tried in vain to whisk her away as soon as possible with her "treasure," to lead her into the kitchen, to make her lower her voice; Mother Olympe, understanding nothing of these precautions, vented her joy and her tenderness in long speeches, in sonorous exclamations, and several times uttered the names of Monsieur and Madame Arsène. So Horace, who at first had taken her for the concierge and had not deigned to lend an ear to her words, then looked her over, observed her, and interrogated us eagerly as soon as she had left. Which Arsène was she speaking of? So, was Masaccio a husband and father? The supposed child of the concierge was actually his? And why hadn't we told him that right away? "I should have guessed; besides," he added, "his baby is already as ugly and pug-nosed as he is."

All this superb disparagement made Eugénie impatient to the point of indignation. She broke two plates, and I believe, despite her sweetness and her habitually dignified manner, that she truly wanted to throw a third at Horace's head. I calmed her down a great deal by resolving to tell the truth immediately. Since Horace would learn it sooner or later, it was better that he should learn it from us and in a moment when we could observe the effect it had on him. Arsène had authorized me several days before, on behalf of him and Marthe, to act as I judged best under these circumstances.

"How is it, Horace," I said to him, "that you have not already guessed that Paul Arsène's wife is a person well known to you, and whom we hold infinitely dear?"

He reflected a minute, looking at us in turn with cloudy eyes. Then, suddenly assuming an offhand pose borrowed from the Marquis de Vernes:

"In point of fact," he said, "it could only be *she*, and I'm quite a fool not to have understood why you were so uneasy just now in front of that old bag who was taking the child away . . . But the child? . . . Oh! . . .the child! . . .I get you! The old woman very distinctly said *his father* when speaking of Arsène . . . an eight-month-old baby . . . since he's eight months old, didn't you tell me this morning, Eugénie? . . .and it was nine months ago that Marthe left me, if my memory serves me well . . . Great God! This is a sublime ending, one I didn't think of for my novel!"

Here Horace fell back onto a chair with a burst of laughter so strong, so harsh, that it hurt us like the rattle of a man in agony.

"Oh! you can stop laughing," exclaimed Eugénie, getting up with an incensed look on her face that rendered her truly beautiful and imposing: "that child whom Paul Arsène is raising and cherishing as his own is yours, since you wish to know. You found him ugly because, according to you, he looked like Paul: and he finds him beautiful, although he resembles, the poor innocent thing, the most egotistical and ungrateful man in the whole world!"

This burst of anger exhausted Eugénie: she fell back into her chair, choking, tears streaming down her cheeks. Horace, irritated by what amounted to a curse vehemently hurled at him, had also stood up; but now he dropped back down, as if struck by the cry of his conscience, and hid his face in his hands.

He remained that way for over an hour. Eugénie, wiping her eyes, had resumed her housework, and I waited silently for the conclusion of the battle that pride, doubt, repentance, shame were waging in Horace's heart.

He finally emerged from this stormy meditation, getting up and walking around the room with long strides and grand gestures.

"Eugénie, Théophile!" he exclaimed, grabbing us both by the arm and staring at us fixedly, "don't toy with me! This is the decisive moment of my life; you hold in your hands my ruin or my salvation. What's at stake is whether I'm the most ridiculous or the most cowardly of men. I'd prefer to be the most ridiculous, I give you my word."

"I believe you!" answered Eugénie scornfully.

"Eugénie," I said to my proud companion, "treat Horace with a little indulgence and kindness, I beg of you. He's very much to be pitied since he's very guilty. You gave into your impetuous heart just now in crushing him with an extremely serious accusation. But that's not how one should treat the soul's infirmities. Let me speak to him, and trust my respect, my affection, my veneration for your absent friends."

"Respect, veneration," resumed Horace, "only that! . . . that's not much: can't you invent some term of idolatry more worthy of the great, the divine Paul Arsène? As for me, I'd very much like to answer your litanies with an amen; but not before you've proved to me irrefutably that I'm really the father—*the only father,* do you understand?—of that child whom they now want to foist onto me."

"Those are not their intentions at all," I said to him with a cool severity. "They want you never to trouble yourself about your son; they never presented him to you as such; they never spoke to you about him. And if you should get it into your head to reclaim him one day, since the law gives you no rights over him, they would be able to remove him from your belated and usurping protection. So don't insult a nobility and devotion that you can't comprehend. That would degrade you in everyone's eyes, even in your own, when the thick veil covering them finally falls. Besides, the matter at hand at this critical moment, as you rightly call it, is precisely the throwing off of this disastrous veil. You must overcome those feelings that are unworthy of you, and that you would deeply repent. You have to leave here full of respect for the mother of your child, and gratitude for his adoptive father, do you understand? You have to tell me that you've acted like a child, like a madman, or bear forever my antipathy and my disgust for your character."

"Very well," he answered, struggling against my sentence, "I must make honorable amends, because I was made father of a child whom I never even heard of and who turns out to be mine! What test must I undergo to prove how repentant I am? What public penitence do I have to do to wash away my crime?"

"None! This entire story is a secret among four people, and you happen to be the fifth. But if you have the madness and misfortune to make it public, to recount it as you tend to do, I'd be forced to tell the truth, and to inform all those who know you that you lied about it. You demand material proof, proof that's irrefutable! As if it could be provided! As if there are proofs other than ethical ones! It's as if you were declaring that your mind was too dense and your soul too base to believe anything but the direct evidence of your senses. According to this hypothesis, any man on earth could deny and spurn his children on the pretext that he has not witnessed each and every moment of his wife's existence."

"What would you have me do, then?" he said with a concentrated fury. "Tell the world my secret, and proclaim Marthe's virtue at the expense of my honor? What you're suggesting is a duel to the death between that woman's reputation and mine!"

"Not in the least, Horace. This is not the world that you just left. Twenty salons are not watching with gawking eyes the secrets of your domestic life, and Marthe's honor does not require, like that of a certain Viscountess, that yours be compromised. The milieu where those events took place is very limited and obscure. At the most, four or five old friends will ask you to account for your love affair with her. If you answer them that she was an unfaithful and undignified lover, this brouhaha could spread and reach her in the more public and envied position that she is beginning to assume. But you can preserve your dignity and hers, which are not in conflict here in the least. If you don't understand how you must conduct yourself in this situation, I'll tell you. You will refuse to offer any explanations; you will never speak of the child whom Arsène recognizes and declares, through a pious lie, to be his own; you will say in the firm and concise manner that becomes a serious man that you have the esteem and respect for Marthe she deserves. And believe me, this declaration will do you honor, even in the eyes of those who suspect the truth. Only that can make them excuse and keep quiet about your strayings. . . If you had acted in this way even in regard to another woman who is less worthy, you would perhaps be rehabilitated today in the eyes of more punctilious and demanding judges than your former friends were."

This insinuation brought up another subject for explanations, and Horace, dismayed, received my admonishments in silent dejection. But he argued about Marthe for a long time, and for two hours I had to struggle, not against his incredulity, which was weak enough, but against his obstinacy and spite. Despite his resistance, I still saw clearly that he was teetering and that I was gaining ground. At nine o'clock that night he went out, telling me that he needed to be alone, to get some fresh air and take a walk to think it over. "I'll be back before midnight," he said to me, "and I'll let you know then quite frankly what my conscience has told me. We'll chat again about all this, if you're not horribly weary of me."

He returned around one in the morning with a lively look on his face, though still very pale, and had a warm and communicative manner. "Well?" I said, squeezing the hand he held out to me.

"Well!" he answered, "I won a victory, or rather it's Marthe and you who have vanquished me, and from now on you may do with me as you please. I was mad, unhappy and tormented by a thousand piercing doubts; but the rest of you, you're strong, calm, and wise. You're helping me find the face of truth again, when it clouds over in my imagination. Listen to what happened to me; I want to tell all. After leaving you, I went to the Gymnase; I wanted to see Marthe, a parody of an actress on that shabby stage, reciting in a simpering voice the sentimental smut of our little bourgeois dramas. Yes, I wanted to see her like that, to cure myself forever of the spite she left in my soul, to despise her image within me and to despise myself for having loved her. I hadn't been sitting there five minutes when I saw an angel of beauty and heard a pure and touching voice like Mademoiselle Mars's. It was really the beauty, the voice of my poor Marthe; but how poeticized, how idealized by the culture of the mind and by the serious work of seduction! I said it to you before; a woman who does not make her main occupation that of pleasing is not a woman; and in those days, Marthe, despite all her natural gifts, had a melancholy laziness, a humble and sad reserve that made her lose, most of the time, every advantage she had.

"But what a metamorphosis, great God! had taken place in her! what an abundance of beauty, what distinction in her bearing, what elegant diction, what aplomb, what nonchalant grace! And all that without losing that simple, chaste, and sweet manner, which used to bring me back to myself and make me fall on my knees in the midst of my suspicions and frenzies! Tonight she had, I can assure you, a success that was not merely dazzling, but real and well deserved. Her part was bad, false, even ridiculous, but she was able to make it true, noble, and thrilling, without exaggerated gestures, without rash measures. They only applauded a little; they didn't say: Sublime! Fantastic! But everyone turned to his neighbor and said: Now, that was good; really good! Yes, *good* is the right word. I learned in society, where one learns a few good things in the midst of any number of bad ones, that the good is harder to attain than the beautiful; or, to put it better, the good is a more refined facet of beauty, more polished than any other.

"Oh! the truth is, I'd be delighted if all the impertinent giddy creatures they call 'women of the world' could see how this poor grisette knows how to walk, to sit down, to hold her bouquet, to chat, to smile, with more decorum than all of them rolled into one! But where the devil did Marthe learn all that? Oh, intelligence is such a quick and penetrating force! On my honor, I never suspected that Marthe had so much of it; and that thought made me open my eyes. How little I understood her! I said to myself, watching her. So often I thought she was limited or foolish, and here she is contradicting me, and this seems to be her revenge for my mistake, to show how accomplished and triumphant she is, before my very eyes, before that whole audience, before everyone who is anyone in Paris!—since everyone who *is* anyone in Paris will soon be talking about her, and squabbling over who will have the pleasure of seeing and applauding her!

"I blushed a good deal at myself, I confess. And when the play was over, I ran to the stage door, I broke all protocol, I infuriated all the porters and watchmen of that strange sanctuary; I searched for her, I found her dressing room, I shoved open the door after I'd knocked, and, without waiting for them, according to the custom, to negotiate with me, I dared to penetrate to where she was. She was still in her elegant costume, but she had wiped off her makeup; her hair, from which she had removed the flowers, trailed down, longer, blacker, more beautiful than ever, onto her regal shoulders. She was even more gorgeous than she had been on stage, and I threw myself at her feet; I pressed her knees against my chest, scandalizing to no end her maid, who seemed to me a very naive village girl for a dresser in a theater.

"I knew I wouldn't find Arsène by her side; I remembered clearly that he was a ticket seller, that he would be busy with administration while his wife was getting dressed. My friends, say what you will to me: she's married, she cherishes her husband, she respects him, she prizes him; all that is well and good: but she loves me! Yes, Marthe still loves me, she will always love me, and although she told me the exact opposite, I can't doubt it. She turned, when she saw me, pale as death; she tottered; she would have fainted away if I hadn't held her up in my arms and sat her down with me on the settee. It was a full five minutes before she could manage a word, she was so distracted; and finally, when she spoke to me to boast of her happiness, her tranquillity, her marriage . . . her moist eyes and her heaving bosom told me something entirely different. And I, only vaguely hearing with my ears the words that came out of her mouth, I understood with my whole being the voice of her heart, which was speaking louder and more eloquently.

"She wanted me to wait in her dressing room for Arsène to arrive; I think she feared his suspicions, if it seemed that she was receiving me in secret. But Monsieur Arsène worried and tormented me for a year, so I had no scruples about giving him some of his own medicine for one evening. Besides, I was not at all disposed to see that vulgar and prosaic being speak intimately with, kiss, and lead away the woman whom I was not yet ready to stop viewing as my mistress and companion. I stole away, promising her only to come and see her again when she wanted, and in the presence of whomever she wanted. But for at least an hour I was excited, moved, and, since I should tell all, smitten as I haven't been for a long time. I said it to you twenty times in the midst of all my follies, remember, Théophile: I have loved only Marthe, I feel strongly that I will never love anyone but her, despite it all, despite her and myself.

"But why are you knitting your brows? Why is Eugénie shrugging in that sad and worried way? I'm an honest man; and since Marthe is a proud and upright woman, since she will certainly only want to see me now in the presence of her husband; since, if her husband consents to it, it would be a tacit agreement on my part to respect her trust and honor, you hardly need fear, it seems to me, that I'll cloud the serenity of their household. Oh, don't worry, I beg of you; I don't have the slightest desire to run off with his wife, even though he ran off with my mistress. He has behaved admirably toward her, and toward my son . . . since he is my son! Marthe didn't say a word to me about the child, nor did I, as you may imagine . . . But in the end, a sacred, indissoluble bond definitely unites me with her, and if I ever become wealthy, I won't forget I have an heir. Then I'll be able to pay Arsène back indirectly for the care he's provided him; and since they wish me to withdraw my parental rights, I will only exercise my paternity in a mysterious way, one might say providentially. You see, my good friends, I do not intend to be either as cowardly or as perverse as you thought this morning. In fact, far from being Marthe's enemy and slanderer, I remain her admirer, her servant, and her friend. I don't think Arsène can fault me for that: when he attached himself to the woman who used to belong to me, he should certainly have foreseen that her feelings for me wouldn't completely die, nor mine for her. He's a wise and coolheaded man, who won't lord it over her, since he knows me. As for me, I feel relieved, consoled, and almost revived by today's events. I was absurd and sullen this morning. Forget that, and look on me from now on as the old Horace whom you loved, respected, and whom the world has been able neither to debase nor corrupt. Let me tell you that I love Marthe more than ever, that I'll love her all my life; because I say in answer to you that my love will never give her cause to tremble or suffer, just as nothing in my conduct toward her will ever give you cause to stifle or condemn it."

While Horace, caught up in a thousand boasts, a thousand plans, and a thousand hopes, all contradicting one another, made us the boldest promises of virtue and reason, Marthe, who had returned home with her husband, recounted to him as candidly as possible the exchange she had had with Horace. Arsène felt a terrible fear and a terrible rending of his heart at this news; but he didn't let it show at all, and he approved in advance of all that his wife was planning.

"Are you then of the opinion," she said to him, "that I should see him again, and that I should be friendly to him?"

"I have no opinion on the subject, Marthe," he answered. "You owe him nothing. And yet, if you make up your mind to see him, you're obliged to treat him in a gentle and friendly way. For one thing, you might not have the strength to be severe and cold with him, and if you did, what good would it do, unless he tries to coerce you with new claims? You tell me he's not making any, that he can't make any more, that he only wants you to forgive him for the past and show him a bit of generous pity for his repentance. If it happens that you're satisfied with the way he conducted himself with you today, and you fear nothing from him in the future . . ."

"Paul," said Marthe, interrupting him, "as you're saying this to me, your face is turning pale and your voice is becoming muddled: in the depths of your soul, are you anxious about this?"

Arsène hesitated a moment, then answered her: "I swear to you before God, my beloved, that if you have no anxiety yourself, if you feel as calm and happy as you were this morning, then I, too, am happy and tranquil."

"Paul," she cried, "I don't want to lie to you of all people, whom I cherish more than anything in the world. I don't feel that I'm in the same situation I was this morning. I feel even happier to belong to you now that I've seen again the man who did me such a horrible wrong; but I didn't feel calm in his presence, and at present, I'm still shaken and unsettled as if I'd seen lightning strike near me."

Arsène kept silent for a few moments; and when he felt strong enough to speak, he begged Marthe not to hide anything from him and to explain to him the sort of emotion she was feeling, without fear of grieving or worrying him.

"It would be absolutely impossible for me to define it," she answered. "For an hour I've been trying in vain to define it for myself. It seems to me a sensation of terror that smarts, a shiver such as one would experience in seeing the instruments of a torture one had endured. What I can tell you with certainty is that everything about this emotion is painful, even horrific; that it's mixed with shame and remorse for having misjudged you for so long, with regret for having suffered so much for a man who has so little seriousness in him, with a sort of disgust and hatred for myself. In short, it makes me ill, without the slightest bit of satisfaction or tenderness: everything that man says seems affected, vain, and false. I pity him; but how bitter and humiliating that pity is for him and me! It seems to me that when you see him again as he is now, elegant and slovenly, humble and pretentious, withered and puerile, you won't be able to keep from feeling contempt for me, for having preferred to you this actor who is worse, alas! than all the ones I had the misfortune to play love scenes with in Belleville."

Marthe spoke her thoughts sincerely, making no hypocritical effort to reassure her spouse. Still, she couldn't sleep that night. To the unsettling effect her debut had had on her was added what Horace had thrust upon her. She dreamed exhausting dreams, during which she imagined, over and over, that she had fallen back under his fatal domination, where the cruel scenes of the past appeared to her imagination more violent and horrible than they had been in reality. Several times she threw herself into Arsène's arms with stifled screams, as if seeking a haven from her enemy; and Arsène, reassuring her and blessing her out of his instinct for trust and tenderness, felt much more unhappy than if he had found she was indifferent to the memory of Horace.

On waking, Marthe went to hold her baby, hoping, while caressing it, to forget all the night's anxiety. Mother Olympe delivered a letter to her that Horace had spent that very night writing to her. He had shown it to me before having it delivered to her: it was truly a masterpiece, not just of style and eloquence, but of feelings and ideas. Never before had he been inspired to express himself so well, and never had he seemed so full of such noble, pure, tender, and generous instincts. It was impossible not to be won over by the grandeur of his impulses, and not to give credence to his promises. Ardently he asked for Marthe and Paul's forgiveness, friendship, trust. He condemned himself with complete candor; he spoke of Arsène with deeply felt enthusiasm. He implored, as an act of grace, that he be allowed to see his son in their presence, and to deliver him, humbly and courageously, back into the arms of the man who had adopted him, who was more worthy than he of being his father.

Paul discovered his wife reading the letter, her eyes full of tears.

"Look," she said, handing it to him, "it's a letter from Horace, and as you see, it's making me cry. And yet something tells me that these are merely words, as he knows so well how to use them."

Arsène read the letter carefully, and, returning it to his wife with grave emotion:

"It's impossible," he said to her, "that this could be anything but the expression of true feeling and generous resolutions. This letter is beautiful, and this man is good despite his vices. It's impossible for me not to believe that he's better than he knows how to demonstrate by his conduct. A person doesn't speak that way for fun. He cried when he wrote to you. Let me assure you that you shouldn't blush at having believed he was stronger and wiser than he is: he had all the good intentions of the virtues he lacked. You owe him the forgiveness and friendship he asks of you; and if I were to turn you against him, I'd be giving you self-centered and cowardly advice."

"Well then, I'll see him again, but only in your presence," answered Marthe. "The one thing that makes me suffer is to think that he will see Eugène, kiss him in front of us, call him his son, and see in me the mother of his child. No, I didn't want to reawaken and bring back the past in any form. I was used to seeing this child as yours. I only very rarely remembered that he was not; and now, he's going to take him from us in a way, by stealing one of his caresses!"

"That idea is even more painful to me than it is to you, my poor Marthe," Arsène said; "but it's a duty that we must perform. I thought all night about these things, and I said something very serious to myself that you will understand. Above our desires, our choice and our will, there is the design, the choice, and the will of God. God does nothing that is not necessary, and his mysterious intentions should be sacred to us. He wanted Horace to be a father, although Horace pushed away the joys and sorrows of a family. He wanted Horace to see you again, and feel the desire to embrace his son, although he had up till now forsworn the sweetness and responsibilities of fatherhood. Only God knows what hidden and powerful influence this child could have on Horace's future. It's a bond between heaven and him, which it is in no one's power to break. It would be sacrilege, a crime, to interfere. To rob him of his ability to know and love his son, even if he is to know and love him feebly, would be a sort of kidnapping and an irreparable injury we would cause to his moral being. So we must, far from monopolizing our treasure to his detriment, allow him to enjoy him, since God is calling on him to profit from this good turn. I don't want to believe that the sight of this child would not make him better and would not bring about a serious change in his soul."

Marthe yielded to those high, spiritual considerations, and her veneration for Arsène increased. A luncheon was organized at my apartment for the meeting. Marthe and Arsène brought the baby; and this time Horace, who was once again displaying his affectionate, naive, and sensitive ways, behaved admirably in all respects toward him, toward his mother, and above all toward Arsène, whose noble and serene attitude surprised him into respect and tenderness. It was the most beautiful day of Horace's life.

Mere vanity made this beautiful change blossom in his soul, it must be admitted. Disgraced and insulted by those in society, humiliated and wounded by us, in the end he felt diminished and soiled in his own eyes. He felt a violent need to escape this debased condition and to rehabilitate himself in our minds and his own, while waiting for a chance to cleanse himself in the eyes of the world. He didn't want to get only halfway out of his predicament, to be content with appearing good and repentant: he wanted to appear great, and turn our pity to admiration. He succeeded for one whole day. His ostentation had at least the advantage of familiarizing him with certain conceited joys that he hadn't yet known, and that he recognized as preferable to the shabby satisfactions of a narrower vanity. He entered, from that day on, into a phase of pride; and his being, without changing its nature, expanded at least in the path that was now open to it.

The next day he woke up somewhat tired from all these new emotions and from the great crisis that had taken place in him a bit too rapidly. He thought of Marthe a little more than he thought of Arsène, and of himself a little more than of his son. His enthusiastic friendship for Marthe resumed its character of a reawakened passion, which cannot give up all at once certain chimerical and guilty hopes. Finally, as Eugénie put it, recalling a scientific phrase, his star began to dim. It was time for Horace to leave so he would not have the chance to go back on his noble resolutions. I forced his hand in a way, and not without difficulty and struggle; although he was charmed by the idea of a journey, he tried to buy time for a few days. But I was excessively firm, feeling that his entire moral future depended on how he conducted himself toward Marthe in the present circumstances. I made him accept, as if it came from me, the sum that Louis de Méran had sent to me for him, and I set a date for his departure for Italy without letting him see anyone else.

The joy of possessing again a small fortune, and of realizing one of his dearest plans, so completely intoxicated Horace in his last days here, that I became alarmed by the mad frame of mind I saw him in as he was preparing for his journey. He was cooking up illusions about all sorts of things that made me fear seriously imprudent actions or bitter disillusionment. After the week of despondency and deep depression caused by his fiasco in high society, he had a week of enthusiasm, delirious expansiveness, and sublime pride. All these emotions had broken his body, already decimated by the life of pleasure he had led for the entire winter, and I saw him fall prey to a fever that seemed all the more real for his not complaining of it or even perceiving it. Afraid that he might become ill en route, I resolved to escort him as far as Lyon, in order to make him rest there and to look after him if the first days of travel, instead of being a happy diversion, hastened the onset of an illness.

So we made our preparations for departure together, and I kept him always in sight so that he wouldn't run our plans aground with some precipitously extravagant act. I had a foreboding of an imminent crisis. His ideas were disordered, his preoccupations were strange down to the smallest details, and there was something veiled and bizarre on his face that also struck Eugénie. "I don't know why I can't look at him anymore," she said to me, "without imagining that he's doomed to die a madman. Those grandiose sentiments we've seen in him for the last few days seem to spring from a secret derangement of his whole being; in the end he's no longer acting these sentiments, I see that, and yet they're not natural to him. A person can't shed a lifetime's habits in one day!"

I scolded Eugénie for doubting the divine influence on the human soul; but in the depths of mine, I wasn't far from sharing her apprehensions.

The truth is that Horace, for the first and last time in his life, was not master of himself. He didn't realize the violent impulses that, up till then, he had provoked in himself and almost caressed with love. The affront he had received at society's hands had left him with a secret but biting sorrow; he succeeded in distracting himself and in chasing it away by exalting himself in his own eyes in a new emotional vocation. But this nightmare pursued him, and made him turn pale in the midst of his purest joys. The more he believed he could triumph over it by steeling himself against that bitter memory and by seeking to raise himself in his own estimation through internal oratory, the less he succeeded in attaining that stoic calm, that contempt for cowardly attacks and foolish words which he boasted he had. To sum him up and define him one last time, as I'm concluding the narrative of this period of his life, I will say that he had a very organized brain, very intelligent and firm, which could nevertheless become muddied and deteriorate instantly, like a beautiful machine with its motor broken.

The great strength of Horace's brain was the faculty that Spurzheim, founder of a new psychological language, has, with an ingenious neologism, styled *approvativity;* and Horace's approvativity had received a terrible shock the night of the dinner at *Proserpine's*. Despite the bandage that the sweet effusiveness of the lunch at my apartment with Marthe had placed over that wound, turmoil and confusion still reigned in the depths of Horace's mind.

The morning of May 25, 1833 (we had reserved seats on the Laffite & Caillard coach for that very night), Horace, seeing that all his preparations were finished, and feeling worn out by my surveillance of him, adroitly escaped me and ran to Marthe's. He felt an insurmountable desire to see her alone again and to say farewell to her. Perhaps the calm and sweet way she had taken leave of him at our last meeting had left him secretly discontent. He was willing to be magnanimous and leave and renounce her forever; but he understood that in so doing he was

making an admirable sacrifice of his rights and his power over this
woman's soul; whereas she, seeing her role differently, believed, when
she let him squeeze her hand and kiss his son, that she was bestowing on
him a sort of religious absolution. Horace, by accepting this position,
didn't feel high enough in the estimation of Marthe, whom he wanted
to leave with regrets; or in that of Arsène, in whom he wanted to inspire
gratitude; or in that of Eugénie and myself, whom he wanted to dazzle
in every way. The day of the luncheon, I don't think he had any second
thoughts about it; but he did the day after; and finding us all resolved
not to repeat this delicate scene, he was dissatisfied with all of us, and
with the position he had been forced to assume with regard to us. He
wanted, in a word, to take away with him some of Marthe's kisses and
tears, in order to make his entry into Italy as the generous victor over a
woman, and not as the victim, left by three or four of them.

Let us say at the outset, to excuse him, that these thoughts were not
clearly formulated in his mind, and that it was not the cold disciple of
the Marquis de Vernes who came to take his revenge on Marthe, but
the true Horace, riled by the fever of his wounded vanity, proceeding
despite himself and without any fixed plan, seeking any type of relief,
even if it were only a glance and a word, for his unbearable suffering.

He went into a café three doors down from where Marthe lived, not
far from the Gymnase. There he jotted down in pencil a few discon-
nected words that he had a guttersnipe take to her. The child came
back a quarter of an hour later with this reply:

"I would be happy to say a last farewell to you: we will go, Arsène
and I, with Eugène in our arms, to see you off in the coach. At the
moment, I can't possibly receive you."

Horace smiled bitterly, crumpled the note in his hands, threw it on
the ground, picked it up, read it again, asked for coffee several times to
clarify his thoughts which were straying more and more, and finally settled on this hypothesis: Either she is hiding a new lover, and in that case
she is the lowest of women; or her husband is absent and she doesn't
dare see me alone, which would make her the most adorable of lovers
and the most virtuous of spouses. In the latter case, I want to press her
to my heart one last time; in the first case, I want to be convinced of
her shamelessness, so I can be forever free of her memory.

He put the note in his pocket, rearranged his hair in front of a mirror, and, seeing that he was quite pale and shaky, asked for a glass of absinthe, believing it would sharpen his wits, thanks to its stimulants, which had just the opposite effect on him.

Finally he crossed the threshold of that unfamiliar house, walked up five flights, rang the bell, pretended that he didn't hear the definite *No* of old Olympe, easily pushed her aside, passed through two small rooms, and penetrated to the simplest and most chaste of boudoirs, where he found Marthe alone, studying a part, with her child asleep beside her on the sofa. Seeing him, Marthe cried out, fear etched into all her features. She got up and complained in a dry and trembling voice that Horace was being obstinate. But he threw himself at her feet, shed tears, and depicted his insane love for her with all the ardor his natural eloquence was able to lend him. At first Marthe received his words with a bitter coolness; then she tried, with a nearly evangelical speech, completely borrowed from the pious goodness that Arsène had been able to inspire in her, to bring Horace back to the noble sentiments that he had formerly displayed.

But the more she showed herself to be lofty, strong, full of heart and intelligence, the more Horace felt the value of the treasure that he had lost through his own errors; and a sort of despair, a somber and violent pride, like that of a true love, seized hold of him. He surrendered to it with extraordinary energy; and Marthe, afraid, was going to call Olympe and have her run and fetch her husband from the theater, when Horace, drawing from his bosom a real dagger, threatened to stab himself if she didn't consent to hear him out. Then he told her, from his own viewpoint, the story of the solitary and horrible life he had led apart from her, the furious attempts he had made in the arms of other women to drive the memory of her away, the brilliant conquests he had made, none of which could assuage him for even a moment. He announced to her that he was leaving for Rome with the intention of drowning himself in the Tiber if he couldn't cure himself of his love; and after a long tirade, so beautiful that he should have saved it for his editor, he made her the maddest offer: he begged her to flee with him or to commit suicide along with him.

Marthe listened to him with that extreme incredulity one acquires from love at great expense. She found his conduct absurd and his intentions reprehensible and cowardly. Yet, although her heart was closed to him and there was no going back, she felt with terror that the old magnetism this man had exerted on her, so deadly to her peace of mind, was on the verge of coming back to life, and that a mysterious influence, satanic in a way, and which she had a horror of, began to penetrate her veins like the chill of death. Her heart tightened, a convulsive trembling moved through her hands, which Horace held by force in his own; and when he threw himself on his knees before his sleeping son, when, in the name of this innocent creature, who bound them forever to each other despite fate and men, he asked her for a little pity, she felt reawakening, for him who had made her a mother, a sort of fatal tenderness, mixed with compassion, contempt, and concern. Horace saw her eyes filling with tears, and her chest swelling with sobs; he encircled her with his arms energetically, exclaiming, "You love me, ah! You love me, I see it, I know it!"

But she extricated herself with a greater strength; and, suddenly making a desperate resolution to free herself forever from her evil genie:

"Horace," she said to him, "your passion is misplaced, and you should cure yourself of it as quickly as possible. I could no longer keep your respect for long at the expense of your peace of mind and your dignity. I don't deserve the praise you overwhelm me with, I broke my word to you; your suspicions were all too well grounded: this child isn't yours. It truly is Paul Arsène's, whose mistress I was at the same time I was yours."

Marthe, by uttering this lie, was performing a true act of fanaticism. It was like an exorcism *to drive away all the demons in the name of the prince of the demons.* Horace was in such a wild state that he didn't even think how unlikely this assertion was, given the way Arsène had behaved toward him. He didn't hesitate to accuse that virtuous man of conspiring with a shameless woman to make him accept the paternity of the child. He forgot that he had neither name, nor wealth, nor position, and that consequently Arsène could have no stake in such an outlandish trick. He only believed at that remorseful moment that Marthe had just fooled him to rid herself of him; and overcome by a sudden fury, seized by a fit of actual insanity, he rushed at her, screaming:

"Die, you prostitute, and your son, and me with you."

He held his dagger in his hand; and although he certainly had no clear intention except to frighten her, she received, throwing herself in front of her son, not a death blow, but, alas! since it must be said, at the risk of deflating the one slightly serious tragedy Horace had acted in his life . . . a little scratch.

At the sight of a drop of blood which reddened Marthe's beautiful arm, Horace, convinced that he had murdered her, tried to stab himself. I don't know if he really would have pushed his despair that far; but he had hardly skimmed his vest when a man, or rather a specter who seemed to emerge from the walls, bounded onto him, disarmed him, and, shoving him by his shoulders, hurried him down the stairs while shouting at him with a bitter laugh:

"Run, my dear Orestes, make your debut at the Funambules, and above all, get lost!"

Horace staggered, knocked into the wall, caught hold of the banister; then, hearing Arsène's footsteps coming up the stairs toward him, he quickly fled, his head bowed, his hat pulled down over his eyes, and saying to himself: "I really must be mad; everything that just happened is a dream, a hallucination, above all that vision I just had of Jean Laravinière, killed last year at the Saint-Merry cloister, before the eyes and in the arms of Paul Arsène."

He leapt into a hansom cab and had himself driven, as fast as that broken-down horse could carry him, to Bourg-la-Reine, where he seized the opportunity of taking the first coach that went by, believing that he would soon be wanted for murder, and impatient to flee Paris as quickly as possible. I waited for him in vain that whole evening; I lost the deposit I had put down on our seats, but I couldn't imagine that he would have left without me, without his belongings or money. When I saw the carriage that was to have taken us pull away, I ran to Marthe's, and there I got a brief account of what had happened. "He wouldn't have killed me," said Marthe with a scornful smile; "but he might have done himself a bit of harm, if I hadn't been rescued by a ghost."

"What do you mean?" I asked her. "Don't tell me you're mad, too, my dear Marthe!"

"Just try not to go mad yourself," she answered me, "since there's reason to, both from joy and astonishment. Well, are you prepared for the most extraordinary and happy event that could happen to us?"

"Not such a long preamble!" said Jean, emerging from Marthe's boudoir. "I wanted to give her time to prepare you to embrace a dead man, but I can't contain my impatience to embrace the living whom I love."

It truly was the President of the Bousingots in the flesh, in the spirit, and in truth, whom I held in my arms. Tossed among the dead in the church of Saint-Merry on the day of the massacre, he had felt himself holding onto life by a thread, and, dragging himself along the bloody flagstones, he had succeeded in huddling in a confessional, where the next day a good priest had found him, sheltered him, and helped him. This worthy Christian had hidden him and cared for him during the several months Laravinière stayed with him, always hanging in the balance between life and death. But since he was a timid and fearful man, he had greatly exaggerated to Laravinière the results of the persecutions attempted against the victims of June 6th, and had prevented him from letting his friends know of his fate, asserting that it was impossible to do so without compromising them and exposing him to the rigors of justice.

"My mind and body were so weakened," Laravinière said, telling us his story, "that I let my benefactor direct me however he chose; and this man, who was, in fact, quite admirable, was so afraid that he didn't wait until I was fit to be moved before transporting me to his province. He left me there at the home of some good peasants of Auvergne, his father and mother, who kept me till now, hidden in a mountain hollow, caring for me as best they could, feeding me very little, and tormenting me a great deal to make me take confession: since they are extremely devout, and my continual state of agony made them think that any day the moment would come to settle my accounts. That moment isn't far off; don't get the wrong picture, my friends, though you see me standing on my own two feet and strong enough to give chase to Monsieur Horace Dumontet. I'm wounded to the core, and at every seam. I stopped two bullets with my chest, and roughly twenty other blows that are unforgiving. But I wanted to come back and die under the gray skies of my beloved Paris, in the arms of my friends and my sister Marthe. Now I'm quite content, used to suffering, resolved not to nurse myself along anymore, delighted to have escaped confession, and calm for the small measure of time I have left to live, since the indictment of the June 6th patriots didn't mention my ugly face. Oh, yes indeed! I'm not any more beautiful than before, my poor Marthe, and you no longer have to worry about falling in love with that Jean whom you knew as so handsome, with such a smooth complexion, such a thick beard, and such big dark eyes!"

Jean made jokes of that sort all evening, and once Arsène, who had already embraced him (but from whom they had hidden Horace's impetuous attack), had come home, we all dined together, and the heroic jollity of the "ghost" never flagged. Seeing him so happy and playful, Marthe couldn't persuade herself that he was incurable. I myself, observing how much strength and liveliness remained in that extenuated body, didn't want to renounce any hopes; but, fearing that I was building castles in the air, I had him submit to a long and minute examination. How happy I was when I found that the organs Laravinière thought had been attacked were actually intact, and when I convinced myself that it was possible to administer an effective treatment! For several months it was my most constant preoccupation; and, thanks to the good constitution and the admirable endurance of my patient, we saw him take root in life again, and quickly recover his health. The tender care of Marthe and Arsène also helped. From then on he joined this young household, where he watched with joy their happy and noble union. "You see," he said to me one day, "I used to imagine that I was in love with that woman, when I saw her unhappy with Horace: it was an illusion produced by the ardent friendship I feel for her. Now that she has been restored, purified, and requited by another, I feel, from the joy in my soul, that I love her like a sister and in no other way."

I certainly won't tell you the rest of Laravinière's story: the remainder of his life encompasses too many things, and would introduce reflections that should be developed elsewhere and in their own time. All that I can inform you of in this regard is that, persisting in his incorrigible and savage heroism, he perished, and this time, alas! in earnest, in the streets, and with his rifle in his hand, near Barbès, happy at least to escape the tortures of Mont Saint-Michel!

As for Horace, several days after his abrupt departure I received a letter from him postmarked Issoudun, in which he confessed the truth to
me, evinced his shame and repentance, and begged me to send him his
wallet and his trunk. I was touched by his sadness, and keenly distressed
by the miserable position into which he had put himself, when it
would have been so easy for him to be in quite a beautiful one. I still
had some fear for him, and still thought of joining him in order to lecture him and console him as far as the border; but since his letter
seemed very rational, I limited myself to sending him his personal
effects and his funds, and promised him, on behalf of Marthe and all of
us, to forgive, forget, and keep his secrets.

The publisher of this account trusts that each reader is willing to
make the same promise, even more so since Horace's last fit of madness
did not compromise Marthe's happiness in any way, and since Horace
himself became an excellent young man, steady, studious, inoffensive,
still a bit declamatory in his conversation and bombastic in his style, but
prudent and reserved in his conduct. He saw Italy; he sent back to the
newspapers and magazines fairly remarkable and poetic descriptions, to
which no one paid any attention: these days talent is everywhere. He
was a tutor at the home of a rich Neapolitan lord, and I suspect him of
having left there before he had guided his pupils into secondary school
because he courted their mother. Then he wrote a flamboyant play that
was booed at the Ambigu. He rewrote three novels on his love affair
with Marthe, and two on his affair with the Viscountess. He wrote the
first lead articles about a fairly wise politician in several of Paris's opposition newspapers. Finally, having had less literary success than talent
and needs, he courageously decided to finish his law degree; and now
he is working to build a clientele in his native province, where he will
soon be, I hope, the most brilliant of lawyers.

Selected Bibliography

Alexandrian, Sarane. *Le Socialisme romantique.* Paris: Seuil, 1979.

Barry, Joseph Amber. *Infamous Woman: The Life of George Sand.* Garden City, N.Y.: Doubleday, 1976.

Beecher, Jonathan. *Charles Fourier: The Visionary and His World.* Berkeley and Los Angeles: University of California Press, 1986.

Booth, Arthur John. *Saint Simon and Saint-Simonism: A Chapter in the History of Socialism in France.* London: Longmans, Green, Reader, & Dyer, 1871; reprint Amsterdam: Liberac, 1971.

Cates, Curtis. *George Sand: A Biography.* Boston: Houghton Mifflin, 1975.

Collingham, H. A. C. *The July Monarchy: A Political History of France, 1830–1848.* London: Longman, 1988.

Evans, David Owen. *Social Romanticism in France, 1830–1848.* Oxford: Oxford University Press, 1951.

Graña, César. *Bohemian Versus Bourgeois: French Society and the French Man of Letters in the Nineteenth Century.* New York: Basic Books, 1964.

Maurois, André. *Lélia: The Life of George Sand.* New York: Harper & Brothers, 1953.

Murger, Henri. *Bohemians of the Latin Quarter.* New York: Howard Fertig, 1984.

Powell, David A. *George Sand.* Boston: Twayne, 1990.

Sand, George. *Consuelo.* Meylan, France: Editions de l'Aurore, 1983.

———. *Lélia.* Translated by Maria Espinoza. Bloomington: Indiana University Press, 1978.

———. *Story of My Life.* Albany: State University Press of New York, 1991.

Siegel, Jerrold. *Bohemian Paris: Culture, Politics, and the Boundaries of Bourgeois Life, 1830–1930.* New York: Penguin Books, 1986.

Winegarten, Renée. *The Double Life of George Sand: Woman and Writer.* New York: Basic Books, 1978.

Notes

I am indebted to Nicole Courrier's introduction to the most recent French edition of *Horace* for much of this information.

CHAPTER 2

Page 17, Antony: Reference here is not to Shakespeare's *Antony and Cleopatra* but to the romantic drama *Antony* by Alexandre Dumas the Elder, which premiered in 1831. The play concerned a passionate younger man who stabs his married lover. The original production starred Marie Dorval (an intimate of Sand's) and Bocage (who appeared in several of Sand's own plays).

Page 18, *the Code and the Digest:* Parts of the body of French law. Robert-Joseph Pothier and Auguste-Marie Du Caurroy were leading jurists of the eighteenth century, and J. A. Rogron of the early nineteenth century.

Page 19, *grisette:* A grisette was a young woman of the working class who had "been around." She was either the mistress of a student or she exchanged her sexual favors for money. See Translator's Introduction.

the Chaumière: Literally, the "thatched-roof cottage," after its rustic front. The Chaumière was a popular outdoor dance hall on the Left Bank, frequented by student radicals and grisettes. It was known for brawls and for the shadowy recesses of its garden, to which couples retreated.

CHAPTER 3

Page 24, Paul et Virginie: A romantic tale written by Bernardin de Saint-Pierre, pen name of Jacques Henri (1737–1814). This novel tells the story of a star-crossed but idyllic love on a tropical island.

Page 25, René *and* Atala: Two novels of thwarted passion by François-René Chateaubriand (1768–1848) that introduced many of the themes of Romanticism.

Page 27, *a follower of Lavater:* Johann-Kaspar Lavater (1741–1801), a Swiss clergyman, wrote a book on how to tell a person's character from facial characteristics. It was translated into French as *Fragments philosophiques* in 1783. In this section, and elsewhere in *Horace,* the narrator refers to the ideas of phrenology, a nineteenth-century pseudo-science that purported to be able to determine personality and intelligence by means of the structure of a person's head.

CHAPTER 4

Page 34, Iambes *by Barbier:* Auguste Barbier (1805–82) wrote a series of satirical poems that he called *Iambes,* published in 1832. Though the poems were not written in iambic lines, he took the title from the poetic meter the Roman satirists used.

CHAPTER 5

Page 43, *Polyhymnia in the museum:* A classic sculpture in the Louvre Museum in Paris, depicting Polyhymnia, the muse of sacred lyric, in a meditative pose.

CHAPTER 6

Page 52, *Fénélon's Calypso:* Calypso appears in the novel *Télémaque,* by François de Salignac de la Mothe-Fénélon (1651–1715). *Télémaque* uses characters from the *Odyssey* in an original plot. In Fénélon's story, Telemachus lands on Calypso's island and is almost seduced by her.

Page 53, *Friar John Hackem:* A character in Rabelais's tale *Gargantua*. Friar John Hackem, in contrast to the fearful monks of his abbey, leads the successful counterattack against the army of Gargantua's aggressive neighbor, Picrochole.

CHAPTER 7

Page 55, *Hebe:* Hebe, goddess of youth, was the cup-bearer for the gods in Greek mythology. She was believed to have the ability to restore youth.

CHAPTER 8

Page 67, *Taitbout Hall:* This Paris meeting room was the center for the Saint-Simonian movement, a quasi-religious, utopian socialist group that Eugénie follows. The Saint-Simonians wanted to replace the existing world order with an international government where leaders would be chosen for their technical expertise. They also held that these changes would be brought about by a new messiah, who would be a woman. They were the first organized movement to advocate equal rights for women.

CHAPTER 9

Page 69, *the arrival of Louison:* Paul's sisters are named Louise and Suzanne but they are sometimes called by their nicknames, "Louison" and "Suzon," just as Marthe is sometimes called "Marton."

Page 74, *his Vitellius profile:* Aulus Vitellius (A.D. 15–69) was briefly emperor of Rome before his murder. He was famed for his gluttony and cruelty.

Page 76, *a latter-day Beatrice, escaping the sinister violence of a latter-day Cenci:* Beatrice Cenci was a sixteenth-century Italian noblewoman, whose father, Count Francesco Cenci, abused and imprisoned her. She was later beheaded for plotting his murder. Percy Bysshe Shelley's play *The Cenci* (first published in 1819) dramatized this historical incident.

CHAPTER 10

Page 78, *phalanstery:* The name Charles Fourier gave to his utopian communities. In Fourier's system, a phalanstery was a much larger and more elaborate commune than the one Sand depicts here. The cooperative that Sand describes in this chapter, however, does share certain critical elements with Fourier's socialist enterprises: each person performs a task suited to his or her abilities for the common good.

Page 82, *the work of the Cyclopes, which was evidenced by the glow of Aetna:* In the *Dictionary of Classical Mythology,* Robert E. Bell writes of the Cyclopes, "Later tradition regarded them as assistants of Hephaestus [god of fire]. Volcanoes were the workshops of the gods." Mount Aetna is located in Sicily.

Page 85, Marion Delorme: A poetic drama by Victor Hugo, based on the life of a famous courtesan in the reign of Louis XIII. The real Marion Delorme lived circa 1611 to 1650.

CHAPTER 11

Page 90, *the Faubourg Saint-Germain:* The neighborhood on the Left Bank in Paris where many of the aristocracy had their town houses. It became synonymous with that class.

Page 96, Meditations . . . *Lamartine:* Alphonse de Lamartine (1790–1869) began publishing his *Poetical Meditations* in 1823. They quickly established him as a leading voice in French Romantic poetry. He later served in the government in the Second Republic, as did George Sand.

CHAPTER 15

Page 133, *Figaro's "irresistible arguments":* This is a quote from Count Bazile in Act IV, Scene 8 of Beaumarchais' play, *The Barber of Seville:* "That devil [Figaro] always has his pockets full of irresistible arguments."

CHAPTER 18

Page 147, *the Pompadour:* a rococo or ornate style that had an old-fashioned flavor.

Jules Janin: A French critic of drama and other literature as well as a novelist. Janin lived from 1804 to 1874, and edited the weekly feuilleton of a popular Paris newspaper. He was eventually elected to the Académie Française.

Page 148, *Daughters of Eve: A Daughter of Eve* is the title of a novel by Balzac.

Portia *or* La Camargo: *Portia* was a short story in verse by Alfred de Musset. La Camargo was the stage name of Marie-Anne Cuppi, a famous dancer of the eighteenth century, who performed at the Paris Opera. She appeared as a character in de Musset's *Les Marrons du feu.* Alfred de Musset was a poet and dramatist, as well as a contemporary and, at one time, a lover of George Sand.

feuilleton: The Oxford Companion to French Literature defines a feuilleton as "a supplement issued with a newspaper. . . . It formed an appendix to the rest of the paper, being printed across the lower part of the page and detachable at will." *Horace* was first published as a feuilleton, as were many other nineteenth-century French novels.

Page 154, Memoirs of a Contemporary: A work written by Malitourne in 1827 but inspired by the life of Elselina Vanayl de Yongh, who called herself Ida Saint-Elme.

CHAPTER 19

Page 160, *Babouvism:* A philosophy, named for and championed by François-Émile Babeuf during the most radical period of the French Revolution. Babeuf believed in equality of income and collective ownership of property. His conspiracy to seize power in 1796 was betrayed, and Babeuf and thirty supporters of Babouvism were condemned to death.

CHAPTER 20

Page 165, *political trials of that era:* Trial on the right of association, December 1832 [author's note].

he didn't hear the other pleas made that day: Yet it was during the same session that Plocque uttered these handsome words: "Can't destitution and need logically demand the power to designate their own representatives, public defenders for hunger, poverty, and ignorance?" [author's note]

Page 167, *Godefroy Cavaignac and the Friends of the People:* Godefroy Cavaignac (1801–45) was a leader of the movement that helped produce the July 1830 revolution. He was also a personal friend of George Sand. The Friends of the People was founded in 1830.

Page 168, *Saint-Simonianism, Fourierism:* The two leading social theories of the left opposition in the 1830s. The Saint-Simonians, critics of the economic system, also believed in the coming of a female messiah and defended the rights of women. Charles Fourier laid out a plan for a utopian society in which prosperity resulted from each person contributing to a communal village according to his or her nature.

Page 170, *he also read l'*Avenir *and ardently venerated Monsieur Lamennais:* George Sand was a supporter of Abbot Lamennais (1782–1854), whose ideas foreshadowed Liberation Theology. In his newspaper *l'Avenir (The Future),* Lamennais preached a version of Christianity that stressed freedom and equality for the poor.

CHAPTER 21

Page 180, *Bocage playing Buridan:* Pierre-Martinien Tousez (1797–1863), whose stage name was Bocage, was a major figure in the theater of George Sand's day. He played the role of Buridan, fourteenth-century rector of the University of Paris, in *La Tour de Nesles* by Alexandre Dumas and Gaillardet. Bocage also acted the title role in Dumas's *Antony* and starred in several plays by George Sand.

CHAPTER 24

Page 209, *Bicêtre:* A nineteenth-century insane asylum for the Paris region, the French equivalent of Bedlam.

Page 213, *Duchess of Berry:* Marie-Caroline de Bourbon-Sicile, the Duchess of Berry, led the unsuccessful royalist revolt against Louis-Philippe's government in the summer of 1832. The uprising, based in the Vendée region of western France, was intended to put the Duchess's son on the throne.

CHAPTER 25

Page 222, *Desdemona singing the willow song:* This song appears in Act IV, Scene 3 of Shakespeare's *Othello.* Sand, however, is referring here to Rossini's opera, *Otello,* where the song occurs in Act III, beginning with the line, *"Assisa a piè d'un salice."* In Sand's day, the role of Desdemona was sung by Malibran, the diva with whom Horace becomes infatuated in chapter 10.

CHAPTER 26

Page 230, *Lauzun, . . . Créqui, . . . Duke de Saint-Simon:* Illustrious and literary members of the nobility before the era of this novel. Armand-Louis de Gontaut-Biron, Duke de Lauzun (1747–93), was a famous Don Juan who wrote memoirs of his romantic and military adventures. Renée-Caroline de Froullay, Marquise de Créqui (1714–1803), had memoirs attributed to her which were actually written by someone else. The Duke de Saint-Simon, Louis de Rouvroy (1675–1755), wrote a well-known memoir of the reign of Louis XIV, in whose government he had served.

CHAPTER 27

Page 241, *these new Thermopylaes:* At the Battle of Thermopylae, in 480 B.C., a heavily outnumbered Greek force held off the Persian invaders for three days before succumbing.

CHAPTER 30

Page 277, *a Calderón hero:* Pedro Calderón de la Barca (1600–1681) was one of the major Spanish dramatists of his generation.

CHAPTER 32

Page 313, *Mademoiselle Mars:* Anne-Françoise Boutet-Montvel (1779–1847) used the stage name Mademoiselle Mars. She was a classical actress whom Sand did not admire.

CHAPTER 33

Page 322, *Spurzheim, founder of a new psychological language:* Jean-Gaspard Spurzheim (1776–1832) was a phrenologist who continued the work of this pseudo-science in associating the protuberances on the human skull with various psychological qualities.

Page 326, *the Funambules:* A Paris theater Sand frequented, located on the Boulevard du Temple on the Right Bank.

ZACK ROGOW's numerous translations (from French and other languages) have been widely published, including his co-translation of André Breton's *Earthlight,* which won the 1994 PEN/Book-of-the-Month Translation Prize. For his own poetry he has received a fellowship from the California Arts Council. He is also the writer of numerous articles and a children's book entitled *Oranges.*

Edited by Anne Canright, Leslie Tilley, and David Peattie.
  Proofread by Kim Zetter.
Designed by Thomas Christensen using Monotype Bembo 11.5/14.
  Composition by David Peattie.

Table of Illustrations

The images in this edition are intended to *accompany* rather than *illustrate* the text. (For some, we are indebted to the Editions de l'Aurore edition of *Horace*, published in 1982; for years this Swiss publisher has heroically been reissuing the original French-language works of George Sand.) The illustrations reproduce or are based on the following sources: p. iii (title page): Lucien Boilly, *George Sand in 1837*; p. 5: Janet Lange, *Salon de 1849*; p. 13: from the journal *L'Illustration*, 1857, after Jules Gaildrau; p. 21: Gavarni, *Modes*; p. 30: *Souvenir de Charles X*; p. 39: Nodier, *Histoire du roi de Bohême et des sept châteaux*; p. 47: Gavarni, *Le Bousingot*; p. 54: Gustave Doré, *Jeune femme de Valence*; p. 61: Maurice Sand, illustration for *Le Secretaire intime*; p. 68: Gustave Janet, *La Pavana*; p. 78: wood engraving after Nanteuil, from Balzac, *Un Grand Homme de province á Paris*; p. 88: Boilly, *Le Libéral*; p. 98: Gavarni, *Pas le sou, un jour de Chaumiere!*; p. 105: Boilly, *L'Ultra*; p. 114: Gavarni, *Modes*; p. 123: Jules David, *Vie d'un joli garçon*; p. 135: Lix, *Vignette*; p. 142: Lix, *Vignette*; p. 147: Alfred de Musset, *George Sand á l'évential*; p. 157: G. Engelmann, *Le Vieilleur de la main droite*; p. 164: wood engraving after Monnier, from Balzac, *Un Ménage de garçons*; p. 173: Grandville, *Chapellerie au XIXe*; p. 185: Daumier, *Souvenirs du Choléra-Morbus*; p. 194: Daumier, *Souvenirs du Choléra-Morbus*; p. 205: Pigal, *Recueil de scènes de société*; p. 217: Maurice Sand, from the 1852 edition of *Horace*; p. 230: Sue, *Le Juif errant*; p. 241: Eugène Delacroix, *Buonaparte and Other Sketches*, 1814; p. 254: Holmant Hunt, *At Night*, 1860; p. 265: from Jim Harter, *Food and Drink: A Pictorial Archive from Nineteenth-Century Sources*; p. 277: Grandville, *Un Autre Monde*; p. 289: François Grenier de Saint-Martin, *The Amateurs*; p. 302: Henriquel-Dupont, *Louis Pierre Louvel*; p. 321: Janet Lange, *Salon de 1849*.